EMPRESS

THE SECRET HISTORY of ANNA K.

GREG OLEAR

ISBNs:
Paperback: 979-8-9859319-0-7
Ebook: 979-8-9859319-1-4

Publisher: Four Sticks Press

TABLE OF CONTENTS

INTRODUCTION TO THE FIRST EDITION

By Greg Olear

IN THE EVENT THAT YOU RECOGNIZE MY NAME AT ALL, it's almost certainly in association with my political writing. Perhaps you subscribe to my Substack (PREVAIL) or listen to my podcast (also called PREVAIL). Maybe you follow me on Twitter, where my frequent "threads" on Trump/Russia were widely shared during the administration of the Defeated Former Guy, thus catapulting me from obscure novelist to obscure novelist with 190,000 followers.

Nothing there hints at how I might have come into possession of the medieval manuscript you are about to read—an honest-to-God, genuine artifact from the High Middle Ages. Something like this is usually published in association with an august museum or a fancy university, and shepherded by a scholar of great renown, not an English major who tweets too much. So I understand the confusion.

Let me come clean. Writers, and novelists especially, like to cultivate the impression that we are well-off—that we bank so much coin from book royalties that we can afford to sit around all day eating bonbons and working the Twitter machine. This is mostly fantasy. The novel (what a misnomer, that!) is a dying art form, like opera or ballet; the average novel sells fewer than a thousand copies, and has a total readership that would fit comfortably in the auditorium of your local high school. With the obvious exception of fiction-writing royalty like Stephen King and J.K. Rowling and, I don't know, Dean Koontz and the like, novelists must hustle to make ends meet. We teach classes in creative writing. We freelance for what few publications still pay for content. We run social media for corporate websites. We moonlight at advertising agencies. We sell real estate and life insurance. We marry investment bankers.

I am no exception. I, too, have a "day job." For the last ten years, I've worked for a wholesale company that deals in ancient coins: Greek, Roman, Crusader, and so on. I handle product development. My job is to concoct stories about the various coins to make them more appealing to our customers. For example: no one has heard of Sigismund of Luxembourg, a minor Hungarian king of the early fifteenth century, and thus no one much cares about the crappy little silver coins struck half a millennium ago in his long-forgotten kingdom. But Sigismund of Luxembourg founded the Order of the Dragon, a secret society whose mission was to repulse the Turks—and which membership gave Dracula his nickname. ("*Draculea*" is Romanian for "Little Dragon.") Packaged in a snazzy "Dracula" box, and attractively priced, those same crappy little silver coins, thousands of which had languished in our company's vault for decades before my arrival, quickly sold out.

Our company is active in the ancient coin market. We buy big lots of relatively inexpensive coins, which we then wholesale to retail coin dealers. Late Roman bronzes are our bread and butter. (I know so much about Constantine the Great that I could walk into a classroom right now and give an hour-long, off-the-cuff lecture, the same way a car dealer could riff for hours on this or that iteration of Ford Mustang.) Judaean prutahs, which we sell as "Biblical Widow's Mites," are also perennial best-sellers. That's usually what's on offer, and that's typically what we buy.

But every so often, we come across something novel. Once we bought a lot of Norman silver deniers struck by William the Conqueror from a newbie dealer from Rouen who barely spoke English; my boss negotiated the deal in his rudimentary schoolboy French, and the agreement was literally drawn up on a napkin. That lot sold at a tidy profit a few weeks later.

The Frenchman found us at the big Berlin coin show, referred to us by another dealer. Word of mouth is also how we came into possession of a hoard of medieval coins, some three thousand total, struck by various Byzantine emperors from the late eleventh through the early twelfth centuries. Scyphates, or "cup coins," are roughly the size of a quarter, but convex in shape, like a contact lens. On one side is a portrait of Jesus Christ; on the other, the Emperor, sometimes with his wife or his sons. The portraits are all rendered in that strange Byzantine style that looks like something from a medieval sci-fi comic:

The coins are struck in billon, an alloy best described as "bad silver."

This particular hoard was discovered on 2 September 2016, in a sealed lead pot, by construction workers building a strip mall in the Zeyrek neighborhood of Istanbul. Initially thrilled at their apparent good fortune, executives at the construction company were disappointed to learn that the coins were dirt-common. Byzantine scyphates in extra fine condition retail for something like 20 bucks—if you can find a willing buyer. The buried treasure wasn't much of a treasure—not to a big corporation, anyway.

After clearing it with the Erdoğan government, the executives unloaded the lot to a Bulgarian coin dealer—a slight man with a horror-movie aspect, owing to his hairlip and his vampiric accent—who in turn sold it to my boss, lock, stock, and proverbial barrel, for twelve thousand euros. My boss immediately flipped a thousand of the coins to a dealer in Canada for the same price, which means that, in effect, we acquired two thousand Byzantine coins for nothing.

When the shipment arrived in our upstate New York warehouse, we were shocked to discover, inside the original container, a rolled-up stack of yellowed parchment. My boss freaked out. He was wary of getting involved with antiquities. There had been, half a decade earlier, a series of high-profile arrests of antiquities dealers of his acquaintance—Syrians living in London, alleged to be fencing stolen artifacts to finance jihad—so he preferred to stick to cheap coins, which tend to move more easily through Customs. When I offered to take the thing off his hands for a thousand dollars—and, more importantly, to handle whatever paperwork was necessary to make it good with the Office of Foreign Assets Control—he happily agreed.

I reached out to an old college friend, Marina Gavaris, a tenured professor of Medieval Studies at Georgetown, our alma mater. She's one of those freakishly brilliant people who speaks seven languages, including Medieval Greek. She agreed to translate the pages—and also, critically, arranged for Dumbarton Oaks, a prominent Byzantine research library within walking distance of her office, to both finance the project and clear it with the OFAC. As part of the deal, Dumbarton Oaks would retain the physical codex, once she was finished with the translation. Which was fine by me. For my troubles, I would get the publishing rights—although, when I drove down to Washington to hand-deliver the thing, I had no idea what those publishing rights might involve. Marina warned me that the codex was likely nothing—an inventory of goods, a household budget, liturgical documents, something prosaic like that. When she began to read the faded Greek minuscule letters, however, her eyes widened so much I was afraid they might pop out of her head entirely.

"Holy shit!" exclaimed the learned Byzantine scholar. "Holy fucking shit!"

THE CODEX WAS NEITHER inventory of goods nor household budget nor liturgical document, but rather a lost manuscript by the Byzantine princess Anna Komnene (1083-1153). Anna, the firstborn daughter of the Emperor Alexios I Komnenos (1053-1118), is the author of the *Alexiad*, an exhaustive history of her father's long and eventful reign. Both princess and book are largely forgotten now, familiar only to Byzantinists like my friend Marina, but her chronicle remains one of the finest extant primary sources on the First Crusade.

This newly discovered codex, known as the *Anekdota*, or *Secret History*,[1] is a shockingly modern companion piece to the *Alexiad*. The pages that follow comprise the first English-language edition of what Marina insists is one of the great literary works of the High Middle Ages.

A random twist of fate led me, a novelist, to be the publisher of this remarkable work—appropriately so. Unlike the *Alexiad*, which is part history, part hagiography, and frankly a bit on the dull side, *The Secret History* reads like a novel. Perhaps that art form *isn't* dead after all? Here is a book, painstakingly compiled (and stashed away before anyone could ever lay eyes on it!) nine centuries ago, read for the first time by a Medieval scholar—a woman, which seems significant—at a university on a continent that Anna Komnene herself did not know existed, almost a full millennium later . . . and those faded scribbles of ink on decaying parchment—the very

---

[1]   Literally, "unpublished." A nod to the alternate and damning chronicle of Justinian I and Theodora by Prokopios (500-560 CE), known in English as *The Secret History*.

words an incantation—somehow have the power to restore, to *reanimate*, a world long since vanished. Is that mere art? Is it not closer to magic?

—*Greg Olear*

P.S. Unless indicated by "A.K." for "Anna Komnene," or "G.O.," for me, the footnotes are by Marina Gavaris, the translator.

Ἀνέκδοτα

Ἄννα Κομνηνή

THE SECRET HISTORY

ANNA KOMNĒNĒ

PREFACE

THE STREAM OF TIME will wash away the dark stain of our delible memory, sure as the rushing river smoothes the stone on its bank. No man mortal or otherwise is impervious to these relentless waters: even the gods are forgotten. This, the astute reader will recall, was my stated motivation for writing the *Alexiad*—to give account of the deeds of my esteemed father, the great Emperor Alexios Komnenos.

It is with some irony, then, that my own memories are refusing to wash away, or at any rate are not washing away fast enough. Time takes its time. Ancient as I am at sixty-nine, withered and broken in my modest rooms at Kecharitomene,[2] I find that not an hour passes without my mind turning to the events chronicled in that book of mine. And not for the reasons one might suppose. The historian, as I

---

[2]   Convent of the Mother of God Kecharitomene ("Full of Grace"), a nunnery built by Anna's mother, Irene Doukaina. It no longer exists, although a typikon written by Irene survives in the Dumbarton Oaks collection.

wrote therein, must shirk neither remonstrance with his friends, nor praise of his enemies; he is in the service only of Truth. And this, more than anything, is what gnaws at me now. While I did not bear false witness, nor did I tell the full story. Much was left unsaid or unremarked upon, much ignored in order not to bestow credit upon some heroic character other than my father. The women, especially, I have marginalized: my irrepressible grandmother and namesake Anna Dalassene, the formidable Empress Eudokia Makrembolitissa, and most of all the lovely Maria of Alania, who was so forthcoming in relating to me the momentous events of her incredible life. These egregious omissions fill me with shame. Of all people, I should have known not to downplay the female contributions to our proud history!

It is Candlemas Day,[3] *Anno Domini* 1153. John II Komnenos, my hapless half-brother and my father's unworthy successor, is sixteen years dead. His flouncing son Manuel now occupies the throne. My throne. Or, rather, the throne that would have been mine were I not of the weaker sex. The throne that should have been mine regardless.

I, Anna Komnene, Lost Queen of the Byzantines.

Men cannot know the anguish of being ruled ineligible on anatomical grounds beyond one's control. Slaves can perhaps understand, eunuchs too, and perhaps even those doomed nobles, like the

---

[3]   February 2.

deposed Emperor Romanos Diogenes, whose eyes have been put out. But not men! How apposite is the Scripture, Adam content in his slothful ignorance, lazy ruler of all he surveys; Eve ripe with fecund curiosity and grand ambition; Eve punished for the selfsame willful attributes gifted her by her Creator.

The cruel vicissitudes of fate, of which the tragedians sang so plangently: my tale is worthy of Aeschylus or Sophocles. I will not lie, it is a struggle to avoid bitterness. Tragedies often end in death, as a cursory survey of Greek drama shows, but death at least is respite from bitterness and rage and humiliation. Real tragedy is confinement to a convent, house arrest in this forgotten place, exile to irrelevancy. The blind Oedipus (or Diogenes!) wandering the earth. Impotence, celibacy, boredom. Intellectual stagnation. Rot.

The machine of government grinds on without me, entombed as I am in this mausoleum-by-another-name. My nephew, traipsing 'round the Grand Palace in those ridiculous pantaloons, entertains infidels, but will not grant his aunt an audience.[4] My own children scorn me. My friends—there were never, let us be true, very many—have all passed on.

I have managed the best I could. When my husband[5] died a dozen-and-a-half years ago, he

---

[4]   Manuel Komnenos (1118-1180), the first emperor to forsake robes for pants.

[5]   Nikephoros Bryennios the Younger (1062-1137)

left behind fragments of a manuscript, a history he'd intended to continue to the present day, or at least through the reign of Alexios that ended in *Anno Domini* 1118. I picked up where he left off—although his scholarship was too shoddy to be of much use. My helpmate was more Hannibal than Plutarch. By completing Nikephoros Bryennios the Younger's history of Alexios Komnenos, I could honor both my husband *and* my father. This was the well-intended advice the Mother Abbess put before me: "Serve the memory of the two distinguished men who were your masters," she said. And so I did, to a degree that even my kindly Mother Abbess scarce could have imagined. The *Alexiad* not only far exceeds the immature scribblings of my husband, but ranks, dare I say, with the works of Herodotus and Xenophon. Certainly the blundering Psellos[6] is not my match, as he could never resist the temptation (as I have, although I have more reason to include myself than that old fraud!) to insert himself so prominently in every relevant scene. So long as the *Alexiad* exists, Alexios Komnenos and Nikephoros Bryennios the Younger will never be forgotten. No daughter or wife has ever given greater glory to father and husband!

---

[6]   Michael Psellos (1018-1096). Byzantine orator, statesman, imperial adviser, and historian. Wrote the *Chronographia*, a history of fourteen Byzantine Emperors. Anna detests him, as we shall see.

Selflessly have I acted in composing my history, but History is not well served by selflessness. *Mea culpa*, I have presented a flawed account. O History, I have betrayed thee!—just as I was myself betrayed by my father, by my husband, by my very anatomy. "The reward of suffering is experience," the play-wright wrote.[7] But he has it wrong, it's the other way around: the reward of *experience* is *suffering*. The guilt of my literary deceit weighs heavily on me. I lie awake at night. Beneath the habit, what little hair that remains falls out in clumps.

If the truth is ever to be told, I am the only one left to tell it, and tell it I must. I must atone for the sin of redaction, a sin for which neither presbyter nor Patriarch can offer true absolution.

Let these pages be my penance, O God.

---

[7]   Aeschylus.

BOOK ONE

THE FOREIGNER

Volume One:
Eudokia Makrembolitissa

A.D. 1056-71

I

THE ASTROLOGER

AT HALF PAST TEN in the morning, on the first day of the twelfth month of the Year of Our Lord 1083, a eunuch burst out of the Porphyra and hurried into the nearby chambers of the court astrologer, an Antiochene by birth, who had served the emperors of Rome since the days of Monomachos.[8] The astrologer was at his writing desk, ephemerides at the ready, awaiting the eunuch's arrival.

"What was the time?"

"Just now, sirrah."

The astrologer nodded, ran his silt-brown fingers through his thick white beard, and turned to his books: that year's ephemeris first, then the well-worn copy of Claudius Ptolemy's *Tetrabiblos*. As he made his notations, a crooked smile broke across

---

[8]　Constantine IX. Ruled 1042-55.

his grizzled brown face. After ten minutes of furious computation, he put down his pen and exclaimed "But God is good" to no one in particular, as the dutiful eunuch had already returned to the Porphyra to attend to the new mother and her baby. The old man rose and practically ran down the hall to the royal apartments, dizzy with excitement.

He found the Emperor in the Map Room, anxiously pacing to and fro, wearing holes in the rugs.

"What news?" the *Augustus* cried.

"The child is born," the old man said. "And Your Excellency, the stars are a thing of wonder!" He went on to analyze the natal chart of the Emperor's first-born and heir to the throne. "The position of Mars in the first house, so close to the horizon… Your Grace, you could not ask for better placement." Mars, the astrologer explained—although the Emperor was himself familiar with Ptolemy, and did not require remedial instruction—was ruler of war, and thus its position on the Ascendant indicated an assertive, self-confident aspect well-suited to command. This child was a natural-born leader, the sort of man others would happily follow into battle, even into certain death. "Not unlike yourself," he added, in a tone of well-practiced obsequity. (He had not retained his position for so long without knowing how and when to deploy blandishments). The Emperor nodded, and the old sycophant continued: "And Jupiter, also so close to the horizon… Jupiter is the Great Benefic. This is a lucky child, Your Grace. Lucky indeed."

"This pleases me," the Emperor said. "Thank you, sirrah. That is all."

The astrologer was banished to Proti[9] the very next day, after the Emperor discovered—to his eternal disappointment, given the auspicious astrological reading—that the baby crying in the Porphyra, his first-born child and presumptive heir, was in fact a girl.

The Emperor was Alexios Komnenos.

The baby girl was me.

By the time I was "born in the purple,"[10] of course, my father was firmly ensconced on the throne, having been *Augustus* for two full years. Any lingering questions about his legitimacy had been answered with his Empire-saving military victories over Robert the Fox and the Normans at the beginning of his reign (of which more later). Before Larissa,[11] however, such questions plagued him. For Alexios, let us not forget, was a usurper. That his great-uncle Isaac Komnenos had been Emperor decades earlier indicated that he was of noble stock, but this in itself was

---

9 A tiny island twenty or so miles off the coast of Constantinople, used for purposes of exile and punishment. The Byzantine version of Gitmo.

10 Said only of children born to sitting Emperors.

11 The Battle of Larissa, 1081, at which the Normans were defeated.

not much of a claim. Alexios was not even the oldest of the Komnenoi; his beloved brother, named Isaac in homage to the former Emperor, had held that distinction since the death of their eldest brother, Manuel, at Manzikert[12]. Why should this upstart, this third son of the brother of a former Emperor, wear the purple? Why should Alexios Komnenos, of all people, be the one to supplant the more-or-less rightful ruler, Botaneiates?[13] Divine Providence, some would say—and surely God willed his speedy ascension. Others would credit the kingly mix of charisma, piety, cunning, and ambition that formed his personality—and certainly a lesser mortal would not have pulled it off. But the political genius who engineered the coup, who plucked my father from his post as Domestic of the Schools[14] and installed him on the throne, was neither Alexios nor God. No, there was, as is often the case in the long annals of Rome, a puppet-master (or mistress, as it were) just offstage, tugging at the marionette strings.

My father never told me the story of the astrologer, you see. It was related to me by the other occupant of the Map Room on the morning I was born, when the old stargazer made his blunder.

---

[12] Against the Turks in 1071; one of the biggest defeats in the history of Byzantium.

[13] Nicephoros III Botaneiates, ruled 1078-81. Alexios deposed him in a coup.

[14] The title of the head of the imperial army; has nothing to do with modern-day schools.

For Alexios was not alone on the first of December, A.D. 1083. He was never alone in those days. He was always in the company of his lover, the most beautiful woman in the kingdom, if not all of Christendom, who had been the wife of the decrepit Botaneiates, and also wife to the Emperor before him, Michael VII Doukas. It was this erstwhile Empress, a foreigner by birth, who devised the grand scheme, who set the pieces in motion, and who did not rest until the deed was done.

Without Maria of Alania, there is no Alexios.

In order to fully appreciate how much his improbable rise depended on her benisons—and how my own modest accomplishments would have been impossible without her inestimable influence and exemplary example—we must speak in greater detail of Maria, whose life, it must be said, is just as worthy of an epic as was my father's, if not more so. She is given short shrift in the *Alexiad*, and I must use the requisite pages (there will be scores!) to correct this oversight now. Before we commence that discussion, however, there is one last detail in the story of my birth-day that I must relate. It is a prurient detail, and I disapprove of prurience in all its forms, but I feel that full disclosure is necessary here, as this detail illustrates, more than any discursive editorial I might proffer, the dynamics of the relationship between my father and his comely lover.

You see, Alexios was not "pacing" when the daft astrologer made his fateful entrance in the Map Room; that is a fiction I invented for purposes of decorum; no, adding to his humiliation, the old fool caught the Emperor and his lover *in flagrante delicto*. There lay Maria upon on the lush divan, her fair legs splayed, her pretty head cocked back, and there was the mighty *Augustus* on his knees before her, lapping at her fountain like a thirsty mongrel. (A gorgeous icon of the Virgin Mary hung on the wall behind the divan, smiling radiantly and chastely upon them). At thirty-two, Maria of Alania was already an old woman by then, five years his senior, twice divorced, with a young son of her own—ruined beyond ruination, by any conventional metric, and yet still as alluring as the fairest courtesan half her age. As soon as the door to the Map Room was shut and they were again alone, my love-drunk father, with nary a thought to his wife or his newborn heir, fell prostrate before his lady, and in that base position unbecoming his high office, resumed his obscenity.

"I did not release him," Maria told me later, one of many secrets she was to reveal, "until my desire was satisfied."

Maria, maker of Emperors.

Maria, mother of my betrothed.

Maria, who raised me, who loved me, as her own.

In the convent all these years later, when I offer prayers to the Mother of God, no matter the radiant countenance of the icon before me, the face of the Virgin Mary, in my mind, is the face of the Empress Maria.

II

THE ABBOT

T O THE NORTHEAST of Byzantium, across the Black Sea from New Rome,[15] lies a mountainous region of petty despots and imperial vassals who pay tribute to the Equal of the Apostles.[16] The two most prominent kingdoms in the region, if we must grace these insignificant marshlands with such undeserved grandeur, are Georgia, to the south, and to the north, Alania. For most of the last century, the king of the former was a handsome and clever rogue called Bagrat. This Bagrat was a fearsome fellow in his own land, quick to anger, and overly fond of excessive punishment. Once, when a common thief appealed to him for clemency on the grounds that she was a poor widow stealing bread to feed her starving brood, he personally lopped off her hand with his scimitar. But

---

[15] Constantinople.
[16] Another of the Emperor's titles.

from the Constantinopolitan point of view, Bagrat was a model vassal: a pious (more or less) Christian who was neither late nor short with his tribute, who supplied the Empire with much-needed eunuchs and slaves, and who fought with valor against the odious Turks. North of Georgia, nestled high in the Caucasus, was Alania, a place of higher culture and refinement than Bagrat's uncouth little fiefdom to the south.[17] The king of the Alanoi, as a token of his peaceful intentions, married his sister Borena to Bagrat. As in the case of my own father and mother, the first child born to the Georgian king and queen was a girl, whom they called Mart'a. When she came to Constantinople for the second time in 1065, to marry the crown prince Michael Doukas, she was re-christened *Maria*. Speaking only a word or two of Greek, she was referred to as "Maria the Foreigner" or "Maria of Georgia." Later, when her husband became Emperor, she amended this to "Maria of Alania." Alania, she insisted, was a land of magic and art and learning, quite unlike the rough and tumble Georgia, and also a country known for the pulchritude of its inhabitants (of whom she was, by all accounts, the most pulchri-tudinous). We Byzantines did not have an opinion one way or the other—both backwater rump states were inferior to mighty Byzantium, the pinnacle of Christian civilization; it was only when they were

---

[17]   Alania roughly corresponds to modern-day Ossetia, in Russia.

lost to the Moslem barbarian Alp Arslan that anyone in Constantinople took notice—and honored her modest request. Thus Maria of Alania she became.

But I'm getting ahead of myself. In A.D. 1056, when Maria was five years old, the Georgian royal family journeyed to Constantinople to pay homage to the Empress Theodora. The purpose of the visit is unknown to me, but likely it was undertaken by Bagrat to smooth relations subsequent to some or other misdemeanor. Perhaps he was late paying tribute that year. In any event, Bagrat set out for the Queen City with his wife and children, his retinue of relatives and high nobles and envoys and servants, a parade of handsome eunuchs to present to the Empress, and carriages so laden with gifts that the horses groaned with the weight.

The visit was a success. He charmed the Patriarch,[18] he presented his gifts (the eunuchs especially were much prized, as castration was technically illegal within the imperial borders, and thus all "beardless slaves," so necessary to the administration of government, had to be imported from elsewhere). He made obeisance to the *Augusta*. And when he returned to his palace at T'blisi, he left behind, as a show of good faith, a hostage: his lovely blonde-haired, blue-eyed daughter, all of five years old. She looked, Theodora remarked in awe, like a little angel sent down from Heaven.

---

[18] The Patriarch is the head of the Eastern Orthodox Church—the Byzantine equivalent of Pope.

It was, as it still is, common practice for vassals of Byzantium to send their young children to Constantinople as hostages. This helps ensure good behavior—what father would dare defy the Emperor, knowing that such defiance would spell the death or despoilment of his flesh and blood?—but it also serves to promote cordial relations. Educated by the best teachers in Christendom, the princes and princesses return home enriched by the experience. (This Abrahamic sacrifice is peculiar to high nobles and royals and quite unknown to the peasantry, who operate under the delusion that life in the purple is all garland wreaths and sweetmeats).[19]

Little Maria was not left alone in the Queen City. Also remaining were a clutch of servants, including her beloved nurse Rona, and several of her Alani cousins—enough of a contingency to effect some influence at the court, albeit minor. This cheerful entourage provided ample solace for the young princess, and she was anyway used to the cloistered life of a royal daughter, but she missed the king horribly.

"Father wanted me in Constantinople so that I may one day marry a Byzantine prince," Maria

---

[19] Bagrat was intimately familiar with these arrangements. He himself had been posted to the Grand Palace as a hostage by his father, also named Bagrat, in A.D. 1023, late in the reign of Basil the Bulgar-slayer; as a happy consequence of this experience, he took as his first wife a Byzantine princess, a niece of the Emperor Romanos III Argyrus. (A.K.)

recalled. "He knew how important such a marriage would be, for him as well as for me. Although of course I was too little to understand his reasoning. At that age, a girl needs her father more than anything. When he went home, I made him leave behind one of his cloaks. I slept with it every night, because it smelled like him."

While she made the most of her time in Constantinople, Maria did not particularly enjoy her stay. "When my parents left me behind, I was devastated, as you can imagine. I felt like they had abandoned me, and I cried every night and prayed that God might deliver me home."

The Almighty heard her prayers. Five short months after Maria's arrival at the Grand Palace, in late August of that year, the Empress Theodora was seized with a virulent illness of the bowels, from which she suddenly and explosively died. Maria returned to T'blisi the very next day.

It just so happened that the abbot of the famed Iviron monastery on Mount Athos, one Giorgi, a venerable monk with a long white beard who had lived so many years in piety that he'd developed a knack for prophesy, was also in Constantinople at this time. As the little girl was being conveyed to a carriage to bring her home—this was just outside the magnificent Grand Palace, near the Imperial Gate—the saintly abbot detained her, placing his calloused hands upon her shoulders, and looking her in the eye. "On this day, let it be known," he proclaimed, loud enough for all of her retinue and bystanders on the street to hear, but never breaking his steely gaze with the young princess, "that the Queen has departed, but the Queen"—and here he gripped Maria's shoulders even more tightly—"has arrived." This caused quite a stir, as the abbot was generally serene and stoic and not the sort to accost little girls and make strange pronouncements. Had he gone mad? Or had he seen something no one else could see? In any event, the abbot's words did not go unnoticed by leading members of the noble House of Doukas. In particular, the learned and pious Constantine Doukas, soon to take the purple himself, was friendly with the abbot, and it was suggested later that without what amounted to a ringing endorsement by one of the most blameless holy men in Christendom, our little Mart'a, as she was then still known, would not have been summoned back to the capital ten years later by the same Constantine Doukas, now the Emperor, to wed his son and heir.

Maria, for her part, was traumatized by the scary old mystic appearing out of nowhere, as if a ghost, and assaulting her person. She had not been in Byzantium long enough to learn more than a few phrases of Greek, so his words were but frenzied gibberish to her foreigner's ears. She did not learn of the prophesy until many years later—long after it came true.

In Byzantium, meanwhile, an empire long thought to be on the verge of collapse teetered toward the brink. After years of imperial dissolution and debauchery—including a *ménage à trois* in the Grand Palace itself, a shameful arrangement ratified by both the Senate and the Patriarch![20]—my great-uncle Isaac Komnenos, a retired general of the army, reluctantly took the throne. Humble, shrewd, efficient, and charismatic, he displayed the raw Komnenoi character traits my father would later refine. Isaac immediately took action, reforming the currency, eliminating waste in the bureaucracy, and building up the army, which had devolved into little more than a motley collection of barbarian mercenaries. He alone recognized the dire threat of the Turks mounting along the eastern frontier, and knew that only a well-trained, well-financed standing army could ultimately save Byzantium. The debauched Senators and other aristocrats did not favor his policies, as they were expensive; the clergy regarded his brazen attempts to seize church lands with abject horror; and needless to say the hoi polloi were too simple to understand the gravity of the situation. Isaac was not popular, but he was effective, and he also had the inestimable virtue of

---

[20]   The Empress Zoe, her third husband the Emperor Constantine IX Monomachos, and his lover Maria Skleraina, whom he refused to leave after taking the purple. It was not as prurient as Anna suggests—they were not a "thrupple"—but it was highly unusual.

being right. No matter. He was undone by his own foolish superstition.

Lightning struck a tree he happened to be standing under for shelter during a storm; soon after he fell gravely ill; he interpreted this, idiotically, as a sign of God's displeasure. As he lay dying, his advisor Michael Psellos, widely regarded as one of Christendom's leading lights although he was in fact a self-serving imbecile, convinced Isaac to name as his successor his, Psellos's, bosom chum, the effete and bookish Constantine Doukas. This unfolded in the Year of Our Lord 1059. The coronation of the new Emperor, now Constantine X, proceeded apace; the Senate approved him, magistrates met with him, subjects fell prostrate before him—all the requisite homage due when a new ruler takes the throne. That Isaac, left for dead, eventually and miraculously recovered from his infirmity was either embarrassing inconvenience or cruel joke, depending on one's point of view. What to do with this Lazarus *Augustus*? Shun him, as it happened. The Empire moved on without Isaac, this most excellent man who wanted only to save it, and he retired to a monastery, where he died not long after.

What can be said of the tenth Emperor Constantine, of the House of Doukas?[21] Let his beloved

---

[21] I am myself of the House of Doukas. My mother's name is Irene Doukaina. Her father, Andronikos Doukas, was the son of John Doukas, the Emperor Constantine's younger brother, who for decades held the office of *Caesar*.

friend, chief advisor, and eventual biographer Psellos speak on his behalf (I'm quoting here from the *Chronographia*): "He controlled his temper, did nothing by instinct, always followed the dictates of reason. None were put to death by him, even where the most dreadful crimes had been committed. None suffered mutilation at his command. He rarely uttered threats, and even those were forgotten soon, for he was invariably more inclined to shed tears than resort to cruelty." By way of example, Psellos relates the story of a failed coup, an attempt on the Emperor's life. When the nefarious conspirators were rounded up, Constantine did not have them beheaded, or blinded, or maimed in any other way, as I certainly would have. Rather, he flaccidly condemned them to exile. And even that punishment was too severe for him to dispassionately mete out. The night the miscreants were sent away, he remarked at dinner to Psellos, "What a shame our exiles cannot share in this fine meal. I cannot possibly enjoy myself when others are in distress." Can you imagine! Reading that anecdote, I assumed the obsequious historian simply made it up, to validate his claims of Constantine's vaunted piety...but no, Maria herself assured me that, while

---

I mention this not to boast, but to show that, unlike in the *Alexiad*, I can and will be ruthless when my duty as historian requires objectivity. I will subject my own ancestors to criticism and rebuke. A model Empress I would have been... (A.K.)

she could not vouch for the veracity of the story, it was certainly consistent with his character. "A finer Christian I never knew," she affirmed. Constantine X was described by both Psellos (in his book) and Maria (in conversation with me) as meek, patient, kind, sensitive, compassionate, and merciful. He was, apparently, such a good man that he could not conceive of anyone else being evil.

Ah, but the selfsame qualities that made him a lovely father-in-law and a model Christian made him a bumbling and ineffectual *basileus*.[22] I know that there are heinous human beings who lust for blood and derive sick pleasure in the slicing off of ears and the lopping off of heads. Men of this stripe are infidels, for none who love Christ would revel in the infliction of pain. No true Christian *wants* to condemn another to death. Nevertheless, an Emperor must not shirk the responsibility of his office. He must take it upon himself to enforce the law, however unpleasant that enforcement might be. This, after all, is his primary function. If "the most dreadful crimes" have indeed been committed, retribution must come. If the law requires the guilty to lose his nose, his nose should be cut off, or his hands, his eyes, his testes. And if, in those rare cases, the law mandates a man to die, then die he must. To execute the law, the Emperor must execute the murderer, the conspirator, the rapist, the deserter,

---

[22]   King.

the traitor. Anything less is anarchy. Even Jesus Himself came to bring the sword! Anyone unwilling to discharge this sacred duty has no business taking up the purple. Psellos proffers that the tendency to ignore the sage advice of counsellors—which is to say, the counsel of Psellos himself—is the "incurable malady of Emperors," and the cause of the decline of the Roman Empire. Fie. The cause is *weakness*. Weak men like Constantine Doukas unable or unwilling to exercise their full power. Let history be our guide: Augustus, Trajan, Constantine, Justinian…the Empire thrives when the Emperor himself is strong!

Fortunately for both Emperor and Empire, Constantine's wife, the Empress Eudokia Makrembolitissa, was better suited to the task. A formidable woman both beautiful and abominable, a throwback to Livia and Julia Domna and the great Theodora,[23] she assisted her pusillanimous husband with the diurnal administration of government. She was in charge of it all. This she did while fulfilling her primary queenly duty, producing heirs to the throne.

Her first son, Michael, who took after his father in temperament and thus did whatever his willful mother commanded, however degrading or beneath his station, came of age in A.D. 1065. He did not especially yearn for female companionship, as we shall see, yet as the presumptive heir to the throne

---

[23]   The wives and *Augustae* of, respectively, Caesar Augustus, Septimius Severus, and Justinian. All three are exemplars of female power in antiquity.

he was in urgent need of a wife. Constantinople's leading families vied for the privilege of marrying one of their spoilt daughters to this Michael, but to choose one over another carried some risk for the Emperor. What if the losing families bore a grudge and conspired against him? What if the winning family concocted some scheme to oust Constantine and achieve the throne for their daughter? The marrying of a crown prince is a complicated business!

At this time, fourteen-year-old Maria was still Mart'a—not yet betrothed, although she'd been eligible to wed for two years—and living in her father's court at the Georgian capital of T'blisi. The blonde-haired, blue-eyed little girl had blossomed into a blonde-haired, blue-eyed beauty the likes of which the Empire had never before seen. Her pulchritude was quite without precedent. By the time I was old enough to regard her with any measure of objectivity, Maria was well into her forties, and even then she was an exquisite creature. Slender as a cypress, with snow-white skin and the complexion of a spring flower, her Bosporus-blue eyes radiant. Many a painter's hand has successfully imitated the colors of the various flowers the seasons bring, but her unique beauty, the radiance of her grace, and the charm and sweetness of her manners surpassed all description and all art. Never did Apelles or Pheidias or any of the sculptors produce a statue so beauteous. The Gorgon's head was said to turn those who looked upon it into stone, but anyone who saw Maria walking or met her unexpectedly would have gaped and remained rooted to the spot, speechless, robbed of his mind and wits. That was how gorgeous she was. In a phrase, she was Love Incarnate, come down to pretty up this dull terrestrial sphere. And that was when *I* knew her, and could appreciate her singular appearance, when she was an old woman, when her flower was withering. I could scarce imagine how uniquely ravishing she must have looked at fourteen. Like Semele regarding Zeus in all his glory, one would have had to avert one's eyes or go blind.

Well, word of her Helen-of-Troy-like comeliness reached the Grand Palace (perhaps by Bagrat's deft diplomacy, but no matter; that is a vassal king's job, to see that his daughter marries up) and did not escape the attention of the Emperor and Empress.

"Sire," Eudokia said, "it might be wise to conduct this princess here, for our son to wed. If she is as lovely as they say, Michael may take to her." (Already, you see, there was concern about her boy's peculiar predilections).

"I remember her," Constantine said. "She was here briefly as a child, when Theodora was queen."

Psellos was present during this exchange, as Psellos always was, not having a wife and family of his own to distract him from his insatiable meddling. He could not resist chiming in. "Importing a foreigner would obviate the need to choose one of the families over another," he noted, stating the obvious as was his wont. Doubtless he was imagining how simple it would be to exert his influence over some rube brought in from the frontier. "My only concern," the chief minister said, "is public perception. Is it beneath the station of the crown prince to marry a savage?"

"She's not a savage," the Emperor replied, with more patience than Psellos deserved. "King Bagrat is a good Christian, and I'm sure his daughter will be suitable."

"Besides," added Eudokia, "if her reputation is well deserved, the people will love her. Beauty's veil covers every blemish."

"If you're sure," Psellos said, although he knew she was sure, and was pleased with this outcome.

"Shall we inform Michael?" Constantine asked.

Eudokia dismissed this notion with a wave of her hand and a roll of her imperious eye. "He won't care one way or the other. Let us proceed."

"Attend," the Emperor said. "I want first to send word to Iviron and make sure the abbot has no objections."

But the abbot in question was the same Giorgi who'd foretold that the Alani princess would be queen, and he gave no protest. So it was that Mart'a was sent for. When she arrived in the Queen City the second time, she took a new name, one that reflected her adoption of the Constantinopolitan way: Maria.

III
THE CROWN PRINCE

THE DISTANCE FROM Bagrat's palace in T'blisi to the Boukoleon[24] in Constantinople is almost exactly a thousand miles. Even with favorable winds—which they enjoyed; the trip seemed blessed by Poseidon from the start—it took the princess twenty-seven days to make the journey. On the ship with Maria were her uncle, who acted as chaperone and envoy, Rona her nurse, a few eunuch slaves, her beloved cousin Irina and two of Irina's sisters, and of course heavily armed guard on the decks. When she boarded the vessel, the girl was terrified. She was leaving behind her mother and her father to move to a strange city—yes, she'd traveled there before, but for only a few months, and she had little memory of her adventure beyond a vague feeling of despair—where, she was

---

[24]   The nickname of the imperial palace.

reliably informed, the natives may not well take to her being a foreigner. "It is simply not done to marry an outsider," her father had told her, his austere face beaming with pride. "This has not happened since the Emperor Justinian took Theodora of Khazaria as his wife. And that was five hundred years ago! It is an incredible honor, and one you are most worthy of, my sweet."

Since news arrived of her betrothal, she had been studying Greek with the best tutor in Georgia. But she had no natural flair for languages, and the tutor, esteemed though he might have been, was not equipped to handle a teenaged princess who had a thousand more exigent matters on her mind.

Nervous though she was, three weeks at sea had dulled her initial apprehension. Boredom set in, as it will on long journeys. By the twenty-third day, she and everyone else on board had succumbed to the tedium. That's when Rona her nurse took it upon herself to initiate the young woman into the ways of love. This nurse was in her early twenties when Maria came into the world, and was now in her middle age. She was a short, kindly woman, plump as a pumpkin, with lovely black hair she wore under a babushka, in the Georgian peasant fashion.

"While a princess must remain intact until her wedding day," the nurse told her, "she need not remain ignorant." She went on to explain, as decorously as she could, the mechanics of the copulative operation, which contemplation both titillated Maria and filled her with revulsion. "The first time, the best course of action is to lay back and let the man do what he will, for men, even princes, are often better acquainted with such matters than are their virgin brides. If a young prince beds a courtesan before entering a marriage, it is regarded as a youthful indiscretion. If a young princess does the same, it is a scandal that will bring upon her ruin."

"That doesn't seem quite fair," our innocent Maria said.

"It isn't," said Rona. "But that is the way the world works, my lady. Women have more natural power than men, but tradition prohibits us from using it explicitly. We have to be more…subtle in our methods." The nurse smiled and hugged the princess to her ample bosom. "You are a bright girl, my peach. You'll figure it out."

Two days later, the ship sailed through the Bosporus and into the harbor of the Golden Horn. Although she had been to the Queen City before, Maria had no memory of the actual journey and was thus unprepared for the breathtaking vista that awaited her. The dome of the Hagia Sophia towered high into the sky, gleaming in the noonday sun like a heavenly beacon, and the hillside palaces surrounding it, any one of which would be far and away the most magnificent edifice in her homeland, or indeed any other country in the world, only enhanced the effect of dizzying splendor that strained credulity. This was not a metropolis of men, surely; this was a city of God, somehow brought down to earth.

"I could not believe my eyes," Maria said. "How could human beings have created a place so marvelous? For a moment I thought I had died at sea and was sailing into Heaven."

What the helpful nurse could not teach her, and what Maria could not have foreseen, is that Fortune had smiled upon her marriage in three important ways. First, her betrothed, Michael, was himself only fifteen years old. Just as the Doukids[25] had ignored centuries of custom in selecting a non-Byzantine bride, so had they cast aside the long and unpleasant tradition of older princes taking much younger wives. (I well know what an unspeakable horror that can be for the young wife in question). Not that Michael was in any way her equal in appearance; no one could have been, but he was far from. His swarthy, splotched complexion, combined with a bulbous nose, fat face, and dull, incurious eyes, formed a face not pleasant to look upon. Worse, his entire body was matted with thick black fur, giving him a faintly ursine aspect. Together, they looked like Venus's younger sister being escorted by an anthropomorphic black bear. Still, better a young black bear than an old gray tyrant!

Her second stroke of luck involved her husband's prospects. Fifteen-year-old Michael was heir to the

---

[25] The collective name for the Doukas family.

throne, yes, but this designation in no way guaranteed that he would one day occupy it, or that Maria would be Empress. Any sort of disaster might befall the couple before coronation. Michael might die. Constantine X might decide to name someone else as his successor. The Franks might sack the city. The Rapture might come. Nothing but nothing is certain in life (as I can faithfully and woefully confirm).

The third blessing—I see it as a blessing, anyway; she herself was of mixed feelings on the subject— involved the same salacious subject Maria had discussed with her canny nurse on the voyage to Constantinople. Let me explain. The wedding took place on All Saint's Day, A.D. 1065, a few months after her arrival in Byzantium (it also happened to be Maria's fifteenth birthday, which coincidence the court astrologer—yes, *him*—decided was fortuitous). That night, and every night for a fortnight and a half thereafter, she lay in her bed anxiously waiting for her new husband to enter her chamber and assume possession of her body, as was his conjugal right. He did not come. The marriage remained unconsummated.

She could not conceive of the reason. Michael was pleasant enough to her in their brief daytime exchanges. If, for example, he was off to play polo with Ramwold, the tall blonde slave who was his steward, he greeted her with kindness that seemed sincere. "How are you, my darling?" he might ask, or "How did my lady sleep?" or "You look stunning today, as always." He struck her as aloof and moody and not particularly ambitious—not at all like her own father—and he was so in thrall to his mother Eudokia that he would do whatever she said. If the queen commanded him to fall on the floor and consume dog excrement, he would have done so with alacrity. But he seemed to fancy Maria, or at least not to actively despise her. Had she done something wrong? Was she not beautiful enough? Was he put off by her inability to communicate? Her Greek was still rudimentary, and what few words she knew were pronounced with a thick Georgian accent. Perhaps that was the answer: a true gentleman, he was politely waiting to engage her until she could speak for herself.

After three weeks of this, Maria could tolerate the anxiety no more and resolved to meet the problem head-on. One moonless night, she crept down the hall and opened the door to the prince's own bed-chamber. "I will demand that he discharge his duty," she thought (in her native tongue, for she would not think in Greek for many years). "I will insist that he honor his wife!" She'd rehearsed what she would say, learned the words she needed to learn to articulate her demand. She was apprehensive as she stepped into the anteroom and peeked behind the purple curtain to the majestic bed-chamber proper, but reasonably confident that being there was within her rights as Michael's wife.

As it turned out, she did not have to utter a word. For as she peered through the slit in the royal curtain, she saw something that stunned all speech.

There was the prince, wearing only what God gave him, on all fours like an animal. The matt of fur on his arms, legs, and back, slick with sweat, added to the bestial affect; he looked for all the world like the little bear cub at her father's menagerie, the gift from the envoy of the prince of Rus'. Standing behind him was Ramwold. The slave boy was also naked, but his body, unlike his owner's, was pink and hairless. With his freakishly long and slender arms and legs, the girlishly pretty features of his beardless visage, and his impressive stature (he was a full cubit taller than the prince), he had all the distinguishing characteristics of a eunuch (although he was slim and many eunuchs are plump). Indeed, in her brief interactions with the slave to that point, Maria had assumed that he was just that. But it was now obvious, even to a naïf like her, that Ramwold was in full possession of his priapic faculties.

She stepped away from the curtain, her back against the cold stone wall, and gasped as quietly as she could. Maria was a sheltered girl, her inter-actions with men limited to members of her family and the occasional priest, steward, or tutor. Bearing witness to sexual activity of any kind would have shocked her…but this? Two *men* in carnal embrace? Her husband being ravished like a woman? What did it signify? She could not know that soldiers and sailors routinely resort to sodomy. In the pagan days of Rome, this abomination was countenanced by one and all. Julius Caesar adored his Syrian slave boys, and how Hadrian mourned when his beloved companion Antinoös passed to the Great Beyond! Here Maria's vocabulary failed her. She did not know the words to describe what she saw in her native language, to say nothing of the Greek. She stood still as a statue in the foyer. She caught her breath. But curiosity conquered fear, as it generally does. Again she peeked through the opening in the curtains, and this time she watched, rapt.

It was like some sort of perverted dance. There was a rhythm to it. Ramwold's forward thrusts shook Michael's hirsute body. Over the course of what seemed an eternity but what was probably no more than a quarter of an hour, the force of the thrusts built up in intensity and speed until they suddenly ceased, with both slave and master crying out as if in agony. As luck would have it, Michael was facing the icon of Jesus on the wall and did not notice her. But at the last moment, just before it was over, Ramwold happened to glance at the door, and his gleaming eyes, the same brilliant hue as porphyry, met hers. Something passed between them, an understanding as complete as it was tacit, uninhibited by the barrier of spoken language, and she knew at once that this depraved perversion was Michael's preference, and moreover understood that if the steward had had his druthers, he would rather be with a radiant woman such as Maria than his bearlike young master. Ramwold's kindness, his discretion, his sense of honor and duty, his undeniable erotic appeal: all of this was revealed to her in that single secret exchange of glances.

And this, you see, was the third way that Maria was blessed by God. Her tender body was not sacrificed to the lust of some clumsy, rank old man, just because he chanced to hail from a noble family and was thus regarded as a "good match." Her sleep was not disturbed by a drunken lout demanding satiety for his lupine desires. Her dainty flower was not given over to the relentless battering ram, nor was her inviolate womb filled with the foul seed of an unwelcome sire. No, Maria was to stay intact. She would only explore the exquisite pleasures of the bed-chamber at her own pace, and on her own terms. What a wedding present from God this was!

More than anything—even the very crown itself—that is what I would have wished most for myself.

IV

THE LION AND THE FOX

I F MARIA'S FIRST EIGHTEEN MONTHS in the Grand Palace were of great moment for her personally, so were they too for Byzantium as a whole. In that pivotal span of time, two new powers suddenly emerged to threaten the Empire—one to the East, and one to the West—as if twin daemon hordes had been unleashed from the bowels of Hell by Lucifer himself.

To the East, barbarian tribes begun to coalesce under the sons of a Mohammedan savage called Seljuk, winning a major victory at Dandanaqan[26] in A.D. 1040. (It was news of this battle, in fact, that convinced my great-uncle Isaac of the need to invest in a standing army). Now the new sultan, Muhammad bin Dawud Changri—known to one and all as "The Heroic Lion," or Alp Arslan—resolved to

---

[26]   A Silk Road outpost near the city of Mary in modern Turkmenistan.

expand his dominions in the name of his false god, called Allah. No sooner did Bagrat ship Maria off to Constantinople than Seljuk forces invaded his kingdom, leaving the king no choice but to switch allegiances and bow to Moslem rule. By A.D. 1066, the fearsome and fearless forces of Alp Arslan gathering just beyond the Anatolian frontier represented the gravest threat to the Empire since Attila's Huns— and the Lion was not through roaring.

In the West, meanwhile, a new tribe of barbarians emerged from the North. Although they were duly converted to Christianity, and thus not technically barbarians, their manner and mien was nothing short of savage. One of these Normans, called William, the bastard son of the Duke of Normandy and a peasant seamstress, conquered England in A.D. 1066, not long after one of his brethren, Robert Guiscard, or "The Fox"—one of the most detestable personages in the history of this and every other world—invaded and took most of Italy from us, repulsing the mercenary garrisons the Emperor had stationed there. Only Bari, on the east coast of the boot-shaped peninsula, remained in Byzantine hands. This was the price the Empire paid for not heeding the sage advice of Isaac Komnenos! For Constantine X Doukas, too consumed by piety to place any value on well-trained troops, had foolishly abandoned my relation's prudent plan of investment in the armed forces, as discussed previously, relying instead on hired hands, with predictably disastrous results. He could only watch as these two animals, the Lion and the Fox, nibbled away at his Empire.

"This is the end," he proclaimed idiotically. "The Apocalypse is upon us. The end of the world is nigh."

This was a fashionable idea at the time. Two years prior, Easter Sunday and the Feast of the Annunciation had occurred on the same day for the first time in centuries, a random quirk of the calendar that convinced the foolish and ignorant to make the pilgrimage to Jerusalem before the Rapture, which surely must be due to arrive on 25 March, A.D. 1065. The world did not end that day, needless to say, and by some miracle it managed to survive A.D. 1066 as well, but this inconvenient fact did not stop many a credulous dunce from indulging his eschatological inklings, only to wind up at the mercy of the venal bands of brigands who waited in ambush on every darkling road to the Holy City. That the Emperor's once-estimable powers of reason had stooped to the level of the superstitious hoi polloi was proof of his decline, as his perspicacious wife immediately recognized.

One day Eudokia called Psellos aside. "Father, a word."

He was old by then, Psellos, well into his fifties, and the features of his face visible beneath the gray beard and black cap were so jagged they appeared chiseled out of stone. He may have been a sycophant, but his priestly gravitas gave considerable weight to his words and opinions—and he was never in short supply of either. "Yes, Your Highness?"

"Something must be done," she said. "The Empire is not ready for a war on two fronts. Our military is strained enough as it is. We must either raise the tax, or else divert funds from the church to the army."

As both a holy man and a fool, Psellos was opposed to this idea. He calmly explained what the vast sums of revenue earmarked for religious purposes were used for: the erection of new monasteries and convents, the restoration of old churches, the living expenses of the priests and presbyters and bishops, gold and silver and precious stones to adorn the sacristies. Such expenditures were absolutely essential, he insisted, to appease God.

"The Hebrews worshipped the same God in a humble tent," Eudokia retorted. "They had neither precious stones nor sacristies in which to exhibit them. And Jesus demanded that His Disciples give up their worldly possessions. Surely you recall the parable of the widow's mite? 'It is easier for a camel to move through the eye of a needle than the rich man to enter the Kingdom of God.'"

The garrulous chief minister said nothing.

"But I'm not here to argue theology with you, Father," Eudokia said. "My concerns are of a more terrestrial nature. When the Franks sack the city, they will simply plunder all our silver and gold. And the Turks, if they are our conquerors, will turn the churches into mosques. Is that really the most expedient way to honor God? So you see that maintaining the security of the Christian Empire trumps all."

Whereupon the old monk, who also served as the prince's royal tutor, launched into an interminable soliloquy about God and Christ and the soul and eternal life. Psellos was renowned for his eloquence, but on this occasion, the tone of his voice was more than a little condescending and not a jot convincing. He was an oh-so-wise man who felt the need to retard his speech so that one of the gentler sex might understand it. (How frequently this happened to me at court!). The fool speaks because he has to say something, to paraphrase Plato.[27]

The Empress indulged him, this was how best to handle Psellos, but she was unmoved. "I had hoped," she said, "that you would help me convince my husband of the urgency of the situation, but I see now that I have misplaced my confidence in your alleged wisdom."

Psellos, as was his wont, prevaricated. "I could neither offer that advice to the Emperor nor seek to persuade him by argument, but as a show of good faith, nor will I use my eloquence to oppose you if the opportunity presents itself."

She dismissed him, and then went to see the Emperor.

"We have to take action," Eudokia told her husband. "The time has come." In spite of her lack of familiarity with the military, the shrewd Empress recognized the precarious dangers lurking, and was

---

[27]   This may well be the first recorded instance of "mansplaining."

desperate to locate a solution. "Raise an army. Call on our allies. Something."

To which the Emperor replied, "Yes, we must do something—we must pray," and took to the nearest church.

But God helps those who help themselves, as the playwright says, and no amount of devotions, however heartfelt, was going to make the Turks and the Normans scatter. No, that's not fair to the Almighty, who moves in mysterious ways. The Lord *did* answer His petitioner's prayers to save Byzantium, albeit in a manner the *Augustus* may not himself have chosen: God summoned Constantine to Heaven.

When the Emperor died of grippe on the Feast of the Annunciation, A.D. 1067, "he left abundant material for would-be eulogists," the ever-obsequious Psellos would later insist. Rubbish! The lone virtue of the seven-year reign of Constantine X Doukas, aside from his importation of Maria, is that he had the good sense to expire before losing the Empire entire.

With his father gone, seventeen-year-old Michael Doukas was next in line for the throne, which would have made Maria, then sixteen, the new Empress. While young, Michael was of legal age, and he was the rightful heir. Indeed, as he lay dying, Constantine insisted that Eudokia make two vows: that she would, first, keep the crown in the Doukas family, and, second, that she would never re-marry.

The Empress swore to honor the dying man's last request, going so far as to sign a written contract, notarized by the Patriarch himself. In this official manner, Eudokia made the two promises—only to break them both before the Feast of the Annunciation came again.

V

THE SLAVE

Once Maria realized the queer reason for her new husband's nocturnal neglect of her bed-chamber, she felt paradoxically more comfortable with him. Michael, sensing that his wife was not going to place any undue demands on his own body, opened up to her in other ways, and they became close. "Like sister and brother"—that is how they were described by almost everyone at court. They were about the same age—I cannot stress enough what an advantage this is for a married couple—and while there was certainly no shortage of royal cousins about, they and they alone were in line for the throne, and this bound them more tightly than the most adamantine wedding vow. Michael was a kind man like his father, gentle and thoughtful, a passionate lover of animals, and with the exception of his bizarre dalliances with Ramwold—with whom he was almost certainly in love, loath though Maria was to admit it—he was entirely devoted to her. It was as if he overcompensated for his lack of sexual ardor with over-exuberant kindness. And since Maria had no genuine erotic desire for him, she was especially grateful for his chaste companionship. It was Michael who taught her how to speak Greek, Michael who instilled in her a love of classical literature, Michael who showed her the hidden delights of the city and the surrounding areas, Michael who held her close and dried her tears when she became homesick. They were together almost all the time, a rarity among wedded couples. Servants called them "the twins."

Despite his lowly status, Ramwold, she had to admit, was worthy of Michael's affections. He was an attractive man, to be sure, but also sturdy in a way the prince was not. He hailed from Gaul—he'd been captured in a raid when he was a lad of twelve, and his superlative physical attributes caught the attention of the Emperor, who gifted the slave to his son—but was, like Maria, an Alan, one of a nomadic Alani tribe that migrated from the Caucasus centuries before. While they did not share the same native language, neither did they speak unaccented Greek. They were beautiful blonde foreigners, both of them the property of this dark and homely prince. In short, there was much common ground between them. Soon Maria began to develop concupiscent urges toward Ramwold, mirroring her husband's own. In her case, however, the feelings were reciprocated, if not yet consummated.

"Oh, it was a zany time," she told me later. "Michael was in love with Ramwold, Ramwold was in love with me, I was in love with Ramwold. The self-evident solution was for the three of us to take to the boudoir, but I was a naïve girl and could not even conceive of such an unorthodox arrangement back then, let alone orchestrate it. Not that Michael would have been inclined to share. So I pined for Ramwold silently, as he did for me, and Michael seemed completely unaware that any of this was going on."

"How could he not be aware?" I asked, with genuine puzzlement. I was eight years old at the time, mature for my years to be sure, but untutored in the esoteric subtleties of love.

Maria only laughed. "My poor dear girl," she said, shaking her head, "we see what we want to see, that is all."

Also at this time, Maria made a concerted effort to spend as much time as she could in the company of the Empress. Although the princess was of course the more beautiful of the two, Eudokia was hardly a festering sore. At the phase of life when looks begin to fade—she was in her late thirties—the Empress was the sort of handsome-rather-than-beautiful woman whom middle age becomes. Maria could paralyze onlookers with beauty alone, while Eudokia could summon the same effect with her stately bearing.

If Maria were Venus, Eudokia was Minerva, the helmeted goddess of war, as chaste as she was wise. One was more beautiful than the other, perhaps, but both were divine. Thus the Empress was not even remotely threatened by a foreign blonde teenager, however pretty. To the contrary, as an aficionado of beautiful things, she enjoyed having Maria around.

In the intimidating presence of the Empress, Maria smiled often but spoke little if at all. By the time the Emperor Constantine died, her proficiency with Greek had improved to the degree that she was more or less fluent, thanks to her husband's patient tutelage, although she would never completely lose her accent. Eudokia did not realize this, and Maria made it a point not to reveal it to her. In this way, she could be privy to private conversations. Why should the Empress dismiss her delicious daughter-in-law to have a confidential discussion, if the silly little girl couldn't even understand what was being said?

"Back then, she thought of me as a statue, or maybe a painting on the wall," Maria recalled later. "I was always quiet and still. She would talk to her envoys as if I were not there. But I understood every word. I learned a lot from Eudokia. She was both paradigm and object lesson."

This was how Maria managed to be present during a heated discussion between the Empress and Psellos, the day after Constantine died. By this time, the priestly chief minister was sixty years old. He'd held the same lofty post for decades, and he naturally assumed that he would continue in the same capacity upon the death of his dear friend, especially considering that the replacement on the throne would be the son of that friend, and his own teenaged pupil withal. The three of them—pompous Psellos, shrewd Eudokia, and silent Maria—were in the lavish Empress's Loge on the balcony of the magnificent Church of the Holy Wisdom, the women in mourning dress, the monk in priestly black. It was late in the afternoon on a rainy day, raindrops crashing against the windows of the vast dome, but little light coming through. The dim yellow candlelight gave the place the feel of the world's largest crypt. They had just finished praying when the discussion began.

"When shall we arrange the coronation?" Psellos asked.

"Yes," Eudokia said. "About that. I think we should wait as long as possible."

"Wait? Whatever for? Michael is the rightful heir, and he is of age."

A strange expression crossed her face, one Maria had never seen her make before. "We must be honest with ourselves, Father. There are barbarians to the left of us, and more barbarians to the right. They have their greedy, godless eyes set on Constantinople. I don't think I'm exaggerating when I suggest that the very fate of the Empire depends on how we respond to these dire threats in the next few months. The transition is a time of confusion, and thus of weakness; we are in danger. You know my son as well as anyone, Father. He is a fine boy, and

I love him more than anything else in this world, but he is not ready for this."

"Not ready? That is of no concern. Ready or not, he must take the purple."

"No."

Psellos's face turned red (the part that was visible beneath the beard, that is). He opened his mouth to say something, revealing his tar-black teeth, thought better of it, and held his tongue. He made the sign of the cross and muttered a prayer or two. Then he again looked at the Empress and asked, with thinly-veiled contempt, "What then is *your* plan, Your Highness?"

"I myself will act as regent until such a time as I deem him ready."

"And when will that be?"

She gazed at the marvelously-rendered icon of Christ in the niche before her and smiled. "Only God knows."

"The Senate will never grant its approval."

"They will if Michael requests it."

"And you think he will consent?"

"Yes, I do." Here she turned to Maria, who beamed as innocently and brightly as she could, as if the import of the conversation was beyond her reckoning. "My husband, may Christ have mercy on his soul, interfered constantly with my attempts to build up the military. I will re-implement the plan devised by Isaac Komnenos, and in another year or two, with God's mercy, we will be in better shape to withstand the barbarian incursions. Let us pray they don't invade before that time."

"This is madness," Psellos said. "Your Majesty, I beg you to reconsider."

"My decision is final," she said.

He rose unsteadily, almost tripping over the pew, and began to walk away.

"One more thing, Father."

"Name it, Your Highness."

"The history that you are writing…how is that going?"

Psellos had discussed on numerous occasions the *magnus opus* he planned to one day compile, a collection of biographical sketches of various emperors. *My gift to posterity*, he called it, as if posterity had requested this from him specifically and would be heartbroken at his refusal.

"I have only just begun," he said. "With my duties at the court, I have not had much time to devote to it."

"Well, then I bring you glad tidings," Eudokia said, with a wicked grin. "As of this moment, I'm relieving you of all of your court duties. You'll now have ample time to finish what I'm sure will be a monumental and important work."

Psellos again opened his mouth, and again his vocabulary failed him. When he finally decided upon what to say, he stumbled over the words, the stammer that had earned him his nickname—for "Psellos" means "Stammerer"—revealing itself in his moment of ruin. "B-b-b-b-but…"

"Iviron is lovely this time of year, and they have a wonderful library, from what I hear. I've already notified the abbot. I want you to leave first thing in the morning." And the Empress gave him a smile that was at once warm, kind—and unmistakably and gloatingly triumphant. "On behalf of my late husband, I wish to thank you for your years of loyal service."

Anger flashed on the monk's age-lined face. His eyes gleamed with malice. "No," he said. "I do not accept this. I will speak with Michael, and I will speak with the *Caesar* and the Patriarch and my friends in the Senate, and we'll see just how eager the Empire is for a wanton harlot to usurp the throne."

The charge of harlotry stemmed from the persistent bit of hearsay that Eudokia took lovers from the highest ranks of the military. When an insolent court eunuch called Nikephoritzes (of whom more later) formally accused her thus before the Senate, he was censured and removed to Antioch. Nevertheless, rumors of infidelity had followed her like a shadow ever since.

"No, you won't." Now the Empress stood. She was very still, her back straight as a lance. She looked every bit like the ruler of the kingdom that she in fact if not in name was, and indeed had been for quite some time. She spoke quietly, as if in prayer, and Maria had to concentrate to hear what was said. "If you dare defy me, I will go to the *Caesar* and the Patriarch and the Senate, and I will bring charges against you."

"Charges? What charges?"

"Sodomy."

Judging by the gasp of horror that issued forth from beneath his gray beard, Psellos was unprepared for this line of attack.

"I will maintain that you used my eldest child as a plaything to satisfy your ungodly lust, and you thus corrupted his true nature and turned him into a vile pervert."

At this point, Maria was so aroused by the conversation that it took all the force of her will to remain still. The beating of her heart was like a Turkish war drum. She had no idea that Eudokia knew of Michael's sexual predilection—or, indeed, that it had a name. And she could not help but note the fact that as enraged as he became, Psellos did not deny the charge.

"You would risk destroying your own son's reputation to spite me?"

"I have more than one son," she said, flashing a truculent smile. She knew that in this chess game, this marked the capture of his king.[28]

"You can't do this," he said, without much conviction.

"I just did. Now if you don't mind, I'd like to finish my prayers in silence."

---

[28]   This is not an anachronism. A rudimentary form of chess, called *zatrikion*, was introduced to the Byzantine Empire from Persia in the tenth century.

Humiliated, Psellos hurried out of the chapel. Eudokia glanced over at Maria, who again smiled dumbly and did her best to convey the impression that she was unaware of the veritable volcano that had just erupted beneath Justinian's majestic dome.[29]

"Never in my life have I had more respect and admiration for another human being," Maria told me. "I looked at this hard woman, this cold and calculating creature, and my heart just about burst with affection. I thought, '*This* is what I want to be. *This* is the path I must follow.'"

Observing the desperate and wily machinations of the Empress after the death of her futile husband, Maria learned an important lesson: while a man, even a lesser mortal like one of the rogue's gallery that held the Western throne before the fall of the city of Rome, could assume command exclusively and explicitly, a woman, even an one as formidable as Eudokia, required the intercession of a husband or son if she wished to rule. A fact of female life, as unjust as it was inviolate. The Empress had been ably handling the administration of the government for years, the nominating of officials, the monitoring of the Treasury, the scheduling of public events at the Hippodrome—thankless tasks Constantine would sooner ignore than perform. But as soon as he breathed his last, it was as if she had perished with him. While plenty of women had wielded enormous

---

[29]   Justinian I built the Hagia Sophia, proudly remarking, when it was complete, "I have outdone Solomon."

power since the dawn of the Empire ten centuries ago, none ruled independently. Livia required Caesar Augustus, Julia Domna required Septimius Severus, Theodora required Justinian, Eudokia required first Constantine and now Michael. The lesson of the exchange that night was this: If Maria was going to have any real power, if she was ever going to be more than just a fetching figurehead, if she was going to make her indelible mark on History, she needed at least one male child. Given the abnormal nature of her husband, this was a task that required the cunning of Odysseus—cunning that Maria possessed.

VI

THE STAMMERER

I HAVE NO IDEA IF EUDOKIA'S CHARGES WERE TRUE, if the old monk had really slaked his ungodly urges with the young prince. That Psellos harbored depraved predilections seems plausible; we all have our dark sides, and a lifetime of celibacy does queer things to a man. In any event, the old fool clearly took the Empress's threat seriously. He was not about to end his long and illustrious career at the hands of some upstart strumpet, no matter what her rank, or how much leverage she had over him. Like many men of the cloth, and indeed many men in general, he despised women because they were women—the weaker sex, he believed, was lesser in every way to his own exalted gender—and thus he was willing to go to more savage lengths to avenge himself upon Eudokia than he might have, had he been dismissed by an Emperor instead of an Empress.

Four hours of fitful sleep and two hours in penitent prayer had eased his mind somewhat, and Psellos was able to approach the situation more objectively when dawn broke the next day. Whether or not he was found guilty of sodomy, he reasoned, bringing those explosive charges before the court would ruin him for certain…but it would also ruin Michael. In this chess match, to continue our strategy-game metaphor, it was an exchange of a queen for a queen. Was Eudokia ready to play the part of Abraham, to sacrifice her own son to satisfy her grand ambitions? The odds were against it, Psellos concluded. This was a bluff, nothing more. Still, it was prudent for him to be cautious. So he packed his things and set out forthwith for Mount Athos, as Eudokia instructed. But on the way there, he called upon an old friend.

Psellos knew that he had two powerful potential allies: the Patriarch and the *Caesar*. The former, John Xiphilinos,[30] was present when Eudokia made her vows to the dying Constantine; the latter, John Doukas, was the late Emperor's younger brother. Of the two, Psellos figured that he could reliably depend on the support of Xiphilinos, as they were both men of the cloth, and moreover the Patriarch would have to give his express consent for Eudokia's scheme to work. Doukas was the one who might need convincing—and also the one in a better position to offer aid. So on the way to Mount Athos, Psellos went to see the *Caesar* at John's country estate in Thrace.

---

[30]   Pronounced *ziff-ill-LINE-os*.

A brief word about John Doukas: he was living proof of the inherent foolishness of the policy of primogeniture, for there are often occasions when the first-born is not the best suited to rule.[31] Where his older brother Constantine had been a man of peace, reluctant even to exile conspirators who tried to kill him, John Doukas had no such illusions. He was a realist. He knew how the wicked world worked, he'd led armies, he was unafraid to fulfill his imperial duties. Above all, he had an uncanny ability to read the lay of the land and to quickly and accurately assess a political situation. Whereas members of the other leading families privately groaned about Constantine, they had no ill words to speak of the *Caesar*. Were he in command instead of his brother, in fact, the situation in the Empire would not have been as dire. John Doukas was a smart, savvy, tough, well-respected man of enormous influence. Physically, he was short and stocky and strong as Heracles; his physiology bore a striking resemblance to one of the stone watchtowers along the Theodosian Wall.

Psellos found him in good spirits. While he was still mourning the loss of his beloved brother, his grief was mitigated by the arrival of a new member of his Doukid clan, a baby girl, his grand-daughter.

"We call her Irene," he told the old monk.

"For your dear wife," Psellos said. "How lovely."

---

[31] This was not the case in my own family. (A.K.)

They repaired to the verandah, where they lounged on divans and admired the lush Thracian countryside. The *Caesar*'s bucolic estate offered a particularly breathtaking view of rolling hills and verdant meadows, of oxen and cattle and horses, of swarthy peasants working the land. Joining John Doukas and Psellos were the former's chamberlain, a beardless man called Nikephoritzes[32] who looked not unlike an older, fatter, homelier version of Ramwold; and John's eldest and tallest son Andronikos, father of the newborn Irene. They all four drank wine and ate sturgeon roe spread on crisped bread.

"I humbly request," Psellos began, as if there were anything humble about him, "that you keep what I am about to say confidential. If the Empress finds out I'm here, we may all be in grave danger."

There was no question of this. The Doukas family was above reproach, and Nikephoritzes the chamberlain, the astute reader will recall, had once been a court insider, only to be removed to Antioch for accusing Eudokia of adultery—one of Constantine X's many questionably clement sentences. They all quickly agreed to these terms.

"Very well," said the freshly-sacked chief minister, and he told them what had happened—conveniently redacting the part about Eudokia charging him with sodomy.

---

[32]   Pronounced *ni-KEY-for-EAT-zees.*

John's expression did not change as he took in the news, almost as if he had anticipated just this plan of attack from his shrewd sister-in-law. "She's a usurper," he said matter-of-factly. "A pretender to the throne."

"My sentiments exactly," Psellos hissed.

"What says my nephew of this treachery?"

"He says nothing. He does as she commands."

"That boy." John Doukas exchanged a glance with his son, and both shook their heads. "The irony is that on some level, the Empress is correct. At present, Michael is unfit to rule, and it *is* a crucial moment with regards our enemies."

"But we can't have a woman on the throne by herself," Psellos protested, "in the ultimate position of authority!"

"Of course not," the *Caesar* agreed. "That goes without saying."

"You have more claim than she does, father," Andronikos put in.

"Maybe, maybe not. But if Michael does not object to her acting as regent, there's not much to be done. This has been done many times before, by plenty of *Augustae*. But I wonder if this is merely her first move." John rubbed his fingers through his beard. "Eudokia is very smart. Don't underestimate her. Her political instincts are formidable. And she's had a lot of time to think this through."

"Time?" Andronikos said. "My uncle has only just passed."

"Believe me, she's been planning this moment for years."

"The question is," Psellos said, "what do we do about it?"

John Doukas took a bite of his sturgeon roe and washed it down with a swig of wine. A wide smile broke across his face, and he wagged his plump finger. "I know what she's going to do," he said. The others regarded him expectantly. "What's the first thing that happens when a new Emperor is decided upon?"

"The coronation?" Psellos said, and John Doukas shook his head.

"A blessing by the Patriarch?" suggested Andronikos. "No, no, no."

"The generals will be summoned to Constantinople to pay obeisance to the new Emperor," said the eunuch, the first words he'd spoken since they sat down. "The summons, in fact, has already gone out, according to my sources. Eudokia will simply interview the generals, find the one that suits her best, and marry him, thus elevating him to *Augustus*. There is long precedent on her side. Even if he is of low birth, her station as sitting Empress will legitimize the new Emperor's claim to the throne. She has already outlined her plan to invest heavily in the army—to rob the church coffers to do so, if it comes to that. Taking a general as a husband instead of allowing her son, who is green in the ways of war, to wear the crown, will further endear her to the soldiers, who incidentally already adore her.

So what if the church and the Senate disapprove of her? She has the army on her side. He who has the support of the military wins the civil war."

"The real question," John Doukas said, nodding at Nikephoritzes, "is which general will she choose?"

"Botaneiates," Psellos said. "Or perhaps Nikephoros Bryennios."

"Manuel Komnenos has potential," the *Caesar* said. "Although he's probably too young."

"It won't be either of them," the eunuch said. "I hate to say it, my lord, but the next Emperor is going to be Romanos Diogenes."

Here John Doukas cursed. There was bad blood between him and Diogenes—no one knew the cause, although some say Diogenes, who was something of a rake, had been overly and demonstrably fond of the *Caesar*'s wife—and they loathed each other.

"Do you think the rumors are true?" Psellos asked.

"I know for a fact," the eunuch said. "They have been lovers for some time. It is common knowledge among my kind."

"But Diogenes is married," Andronikos said.

"Isn't his wife dead?" asked Psellos.

"It makes no difference either way," John Doukas said.

"There's also the matter of the vow that Eudokia made," Psellos said, "to never re-marry, and to keep the throne in the family. She swore to honor her dying husband's wishes. The Patriarch himself notarized the contract. "

"Vows," said the *Caesar*, "are easily broken. No, we have to operate as if this is *fait accompli*. We may not be able to stop Diogenes from taking the purple—at least not for now. I think our best course of action is to meet with my nephew and help him assert his claim. One thing's for certain: If Diogenes is to be Emperor, his reign must be short."

Thus agreed, the men poured more wine and drank to their success and Diogenes's failure. From inside the house sounded the plaintive wail of the newborn, the baby Irene.

My mother.

VII
THE LOVERS

B Y ALLOWING HIS MOTHER to rule in his stead, Michael was also denying Maria the opportunity to be crowned Empress. How did she feel about this? Did she seethe with jealousy and bitterness and plot her revenge, as I myself would have?

"I was relieved, to be honest," Maria told me. "It's true, I swear! I wasn't ready for the job. It was too much responsibility. I was, what, sixteen years old? I was not yet fluent enough in Greek not to embarrass myself at court. True, the court eunuchs were so efficient that you didn't need to know much to do the job. But I loved and admired Eudokia, and the idea that I would supplant her as Empress was, at that moment, frankly unthinkable. She deserved to be in power. I knew my time would come; the good Lord had not delivered me to this foreign land if I was not going to one day rule over it. Even that silly old abbot thought so! No, at that particular time, my primary concern was procreation. I needed to produce children, male children. I'd read enough history to know intellectually that it was through one's son that one achieved power, and watching Eudokia manipulate Michael so expertly only reinforced this lesson for me."

So one day, as the royal couple strolled back to the palace from a parade at the Hippodrome—there was a secret passage that allowed the imperial family to process from the Kathisma to the Royal Gate securely—she broached the subject with her husband, her "twin."

"My lord," she said, "you know I adore you, and I love you with all my heart. If it were not for you, I would cry every day to go back to T'blisi. But recent events have made plain the need for us to take aggressive action in the procreative arena."

Michael smiled at her. "Your Greek has become so good, my princess, that I don't even know what you're talking about."

"I need a baby."

"Oh. Yes. That."

"*We* need a baby. You need an heir, my lord. And it's likewise my duty to produce one for you, the solitary task assigned to me."

"We are young yet, Maria."

"Youth fades. And it might take some time. What if the first baby is a girl?"

His face contorted in what could only be described as horror. "We need to have more than one?"

"Well, no, I suppose not. But a son is compulsory."

"Julius Caesar didn't have a son. Caesar Augustus didn't have a son. The first Constantine had four sons, and they all killed one another. Is that what you want?"

They walked a bit in silence. The roar of the crowd could still be heard—it had been a particularly rousing parade, with live bears and acrobatics and music—muffled by thick stone in the ancient passage.

"There is but one solution to this problem," Michael said finally.

Maria nodded.

"Prayer."

"Prayer?"

"Pray to the Lord. He gave a son to Mary your namesake. Perhaps He will bestow the same favor upon you."

She smiled and started to laugh—she had such a beauteous, infectious laugh!—but stopped herself when she realized that Michael was deathly serious. She had no carnal desire for him, but it was still a blow to her self-esteem to learn that he would sooner resort to an unlikely miracle of immaculate conception than even once deign to sully her with his sodomite's seed. His unadulterated faith in Christ had mutated into unhinged delusion.

"Thank you, my lord. I will do just that."

And she did. She went immediately to the Hagia Sophia, which was but a few steps from the Royal Gate, and prayed. She prayed as hard as she ever had. And the Good Lord in His infinite wisdom advised her what to do.

That very night, she began sleeping with Ramwold.

The blonde steward was legitimately fond of Michael, who always treated him with kindness and respect—or, to be more accurate, as much kindness and respect as one can bestow on one's chattel. But Ramwold's natural proclivities did not hew to buggery, and he was weary of having to thus perform. He adored Maria regardless—how could any red-blooded man not?—but when she invited him to her bed-chamber, he was so grateful to engage in normative carnal relations that he went to almost superhuman lengths to please her. The first time, he was gentle and patient, taking great care not to hurt her—Maria was petite, a wisp of a thing; Ramwold a giant in every way—and he somehow managed to pluck her rose without inflicting undue pain. He put his powerful hands to work, caressing the contours and crevices of her body, elucidating secret phrases in strange tongues so to speak, and devised other ways of giving pleasure that never would have occurred to her, and that she would later insist that my father perform. Over the next few months, under his diligent tutelage, she acquainted herself with principles of erotic ecstasy simple, intermediate, and advanced.

The logistics of these lustful liaisons she left to her lover—no simple feat. Ramwold had to contrive to appear in her bed-chamber after the rest of the house had retired for the evening. This required the bribery of several of the court eunuchs, particularly the ones assigned to guard the gynaeceum[33]. Once payment was accepted, the eunuchs were complicit, and thus vested in maintaining secrecy. But just to be sure, Ramwold threatened to accuse them of rape if they ever spoke a word. Fortunately this was never necessary, as the eunuchs were pleased with their extra income, and anyway they liked both Ramwold and Maria and had no wish to betray them.

The dalliances went on for a long time, for months and months—not every night, for Ramwold still had to service Michael, but at least twice a week. Michael was happy. Ramwold was happy. Maria was happy, too, and would have been euphoric, but for the pesky fact that while her lover had revealed to her pleasures of the flesh beyond her wildest imagination, the impetus for her infidelity had not been satisfied. Countless times the handsome blonde slave had filled her with his seed, and still her womb was barren. The child did not come.

---

[33]   The women's quarters.

VIII
THE DOUKIDS

NIKEPHORITZES THE EUNUCH WAS CORRECT in citing the long history of widowed Empresses creating new Emperors through re-marriage. Back in the Year of Our Lord 491, when Queen Ariadne wed a nobleman named Anastasios upon the death of her imperial husband, elevating him to *Augustus,* she established the precedent, which oft repeated itself through the next six centuries. Maria herself would utilize this quirky tradition of matrilineal inheritance—one of the few ways Byzantine women could exercise real power, albeit vicariously—as we shall see. But I'm getting ahead of myself again.

Eudokia was no Ariande. With no viable heir to the throne, the latter had to either take a new husband or remove herself to a convent. This was not the case with the Empress, who had not one but three young sons, all of them soft like their father, all of them under her imperious thumb. She could have reigned by herself, as Michael's regent, with nary a batted eyelash. Instead she chose to do what the prescient eunuch had predicted, and follow the path set by Ariadne. She decided to take a husband.

Initially, Maria was puzzled by this course of action. She struggled to understand Eudokia's strategy. After all, once a man became Emperor, it was impossible to predict what he might do. Only a special kind of individual does not grow drunk on power. And generals, who after all make their living by plunder, are notorious for sacrificing ethics for expediency. Even my own father was not above this. There was no telling how a general, however respectable, might behave once installed on the throne. Why alter the dynamic by bringing in an outsider? Why risk upsetting the Senate, the church, and the aristocracy by changing horses midstream? Why not elevate Michael in name if not in fact, and continue apace?

Eudokia's decision was informed by three factors. First was legitimate concern for the security of the Empire. Assessing the situation, she concluded unhappily that a woman running the show for an effete boy-king would only entice the Fox and the Lion to pounce. Choosing as her new husband a military commander, a rough-and-tumble general with a reputation for bloodlust and bellicosity, might have a prophylactic effect on the imperial designs of both the Norman and the Turk.

Second, given Michael's age and the existence of her other two sons—and the presence of Maria herself, who, while a foreigner, was still a *bona fide* princess—she discerned that she would remain longer in power if she brought in a new husband than if she relied on her children, in whom, as we have seen, she did not have much confidence regardless.

Finally, and perhaps most saliently, Nikephoritzes's accusation of adultery had not been without cause. For Eudokia had indeed had an affair with one of her generals, just as the eunuch had charged. In her defense, it must be said that the fatefully faithful Constantine X Doukas, soon after taking the purple, proclaimed carnal relations to be beneath his godly office and took a vow of celibacy. As virtues go, chastity is well and good, as I can myself attest—the distasteful congress of sweaty, rank bodies I have gratefully eschewed for many years—but for a ripe woman of prime age with an Empress's outsized appetite for salacity, the situation was frankly intolerable. When she confronted the Emperor about his circumlocution of this essential nuptial duty, he remained steadfast in his decision, and gave his blessing for her to look elsewhere for satisfaction. So when she took up with Romanos Diogenes—for it was Diogenes who had been her lover, also as Nikephoritzes had charged—she was not betraying her husband, but rather, and to the contrary, following his imperial command. How dare she defy his unwritten chrysobull and deny herself satiety? There was no way for Nikephoritzes to know this, of course, and he may have passed judgment even if he had; like many eunuchs, he was something of a prig. But now she had the opportunity to marry her lover, and thus legitimize their unholy union, such as it was.

So: Events unfolded exactly as John Doukas and Nikephoritzes the eunuch had foreseen. One by one the generals arrived in Constantinople, the order of arrival largely determined by how far they happened to be from the capital when the summons was received. Each was given a parade and a spectacular entertainment at the Hippodrome, over which the Empress presided regally in the Kathisma, Michael sitting meekly behind her, with Maria watching the spectacle as if it were the most astounding stage-play the Greeks had ever conceived. This began in the spring, right after Easter of A.D. 1067, and continued well into the summer.

First to arrive was Botaneiates. In his late sixties, with more scars on his body than Pythagoras himself could count and not a tooth left in his mouth, he was nonetheless a paragon of rugged toughness and boundless energy, and arguably the finest general in the Empire. He was gracious enough to Maria, but she got the impression that he'd been the sort of soldier who particularly relished the plunder of hard-won cities, mainly for the opportunity to rape with impunity. His voice was loud and his language course. Even when given an audience with the Empress, Maria recalled, he accidentally let slip a few choice expletives.

Nikephoros Bryennios the Elder was next, the father of my future husband. Made of better stock than Botaneiates, and thus given more to mercy and less to rapine, he was as polite and gracious as he was quiet. He hardly spoke, even when asked direct questions by Eudokia, although his eyes raged like twin volcanoes, and he thus conveyed the not-unfounded impression that he was up to no good. "My least favorite of the bunch," Maria recalled. "A snake in the grass."

Andronikos Doukas—my maternal grandfather and the nephew of the Empress—came next, accompanied by his father, the *Caesar*. The former was in no way the equal of the latter (this I must admit if I'm being honest, as I've vowed to be), but he was nevertheless tall—one of the tallest men at court—handsome and cunning and fearless on the battlefield. Eudokia had long fancied him, despite their relation by marriage, but Andronikos was loyal to a fault, to his wife as well as to the House of Doukas.

The interview between the Empress and the Doukids took place in the Empress's Loge in the Church of the Holy Wisdom, the sumptuous balcony that doubled as a lounge, and, unusually, Maria was not there to witness it. I know what took place from my mother, who heard the story from her father, Andronikos, one of the three people present.

John Doukas had been displeased with Eudokia's erratic behavior after the death of his brother the Emperor, and it was with that that the conversation began. "We're here," the *Caesar* began, "to advocate on behalf of our nephew, and to see that the prudent and proper course of action is undertaken."

"Dear brother," Eudokia said, "dear nephew, your concerns are well considered and in fact shared by me. But I ask that you understand my position." She related to them what she'd already told Psellos, about the dire threats mounting to both the East and the West of the Empire. "Just this morning I have received word that the Turks have sacked Caesarea. Caesarea, can you imagine? The Lion is a megalomaniac, and he will not satisfy his hunger until he takes the Queen City itself as his capital. Our very survival is at stake."

"Yes, I heard about Caesarea," John Doukas said, "and I agree with your assessment. What sense does it then make to prolong the inevitable? Or, for that matter, to summon your generals away from the front? You are creating a golden opportunity for Alp Arslan to attack, you must realize."

Eudokia smiled but cannily avoided his questions. "The battle plan is clear. We must show strength now. First, we must declare a state of emergency. We must behave as if Constantinople is already under siege, and see that the cisterns are full of water, and the silos of grain. We must take whatever funds are necessary, by whatever means necessary, and build up a standing army, not some motley crew of goons for hire. In the meantime, we must make hard choices. Recall some of the legions from the West to the East. I don't want that barbarian Robert the Fox to take Bari, but Italy can be lived without in the short term. If Anatolia falls to the Turks, we are doomed." She pounded her fist into the palm of her hand dramatically. "This *will not happen* on my watch."

John Doukas was unprepared for such an astute presentation. How could a woman know such things, and speak with such manly wisdom? He nodded, ran his fingers through his beard, and offered, "I assume you are merely parroting my good brother's opinion?"

Eudokia laughed, but there was no joy in it. "Brother, you discredit me. My husband, may God rest his soul, was the kindest man I ever knew, but he had no mind at all for military strategy. This is *my* assessment. Women are capable of independent thought from time to time, strange as that may seem." She turned to her nephew. "Andronikos, my child. You have known your cousin all your life. Tell me, is it your sincere opinion that he is up to a task of this magnitude? We are in a house of God. Be honest."

The younger and taller Doukas took his time, trying to formulate a response that was respectful, diplomatic, and true. He soon realized this was impossible, and wisely held his tongue.

"I *am* up to the task," she said. "I know what to do, and I know how to do it. Unfortunately, a thousand years of Roman precedent prevents me from the expedient discharge of my duties. A woman has never, since the founding of the Empire, served as *Augusta* by herself. Not once. And as much as it pains me to admit it, this is not an opportune moment to break with tradition. If *you* don't take me seriously, brother, neither will anyone else, especially Robert the Fox and Alp Arslan. At all costs, we must flex our muscles!"

They sat there in silent contemplation for a moment, as sunlight streamed through the bright dome of the church. Then John Doukas spoke: "Then you have but two options. You let Michael take the purple and serve as his chief advisor…"

"Or I re-marry. Yes, I know this. I would prefer the latter option, as it gives us the best chance of success."

"Hence the summoning of the generals to Constantinople," Andronikos said. "Have you decided whom to elevate to the throne?"

"I have."

"Romanos Diogenes?" John asked.

"That rake? Never," Eudokia said, scowling. And now she managed to surprise the *Caesar*. "My choice is you, John."

"Me?"

"You. As my late husband's brother, and thus Michael's uncle, it is the inspired choice. You become *Augustus*, Michael remains co-Emperor, for the sake of appearances, and Andronikos, you can succeed your father as *Caesar*. We keep the throne in the Doukas family, you see, as I swore to Constantine that I'd do." Sensing his hesitation, she added: "This is a marriage of convenience, John. It need never be consummated, if that is your concern."

"But my wife…"

"Irene has a crisis of faith, decides to dedicate her remaining years to God. We install her in a convent here in the city. You can visit her whenever you want. It will be as if you're still married. Our union is for show, a stage-play for the hoi polloi, and nothing more."

"Eudokia, we cannot wed. It is incest. The church will never allow it."

"The church has made exceptions before. And we're not *really* brother and sister, after all."

"I'm sorry, but I can't. I could not dishonor my wife in such a way."

The Empress rose and walked slowly to the rail. She watched the activity in the church proper below. "Think this through, John. This is your chance to be *Augustus*. You've never even sat on the throne, have you? It's quite something."

"I don't have to think it through. The answer is no."

Eudokia turned to face him and nodded. This was all going exactly according to her plan, although to look upon her face just then one would never know it. She was an accomplished actress and a masterful liar. "Very well. What about you, Andronikos?"

My grandfather practically leapt out of his chair. He was not expecting this at all. "Me?"

"I'm your aunt, I realize, but only through marriage, not through blood. You would wear the purple, and your father would remain as *Caesar*. What could be better? You're a young man. Your reign might last for decades, God willing."

My grandfather was more tempted by the idea than was his father. His mind flashed on himself in the purple robes, the crown on his head, the globus crucifer[34] in his hand. He pictured himself in the royal box at the Hippodrome, being wildly cheered by the appreciative crowd. He even, right there in the church built by Justinian, under the grandest cupola in Christendom or beyond, imagined himself in bed with Eudokia. She was not a young woman, but still beautiful in her stately, voluptuous way, and his own wife, my grandmother Maria of Bulgaria, was rather plain. Yes, this was a fantastic offer, and likely his only chance at ever attaining the highest office.

Then he thought of his wife, and his children, and even his cousin Michael, although he never really cared for that accursed bugger. Guilt seized him. His desire waned. Prudence won the day. The truth was, his father would have struck him dead right there in the Hagia Sophia before he let him accept the offer.

"I am flattered, aunt. But I stand with my father. I cannot in good conscience dishonor my wife in that way."

It is ironic that the Doukas men held their wives in such high esteem that they would reject the power of Empire rather than subject them to humiliation, yet also lacked the capacity to allow a woman to

---

[34] A globe on a scepter, an image often seen on Byzantine coinage.

assume sole command. How strange and obdurate are our traditions!

"I must confess to being disappointed," Eudokia said, although she'd anticipated—and, indeed, hoped—that they would decline her offer. This was a courtesy, nothing more, a pre-emptive strike so that when she took the husband of her choice, the Doukids would have no cause to complain. Her plan was working to perfection. "I'm going to wait a while regardless, in case either one of you changes his mind."

"That's not necessary."

"So you say."

"Who, may I ask, will you pick now?"

"I have not yet decided," she lied. "Botaneiates, I suppose. Although Manuel Komnenos will be here in two weeks, and he is not yet married."

"As long as it's not Diogenes, I will approve."

The sound of a choir could be heard from somewhere in the nave—the chorus rehearsing for Mass.

"Tell me," she asked, "what is your quarrel with Diogenes?"

The *Caesar*'s eyes narrowed, and she would not have been surprised to see fire shoot out of them. "I will not go into detail," he said. "Suffice it to say, he is an evil man. I understand why you find him appealing," he went on. "He is a handsome fellow, and egregiously charming, in an arrogant way. But he is an agent of the Adversary sent here to Earth to ruin us all, and I prithee you don't allow him to take the purple."

Eudokia's stony face betrayed nothing, but inside she was highly amused. For there was no question in her mind that Diogenes would be the next Emperor. "I will take that under advisement," she said. "Although I think Manuel Komnenos is the superior choice."

"I concur."

"Please keep this in confidence. I don't want word getting out."

"Attend, aunt," Andronikos said. "What of your vow to the Patriarch?"

For the Empress, recall, had sworn before the Patriarch to never remarry. She had signed a contract to that effect, which he had personally notarized. Breaking that vow would require his approval—which he would be loath to give, as he and the late Emperor were the dearest of friends.

"Leave that to me," she said. "Just keep quiet about what we discussed today, and I will handle the Patriarch."

Thus agreed, the uxorious Doukids went home to their wives—John convinced he did right by refusing Eudokia's offer, Andronikos not so sure.

IX

THE KOMNENOI

WHILE MARIA WAS SOMEWHAT CURIOUS about Eudokia's machinations, she was not overly concerned by what outcome they might produce.

"Remember, I had not been at court very long," she told me. "For all I knew, this sort of thing happened all the time. And Eudokia seemed to know exactly what she was doing. Never once did she evince the slightest bit of fear, anxiety, or doubt. She was an amazing woman, Anna, and might have been the greatest *Augustus* of her age, had anatomical circumstances allowed her to rule solely. A tragedy, truly, that she was denied that chance, for both her and Byzantium. Oh, she had her flaws, we all do, but Eudokia was made of finer stuff than most. I could not hold a candle to her. But soft…what was your question, my peach?"

"I asked if you were vexed that Michael had been passed over."

"Not one iota. I trusted Eudokia implicitly. It was literally unthinkable to me to rise against her in any way. She was Goliath, and I was David…no, I was less than David, I was his toenail, a scab on the bottom of his foot. No, my peach, I had no such illusions at all," and here Maria broke into her biggest, most electrical smile, and her sapphire eyes twinkled like twin stars, and my entire body turned to pudding. "That is, until the day I met your grandmother."

Anna Dalassene arrived in Constantinople from her summer estate late in the summer of A.D. 1067 to meet with the Empress. In her forty-two years on earth, she'd given birth to twelve children, eight of whom survived to adulthood. Three of her large brood accompanied her to the Queen City—her three oldest sons: Manuel, twenty-one; Isaac, seventeen; and Alexios, not yet twelve. A month prior, cancer had claimed the life of her husband John Komnenos, a brother of the Emperor Isaac who'd served briefly as Domestic of the Schools under his reign, and Anna was still in mourning dress. Now, one might expect a woman of that advanced age, a recent widow, with that many children, to be halfway to the grave herself. Not so Anna. A more vivacious woman never breathed air. My grandmother made St. Helena[35] look like a plagued-addled sluggard.

---

[35]   Constantine the Great's mother, who in her late seventies took a pilgrimage to the Holy Land, where she

"She wore her age well," Maria said. "She was voluptuous, like a pagan sculpture of Gaea, and her black garments flattered the smooth contours of her body. She was never a great beauty, but instead of looks she had that tremendous vivacity, which was in itself attractive. She was possessed of a certain magnetism that I've not seen before or since. She could have gone to a convent right then and there, and no one would have spoken ill of her. Instead she stuck around, managed things behind the scenes, and wound up running the Empire for twenty years. What a remarkable woman!"[36]

As for the three sons, they looked identical but for their physical sizes and the extent of their facial hair. Manuel was tall and powerful, with thick black curly hair and matching beard. Isaac was shorter than his older brother, a bit stooped, his beard less full. Alexios was still a boy, with no hair yet on his face, and still shorter than his mother. Yet all three carried themselves in a kingly fashion, and even then, the older brothers seemed to coalesce around the precocious youngster.

Unlike the others, the Komnenoi paid homage to Maria as well as Eudokia and Michael. They all in turn fell prostrate before her and kissed the floor.

---

busied herself discovering old relics—one of them the "True Cross" of Jesus Christ. A woman of great energy.

[36] I am quoting Maria here so as to recuse myself from having to describe my grandmother in my own words, and thus be accused of familial bias. (A.K.)

"Salutations, princess," said Manuel.

"Salutations, princess," said Isaac.

"Thalutationth, printheth," said Alexios. For my father had a severe speech impediment, rendering him incapable of making the "s" sound. Through perseverance and practice, he'd manage to check the disability by the time he took the purple—I only heard it slip out in rare circumstances—but when he was eleven, his lisp was atrocious. Not that he minded. If he felt shame or embarrassment by the way he spoke, he did not show it at all. It was as if he was unaware that the defect existed.

The parade of Komnenoi men made a lasting impression on the young princess. "If I were Eudokia, no question I would have picked one of them," Maria recalled. "Manuel, probably, at that time—your dear father was too young. But they were all more viable candidates, in my mind, than the sweet-talking rogue she ultimately chose."

What surprised Maria most that day, however, was the first-class treatment she received from Anna Dalassene. My grandmother sent her sons to engage the Empress, and then asked to speak to Maria privately, a request that was eagerly granted. The two women repaired to the gynaeceum and sat on a terrace overlooking the shiny blue Propontis,[37] where they could converse undisturbed by male ears.

"Can you understand me when I speak, princess?"

---

[37]   The Sea of Marmara, to the south of the city.

"Yes, of course."

"That's what I thought," and Anna laughed. "The Empress believes you deaf-mute. She has no idea how much you understand of what you hear. Clever, my dear. Very clever."

Maria held her tongue, but could not suppress a smile.

"You realize, then, what Eudokia is doing?"

"Yes."

"Tell me."

"She's going to re-marry, and thus create a new Emperor."

Below, two ships passed each other, expertly navigating the chaotic currents of the Bosporus, as a ray of sunlight shone between them. The image was so perfect it looked like a painter's rendering of the harbor.

"And this doesn't concern you?"

"Why should it?"

"Because your husband is heir to the throne! A throne that is currently vacant! Don't you want to be Empress?"

"Yes, of course."

"So why are you allowing this to happen?"

"Well, I..." But Maria had no ready response.

"You trust Eudokia. I understand. And it may very well be that she has no intention of betraying you. But she will. That's what you need to understand, princess. She will betray you, she will betray Michael, she will betray anything and everything to remain in the purple. Love Eudokia with all your heart. Admire her. Enjoy her company. But do not trust her. Do you understand?"

"Yes."

Anna took Maria's hand in hers and gave it a proprietary squeeze. "I'm only telling you this for your own good, princess. You may wind up on the throne beside your husband, as is good and proper. Or you might be in a convent by this time next week. Once the blocks are stacked up, they tend to fall very quickly."

"A convent?"

"That's where they put princesses," Anna said, "to get them out of the way. Men are blinded, a far worse fate, but we women are locked away in convents. Not that a convent is a bad place, no, not at all, I hope to retire to one myself someday, but there's a difference between choosing to enter a convent at my age and being forced to do so at yours. You are far too young and far too pretty to be discarded like a pair of worn-out slippers."

This gave her pause. Maria had never before considered that this unappealing fate would be an option. But now that the possibility was revealed to her, she saw, as clearly as she did the ships on the blue Propontis, just how likely it was. "What should I do?" she asked. "If you were I, what would you do?"

"May I ask a personal question?"

"Ask anything."

"Are you with child, princess?"

"No," Maria blushed. "At least, not that I know of."

"You should be. You need children. Sons, preferably, and more than one if possible. Start now, while you're young."

"I assure you, my lady, it's not from lack of trying."

Anna smirked. "Is that so."

"You don't believe me."

"I do. You are every bit as enchanting as advertised, my dear, but your husband…let's just say I was under the impression that he did not take to such endeavors with the requisite fervor."

Maria opened her mouth to speak, to limply defend her husband's honor, but then thought better of it. She had no one with whom to frankly discuss Michael's heterodox perversion, other than Ramwold, and when she and Ramwold were together, frank discussion was not the order of the day. Even Rona her nurse had no idea of her queer predicament. The only living soul who had any inkling of her troubles was her dear cousin Irina, but she was returning to T'blisi in a few weeks to marry some horrible Georgian warlord. Her yen for a confidante in such matters was becoming desperate, she realized. Perhaps Anna Dalassene could serve in that rôle? She leaned back in her chair, feigning comfort, and tried to mimic the knowing smile on Anna's face. "As I told you, it's not from lack of trying."

The older woman laughed, a delightful cackle always too loud for the occasion. "Aren't you the canny one! My dear, I came here holding you in high regard, yet I fear I may have nonetheless underestimated you. My sincerest apologies."

"Thank you," Maria smiled, a genuine smile this time. "Coming from such an one as you, I take that as high praise indeed."

"As well you should. But getting back to your original question, what would I do if I were you? That's easy: whatever it took to get my husband on the throne."

"But the Empress...."

"My dear, I love Eudokia as much as you do, perhaps even more, but I would feed her to the wolves before I took up the habit to serve her designs."

This was a treasonous statement, even if couched in jest, so its mere utterance convinced Maria that Anna Dalassene was worthy of her trust—as, indeed, she was. And yet the macabre subject left an uneasy feeling in the pit of her stomach. She felt like a line had been crossed.

"This is all a charade," Anna said. "The Empress has her mind made up. Romanos Diogenes will be the new Emperor. Everyone knows that. She loves him, and she is blind to the fact that no one else does. This myopia will come back to haunt her. I'm of the mind that the rightful Emperor is your husband. I think most people hold with me."

What Anna already understood, but Maria had not yet pieced together, is that the surest way for one of the Komnenoi brothers to take the purple was for him to marry a sitting Empress—if not the Empress Eudokia, then the Empress Maria. For Manuel to take the throne, Michael must rule first, and then be deposed, one way or another. Outright usurpation was a possibility too, of course, but a far messier and more unsure option. All that was years down the line, however. For the time being, the interests of Maria and Anna were perfectly aligned, as when Venus and Jupiter are in trine.

"I'll tell you upfront that my primary concern is for Manuel, or else Isaac, to take the purple," Anna said. "Every move I make is with that goal in mind."

"Of course."

"But I think we would all be happy with Michael as *Augustus* and Manuel as *Caesar*. It's simply not expedient for one family to serve in both rôles—certainly not when that family is the Doukas."

"If we both want the same thing," Maria said, "then we should work in concert."

"My sentiments exactly. In fact, I don't mind disclosing that that is why I came to see you: to form an alliance. Working in tandem, my dear, we can achieve greatness."

Maria's feelings of uneasiness melted away, replaced by an inchoate sense of excitement. "Tell me what to do, my lady. Provide me your wise counsel. I'll do anything you command."

On the polo grounds below, grooms led a team of horses onto the field. Maria could see Michael mount one of them, preparing to ride; she could identify him by his purple robes.

"The only person who can thwart the Empress's plan is your husband," Anna said. "If he goes before the Senate and demands the crown, the crown will be his. It's as simple as that. Without his complicity, the snake is defanged." Anna clutched Maria's arm, her fingers strong as talons. "Convince him to take the purple. Use every means at your disposal, but convince him. The very survival of the Empire is at stake!"

"I will do my best, my lady."

"Good. Now…is there anything I might do for you in return?"

Maria thought for a moment, but her mind was blank. Just as she opened her mouth to decline the offer, inspiration seized her. "There is one thing," she said. "My cousin…Irina is her name…she is Alani too, but she's been with me at the palace since I arrived."

"She is blonde? Like you, princess?"

"Yes."

"I know who she is. A delightful child."

"Her father, my uncle, has arranged for her to wed this vicious warlord back in T'blisi. He's wealthy, from a good enough family, but he's fifty-seven years old and has already buried two wives."

Anna smiled pleasantly. "You want one of my sons to marry her."

"No, not at all, I would never make that sort of request. I would like one of your sons to *consider* marrying her. That is all. One should have some choice in such matters. This would both obviate the need for my cousin's betrothal to that smelly old man, and also necessitate Irina remaining here in Constantinople—both of which would make me inordinately happy."

"Of course, my lady. It is the least I can do."

And that is how my grandmother and Maria of Alania formed their alliance—and how my uncle Isaac came to marry the princess's cousin, Irina of Alania.

X

THE PATRIARCH

JOHN XIPHILINOS WAS ORIGINALLY FROM TREBIZOND, the ancient port city on the Black Sea. He studied law in Constantinople, joined the faculty and advanced to *nomophylax*[38] of the law school before abruptly quitting to enter a monastery, supposedly at the behest of the Archangel Gabriel, who came to him in a Pauline-style vision—although I suspect he was simply drunk. He was both a pious monk and an able political operator, making him a natural compatriot of both the minister Psellos and the Emperor Constantine X, who installed him as Patriarch of Constantinople in *Anno Domini* 1064. He was not quite as zealous as the latter and not quite as meddlesome as the former, but was capable of both zeal and meddlesomeness when the occasion demanded. As Constantine lay on his death-bed,

---

[38] Literally "guardian of the law." A chief justice crossed with a dean of the faculty, basically.

about to gasp his last, it was these two holy men, the Emperor's closest and dearest friends, who'd attended him, like the two thieves on Golgotha flanking the crucified Christ.

In that darkling bed-chamber, already rank with the smell of death, Eudokia had knelt before the Patriarch, who'd made the Sign of the Cross in the air over her head. He'd muttered some inaudible prayers. She'd bowed down prostrate and kissed the hem of his frock. Then she'd leaned back, still on her knees, and gazed up at him.

"As God is my witness, I, Eudokia Makrembolitissa, Empress of the Romans," and here she'd rattled off her litany of secondary and tertiary titles, of which there were many, "do solemnly swear to maintain the throne of Rome in the Doukas family, where it rightfully belongs." Even as the words left her lips she knew they were false, and she knew that the moribund Emperor knew—but that was the purpose of this exercise. Why subject her to such humiliation if he took her at her word? "To that end, I also swear, as God is my witness, never to take another husband." A vow of celibacy by another word, and this after years of wedlocked celibacy!

Again the Patriarch had mumbled some prayers, waved his beatific hand over her unfaithful head, and blessed everything in the room, including Psellos and Constantine. When the ceremony was done, she'd signed a document validating her promises, which Xiphilinos had notarized as a witness (in lieu of God Himself, who'd apparently had other plans that evening). The contract was an official church document, binding before the law, and while as Empress she had some power to circumvent that law, to brazenly renege could have grave political consequences. (It could also subject her soul to eternal damnation, but I don't think Eudokia put much stake in such obvious claptrap).

Invalidating the pact wouldn't be easy—but it could be done. The Emperor was dead. Psellos had been sent away. As regent, Eudokia had the authority to remove the Patriarch from office, to recall him to Trebizond, but to do so would be suicidal to her ambitions. If she wanted her second marriage to be legitimate, the lawful release from her obligations was a must. Xiphilinos was not eager to comply with her request. And yet the ingenious Empress managed to convince him.

How? Well, the Patriarch had a younger brother, called Leo, who at that moment was himself *nomophylax* of the law school as well as a member of the Senate. He was ambitious, this Leo, and while a staunch Christian, did not share his brother's enthusiasm for monastic life. Both men were vain and somewhat fastidious about their appearance, and both sported immaculately trimmed beards, but Leo was also fussy about his clothes, his shoes, and especially his hair, to which he applied so much pomade that his jet-black coiffure was as hard and shiny as armor plating. Eudokia had known him for years, and preferred him to his stuffier brother. The feeling was mutual. She had the distinct sense, in fact, that Leo Xiphilinos secretly (and at times not-so-secretly) pined for her. The Empress was, the reader will recall, a handsome woman, albeit not in the same league as Maria. As fate would have it, Leo's wife, ill for years with a debilitating cancer, had passed away two months before the Emperor himself died. The die was cast.

Eudokia arrived at the school disguised as a peasant woman, kerchief on her head and frayed cloak covering her black gown, flanked by two Hetaireian[39] guards. She found Leo in his offices, squinting at the scrolls opened on his desk—he had famously terrible myopia—but his nearsighted eyes lit up when he realized the identity of his distinguished visitor.

"Your Highness!" he exclaimed, and practically fell over himself to assume a kneeling position.

"Oh, get up, Leo," she said. "I'm here as your friend, not as your *Augusta*."

He pulled himself to his feet, dusting off his fine clothes. He was shorter than she was, the Empress realized—not a desirable trait in a king. "If I had known you were coming…"

"The Hetairei advised that I move in secret, as it lessens the chance of ambush."

"Yes, yes, of course." He looked around the empty room. "Where are they now?"

"Just outside; fear not." She took his hand in hers. "I was so sorry to hear about Claudia."

---

[39] The Hetairei was the Byzantine equivalent of the Secret Service, charged with guarding the imperial family. They were a subset of the larger, but no less elite, Varangian Guard.

"As I was, and am, about the Emperor."

"She was a fine woman, and it grieved me to see her suffer. She is in a better place now."

"Amen," said Leo.

"But that's not why I came here today. I need you to promise me, Leo, that what we are about to discuss is kept in the strictest confidence."

"Of course, my lady. It goes without saying."

"Yes, it will have to," and she smiled. "The Empire is under attack," she said. "We have received intelligence that the Turks are planning a huge offensive that will be launched in the spring, in concert with a Norman invasion of Italy. If drastic measures are not taken, Constantinople might be in Alp Arslan's hands by this date next year."

"Surely you don't think…"

"Soft, sir. I don't intend to let that happen. But I need to make some changes. My son Michael—he is the love of my life, truly, but he is seventeen and green and frankly not up to the Herculean labors set before him. The trappings of high office are intoxicating, and my fear is that Michael will spend the lion's share of his time pursuing his sybaritic interests. This is not what the Empire needs right now. Could I manage on my own? Yes. But I fear that I don't have sufficient political capital. The military does not respect me because I'm a woman, the Senate has its doubts, and although I've enjoyed collegial relations with your brother the Patriarch, I don't believe I have the full confidence of the Church either. For these reasons, I have resolved to take a new husband."

Leo considered this. "You would have your son be passed over?"

"What good is the throne if the Empire falls? He is young. He will have his time if he wants it."

"And this new husband…I assume you will marry one of the generals? Romanos Diogenes, perhaps?"

"Romanos Diogenes," she said, "is a scoundrel and something of a political outsider. The Doukas clan despises him. It's true his military bona fides are impressive, but the negatives far outweigh the positives in his case. No, I was thinking of someone a little closer to home."

The Empress's piercing eyes met Leo's own half-blind ones, and she held his gaze for over a minute. Slowly the idea began to dawn on him. "You can't mean…"

"A *nomophylax* knows his way around the legal system. As a Senator, he has influence with the Senate. As the brother of the Patriach, he enjoys the support of the church. As a grown man with some military experience, he has the respect of the army. And as a recent widower, he is eligible."

"My lady, I don't know what to say."

"Attend," she said. "Don't let your excitement rouse you. It may well be that this never comes to pass. The obstacle here, alas, is that I am barred from re-marriage."

"Barred?"

"I took an oath on my husband's death-bed, before the Patriarch. I swore never to re-marry."

"Ah, yes," running his fingers through his well-maintained beard, "I heard about that."

"No matter. I will speak to your brother and try and convince him to change his mind. What I need to know, right now, is: if I am able to extricate myself from my legal obligation of permanent widowhood…would you consider taking a second wife?"

"My lady," Leo said, "I would do anything for you. To have your hand in holy matrimony…" And he didn't have to say another word.

Eudokia kissed him on the cheek—he practically melted away—and, donning her cloak, she quit the law school, having set her trap.

Two days later, Eudokia went to see the Patriarch, armed with a long and complicated argument that she would not, as it happened, have to use. Clearly Leo had violated his word and spoken to his brother about the lone obstacle to his taking the purple— which, of course, is exactly what she'd planned. The contract, she saw, the official document she'd signed vowing not to remarry, was already out on his desk.

"It is my opinion that my dear friend the Emperor was not of sound mind when he coerced you into signing this document," the Patriarch said. "I therefore declare it null and void." He held the parchment up to the candle, lit it on fire, and the two of them watched it burn to nothingness.

Eudokia was free.

XI

THE HORSEMAN

THE DEGREE TO WHICH MICHAEL DETACHED HIMSELF from his mother's careful intrigues was alarming. He appeared to be operating under the hopeful delusion that things would forever continue as they were—a dangerous mindset, for if there is one absolute certainty of life in the purple, it is that nothing is certain. He spent most of his days either hunting foxes, playing polo, or inspecting the imperial stables. Horses became more important to him than men. Since the day Maria arrived in Constantinople, he had been her constant companion, but ever since his father died, he was a stranger. Even Ramwold did not see him as frequently.

One achingly beautiful summer day, when the sun gleaming on the crystalline sea made the Propontis look like a polished gemstone, Maria called on her husband at the stables, as Anna Dalassene had suggested she do. Her womanly presence there was unusual—the care and feeding of horses was generally the provenance of men—but not explicitly frowned upon. She found him brushing the forelocks of his favorite steed, a dun mare called Humility. (Michael named his favorite horses after the heavenly virtues). He seemed neither surprised nor pleased to see her.

"So this is where you've been hiding."

"Not hiding," he said. "The weather has been so lovely, it's a shame not to ride."

"Michael, we need to talk. In confidence."

He issued curt commands, and his two grooms quit the room. Now they were alone in the stable, just the prince and princess and a horse named Humility. "What is on your mind, wife?"

Maria decided to employ the same strategy she routinely used on Eudokia—she played dumb. "I am still a stranger here," she began, putting on a thicker Georgian accent for effect. "At times, the mores of this land puzzle me."

"Maria," he huffed, "what is the matter?"

"Your father is dead. You are of legal age, no longer a child. And yet you have allowed your mother to rule as regent. This is highly unusual, is it not?"

"The Empress," he said, struggling to conceal the ire in his voice, "is still the Empress. The death of my father does not change the rank of my mother, not in my mind."

"Prithee, do not be cross with me, sire. I love the Empress with all my heart. She is a kind, generous, and brilliant woman. I can scarce imagine anyone being more suited to the rôle than she. But… Michael, don't you *want* to be Emperor?"

"No." He resumed brushing Humility, the fetlocks this time. For a moment she thought the interview was over, that this was his pusillanimous way of dismissing her, and she almost lost her temper. But then he added quietly, "Not yet."

"Not *yet*?"

"I don't know how much history you had in T'blisi, Maria, but if one's aim in life is to live as long and as happily as possible, taking the purple is an unwise move. Emperors die in office, often in bloody coups, or they have their eyes gouged out, or, in those rare cases where Fortune smiles upon them, they are allowed to retire intact to some bleak monastery. Emperors may fully trust no one. Even their own relations may be plotting to do them in, to say nothing of rival families and other factions. *Augusti* are forever waging war or else condemning criminals to death or dismemberment, accruing enemies as they go, and thus are the natural locus of popular anger. Emperors are to be feared, never to be loved. It is a lonely, solitary, horrible life. Say what you will about my father, but Constantine was a good man, and the high office drove him mad. You witnessed this yourself, remember? The poor sot chattering idiotically about the end of the world? I have a good life right now. A blessed life. Why would I give that up? For power? Power does not interest me. Power cannot seduce me. Power brings nothing but madness and death, as I've seen up close. Let the Empress do what she will. I am grateful to her for taking the reins."

The dun mare chuffed, as if in agreement.

"I understand your concerns," Maria said, mollified somewhat by the fact that there was some well-reasoned method to his mad stolidity. "Moreover, I agree with you. My life is also a happy one at present, and taking the purple is unlikely to make it happier. To the contrary, as you sagely suggest. But it seems to me—and, again, I am both a foreigner and a woman, and thus prone to stupidity—that your life, that *our* lives, are going to change no matter what. In that case, is it not better to act than wait to be acted upon?" She took up a brush and helped him tend to the mare. "How would your philosophy be affected, for example, if your mother were to take another husband?"

"She cannot," he replied. "She vowed before the Patriarch, and thus before God, not to."

Maria pursed her lips, waiting for some indication that he spoke in jest, but found none. He was completely and utterly serious, the gullible fool. "But Michael," she said, "what if she changes her mind?"

"Then she changes her mind. She is the Empress. That is her prerogative."

"Very well." She moved to quit the stable—the foul reek of horse excrement was making her woozy; Maria never cared much for horses—but an abrupt change in the tone of his voice arrested her.

"You starry-eyed fraud," he snapped.

"I beg your pardon?"

"Your transparency has betrayed you, wench. You don't give a jot about my legacy. You just want me to take the crown so you can be Empress."

"My lord, that…"

"Is it your sincere belief that the sixteen-year-old daughter of some *savage* is better equipped to wear the purple than Eudokia Makrembolitissa?" And he hurled the brush at her, striking her in the arm.

Michael could be moody when his humours were not in the proper alignment, and she'd witnessed his outbursts before, but this was the first time she was the target of his wrath. She had not expected this. She bent down slowly and retrieved the brush. Her voice was calm, quiet, direct, and she spoke with as little of an accent as she could. "You misunderstand my motives, my lord, just as you misunderstand your mother's. The Empress is planning to take another husband. The Patriarch has already given his consent. That is the nature of the recent appointments with her generals. One of them will take the purple—instead of you."

"You speak falsely."

"This is an open secret at court, my lord. Ask anyone. If you spent more time there instead of out here, knee-deep in horse-shit, you would know this. She will elevate a stranger over her own flesh and blood. It's true, sire. The only question is which of the generals she will choose to usurp you. There is hope among the nobility that you will put up a fight—none of the families want to see this happen; all of them support you, every last one—but there is no such expectation. They see what I see: a coward hiding away in a horse barn."

Michael stepped toward her. Was he going to embrace her? Strike her again? Neither. He took the brush from her trembling hand and resumed the grooming of his steed.

"Leave me."

"I am your wife, Michael. It is my sacred duty to look out for your interests above all."

"Begone, perjurer."

She left her husband with Humility—a horse and a horse's arse—and took the long route through the warren of stables. She came across Ramwold, whom she asked about her husband's state of mind.

"He has been aloof these last weeks," the handsome slave said. "He has not called upon me more than once or twice. I think his mind is troubled."

"The Empress has deceived him."

"Yes, I know."

"Do you think we can convince him to stand up to her?"

He shook his head. "He will not injure his mother, even as she injures him."

"That's what I thought." To change the subject, Maria gave him a melting smile. "Will I see you this evening?"

Ramwold flashed a naughty smile of his own. "I am yours until the cock crows."

XII

THE NEW EMPEROR

THE DIOGENES CLAN HAILED FROM CAPPA-
DOCIA—one of the most affluent families
in one of the most affluent regions of Asia
Minor. The scion of this proud house, Romanos was
named for his mother's uncle, the Emperor Romanos III Argyros. Diogenes was brash, charming,
extravagant, and generous, which only enhanced
his enviable good looks. He came from money and
enjoyed throwing it around, lavishing his friends and
subordinates with gifts, bankrolling saturnalian banquets, and procuring for himself the finest clothes,
horses, estates, foodstuffs, vintages, and courtesans
that money could buy. He was a swashbuckler, reck-
less and fun. His philandering too was the stuff of
legend; at camp, he was known to engage in orgies
with a dozen girls at a go; his virility was Jovian; by
some estimates he'd fornicated with thousands of
different partners, girls as well as scores of catamites
and eunuchs who filled in when ready females could

not be supplied. He literally humped his way across the Empire, spreading spunk and venereal disease from Dyrrachium to Manzikert, and leaving in his wake enough bastard spawn to garrison a provincial capital.

In his youth he'd been a charioteer, one of the greatest of all time supposedly, and no stranger to the roar of an adoring Hippodrome crowd. After quitting the races he proved himself an able if vainglorious general, veteran of many a pitched battle along the Danube, and he was adept at making sure his thrilling successes were widely recognized. Insofar as celebrity can be quantified, he was probably the most famous public figure in the Empire outside of the royal family, except perhaps for Psellos, and certainly the most admired. Men, and soldiers especially, looked upon him with envy, and women swooned in his wake. His valet kept smelling salts on his person, in fact, for the sole purpose of reviving fainted ladies.

His most fervent admirer was the Empress herself. Their love affair, such as it was, consisted of a series of enchanted evenings at the summer palace at Chalcedon, followed by a voluminous exchange of letters, now unfortunately lost, but reportedly full of flowery language and saccharine sentiment. For Diogenes, the tryst represented his greatest romantic conquest, the dandiest feather in a well-feathered cap; for Eudokia, voluptuous wife of the chastely dull Constantine, it was without question the best holiday of her life. She thought about it all the time.

She was not in love with Diogenes as much as she was infatuated with him. This infatuation clouded her otherwise impeccable judgment, and, indeed, proved her downfall.

"What Eudokia saw in him was obvious," Maria told me later. "With his cocky, rugged swagger, Diogenes was larger than life, a hero of old reincarnated, an Achilles or Jason come to Byzantium. Any woman would have delighted at the prospect of ensnaring him. The difference was that the rest of us could control ourselves."

His reputation has now been irrevocably tarnished, but I should iterate that, whatever happened subsequently, Diogenes possessed certain key qualities desirable in an *Augustus*. This cannot be denied, even by his detractors; John Doukas himself would acknowledge this. Diogenes was a fearless warrior, a charismatic leader, and a formidable presence—even at Manzikert he fought bravely, as we shall see. Furthermore, his strategical instincts were not unsound. Like Eudokia, he recognized the imminent threat of Turkish incursion, and resolved to bring the fight to them—quite unlike his diffident predecessor.

But he was not without flaws. First and foremost, while he enjoyed great popularity with the hoi polloi (popularity he was almost immediately to squander), he had few friends in high places. The Doukas family in particular reviled him, and Psellos was not a fan. When Leo Xiphilinos was spurned, the betrayed Patriarch turned against him, and the generals whom Eudokia passed over in his favor—Botanaietes, Bryennios, and to a lesser degree the Komnenoi—had no particular affection for him. The conservative Varangian Guard, the elite company that protected the imperial family, were sticklers for tradition, proper rules of succession in particular, and regarded his fly-by-night coronation as a slap in the face.

Then there was the matter of his impetuosity. Romanos Diogenes moved at a breakneck pace and waited for no man—even, and perhaps especially, when prudence dictated patience. Here is an example of what I mean. In the fall of A.D. 1067, he knew full well that the crown would be his in a matter of months. He had as confirmation a stack of *billets-doux* from Eudokia. All he had to do was cool his heels at the Danube frontier until his lover the Empress gave her summons. This he could not manage. Events were not moving fast enough; he feared inaction would cost him the throne. Instead, he gathered his army and prepared, somewhat noisily, for an outright siege of the Queen City! His treasonous activities were so brazen that the *Caesar* sent the Varangian Guard to arrest him, which they promptly did.[40] The man widely rumored to be the next Emperor arrived in Constantinople late in the

---

[40] Romanos's father, Constantine Diogenes, had himself been apprehended for attempted revolution years before, and threw himself off a precipice rather than face charges; perhaps this sort of treachery runs in a family. (A.K.)

night, on the night before Christmas, a prisoner in chains.

"This man has fomented revolution," John Doukas told the Empress, "and plotted against both you and the co-Emperor my nephew. This is high treason, and I recommend he be executed at once."

"What say you to this charge?" the embarrassed Empress demanded of her disobedient correspondent.

"I am guilty," Diogenes admitted, smirking—daring her to put him to death.

"On your command, fair sister, I shall happily separate the traitor from his head." The *Caesar* raised his broad sword to show that he meant his words.

"Release him," Eudokia said.

"But Your Majesty…"

"You heard me."

The Empress regarded this bumbling attempt at insurrection a blessing in disguise—after pardoning the obstreperous general, he would be all the more indebted to her, and thus never again oppose her wishes. Or so she reasoned, drunk as she was on love. This would prove a grievous error in judgment that would have dire consequences for everyone involved, Diogenes included.

Maria was with Ramwold that Christmas Eve. Indeed, the sudden and unexpected arrival of the famous personage, in Varangian custody no less, caused such a ruckus in the palace that their rendezvous was almost found out.

"Ramwold fled, and I crept down the hall to my husband's room," Maria recalled. "Michael was asleep in his bed, buried beneath a vast pile of blankets and pillows. His mother and Diogenes stood there in the light of a single flickering candle. Then Eudokia sat on the bed and roused him. 'My Emperor,' she said, 'my best of sons. Rise up and receive your step-father. Although he takes the place of your father, he will be a subject, not a ruler. I, your mother, have bound him in writing to observe this arrangement.'[41] All lies, of course. Well, Michael emerged from the bed-sheets—he could not hide any longer—and embraced his new lord and master. He should have stabbed the weasel in the back."

They were married, and Diogenes crowned, one week later, on the first of January, beneath the great dome in the Hagia Sophia. At the marriage-ceremony-cum-coronation was the entire Doukas clan—the *Caesar*, his son Andronikos, Michael and his brothers, and an army of cousins, as well as Psellos—all shooting daggers at the new Emperor from hateful eyes. Presiding over both ceremonies was the Patriarch, whose displeasure was obvious by the glower on his face and the contemptuous, almost disgusted tone of his voice. The Komnenoi were also in attendance, the three brothers behaving more respectfully than the shameless Doukids, but all of them disappointed,

---

[41]   This passage is lifted almost verbatim from Psellos's *Chronographia*, although some of the details are changed.

if not surprised, that Manuel was not the one at the altar. Diogenes looked out at this hostile crowd with his trademark smirk, either oblivious or indifferent to the palpable ill will in the cathedral, and waved regally to his recalcitrant new subjects.

Maria watched the wedding from the women's pews with her cousin Irina and Anna Dalassene.

"Poor Eudokia," my grand-mother said. "Look at her! She is smitten, you can see it on her face. I feel for her. Her heart is about to be broken."

As usual, Anna was right.

The lengthy epistolary exchange between Eudokia and her new husband had afforded them ample opportunity to iron out the details of how power would be shared in the proposed Romanos IV administration. She'd envisioned an arrangement similar to what had existed under the reign of Constantine X, in which she oversaw the administration of affairs of state, while he handled military matters and foreign policy. In his cloyingly sweet letters, Diogenes had ardently agreed with her every suggestion. No sooner was the crown placed upon his haughty head, however, than the new *Augustus* blithely ignored these promised arrangements and did whatever he wished, without bothering to consult her or indeed anyone else. (There was no small irony in the fact that a woman who had broken her own written promises had now had written promises made to her broken; the Greek tragedians would smilingly approve.)

In his first month in office Diogenes managed to alienate every last man in the commonwealth, nobleman, priest, and peasant alike. His first dictate was to permanently recall Psellos from Mount Athos, where the old meddler had scarcely begun his book, and reinstate him as chief minister. Most of the administrative duties previously performed by the Empress were given to her hated rival, which vexed Eudokia mightily. Not that Psellos was able to accomplish much. Diogenes was not given to delegation; he did not permit Psellos to do much of anything, however trifling, without approval. And he was fond of arguing with the (supposed) intellectual, as engaging in such brainy bouts, he reckoned, would boost his own reputation for genius. Psellos loved debate, but he did not enjoy having even his most minor and perfunctory decisions nit-picked. Almost immediately, he was scheming of ways to remove the new *Augustus*.

Next, Diogenes took a hatchet to the imperial budget, slashing as much as he could and reallocating other funds according to his whim. Welfare programs that underwrote bread for the needy, for example, he abolished, and he raised the levy on the poor, who under the exemplary Christian Constantine X had carried a small tax burden. As a last insult, he ceased funding for the games at the Hippodrome, not realizing that those games were for many peasants the sole ray of light in a life of dreariness and misery.

Thus with three strokes of the pen, he guaranteed that the hoi polloi, once his most fervent supporters, would loathe him.

He did not stop there. The salaries of the court nobility were dramatically reduced, and he imposed a prohibitive tax on the income of merchants and tradesmen, with deleterious effects on the economy. And what Diogenes *did* underwrite was just as injurious: lavish court ceremonials which sole purpose was to honor him, renovation of all imperial palaces and other land holdings, and the erection of statues around the city of the dashing new Emperor on his favorite steed. He even tampered with the designs on the coinage, insisting that his own portrait be the same size as the one of Christ on the obverse! Maria told me this was intentional: Diogenes wanted his image spread hither and yon, so his subjects would get used to the idea that he was the *Augustus*. But power is virulent stuff, as Michael had remarked to Maria, and consumed in such heavy doses and so quickly, it is invariably fatal.

Diogenes's military reforms, it must be said, were prudent. This was ultimately why Eudokia chose him, and he proved, at least initially, equal to his reputation. To weed out corrupt officials, he attempted to centralize authority, to the consternation of crooked provincial governors and rank-and-file officers, and in that way to instill much-needed discipline in what was largely a sundry collection of foreign mercenaries. The purpose was to end, or at least curtail, graft, and this worked to some degree, but the unfortunate if predictable repercussion was that the military, like the other segments of society, grew to despise him.

Eudokia stood by helplessly as Diogenes ran roughshod over the government. What else could she do? She had selected him, after all, and to repudiate him two months hence would be to admit humiliating defeat. She had no choice but to support her new lord, even as he undermined her authority, going so far as to physically remove her apartments in the palace to a smaller space further away from his own. Her old rooms he filled with concubines. She did not seem to mind, or even realize that she was being played—at least not at first. She was blinded by his charms. There was love in her eyes and wool over them.

And Diogenes conceived of a clever if time-honored way to shelve Eudokia for most of this period: he kept her *enceinte*. In the fall of A.D. 1068, and again in the summer of A.D. 1070, the Empress gave birth to two sons, called Nikephoros and Leo Diogenes. Indeed, her womb was ripe for most of the first two years of her new husband's reign. At her advanced age—she was in her late thirties, when many women can no longer conceive—she suffered on both occasions from difficult pregnancies that demanded constant bed-rest, and complicated births that threatened her life. When Leo Diogenes was born she almost bled to death in the Porphyra. The ill-starred effect of all this baby-making was that the Empress was kept in a state of constant weakness, and thus was in no position physically or emotionally to provide the counterweight to the increasingly megalomaniacal ambitions of her feckless new husband.

The Empress was not the only woman at court with child. After months of vespertine visits, Ramwold finally succeeded in fertilizing Maria's womb. The time for her menses came and went in January and February, and again in March. By early April A.D. 1069 she noticed that her gowns were tight to the fit. She had a few months before anyone else might notice—much could be concealed under the many layers of her fine raiment—and then she would be obliged to tell Michael the truth: that at his wise suggestion she had prayed to Jesus, and the good Lord had answered her prayers.

By the middle of April, alas, it was clear something was wrong. She experienced sharp pains in her belly, always concentrated on her left side. Thick brown-red blood, looking and stinking like dank earth, trickled from inside. She was frequently dizzy, so much so that she had difficulty standing, and spent at least two hours every day spewing yellow bile into her chamber pot. The pain in her belly worsened, accompanied by a burning fever. Late in the night of Good Friday the nurse ran screaming for the midwife, an elderly woman who had attended the births of every child born in the Porphyra for three decades, and the peril of the situation was evident by the grave expression on the latter's face when she arrived.

Maria was laid on a litter of fur rugs before a raging fire, to keep her warm, and her nightclothes were removed. The midwife felt her forehead and then her wrist. A poultice of comfrey and horse chestnut was placed on her abdomen, which eased the pain somewhat. Then the midwife ground some herbs, bugbane and mugwort and others with stranger names—from China, the midwife said—and made of this a tincture.

"Bugbane?" the nurse Rona said, concerned. "She is with child."

"Not anymore she's not," the midwife said. "That is the cause of her complaint, I'm afraid."

"I don't follow."

"The pregnancy did not take."

Maria choked down the foul-tasting tincture. The pain in her belly intensified, like a volcano on the verge of erupting, and then, suddenly, ceased. She fell asleep on the fur by the fire, huddled in blankets, the poultice still pressed to her belly. She was dimly aware of the midwife and the nurse on their knees before her, heads bowed, hands clasped, praying. In her dream she was flying over the city, soaring like an eagle (or like Icarus) over the vast dome of the Hagia Sophia. How beautiful it looked from the eye of the proud bird! Over her shoulder she could make out the angelic propulsion system: wings, wings like a cherub's. Bright light shone down from above, glinting off the gilded dome, blinding her. Shielding her eyes, she nonetheless could not help but look up at the source of the light. It was Jesus, and she was surprised at the uncanny resemblance between the Son of the God and her own father Bagrat.

"The hour has come," Jesus told her. "The hour has come." And then He called out to her: "Maria… Maria…Maria…"

She woke to the nurse repeating her name, over and over again, like a sort of prayer. The midwife sat by the hearth, the same grave expression on her face. The fire had died down but still generated heat. Maria felt something warm and sticky between her legs: blood, the earthen color of clay, had stained the white fur of the rug. But the pain was gone. The nausea was gone. The fever had broken.

"Maria!" And Rona kissed her hand.

"What happened?"

"You had a miscarriage," the midwife said. "One of the worst I've ever seen. You're lucky to be alive."

"Has it passed?"

"Yes, I think so."

"Thank you." She sat up on her litter of fur. "Where is Michael? Does he know?"

"Under the circumstances," Rona said, "I thought it was best not to tell him."

Maria nodded and sank into the nurse's warm embrace. Later, she would give the midwife a gift of ten gold *solidi*, more than twice her yearly salary, and donate the same amount to her favorite convent, as a gesture of thanksgiving.

"At that instant, I knew that I was meant for the throne," she told me later. "If the Lord were going to take me away, He would have done so that night. He left me on Earth for a reason, you see."

"What reason is that?" I asked her.

"If you find out, please tell me," Maria said, laughing.

XIII

THE WIFE OF CAESAR

HANDED ALL THE POWER IN THE WORLD, Diogenes desired solely what his high office could not automatically provide: glory. Only by defeating our imperial enemies, by parading Alp Arslan in chains at the Hippodrome, would the people truly embrace him. However ulterior or self-serving his motives may have been, his rationale was sound. A decisive, game-changing military victory would erase the ill will he'd accumulated in his first few months in charge. Otherwise, everyone wanted him gone. Indeed, when he personally led an army against the Turks that spring, some three months after taking the purple, the prevailing hope in the Empire was that he would die in battle.

This did not come to pass. His campaigns that spring, and again in A.D. 1069, were modestly successful, although he did not achieve the major military triumph he desperately sought, and desperately needed. And his decision to go on the offensive against Alp Arslan, rather than defend Bari, the last Byzantine possession in Italy, from Robert the Fox, was second-guessed by his ministers at court and learned men throughout the Empire. Psellos in particular was apoplectic when news came in A.D. 1070 that Bari had fallen. When the *Caesar* groused publicly about this, giving a rousing speech on the floor of the Senate, Diogenes threatened him with arrest; for a few weeks, John Doukas was on the lam before tempers cooled and he was able to retire quietly to his estate in Thrace.

I hesitate to include this next story, as the events are murky, the sources questionable, and the topic salacious. I've no wish to implicate an innocent woman, and certainly not one of my own ancestors, nor to dredge up muck best left at the bottom of the lake. With that caveat, I've decided to present it here as objectively as possible, for the simple reason that without knowledge of the story, the reader cannot hope to appreciate the depth of the Doukid hatred for Diogenes—hatred that burned so hot and fierce that it overpowered love of country, as we shall see. No, I've come this far, I must not hold back, I must tell all.

During this period, the *Caesar* and his family were living in their palace in Constantinople, a short walk from the Boukoleon. No sooner did John Doukas flee to Thrace than the Emperor called upon Irene, wife of the *Caesar*, in person. That much I can ascertain. As to what transpired once he entered her parlor, that is more open to interpretation.

Although Irene was my great-grand-mother, she is something of a shadowy figure in the family annals. She died before I was born, and I cannot recall my grand-father Andronikos saying a single word about her, other than perhaps some generic praise of her piety. My sense is that she was a quiet, shy woman, a delicate soul, one who was not comfortable in the spotlight. A few years later, when John Doukas could have taken the throne himself, he chose instead to remain in the background; my mother once suggested to me that this was out of deference for the diffident Irene, who did not want the attention and fuss that comes with being Empress.

What Diogenes saw in her I cannot say. He was famous, attractive, charming, and experienced at the art of wooing women; he could have had anyone in the Empire. Yet he desired Irene. Why? I think it had less to do with any inherent qualities she possessed—from what I can gather, she was a bit dull, and not much to look upon—and more with context. He wanted Irene not because she was Irene, but because she was the *Caesar*'s wife. We all want what we cannot have; it is human nature. In the event, Diogenes arrived at the *Caesar*'s palace with one singular and devious objective: to compromise her virtue. Was Irene flattered? Terrified? Titillated? Probably all three at once. That the Emperor got what he came for is exceedingly likely if not absolutely certain. The only lingering question, at least in my mind, is whether Irene fought to preserve her chastity, acquiesced to the imperial advances reluctantly, or participated with ardor. The fact that the presumed cause of the rift between *Augustus* and *Caesar*, a gaping fissure that existed long before this incident, was the former's illicit attitude toward the latter's wife suggests that this was not the first example of questionable behavior on the part of Diogenes regarding my great-grand-mother.

Irene did have a soft spot for the Emperor, I believe, although such fondness does not necessarily implicate her. As a member of the House of Doukas, I would like to believe that Diogenes forced himself upon her, so that would not bring dishonor upon the family. As a woman, however, I prefer to imagine that she both consented to and reveled in the infidelity, as I would not wish sexual violation on any woman, friend or foe, and certainly not my own relation. That Irene went to great pains to conceal the encounter—John Doukas heard of the Emperor's visit from Psellos, not from his wife—might be construed as evidence in support of the latter possibility. We cannot know for sure. Whatever the details, something untoward did transpire between Irene and Diogenes, and the *Caesar* did believe the *Augustus* guilty of rape—although by the time my great-grand-father learned of the encounter, Diogenes was already on his fateful way to Caesarea to wage war.

XIV
THE DEBACLE

BEFORE WE MOVE ON to the Emperor's ill-starred foray to Manzikert—even eighty years hence, that exotically sonorous place-name is shorthand for unspeakable disaster!—I shall have to invest a few paragraphs in a description of my late uncle Manuel, my father's eldest brother. A finer specimen of manhood never strapped on armor. Manuel surpassed his lisping kid brother in every way, from the fullness of his beard to the purity of his speech. He was taller, stronger, handsomer, wiser, better at military strategy and truer in love (this is the general consensus of everyone I surveyed, including Alexios himself). The deeds of the imperial generals during the reign of Diogenes ranged from reprehensible to outright treasonous; only Manuel was loyal to his *Augustus*, although there was not, according to my grandmother, much love lost between them. My noble uncle was able to put the concerns of the commonwealth above his own petty cares. For this alone, he is a veritable saint.[42]

Early on, Diogenes promoted Manuel to Domestic of the Schools, ordering him to retake some of the territory in Syria that had been lost under Constantine X. This my uncle promptly did, capturing the important city of Hierapolis Bambyce in the summer of A.D. 1069. In the battle that followed, however, Manuel was defeated and taken prisoner by the dreaded Alp Arslan. Contrary to his bloodthirsty reputation—perhaps enhanced by his mustaches, which were so long they had to be bound behind his head so he would not trip on them when charged in battle—the Lion was a kind and generous man, levelheaded and wise, and unlike Attila was not interested in violence for violence's sake.

"I have no wish to make war with Rome," the sultan told Manuel, as they dined at his sumptuous table. As a Moslem, Alp Arslan did not drink wine, but that libation excepted, the banquet set up in his roving tent, I'm reliably informed, rivaled a Christmas feast in the Queen City. "I have a more important calling."

"If you wish to pay tribute and vow fealty as our vassal, I'm sure the Emperor would accept," Manuel said, smiling to show that this was a joke.

---

[42]   If the Komnenoi are the Kennedy clan—and there are many similarities—then Manuel was Joseph Jr., the eldest and the chosen one killed in battle, in the latter's case during the Second World War.

The Lion laughed, a mighty uproar.

"What, then, are your aims," my uncle asked, "if I might inquire?"

"Ægypt."

There were, the Lion explained, two distinct strains of this risible heresy known as Islam, from a schism in the faith that had formed long ago, a few generations after the death of the illiterate blasphemer who founded the cult in the seventh century—not unlike the rift between the Orthodox Christian Church in Constantinople and the oft-heretical one in Rome. The sultan's aim was to conquer the heathen Moslems in Ægypt and establish a catholic Caliphate, a universal Islamic state.

"I cannot wage war on two fronts," he admitted. "I don't have the forces. And it behooves both of us to make peace, does it not, and put a stop to these constant and ill-advised squabbles in the borderlands."

Manuel was an avid student of history, and thus knew that the last time the Empire had held both East and West was during the reign of the inimitable Justinian—and for all of his considerable genius, Justinian was only able to make his wars of conquest *after* he made his peace with the Persians. Here, my uncle thought, was a golden opportunity. If Alp Arslan was to be taken at his word—and by all indications, he was; Manuel interviewed him for days and found him singularly honest, a no-nonsense fellow—then a suspension of hostilities to the East would allow Diogenes to focus his energies to the West, on the repulsion of Robert the Fox and his Normans.

"I concur," Manuel said. "And while any agreement would have to be ratified by the Emperor, I am qualified to negotiate on his behalf."

And negotiate he did, convincing the Turks to surrender all ambitions in Anatolia for two years in exchange for practically nothing. The terms were so generous they strained credulity, and yet the sultan proved a man of his word—marauders did not again raid Byzantine territory until twenty-four months had passed. Alp Arslan returned Manuel to Constantinople with a train of armed guards and a pledge of sheathed swords, and for those two remarkable years, there was peace in the East.

The agreement expired in A.D. 1071—what would come to be a dark year in the sad annals of Byzantium. Manuel smelled trouble when the Emperor dispatched another general, the inept Joseph Tarchaneiotes, to the Turkic capital at Isfahan to parley with the sultan when the two years had passed.

"Your Highness," Manuel asked, "why am I not leading the embassy?"

"Because Tarchaneiotes will do as I command without thinking," Diogenes said. "Also, I do not want to put you in the position of not being true to your word."

"True to my word? Is the aim here not to extend the treaty?"

"The aim," Diogenes replied, smirking, "is for Alp Arslan to *believe* we wish to extend the treaty. And why should he not? We have observed the provisions these last two years, just as he has. Let him be lulled into a false sense of security. Let him move his army south, towards Ægypt. Then, we will strike!"

This underhanded stratagem was so abjectly vile on so many different levels that Manuel could scarce believe the Emperor had proposed it. For one thing, violating a treaty would only demonstrate that the Byzantines could not be trusted; the East would then be a war zone and have to be defended for years to come. For another, what was the point of attacking the Turks now? They had already moved out of Anatolia, and had proved willing and able to adhere to the treaty. The current situation, which Manuel had savvily negotiated, was desirous for both parties.

"If I may be so bold as to inquire, Your Lordship…what is the war objective?"

The brash Diogenes seemed insulted that Manuel would ask such a question. "The war objective? You ask what's the *war* objective? Why, to win, of course."

"Yes, but to win *what*? And to what end? And at what cost?" My good uncle then, as diplomatically as possible, cautioned against invading a foreign power in an area as vast as Asia Minor without a clear war objective or a credible exit strategy.[43]

"Fie," the Emperor shouted. "You whine like a woman. We must act like men, and bring the fight to the barbarians."

---

[43]   The more things change, the more they stay the same.

"That speech would play well at the Hippodrome," Manuel hissed, "but it is not a strategy. You're going to get us all killed."

Psellos was present during this exchange, as Psellos always seemed to be. The Emperor called upon him for his opinion. "I hold with Komnenos," the chief advisor said. "Your plan is suicidal."

That the two men Diogenes most trusted vehemently disagreed with him did not change his mind, but only inflamed his desire to be proven right. His self-regard demanded it. Moreover, the Emperor was influenced by the ephemeral and uneasy nature of high office. Public opinion was already against him. Without a major military victory, complete with vast territorial gains and lavish spoils of war, popular sentiment could spark revolt. These realities inured him to folly. He was obdurate in his foolhardy decision, his proud heart stony as pharaoh's.

"We leave when spring comes," was his final command. "And you will both ride with me."

The army assembled by Diogenes was staggering in both its size and its diversity. Some ninety thousand soldiers comprising professional troops from both the Eastern and Western provinces, infantrymen from Antioch and Armenia and Georgia, much of the elite Varangian Guard, and mercenaries of Frankish, Norman, Uz, Pecheneg, Alani, and Bulgarian extraction, not to mention certain notable juveniles—my father accompanied his brother at the onset, even though he was just fourteen years old at the time—marched toward the rising sun, under the (mistaken, alas) impression that the bulk of the sultan's forces were elsewhere engaged.

My adverse opinion of Psellos is no mystery, but his reading of the blundering offensive happens to square with my own take on the situation—this is how fallacious the Emperor's plan was!—so I will let the grandiloquent meddler speak: "With his usual contempt for all advice, whether on matters civil or military, Diogenes at once set out with his army and hurried to Caesarea. Having reached that objective, he was loath to advance any further and tried to find excuses for returning to Byzantium, not only for his own sake but for the army's. When he found the disgrace involved in such a retreat intolerable, he should have come to terms with the enemy and put a stop to their annual incursions"[44]—he should have, in other words, followed the wise counsel given him by my uncle Manuel. He should have, but he did not.

As *Augustus,* Diogenes was not expected to lead the armies personally; that he did so regardless speaks to his bravery. The man knew no fear: give him that. Bravery does not expiate the tragic result, however. Had Manuel been in command of the troops, the outcome would have been quite different. To begin with, my salt-of-the-earth uncle would not have set

---

[44]   From the *Chronographia.*

out in a baggage train so elaborate and lavish that it was more portable palace than aggregation of tents. Was the royal *gluteus maximus* in such a state of disrepair that its comfortable maintenance required a solid gold throne, encrusted with all manner of gems, weighing more than eight hundred stone? Was it truly compulsory to bring *all* the crown jewels from the Grand Palace? How many changes of opulent purple garments did the peacocky Diogenes really require? This might have been excusable, perhaps, if the army were processing to Thrace, along paved highways—a short march in friendly confines. But the trek through Anatolia was harsh: the terrain was rocky and at times mountainous, the summer heat was brutal, and the men had to be forever on guard against sneak attacks. The presence of so pretentious a baggage train created an obvious target for would-be marauders, with whom the woods were thick. Worst of all, the unspoken message was that the Emperor's creature comforts were of greater import than the safety and security of his troops. Morale consequently was dismal. If any engaged man had commenced the campaign with a neutral view of the Emperor, by the third day of marching he developed antipathy toward him. By the time we took Theodosiopolis[45] in June, the entire army, to

---

[45]   Now the city of Erzurum in eastern Turkey, codenamed "The Rock" by NATO forces, who used the strategically vital site as an Air Force base during the Cold War.

a man, even his most fervent apologists, regarded him with absolute detestation.

Because of its advantages geographical (built at a convergence of major trade routes along Armenia's western frontier) and topographical (sited high on a plateau, and thus easy to defend and difficult to sack), Theodosiopolis was a logical place for the army to bivouac, if not decamp outright. If the purpose of the campaign was to re-establish Byzantine control of Anatolia—if that, in Manuel's phrase, was the war objective—then Diogenes had succeeded just by taking Theodosiopolis.

"Why march on?" asked Nikephoros Bryennios the Elder, one of the generals in charge of the expedition. "Our objectives have been met. We could leave two thousand men here and garrison the city. With a strong military presence in Theodosiopolis, the Turks will think twice about incursion."

"I agree with Bryennios," Manuel said, citing the example of Basil the Bulgar-slayer, who decades earlier had employed just that strategy, with estimable results. "We are here to shore up our position, and by our victory today, we have accomplished that mission. Let us now return to Constantinople in triumph, and turn our attention toward Robert the Fox."

"What say you, minister?" Diogenes asked haughtily.

After a pompous preamble, Psellos said, in his usual diplomatic way, "I believe your generals have given you wise counsel, Your Lordship."

Diogenes sat upon his gilded throne and smirked. He had no intention of turning back now. He needed to engage and defeat the sultan's army, not just win back some former possessions without much of a fight. "Noted," the Emperor said.

Then my grand-father Andronikos Doukas spoke up. "You are all cowards," he cried. "You are fearful of defeat. Remember that we have betrayed our treaty with Alp Arslan. Now we have no choice but to fight him till the death. We must find him, we must kill him, and we must parade his head on a pike through the streets of the Queen City!"

"Hear, hear," seconded the sycophantic general Tarchaneiates.

The lieutenants all whooped and hollered— their lust for plunder and rapine had not yet been sated—and the Emperor himself rose and applauded.

Later, Manuel took Psellos aside. "Father, is not the Lion on his way to Ægypt? Was that not the purpose of the treacherous stratagem?"

"The Lion is in our midst," the chief minister said. "He is closer than the Emperor realizes. If it's a battle he wants, a battle he shall receive."

"This is madness," Manuel said.

"I wholeheartedly concur, but what can we do?"

Manuel studied Andronikos closely. Something rang false in his polemic, something dishonest. Even as the Doukas clapped and cheered, his eyes burned with deceit.

Later that night, when the commotion had died down, Manuel decided to call on Andronikos in the latter's tent.

"Your speech was rousing, general," Manuel said. "But surely you don't believe a word of it?"

"What are you insinuating, good sir?"

Both were generals of the highest order, but Manuel, as the Great Domestic, was the senior officer. He did not back down, even though his subordinate was physically a full cubit taller—one of the tallest men, in fact, in the entire regiment. "What's the game, Doukas? What are you up to?"

"There is no game, sir."

"To engage the Lion now is certain death. This is plain. So you are either a fool or a liar. And I don't think you are a fool."

"My general, the excitement of the skirmish has gone to your head." His teeth showed when he spoke—a tell-tale sign of deception. "Perhaps you need some rest."

"My eyes are upon you, Doukas. And if you betray us, I care not who your father is, so help me God, I'll snuff you out with my bare hands."

Andronikos said nothing, but beads of sweat formed on his brow, and his breaths grew heavier. Manuel turned on one heel and marched out of the tent, almost tripping over his younger brother as he stepped outside. For Alexios was still traveling with the army at this point, although he was kept a safe distance from much of the fighting, and he'd overheard the exchange. (It was Alexios, in fact, who years later related it to me.)

"What do you think the Doukath has devithed?" the lisping younger brother inquired.

Manuel did not answer. "Come, Lex," he said. "Let's get some sleep."

The next morning, when Alexios woke, he found his brother dead, face-down in a pool of viscous blood. An investigation as perfunctory as it was sloppy found that Manuel had been assassinated by some Uz mercenaries who had secretly been agents of the Lion. Although they protested their innocence, the Uz were summarily executed without trial by—*mirabile dictu*—Andronikos Doukas. A funeral was held, and after a rousing eulogy by Diogenes and some prayers by the attendant priest, Manuel was laid to rest at Theodosiopolis.

That same day, despite his protests, Alexios was removed to Constantinople, escorted there by Psellos and a small contingent of troops. "The good Anna Dalassene has lost one son," the gallant Emperor said. "Let us not allow her to lose another."

The (alleged) assassination of Manuel Komnenos only heightened the desire of the troops to annihilate Alp Arslan—my uncle was one of the most popular figures in the army—and Diogenes used it to great effect as a rallying cry. Moreover, with Manuel dead and Psellos recalled, two of the strongest advocates for peace were suddenly removed from the picture. Now there would be no question that the Emperor would march on until he found the battle he sought.

As for Alexios, he returned home in tears, bearer of bad news he himself could scarce imagine. He would believe until his last breath that Manuel had been slain not by traitorous Uz mercenaries but by Andronikos Doukas himself—that my father's brother had been murdered by my mother's father.

The Lion was blessed with one of the finest military minds of his age, against which the Emperor's feeble brain was no match. As Psellos had foreseen, Alp Arslan was in Anatolia, not far from the Byzantine army, biding his time, waiting for Diogenes to err, which he promptly did.

Spurred on by the deceitful Andronikos, Diogenes gathered the troops and headed still deeper into barbarian territory. After four days' march southeast through the miserable midsummer heat, the army came to the small but important outpost of Manzikert. On 23 August, they captured the city, again without much of a fight. The next day, spies in the regiment commanded by Bryennios spotted the Turkish army, looming larger and closer than the Emperor had anticipated. The day after that, thousands of barbarian mercenaries defected to the enemy side.

What Diogenes foolishly believed would be a surprise attack was, to the contrary, exactly what Alp Arslan had been patiently waiting for: the Byzantines to march too far into Anatolia to easily retreat.

The Emperor split the army into four segments: Bryennios controlled the left flank, Tarchaneiates the right, and Andronikos Doukas commanded the rear guard, while the Emperor himself—and here we must again credit him for his courage—led the charge from the middle.

The armies met on the fields outside Manzikert on 26 August. It was a debacle from the start. Almost immediately upon engaging the sultan's forces, the inept Tarchaneiates either lost his nerve or calculated that victory was impossible—reports of what exactly happened remain conflicted on this point—and fled. So within the first hour of fighting, the right flank was lost. Meanwhile the canny Lion arranged his forces in the shape of a crescent moon. As Diogenes charged, the sultan retreated rather than engaging in battle. Impulsive and impatient as always, the Emperor kept charging—he would have his moment of glory!—and Alp Arslan kept retreating. By doing so, Diogenes thinned out his forces, leaving him increasingly vulnerable.

Andronikos was charged with defending the rear—the easiest and least dangerous of the four posts. As the sun began to fall over the mountains, however, he inexplicably signaled for his troops to retreat. "The Emperor is slain!" he shouted, although this was a falsehood. "We must away!" He rode off, and a quarter of the army rode off with him, leaving the Emperor's regiment exposed. By twilight, Diogenes was deep into enemy territory—too deep to return to camp before nightfall. His impatience had cost him dearly, just as the Lion had devised. As the sun began to set, perhaps symbolically, Alp Arslan's troops suddenly went on the offensive, routing the Byzantines with volleys of arrows. Bryennios, who'd fought admirably on the left flank, assessed the situation, (correctly) realized it was hopeless, and beat a hasty retreat as well.

By nightfall, the Emperor's own regiment was fighting alone. Casualties were many, with butchered carcasses heaped on the battlefield. Still Diogenes soldiered on. He slew many infidels by his own hand, but he was one against a well-rested army. The Turks closed in on him, and an arrow pierced his armor, wounding his shoulder. He dropped his sword and fell to the ground, watching helplessly as the Lion's men surrounded him, swords drawn. Muttering a prayer to the Virgin, he shut his eyes and awaited the *coup de grâce*…

XV
THE LETTER

BECAUSE THE SURVIVORS TENDED TO BE those who fled the field straight away, the events subsequent to the Battle of Manzikert remain, to the honest historian, hopelessly conflicted. The one unassailable point of consensus is that the summer months of A.D. 1071, and the month of August in particular, were brutally hot—the hottest in recent memory. Constantinople smoldered like a Hephæstean furnace. The low, hot sun baked the roofs and gleamed so brightly off the Propontis that some went blind. A cholera epidemic swept through the poorer quarters of the city, wending its way through the tortuous roads and houses dense with fetid humanity. Paving stones were so hot to the touch that the horses refused to move. While tending to Humility in the stable, Michael collapsed from heat stroke, although he quickly recovered. Commerce more or less shut down for weeks. And the frustratingly ominous lack of news from the

Eastern front weighed heavily on everyone's mind, as few citizens did not have a husband, son, or brother in the army. The Queen City was Hell on Earth.

During the dog days of this singularly infernal August, Maria spent the long afternoons with the Empress in a secret crypt beneath the palace, cooled by the waters of the subterranean cistern. Only within the vast stone walls of this dark, dank place, crawling though it was with rats and spiders and mice, the women could find respite from the heat. Chaises were brought from the parlor, and wine from the nearby cellars, and Empress and princess lay in repose, sipping at fine vintages and nibbling on cheese, as four eunuchs fanned them. By this time, Eudokia had recovered from her second delivery—Leo Diogenes had been born in May—and had regained her faculties. She would need them in the days ahead.

As August turned to September, news of the cataclysmic disaster in the East finally began to trickle in. As usual, accounts conflicted, but a picture gradually developed: after some initial success, the Emperor had overpursued the barbarians, scattering his army in the process, and all who had not retreated had been slain. The irony is that Diogenes had indeed engaged the enemy in glorious battle, just as he'd wanted—but he'd been defeated, and all glory belonged to Alp Arslan. Many decades later, Manzikert is regarded as one of the worst defeats in Byzantine history, but this assessment was arrived at as early as the fall of A.D. 1071. The silver lining in the debacle, which would not become apparent until well into the new year, is that the losses were relatively few. So much of the army had either fled or defected that the casualty rate was lower than expected. Other than Manuel, whose assassination had little to do with the Turks, all of the generals had survived, and because the battle was deep into barbarian-controlled territory, there was nothing to plunder. The only major material loss of the campaign was the Emperor's sumptuous baggage train—and there was some poetic justice to that.

As for Diogenes, his fate was unknown. Some insisted that he was dead; they had seen him fall from his horse, witnessing the Turk forces hacking at him with broadswords. Others maintained that he had been captured alive, and the Lion would soon be sending his ransom requests. Still more averred that he had miraculously escaped the infidel's clutches, and was marauding his way to Isfahan[46] with a small band of Varangian Guard. News would come soon, these last proclaimed. The Emperor would prevail!

Poor Eudokia did not know what to do. If Diogenes was dead, then Michael should be crowned Emperor, with her as regent. But what if he were still alive? A captive Emperor is still an Emperor, surely? In that case, negotiations with the Lion must begin immediately, and the *Augustus* must be freed as soon as possible...or should he? What sort of

---

[46]   Alp Arslan's capital city.

reception might await Diogenes should he return from the East in ignominious defeat?

And those were just the objective political realities. The Emperor was also her husband, a man she loved dearly, for better or worse, despite his contemptuous treatment of her. Eudokia was better than most at subordinating her heart to her head—women in power must master this skill, and are thus always better at it than men—but under those trying circumstances, how could she not be overwrought? Like Job, she cursed God.

"I have prayed," the Empress said to Maria, in the cool darkness of the crypt. "Every night I have prayed. But I have found no solace. Every course of action open to me is unappealing, a choice between evils. I simply don't know what to do. Part of me wants to stay down here forever. Brick off the opening to the crypt and let this be my tomb. What do you think, dearest Maria? You know what is at stake here. What is your opinion?"

This marked a turning point in their relationship. While the Empress had for some time realized that Maria spoke fluent Greek, and indeed was a fine conversationalist, she had always treated her as a subordinate. She was the Empress, Maria a foreigner here by God's grace, and her own. Now Eudokia spoke to her as a peer, a confidante, an equal.

"I am genuinely flattered and honored, Your Highness, that you hold me in sufficient regard to make such a request," Maria said. And then, for the first time, she spoke to her mother-in-law openly and without fear. "I agree that the road before you is rocky. Whatever decision you make will carry with it undesirable consequences. But here is the thing: I have had the pleasure and privilege of watching you rule all this time, since my arrival in Constantinople, and Your Majesty, there is not an one such as you in the whole of the Empire. The inherent burdens of our sex have unjustly prevented you from taking the crown yourself. This is a tragedy, because no one, man or woman, is more qualified to wear it than you are. It is hard and thankless work to run an Empire, and yet you have done so effortlessly and commendably for years. As I see it, you have made but one error in judgment in all your reign, if I may be so bold: marrying Diogenes and thus elevating him to *Augustus*. And even that can only be termed an error now, in hindsight. At the time, I agreed that it was the best course of action to take. You ask my opinion, and here it is: You, Eudokia Makrembolitissa, should have as much power as you possibly can. Disavow Diogenes, leave him for dead, and reign as regent. Michael will not oppose you; I will see to that. The last thing the Empire needs is another blundering *man* on the throne. Long live the Queen!"

A smile broke across Eudokia's face, which had for weeks had been fixed in a joyless scowl. "You flatter me, princess."

"Your Highness, I speak true. The *Caesar*, Psellos, Michael...they all know it. Only their male vanity clouds their vision and prevents them from accepting the truth, which is that you and only you are qualified to rule."

Eudokia's smile was big now, lighting up the room. Her face fell naturally in a frown, and this sort of smile was as rare for her as it was attractive. "Well, if you really think so."

"It is not an opinion, Your Majesty. It is as plain as the sunrise in the morning."

Meanwhile, at the *Caesar*'s palace in Thrace, Andronikos returned to a hero's welcome. His father embraced him, and Nikephoritzes fell on his knees before him. Only Psellos remained skeptical.

"We may have prevailed outright," the chief minister chided, "had you remained at your post."

"Fie!" Andronikos cried. "The Emperor is an imbecile. I saved my men from certain slaughter. One does not pursue battle without good intelligence, and the fool did not even know that Alp Arslan was in the vicinity. He thought he was in Ægypt, and yet there he was, half a day's march away, keeping careful track of our movements. No number of men overcomes such a disadvantage. I saved the day, minister."

"And what of Diogenes?" John Doukas asked. "There is no word of him."

"He is either fallen or captured, father. In either scenario, crowning a new Emperor is indicated."

"It should revert back to how it was," Psellos suggested—one of his rare moments of clarity. "Much as I detest her, I love the Empire more. Eudokia should reign as regent for Michael, in concert with him."

"No," the *Caesar* said. "It is his turn now. He has waited long enough."

"But he has no desire to rule," Andronikos said, "and no backbone at all. He is effectively a woman in a man's body, a weakling. Under his watch Byzantium will implode. It is my belief that you should take the purple, father."

But John Doukas again declined. "That would be a coup," he said. "We don't need yet another usurper to the throne. We need stability."

"If it's stability we want, then allow Eudokia to remain," Psellos said. "She erred in marrying that wretched blowhard, but she is an extremely capable administrator. I don't think you understand just how much responsibility she had while your brother was *Augustus*."

"I cannot pledge fealty to that whore," Andronikos said. "I would sooner hand her over to a horde of Huns than bow before her. And frankly, minister, I'm surprised you don't want her removed, after how she treated you."

"I will take my revenge on her," Psellos said, "in due time. Fear not. But now is not the right moment."

"The solution is simple," Nikephoritzes the eunuch said. "Michael is a lightweight, which only means he is easily manipulated. He is a weakling, yes, but he can handle presiding over games at the Hippodrome and that sort of thing. Eudokia is the one we have to concern ourselves over, so she must be removed—banished, arrested, killed, however it plays out. Michael must renounce her, and she must leave the stage once and for all. Then, under Michael, Psellos will handle internal affairs, I will be finance minister, Andronikos will be Great Domestic, and John, you will take an extremely active rôle as overseer. With Eudokia as regent, we are sidelined; but with Michael reigning by himself, the four of us can effectively rule the Empire."

"Our biggest obstacle is Michael himself," Psellos said. "He will never betray his mother. He loves her dearly."

The eunuch ran his long ladylike fingers along his smooth chin. "Then we shall have to be very convincing."

Anna Dalassene was in such a state of anguish that Maria thought she'd gone mad. She went from copious weeping to subverbal shouting to tortured moaning to outright collapsing in a heap on a settee. Dying young is an occupational hazard of military life, but Anna was unprepared for her firstborn son to have met his Maker so soon.

"After Manuel was born," she told Maria, "the astrologer read his chart, and then looked at mine, and he was astonished. He'd never seen anything quite like it, he said. My son was destined to be Emperor. He would rule for thirty-seven years. And now he is taken from me, so young?"

"Anna," Maria said, embracing her, and chancing, in a candid moment such as this, to address her by her first name, "perhaps the astrologer saw something in *your* chart and not Manuel's. You have other sons. It could be that Isaac will take the purple."

"No," Anna said, "not him."

"Well, Alexios, then."

Anna laughed, but there was no joy in it, only defeat. "No, that will never happen. Manuel was the chosen one. But you are kind to say so, Maria."

This visit took place at the sumptuous Komneni apartments in the Queen City, a short walk beyond the Imperial Gates. When Anna excused herself to rest in her dark bed-chamber—her headaches were so intense, she said, it was like Athena was about to burst forth from the skull of Jove—Maria decided to call on Alexios, then fourteen years old.

"I'm sorry about your brother," she said. "I bring condolences from my husband and his family."

"Thank you, printheth," he said. "My brother wath fond of your huthband, and held both Conthtantine and Eudokia in the highetht regard."

"Manuel was as fine a man as the Empire has ever seen," Maria said sincerely. "We will all miss him."

"Not all," Alexios said cryptically.

"How do you mean?"

"My mother favorth you," he said. "And her favor ith hard-won. Thuth I mutht prethume you are worthy of trutht. May I confide in you, princeth?"

"Of course."

"What I am about to tell you my mother doeth not yet know. I fear to tell her. It would break her heart utterly."

"I will speak not a word to another living soul. I swear in the name of the Holy Virgin."

Alexios nodded. He was a young man, a child still in many ways, and yet he comported himself as one much older, much wiser. His gravitas was remarkable. "Manuel did not fall in battle, as Pthelloth claimed. He wath athathi…that ith, he wath murdered in hith tent, at camp, in the middle of the night."

"Murdered? But who would do such a thing?"

Here Alexios let out a sigh. "Andronikoth Doukath, acting on orderth from hith father the *Thaethar*."

"But…but why?"

"Thabotage." And here Alexios lispingly told of how Andronikos had abandoned his post, taking his entire regiment with him, thus ensuring the Emperor's inglorious defeat. "John Doukath wanted Diogeneth to fall, and conthpired thuth to make it happen. Manuel never would have betrayed hith Emperor, ever, in a million yearth."

Tears welled up in the young man's eyes, which he wiped away. "You don't believe me."

"Of course I believe you," Maria said. "You have nothing to gain from spreading a tale such as this. To the contrary, if the *Caesar* does take the throne, you could be banished for treason—or worse." She took his hand—already strong like an older man's—in her own and squeezed it. As she did, the entire expanse of his face turned a crimson color, the same shade as sheep reddle. "Alexios, is something the matter?"

"Forgive me, printheth," he said, showing a bashful grin. "I'm not…I mean…your thingular beauty is rather overwhelming. I feel like I'm in the prethenthe…that ith, the *company*, of Venuth."

Maria laughed. "You are a sweet boy."

"Prithee," he said, regaining his composure, "do not tell my mother. I will not keep thith from her forever, but right now, it ith not well for her to know."

"I agree," she said. "Thank you for your confidence, sir. It means a great deal to me to have won your trust. You take after your brother; that is already plain." She rose, leaned over, and kissed him gently on the forehead. "Fare thee well, Alexios."

"Fare thee well, princeth," my father managed, before tumbling backwards out of his chair. For he had fallen head over heels in love.

As September wore on, the heat and humidity continued unabated. Not even the cool Bosporus breezes could alleviate the discomfort. Distraught though she was, Eudokia rose to the occasion and performed her royal duties. The gears of government ground on. Michael, in whose name imperial business was conducted, spent most of the summer submerged in the Propontis. Maria, too, dipped into the waters, although decorum and modesty prevented her from going all the way in. They were at one of the royal houses on the water, Maria, Michael, and Eudokia, when the messenger came, riding fast. He was covered in dust and on the plump side and sweating profusely in the late summer swelter.

"Your Majesty!" he cried, dismounting, and only then did Eudokia recognize him as Maurice, the Emperor's valet. He handed her a letter, falling on his knees as he did so.

"But what is this?" she asked, opening the letter, which read:

His Most Exalted Highness, Romanus IV Diogenes, *Augustus*, Emperor of Rome, to the Empress Eudokia Makrembolitissa, his sweetest friend, his devoted wife, his favored helpmate, his better half, his terrestrial Venus, his sole desire, whatever metaphor his inadequate mind might conjure better or more favorable, I write this from a silken tent in the hinterlands of Anatolia, still stunned that Christ in His Divine Mercy has spared me, and that I am still possessed of the faculties necessary to put pen to paper, after all these lonely months since I last enjoyed your warm embrace—is it mere months? It feels like years, like entire lifetimes have come and gone, so much has happened, I am flushed with excitement to relate all to you, my darling Eudokia, please forgive what I'm sure will be a long and scattered missive, my love for you has seen me through this, the greatest trial of my life, my love for you, yours for me, and Christ's bountiful and boundless love for all of us, hallowed be His Name.

By now I'm sure you've heard about the battle, you likely know more of the details than I do, of the fate of my countrymen, my generals and their men, I know nothing, I pray to the Lord Jesus Christ that they have returned home unscathed. I know only of Manuel Komnenos, may Heaven open its glorious gates to receive him, his sleeping form met the dagger of a Turkish spy ere the battle was ever fought, the poor fellow, although the sultan denies that his agents carried out this treachery, and while he has proved a man of his word, I cannot believe he speaks truthfully in this regard. We captured Manzikert, a wretched little town in the marchlands, with ease, the citizenry dropped their weapons and bade us enter in exchange for a vow not to pillage their property, especially their women, and to leave their houses be, a promise I'm pleased to say we obeyed. Two days later, I led a regiment to seek and destroy the sultan's army, I set upon him, many of our forces apparently fled, having received false word of my death, and with such a massive reduction in numbers, and with morale at low ebb, we were no match for the Lion, who is a brave warrior and a savvy general withal, my men fought bravely but to no avail, I slew many barbarians myself, they are more than willing to die for their blasphemy, on several occasions I believe they came at me with the intention of slaughter, so that they may achieve the glorious death on the battlefield, smiled upon in Islam, so these infidels I dispatched to the underworld post haste, but there were too many of them, an arrow slew my horse, I fell, injuring my shoulder, and took more damage when Turkish infantrymen attacked me as I lay, in the confusion of the battlefield, among the dust and the blood and the fury of weaponry, never in a lifetime devoted to warfare have I witnessed such carnage, in time there was no recourse but to surrender, I was with perhaps twenty of my men, brave survivors, they were silent about my true identity hoping to fool the sultan, if he knew the *Basileus* and Emperor of the Romans was among the captives, they reckoned, I would be put to the sword for certain, so they doffed my purple, my gold, my jewelry, anything that gave an outward sign of my superior rank, and I marched in the prisoner procession like a common footman, but the sultan could not be fooled, he suspected I was not of the hoi polloi, and when several of his envoys recognized me, men we had hosted in the palace, who had enjoyed my munificent table, the game was afoot. Alp Arslan the sultan has long mustaches but not so long as to touch the ground as was reported, that was a falsehood, but certainly to his shoulders, his cheeks he shaves with a sharp blade save for the hair on his chin, which falls as do his mustaches—a most sinister affect—and yet he is quick to laugh, and when he spoke to me, he spoke in Greek! Although his accent was thick and I could not comprehend his words unless listening carefully, but the savage intelligence of the man! I was made to bow prostrate before him, as so many captive barbarians have bowed to me in the past, and he rested his foot upon my neck and pressed my lips to the dirt floor of his yurt. He spoke to me and he sayeth, So you are Romanos who has betrayed my trust and violated our treaty, paraded before me like a peasant soldier, is that so, and I answered that it was so, and he spoke again, and he sayeth, Tell me, *Augustus*, if the rôles were reversed, if I were your prisoner, what would you do, and I answered him, and I sayeth, I would lop off your head, perhaps, or else parade you in chains through the streets of Constantinople and throw you in some dungeon for the rats to dine on, and here the sultan paused and studied me with his slanty black eyes as he ran his fingers through that sinister goat-beard, and he spoke again, and he sayeth, The punishment I exact is a far heavier and less merciful one. I shall set you free. Whereupon he clapped his mighty hands, and attendants emerged as if from thin air to do his bidding, and they rose me from the muck, bathed me, clothed me in silken robes, not as soft as my own but of the highest quality, worthy of my office certainly, my wounds were cleaned and bandaged, and I was provided comfortable quarters and sumptuous meals, and saw that my every need was accommodated at once. For some days I have been his honored guest, eating at his table. Strange are their customs, they eat no pork and drink no wine, but draw fragrant incense into their lungs, the air is redolent with the cinnamon reek of their hookah pipes, and their food while seasoned a bit too richly for my taste is yet delectable. The Mosulman faith is apostasy, Moslems blaspheme the true Word of Our Lord Jesus Christ, and yet there is much to recommend that perverted creed, not least the dedication and devotion of its followers, heathens though they are and damned for that reason to eternal hellfire, they are hospitable, service to their god, whom they call Allah, demands that they take in strangers who are in need and serve and protect them, and that is what the sultan has done for me. He does not renounce Christ, this is strange, he has nothing but blessings to bestow upon Our Savior, His

Excellence is apparent even to the barbarians, it cannot be denied. Once I was healed we sat and negotiated terms. I was expecting to have to agree to a humiliating peace, but lo, the sultan is merciful, and the concessions he demands are a pittance: Antioch, Edessa, Hierapolis, and the wretched dunghole of Manzikert, may he keep it, the rest of Anatolia remains in Roman hands. There was some quibbling over the price of my ransom, his initial ask of ten millions of gold *solidi* is not feasible, and so I agreed to fifteen percent of that total, and some yearly tributes thereafter, which we will of course ignore. I was also made to agree to marry Pulcheria[47] to the Lion's own son, and while I loath having to surrender my flesh and blood to the infidel, the marriage will strengthen the bonds of peace between the two great powers. I march home tomorrow, escorted by one hundred of the Lion's finest Mamluk soldiers, and I hope to be in your arms in a fortnight, my sweetest darling, oh how my loins ache for you. I humbly request that you notify the appropriate parties of the terms, they will not like them, but I have already agreed, and prepare the city for a hero's welcome, and your bed-chamber for a joyous homecoming, for your husband and Emperor will soon return! I send you all my love, in the name of Our Lord Jesus Christ,

---

[47] His daughter.

may He come again to judge the living and the dead. I remain,

Faithfully Yours,
Romanos[48]

Eudokia read the letter. She read the letter a second time. She let out a cry of pure joy. And then the dread combination of heat and excitement flustered her, and she fainted, and might have cracked her head open had not Maurice the sweaty valet caught her as she fell.

---

[48] Psellos references this letter in the *Chronographia*.

XVI
THE SUNSET

THE EMPRESS MADE ONE MISTAKE: she fell in love with the wrong man. While this insidious complaint may be a commonplace in the sad history of womankind, in the pitiable case of Eudokia, her imprudent heart's caprice brought nothing but tragedy, as we shall soon see. The events of this last chapter of Volume One are not so pleasant to relate, and that gives me pause. For no one emerged from the Year of Our Lord 1071 uninjured by the dread events of that *annus miserabilis*, arguably the blackest year in the long annals of Byzantium for both the Empire as a whole and for the individuals heretofore described. Steel yourself, Anna. Best to get on with it.

Once she regained her composure, and indeed her consciousness, Eudokia was elated at the news of her husband's homecoming. Her heart was lifted and her mind was cleared. She now knew how to proceed. It could not be simpler: Diogenes was still alive, and thus still the *Augustus*. Why should it be otherwise? He had erred in making war on the Lion, of this there could be no doubt, but he did so in service of his frontier lands, which were constantly fending off incursions by Turkish raiders. Something had to be done about that. Now he'd met with the sultan and come away with what were under the circumstances generous terms. If there was no historic victory, there was likewise no epic failure, not really, not so long as the treaty held. Her husband was not the first *Augustus* who had bumbled and botched and bollixed, Lord knows. The history of Rome is a chronicle of miscalculation. Even the best Emperors blundered. The first Constantine out of misplaced jealousy slew his wife and his first-born son—what error could be more grievous than that? No, Diogenes would receive a hero's welcome, just as his letter stipulated, and moreover, Eudokia reasoned, he would learn from this terrible mistake and improve himself going forward. His good name would be rehabilitated. She would see to that. She sent word to the *Caesar* and the Patriarch and also to Psellos the chief minister to prepare for the Emperor's imminent arrival, and she began herself to make the necessary arrangements.

Needless to say, the Doukas faction was dismayed by the news. At the family's Constantinople apartments, John Doukas, Andronikos, Psellos, and Nikephoritzes the eunuch met to decide on the proper course of action. That Diogenes should be deposed was their unanimous conclusion. If the stalwart Emperor managed to survive, the cabal decided, he would immediately seek revenge on those who abandoned him at Manzikert. Andronikos would be tried for treason and likely executed, the *Caesar* would be removed from his office and, at best, banished, and John's wife Irene would once again fall victim to the Emperor's lustful predations. None of these outcomes could be permitted to take place.

"What's curious," Psellos said, coughing—for he had been gravely ill for the last few weeks, and was only just well enough to resume his duties—"is that this has happened before, when the Emperor Isaac Komnenos was presumed dead, only to recover from his illness."

"That is uncanny," John Doukas agreed.

"Still, I move that it reverts back to how it was," Psellos said. "How it *is*. Eudokia reigning as regent for Michael."

"That cannot be," the *Caesar* said. "Not while Diogenes lives. Alive, he quite rightly sees himself as the Emperor. How can the Empress reign and the Emperor not? He would be a constant threat. No, no, it cannot be that way." He put his arm around the infirm Psellos's shoulder. "When Isaac was ill, he was replaced by a new Emperor, not a retread."

"True," the chief minister said, unconvinced.

"Why," Andronikos asked, "are you so keen on restoring the Empress, minister? You despise her."

"Yes," Psellos said, "but I love the boy. He is the son of my closest friend, may God rest his soul, and I promised to look after him."

As usual, Nikephoritzes the eunuch had offered not a word to the conversation, until the time when his words most mattered. "Let us summon Michael," he said. "I know what to do." Then, to Andronikos: "Raise an army. Meet the Emperor before he gets to the city. It's not necessary to slay him, but he must be made…ineligible for office."

"I understand," the tall general said, "and I concur."

"As do I," said John Doukas. "In fact, I should like to take on that particular assignment personally."

Psellos also gave his reluctant consent. "If this is what is to be," he said, "I will happily stage-manage the downfall of Eudokia."

"Let it be as humiliating as possible," Nikephoritzes said, and Psellos nodded. "Let her be an example for any woman who dares take on a man's responsibility."

When Michael with great annoyance quit the stables to meet with his kinsmen, he comported himself like a spoilt child whose favorite toy had just broken. None of their concerns mattered to him—which attitude his uncle and cousin and teacher should have interpreted as the ill omen that it was. All Michael wanted was to get back to his horses. If he rode fast enough, perhaps, he could outpace all the worries of the world.

"Diogenes is alive," the *Caesar* told him.

"So I've been told. Thanks be to God."

"We do not share your enthusiasm," Psellos said.

"He is my step-father," Michael said. "There are covenants between us. Moreover, my mother loves him. I am sincerely happy he has survived. For some days, I feared the worst."

"Nephew," John Doukas said, "have you met my friend Nikephoritzes?"

Michael regarded the handsome if plump eunuch with obvious approval and delight. "I know who you are, of course. Your reputation for genius precedes you. But I've not had the pleasure." And the two shook hands, man and eunuch.

"Since his untimely dismissal from the court, Nikephoritzes has been with me in Thrace, managing my affairs," John said to his nephew. "He is particularly good with money. I strongly suggest you recruit him in a similar capacity in your new administration."

"My administration?"

"Diogenes cannot be *Augustus* any longer, Michael. It simply cannot be."

"But…" And he looked at Psellos, hoping for the minister to proffer some bit of wisdom that would counter what his uncle had said.

But the meddler only nodded. "It is your time now, my boy."

"I won't have him killed," Michael warned.

"I assure you, that will not happen," Andronikos said, and the simplest child could see that he was speaking falsely. "Every effort will be made to preserve his safety."

Michael paced around the room. He pulled at the thick curls on top of his head, a nervous habit of his. Then he said, "I suppose you're right. Have you informed the Empress?"

"Your mother's reign as Empress is over," Nikephoritzes said, "so long as her husband the deposed Emperor is still alive. It will send a signal to both your subjects and our foes that you are fragile. We need to show strength now. *You* need to show strength."

"I cannot do that," Michael said. "I cannot renounce my mother."

"Renounce? No, no. You misunderstand our intentions, Your Highness," said Nikephoritzes. "The Empress will willingly abdicate. Her regency will end, and she will retire to a convent of her choosing."

Michael stood silently for a moment, outmatched by the others in the room.

"There is another matter we have not yet discussed," the *Caesar* said. "She has two sons now by Diogenes. She's already made plans to name the first-born, Nikephoros, co-Emperor and thus heir to the throne. Has she mentioned that to you?"

Here Michael turned red. "Lies," he said. "You speak falsely, uncle."

"Would that I do. Shall we ask the Patriarch? He can show documents signed by the Empress indicating that same intention."

"I cannot believe it."

"That does not make it false, Your Highness."

For a full minute no one spoke. Michael's face was red. He looked like he might at any moment burst into tears. But he managed to stem that womanly impulse.

"If Diogenes is alive, your mother must not be at court," Nikephoritzes said, "for reasons of your own safety. Consider the possibilities. If the Emperor returns and re-claims the throne, you are a viable rival and thus a marked man. We can protect you now, but if he is reinstalled, we may well be put to the sword in the inevitable purge, and who will safeguard you then? I appreciate that you and Diogenes have a covenant, but he also had a covenant with the sultan. He is not a man of his word. He is not to be trusted. Do you see?"

"Yes," Michael said. "Yes, I suppose."

"You have a choice, Your Highness," Nikephoritzes went on. "You can order Diogenes to be executed, and thus preserve your mother's place at the court. Or you can allow your mother to retire, and thus preserve the man's life. It is one or the other. There are no other options."

"Say the word, cousin," Andronikos said. "Give us your command. Your day has come."

"I won't have him killed," Michael said again, this time in a whisper.

"We will make all the arrangements," John Doukas said. "Leave the details to us. Return to your stables. Breathe not a word to anyone—not even your horse. When the time has come, you will know."

Whereupon all of the men, Michael's uncle and cousin as well as the two ministers, took a vow of fealty to the soon-to-be-proclaimed Emperor, bowing before him, and the meeting ended.

Once out of the sultan's clutches, Diogenes raised the imperial banner and gathered the remnants of his army—a meager force to be sure, but one sizable enough to menace the defenseless countryside, from which it plundered its way willy-nilly across Anatolia. Puzzled were the citizens who had their lands occupied and their livestock seized by the very man entrusted to protect them against such incursions by their enemies!

Meanwhile, a force led initially by Botaneiates, perhaps the finest general in the Empire but one Diogenes personally detested, set out to intercept him. The two armies met at Adana, a provincial capital in the south of the peninsula, a dozen miles inland from the Mediterranean Sea, which was held by the Emperor. There was little fighting and few if any casualties. The overmatched garrison at Adana, recognizing the superior force coming from the west, threw open its gates and defected, leading Botaneiates straight away to the house where the Emperor was quartered. Already rogue elements in the army had overwhelmed Diogenes, stripping him of his regal garments and clumsily tonturing his hair.

"Surrender now," the aging Botaneiates told him, "and no further harm will come to you."

"On whose authority?"

"The ranking officer Andronikos Doukas, acting on behalf of the sovereign Michael."

"Very well." Here the haughty Diogenes rattled off a list of terms of his surrender. One of these was to be treated with dignity, a condition Botaneiates promptly agreed to, but which did not prevent the general's men from tying the erstwhile *Augustus* backwards to a donkey and parading him around the dirt roads of the garrison town.

In due time the well-travelled Andronikos arrived, this time by ship. Seemingly appalled by the Emperor's humiliating treatment, he freed Diogenes from his shackles, apologized profusely, invited him to his tent, and broke bread with him.

"The Emperor Michael has decreed that no harm shall come to you," Andronikos said. "As you know, he personally has great affection for you, and for this you should count your lucky stars. You will be taken back to Constantinople, where you will retire to a monastery. He asks that you pledge fealty to him, and nothing more. Do you agree?"

"Under the circumstances, I have no choice," Diogenes allowed.

"Do you agree?"

"Yes, I agree."

"Excellent. I shall send word. Rest up, sir. We leave at dawn."

I am writing this as quickly as I can, glossing over smaller battles and near-misses, but that should not suggest that events unfolded with great speed. Anatolia is something like a thousand miles wide and five hundred miles high from the Black Sea to the White,[49] and across this broad expanse Diogenes moved his men haphazardly. It took time for him to be located, more time for him to be subdued, and still more time to convey him to the capital. When at last the ship dropped anchor at the Golden Horn, the summer was long since over, the heat a distant memory, and the leaves on the trees resplendent with red and orange and yellow and brown. It was the twenty-fourth day of October, a Wednesday, when the ship docked at harbor in Constantinople, and on that fateful day, the snail's pace quickened, and events unfolded with lightning speed.

Diogenes had been given comfortable quarters aboard the ship, and although he was no longer permitted to wear his purple garments, he was out-fitted with dashing new clothes. As he gazed through the peephole at the magnificent landscape of the city—the gleaming dome of the Hagia Sophia, the Boukoleon, and the Hippodrome all visible as they

---

[49] Here Anna is using the poetical Turkish system of colors denoting directions: Black/North, White/West, Red/South, and Blue/East. White Sea = Mediterranean.

passed—he prepared himself to meet his wife, his Emperor, and his fate.

Andronikos, who had been at his side all that day, suddenly rose. "This is adieu, I'm afraid," he said, quitting the room with no further preamble, and closing the portal behind him. Diogenes tried to follow, but the passage was blocked by an iron bar. He pounded on the door to no avail. After perhaps two hours, perhaps three, he heard footsteps outside, and the scrape of the lock. Into the room stepped John Doukas, and behind him, a short, stocky, cruel creature whose visage was as grotesque as a gargoyle's, its God-given ugliness made uglier by the inexpert removal of its nose.

"Romanos," the *Caesar* said brightly, subtly insulting the former Emperor with the use of his familiar name. "I trust your passage was comfortable?"

Diogenes regarded the two men with appropriate horror. The *Caesar*, he saw, was carrying a mace. "Yes, thank you."

"I trust you know the *mega hetaireirarches*,[50] Romanos Straboromanos?"

"Only by reputation."

"Apropos, is it not, that you have the same Christian name? The two of you will be spending a lot of time together in the coming days."

"The new Emperor has promised me safe passage," Diogenes pleaded, and while he was outwardly

---

[50]   The head of the Secret Service, essentially.

brave, full of bluster as always, still he must have felt enormous fear. "That was the one condition of my surrender, that nothing ill would befall me. Michael would not betray me thus. Now I ask that you honor the wishes of the *Augustus* and take me at once to see my wife."

"You speak the truth," John Doukas said, smacking the mace menacingly into the palm of his hand. "The Emperor has indeed ordered that not a hair on your head be harmed. The two of you have covenants, he claimed, and anyway he has great affection for you, as does his mother your wife. For my part, I invite you to take the matter up with him later— after. In the meantime, you are in my custody, and I have no intention of honoring the terms of your surrender."

And with that, he swung the mace at the Emperor's right leg. It connected with a thud, fracturing his femur, and Diogenes collapsed at once to the floor, whereupon the *Caesar* kicked him, the blow landing under the fallen man's jaw. He kicked him again, and then once more for good measure. Then John said, "You have violated the honor of my virtuous wife, you vituperous snake, and that supersedes any arrangements you might have made with my molly of a nephew. Much as I'd like to strangle the last breath out of you right here and now, I shall temper that impulse and spare your miserable life, per my nephew's wishes. But I must protect my kinsman, you understand. As a former *Augustus*, you are, in your intact condition, a permanent threat to revolt.

Straboromanos will see to it"—he punctuated that word, *see*—"that this option will be forever taken away from you. You ask to see your wife? No, Romanos, no. You will not see her, or anyone else, ever again." Then John coughed up a viscous ball of phlegm and spat it on Diogenes, who was huddled quaveringly on the floor, and quit the room.

Michael was in the stable, grooming Humility. He had just gone riding at the Polo Grounds, the verdant meadows ranging from the imperial palace out to the Bosporus. Sunshine had blessed his ride, but now a light rain was falling—one of the sudden weather changes endemic to our city. Into the stable burst Andronikos, along with a score of Varangian Guard, all of them bearing long shields. The preternaturally tall general was visibly drunk. "Long live the Emperor!" he cried. "Hail, *Caesar*! Hail, *Augustus*!"

Several of the guardsmen snatched the terrified Michael and hoisted him over their shoulders, bearing him on their shields, bouncing him up and down and shouting *Long live the Emperor*. Thus situated, they paraded him out the imperial gate and through the streets of Constantinople, to rousing cheers from everyone who saw them.

A blind man may not wear the purple: probably this prohibition was intended to protect the Empire from the feeble appearance that a sightless *Augustus* might create. The codicil's unintended consequence lies in its presumptive dispatch: If a blind man cannot by law be Emperor, a rival with his eyes put out is a rival no more. In theory this could not be more logical, but in practice there are difficulties. The result of permanent darkness cannot be achieved by the pull of a lever, alas. The light must be extinguished by hand, which is an unpleasant business, as painful as it is cruel.

As the ship pulled out of harbor and headed to the miserable isle of Proti, where Diogenes was to live his last days in exile, the deformed Straboromanos strapped his prisoner face up to a table, the erstwhile Emperor's head dangling over the edge. The merciful way to blind a man is to hold a red-hot iron close to the eyeballs without touching them; thus the heat blinds without causing other damage. Diogenes would not be so lucky. There was a special tool the torturer used just for this purpose, a long-handled spoon with serrated edges. Straboromanos dug the sharp spoon into Diogenes's left eye socket, hacking through the vessels binding the eye to the skull. Once the proper angle was achieved, he leaned hard on the handle and pushed down. The milky white orb popped out of the socket and plopped to the dirty floor, and the screams of the former Emperor could be heard from dry land. As Diogenes begged for mercy, Straboromanos repeated the procedure with the right eye socket. This one gave more easily, the oculus popping out as if designed to do just that. Then, to stop the bleeding, the slit-nosed torturer jammed two nearby rags into the gaping holes in his prisoner's face, rags that the now-blind now-former Emperor had used to make his ablutions after defecating. Again Diogenes screamed, and continued to scream, but strength and spirit had departed along with his vision, his light and fight both spent.

The erstwhile Emperor would live in anguish for eight miserable months on Proti before dying in unspeakable agony, after his wounds became infested by maggots. The stench emanating from his eyeless face, we are told, defied description.

After some hours of the shield parade, Michael was taken back to the Grand Palace, where he and Andronikos met with the *Caesar*, the Patriarch, the chief minister Psellos, and the eunuch Nikephoritzes—all of them his new cabinet.

"Why is this happening now?" he asked. "Where is the Emperor?"

"You are the Emperor, Your Excellency," Psellos told him.[51]

---

[51] Later, Psellos would write a letter to Diogenes congratulating him on his blindness. "If the Lord took your eyes, that means there is a place for you in Heaven," he wrote, in a hand Diogenes himself could not read.

"Yes, but where is Diogenes?"

"I'm sorry to inform you, Your Highness, that he resisted arrest," Nikephoritzes said. "He was steadfast in his desire to reclaim the throne. He was dealt with accordingly."

"What does that mean?"

His uncle relayed the news, and Michael, whose stomach had been upset by all the bouncing around on the shields, vomited all over his new purple robe—not, it must be said, the most auspicious beginning to his reign.

Eudokia was in the Loge of the Empress in the Hagia Sophia when all this was happening, and Maria happened to be with her.

"Last night I had a horrible dream," the Empress said. "The moon turned red, and the sea was the color of blood. The Apocalypse was nigh. It was terrifying."

"My goodness," Maria said. "I wonder what it could mean?"

"My late husband would have found some deep meaning therein," Eudokia said, "and I perhaps would have scoffed at him. But there is no doubt that it is an ill omen. Perhaps…"

She did not finish her thought, for Psellos burst into the Loge with a sextet of Varangian Guard which seized her, twelve relentless hands ripping off her imperial garments and knocking her tiara to the ground. Eudokia screamed, and although there were priests praying in the vast church below, none so much as glanced up at the Loge. Maria could only watch helplessly as they stripped her almost naked, and Psellos with sheep shears tontured Eudokia's long black hair.

When this was done he leaned close, his lips at her earlobe, and muttered, "Your accusation is false, strumpet. It was Michael who made untoward requests of me, and not the other way round. I did not make him a buggerer. He was formed that way in your sick womb, a product of your own despicable sin."

Before Eudokia could reply the guardsmen threw her, gently weeping, into a burlap sack, bound it with rope, and whisked her out of the church.

As he followed the company out of the Loge, Psellos turned to Maria. "Forgive me, Your Highness," he said, bowing deferentially, and then he too was gone.

The whole episode was over in sixty seconds—a fall from grace as sudden as it was humiliating.

"It was stunning," Maria told me later. "This beautiful woman, powerful and wise, had run the Empire for years and was an all-consuming presence in my life, and in an instant, she was gone. I spent the entire afternoon hysterically weeping, my eyes like fountains. I was completely and utterly devastated. It was like the sun itself, the source of all light and energy, had been suddenly and without warning blotted out of the sky—almost like her dream presaged." Indeed, there was some analog between the arrest of Eudokia and the blinding of Diogenes: in both cases a plunging into darkness.

The coronation was held at dusk, the sun setting over the Theodosian Wall basking the city in gloomy shadow. But for the absence of Eudokia and Diogenes, not to mention the slain Manuel Komnenos, it was a remarkably similar ceremony to the imperial wedding of three years previous. This time, of course, Maria was herself on the dais, in flowing purple robes and whatever crown jewels Diogenes had not lost on the road. Her husband, nervous and sweating profusely, stood beside her, rocking gently to and fro. There was, Maria noticed, a piece of lettuce stuck in his teeth. Ramwold, who had been freed from slavery by his master for the occasion, sat in a back pew, and one can only imagine what was going through his mind.

In the presence of the grumpy Patriarch, Michael was formally declared Emperor, and Maria of Alania, a week shy of her twentieth birthday, crowned *Augusta*. Five years prior she'd been living at Bagrat's court at T'blisi, princess of a minor vassal state who spoke not a word of Greek. Now she was nineteen years old and Empress of all Byzantium—the most powerful woman in the world.

VOLUME TWO:
MICHAEL VII

A.D. 1071-78

XVII

THE ABSENTEE EMPEROR

I BEGAN THIS ENDEAVOR on Candlemas, the second day of February: the dead middle of winter. It is already the ninth of April; spring has come, bathing Constantinople in dreary rain; I have been working night and day on these pages, with no end in sight. I have neglected to keep count, but there must be some six score sheets of parchment in the crooked pile upon my escritoire, and yet I am no closer to the part of the story I'm so eager to reveal, the meat in the narrative stew, which is to say, my own autobiography. To those patient readers who remain, I apologize for my garrulity. I assure you I'm moving as swiftly as I can—so much already have I left out in the service of velocity!—for I know, O verily do I know, how short and how precious is our interval upon this sad terrestrial plane. Death will come for me ere I compose a third history. I must make this one count.

I want now to tell of the radical adjustment Maria suddenly had to make, from pretty princess loitering on the sidelines to full-fledged *Augusta* of Rome—a transition she was nevertheless fully equipped to undergo, having been trained for the rôle by that paragon of Empresshood, Eudokia Makrembolitissa. Before we move to Maria, however, we must remark on the peculiar character of her husband, the new emperor.

Isaac Komnenos had been a reform-minded if superstitious military man, Constantine X Doukas a pious scholar with priest-like inclinations, Romanos IV Diogenes a swaggering, self-absorbed rake. Michael VII Doukas resists such easy adumbration. In some ways he was feeble and cowardly, in others courageous and remarkably strong. He was unquestionably smarter than his predecessors, a voracious reader of all the great books, possessed of a worldly wisdom that belied his twenty-one years and at times approached the divine intelligence of Jesus Christ Himself, and yet too often he could be maddeningly stubborn and incredulously stupid. Maria loved him dearly, albeit in a sororal sort of way, as he loved her reciprocally, but he was also a constant source of frustration for her, libidinous and otherwise.

The reader has already been acquainted with Michael's heterodox bedroom predilections, which informed his personality to no small degree. Homosexuality[52] is a grievous sin; this, Scripture makes

____

[52]   The Greek word Anna uses is *arsenokoitai*, first employed by St. Paul the Apostle in his First Epistle to the Corinthians.

plain. Per Leviticus: *cum masculo non commisce-beris coitu fenimeo quia abominatio est*, and also *qui dormierit cum masculo coitu femineo uterque operati sunt nefas morte moriantur sit sanguis eorum super eos*.[53] In plain Greek: an abomination punishable by death. To put the nature of the sin in perspective, the Holy Book also provides helpful contextual examples. When hosting uncouth travelers in Sodom, Lot as an enticement offers up his own daughters to sway his guests from engaging in carnal relations with one another. Rather than being smote for acting as his daughters' procurer, Lot is instead saved by his angry God—the only Sodomite spared destruction—*because* he took said action. How else to interpret this unseemly tale but that sodomy is a more heinous transgression even than daughter-whoring? An avid scholar and a pious Christian, Michael was intimately aware of these passages, just as he knew by heart St. Paul's own condemnation of sodomy in various of the Pauline Epistles. Too, he was familiar with charges against the various heretical sects, the Manichæans, Albigensians, Paulicians, Patarenes, Cathars, and in nearby Bulgaria, just beyond Thrace, the Bogomils, all of them apostates, all of them eager practitioners of sodomy, all of them apostates *because* they favored,

---

Although it was sometimes used to signify anal intercourse specifically, even between men and women, Anna here clearly refers to homosexuality.

[53] 18:22 and 20:13, specifically.

or in the event did not explicitly prohibit, sodomy. It was a reflexive equation: Sodomy was heresy; heresy, sodomy.

Michael knew this too well. How could a royal sodomite not? And yet the harsh words that Psellos spoke to Eudokia as she was arrested, while witheringly cruel, were nevertheless true. Michael's perverse lusts were not volitional; some external agent (viz., Psellos) had not inured him to this way of being. From the womb of his exemplary mother he'd sprung with these wicked inclinations already lodged in his heart. If God made him that way as some sort of retribution for Eudokia's sins—sins of which he himself was innocent—how was he to reconcile such a malediction with his Christian faith? Was he really cursed, doomed to wander the earth in sin, like Lot's intractable house-guests? Diogenes, for one, engaged in carnal relations with hundreds if not thousands of women, many of that number taken by force; Michael, as far as we know, confined himself to Ramwold. Do mass philandering and rapine really constitute lesser offences in God's eyes than monogamous buggery, however distasteful the latter act may be? How does that square? And yet that is precisely what Scripture made plain, although, most frustrating for Michael, it did nothing to explain the wherefores of the prohibition.

The new Emperor was thus consumed by guilt, so much so that it could paralyze him fast as a Gorgon's glance. Michael sought refuge in the Gospels, finding some solace in the fact that Our Lord and

Savior Jesus Christ did not Himself disparage sodomy, going to far as to make the specious argument to himself that *diliges proximum tuum tamquam te ipsum*[54] was a ciphered sanction of man-on-man love. He hated himself for his passions, he indulged himself regardless, he hated himself for his passions, and on and on went the cycle *ad infinitum* and *ad nauseum.* I do not care for venereal activity at all, whether in the time-honored manner of Adam and Eve or in the Gomorrhean fashion that was the Emperor's exclusive provenance—for erogenous pleasure, I would sooner extract a tooth with rusty pliers that offer my tender flesh to such abuse; if cruel Nature had provided any other way to produce children I would have happily submitted to it—so I harbor more sympathy than most for his uncouth predicament. For this reason alone, it's hard not to feel pity for him; but alas, there is more woe to reveal.

His snap decision to banish Eudokia rather than execute Diogenes weighed heavily on his mind also. His step-father died despite his clemency, eyeless and in excruciating agony—Michael had not authorized the blinding and was horrified when he heard the news—and his beloved mother, for so long a constant and imperious presence in his life, was vanished. Eudokia, once the Mother Earth around which the lesser planets orbited, remained under virtual arrest at Piperoudion—a convent notorious

---

[54]   The Golden Rule: Love thy neighbor as thyself. From Matthew 12:31.

for its strictness in not allowing men to so much as enter the courtyard—deprived of any sort of contact with anyone at court,[55] and may as well have been in exile on one of the aforementioned lesser planets. It was as if she too were dead—and just when he needed her most.

And this leads to what is for me the most confounding aspect of Michael's character. While he was content living under the domineering thumb of his mother as a pampered crown prince, *he did not want to be Emperor*. As an one who desired nothing more than to take the purple—who, indeed, lived her entire life in the service of that singular if unprecedented and unrequited ambition—I find this quirk of Michael's character particularly difficult to fathom.

In the event, despite whatever qualms he had, he deigned to be crowned *Augustus*, he gave grudging consent as Eudokia was sent away, and he allowed the same kinsmen who removed his mother and blinded his predecessor to have the run of the place. If he did not abdicate in fact, he abdicated in kind, for John Doukas and Psellos and Andronikos and especially Nikephoritzes the eunuch ran the Empire. Michael's reign was their reign: for better, and mostly

---

[55]   Attempts by the Emperor to contact her were rebuffed, Michael was made to believe by Eudokia herself but probably by the *Caesar*, who wanted her out of the picture for good. It is not difficult to foment discord between two people who do not communicate. (A.K.)

for worse. The precedent was set a few days after the coronation. Diogenes had been disposed of, in the cruelest possible way, but there was still the question of the deal he'd struck with Alp Arslan—Manzikert's silver lining: The generous territorial concessions, the resumption of friendly relations, the promise of quiet on the Eastern front that would allow the new Emperor to gather himself before turning his attention to the hungry Fox prowling to the West. While Diogenes had certainly erred in making war with the Lion when war was not compulsory, he had at least managed to come away from the bargaining table with a salable peace. To parade prisoners of war around the Ægyptian obelisk at the Hippodrome is better theater, certainly, but hard-won diplomatic gains are ultimately more important to an empire's survival. Humiliate the man, deprive him of sight, exile him to a lonely island and leave him for dead—all tragic but perhaps excusable, given the confused circumstances in the Grand Palace and Diogenes's own chequered history of insurrection. But to then repudiate his Heaven-sent gains at the negotiating table? This was a blunder just as foolhardy as Manzikert.

They were all in the Map Room for this urgent discussion, John Doukas, Andronikos Doukas, Psellos, and Nikephoritzes the eunuch. Maria happened to be present also, as she remained at her husband's side for weeks after the coronation, acting as a sort of bodyguard. At this time, the Map Room still contained maps, many of them laid out on an enormous oaken table, around which the participants sat, looked upon by icons of various saints on the walls. (Alexios would later have the table and chairs removed in favor of the divan, upon which he and Maria would indulge their base desires.)

"Please explain to me," Michael asked of this venal cabal, "why on earth I would reject this deal?" He had been Emperor less than a week and the experience already weighed on him. At twenty-one years old, he'd noticed in horror that the ample hairs on his head and his face were suddenly speckled with gray.

"Sire, we cannot allow Diogenes to speak on behalf of Rome," the *Caesar* said.

"But he was the Emperor when he so spoke," Michael replied. "That makes him as legitimate an ambassador as could be."

"It's a matter of perception," his uncle continued. "What will happen when the hoi polloi learn that the new Emperor accepted the humiliating peace negotiated by his loathsome predecessor?"

"I don't think it's a *humiliating* peace at all," Michael said.

Andronikos tried a different tack. "We must show strength," he said. "That is what your good mother was forever preaching. What will our enemies think of you when you capitulate at the earliest possible moment?"

"But what is the alternative? A second Manzikert?" He turned to Psellos, his longtime tutor and family friend. "What say you, Father?"

Psellos took the opportunity to give a history lesson. Commodus, he said, the son of the enlightened Emperor Marcus Aurelius—remember, sire? we read his *Meditations*—ascended to the throne upon the death of his father in A.D. 180, nine hundred years ago, he was the first Emperor born in the purple in many decades, I believe the last case was Titus succeeding Vespasian a century previous, no matter, he was the well-educated son of the Emperor, doted on by his parents, a complicated fellow, more concerned with his own pet interests, his horses and foxes and so forth, than in rule—does this sound familiar, sire?—well his father Marcus Aurelius was presiding over a decade-long war, he was attempting to expand the Empire across the Danube and subjugate the Germanic tribes there, one of the lofty goals oft-attempted but never realized by his noble predecessors, and Marcus Aurelius was on the cusp of achieving this grand ambition when he fell suddenly ill and died. Did Commodus continue where his father left off? Did he fight for the glory of Rome? He did not. He sued for peace, came away with humiliating terms, the first ones offered him at the table, and returned to his palace and his life of decadence. Rome was never quite the same. "We don't want you to make the same mistake as Commodus, Sire."

This was an imperfect analog, as the Emperor (as well as Maria, who had read her Plutarch and her Tacitus) immediately recognized, for Marcus Aurelius was not captured by the Germans and had not himself sued for peace, as Diogenes had; Michael made this argument to Psellos, who would have none of it. "This is a mistake we simply cannot allow you to make, Sire," he said.

"It would be a fatal error," the eunuch said.

"Fatal," added Andronikos.

"We are here to protect you," the *Caesar* reminded him, "from just this sort of blunder."

The expression on the new Emperor's face was akin to the drowning man who realizes the last piece of driftwood is out of his reach. He was flailing.

In this insular, incestuous, male-dominated environment, not much is left for a twenty-year-old foreigner Empress to do. But Maria saw her opportunity. "Gentlemen, if you please," she said, her accented voice unsteady. She was out of her depth participating in this sort of assembly, but she spoke out of mercy above all, to rescue her drowning husband. "Forgive my impudence in interrupting, and also my ignorance, as I am but a woman, and a foreigner at that, but there is something I don't understand, and I hope that you will illuminate it for me. Again, a thousand pardons for my interposition, but my rôle here is to assist my good husband with matters of state, as yours is, and I am essaying only to fulfill my required duty."

The four advisors, two of them her in-laws, two of them celibates, turned to face her. Probably none of them had ever heard her speak more than a word or two in all her years at court, and they were as shocked as if the icon of Our Lady of Blachernai had suddenly found speech. Once they attributed the strange, soft, soprano voice to Maria, they tripped over themselves in deference to their new Empress. Through egregious and hollow courtesy, they reckoned—through appeal, in other words, to female vanity, the satiety of which simply *had* to have been her sole motivation—she would be easily managed.

"Please," John Doukas said, "speak, Your Highness."

Now the enormity of the moment struck her, and her cheeks flushed red as the roses in the vase on the table beside her. With a glance at her husband, who was clearly grateful for the aid, she gathered herself and spoke: "Correct me if I'm wrong, but is anyone outside of this room even aware that Romanos Diogenes reached an agreement with the sultan Alp Arslan? As I understand it, the terms were communicated only in his hurried letter to the Empress his wife."

"Nay, you are correct," Psellos replied with outsized avuncularity, as if addressing Andronikos's eight-year-old daughter Irene.

"Well," she said, "then what stops Michael from sending his own embassy to the sultan, ratifying the terms, and claiming sole credit for a clever bit of statecraft? Mobilize the army, march a few miles to the east for show, and come home with the same terms: Antioch, Edessa, and Hierapolis for the whole of Anatolia. We can claim that the Lion trembled at the might of the Byzantine army under the youthful Emperor Michael, and immediately sued for peace himself, like a rank coward. How would anyone know otherwise?"

The look of relief on Michael's face as she spoke lifted her heart. He had no interest in serving as Emperor, true, but he was wise beyond his twenty-one years and knew a good idea when one was presented. Before he could give his consent, however, much less issue commands, the others spoke all at once, lambasting Maria's suggestion as "simplistic in a womanly way" and "ignorant of the realities of the office" and "silly." All four agreed that this must not be done, that the only way to show strength was to publicize the terms achieved by Diogenes and then vehemently renounce them, and then march on the infidels as soon as a new army could be raised. "We cannot allow you to make this fatal error," they all said, over and over again, until Michael in frustration threw up his hands.

"Am I *Augustus* or not?" he cried.

"Of course, of course. But still..."

"This is madness," he said. "I will not be party to this. Do what you will, but bother me no more," whereupon he quit the room.

They were surprised when Maria did not follow him.

"Your Highness," Psellos said, "you should leave matters to us. This is no place for a woman."

"Your husband and master has withdrawn," added Andronikos. "You should follow his lead."

"No," said Maria, and now they had a better understanding of the exquisite creature they were dealing with. "I will not be a figurehead, and I will not be my husband's wet-nurse." She had observed that of the four others in the room, Nikephoritzes—the least manly among them, ironically—was the one to whom the others ultimately deferred. It was to the eunuch that she spoke: "If you wish me not to meddle further in affairs of state, then you need to give me responsibilities. Real ones, like Eudokia had. That is the only way to be rid of me, I'm afraid."

Nikephoritzes's blue eyes gleamed, and he smiled admiringly. He was handsome when he smiled, not as handsome as her lover Ramwold, but cut from similar cloth. This trait would carry him far with Michael. "As you wish, Your Majesty," he said. "You are hereby in charge of the court and the palace. The ceremonial, the staff, the décor, the banquets—all of it. Will that please you?"

"For now," she said, smiling. "For now."

XVIII
THE PALACE

I F I HAVE BEEN REMISS IN PROVIDING a full picture of the Grand Palace, neglecting to furnish detailed descriptions of the complex of halls, apartments, churches, recreation rooms, gardens, fountains, meadows, servants' quarters, kitchens, cellars, and reliquaries that comprise the Boukoleon, eliding the royal inventory of icons, statues, jewels, artefacts, and relics from any number of saints, including the Virgin Mary Herself, it is because these things are frankly of no interest to me. I was born in the Palace, and aside from a few formative years spent at a different but no less lavish palace within the imperial walls, I lived most of my life at the Palace, from the age of eight until my banishment to the convent. Even when my father removed his court to Blachernai, after the Franks took back Jerusalem, I remained at the Boukoleon. First-time visitors to Constantinople may regard with righteous awe the Serpentine Column at the Hippodrome, or the imperial diadem laden with a piece of the True Cross, or the mosaic of Christ Pantokrator on the apse in the Throne Room, but to me, these were as yawningly familiar as the pigsty to a swineherd. One can be inured to riches just as one can to dreck, and a surfeit of the finer things can have much the same impact on one's deportment as a lack. A peasant celebrates Christmas upon the dirt floor of his hovel, a princess in the Hall of the Nineteen Couches at the Palace; both are unremarkable because both are diurnal.

I must apologize, then, for my inability to adequately render the magnificence of the place. Maria, however, who grew up in her father's simple residence at T'blisi, never lost the sense of wonderment concerning her new address—especially after her creation as *Augusta*.

"I had become somewhat accustomed to luxury, after so many years at the Palace, but when Eudokia left I moved into her apartments," she recalled later. "All of it was now mine: the furniture, the art, the elegant garments, the jewels, the breathtaking view of the Propontis. I couldn't believe it. It was beyond a gift from God. How could Heaven itself be any more lovely than those sumptuous rooms?"

Not that Maria spent her days lounging around. Running an Empire was difficult work, especially with an Emperor who was not much interested in the job. Court ceremonial, which was now her bailiwick, was a particularly detail-oriented and thus onerous task. There was a constant stream of important guests, provincial governors or lesser generals or influential family members from within the Empire, or else embassies from beyond. On any given day, there would be some foreign element at court, Bulgarians or Franks or Turks or Rus' or what have you. Thankfully, the staff of eunuch administrators expertly ran the day to day operations, as they had for Diogenes, for Constantine, for Isaac, and for all the Emperors before them. What would we do without our blessed beardless ones! But Maria could not simply repair to the stables, as Michael did, while they did the work; her regal presence was requisite. Indeed, in the absence of the Emperor, the Empress became the face of Michael's reign. She had to meet those dignitaries, entertain them, be present for them. This does not take into account the feast days and other celebrations which compelled her to perform some or other public service: Easter and Christmas and dozens of lesser liturgical holidays, as well as secular celebrations like the Eleventh of May[56] and the Memorial Day for the repulsion of the Arabs four hundred years before.

She was furthermore in charge of the Grand Palace itself, an operation that required her to oversee, directly or otherwise, hundreds if not thousands of people. Scores of them lived at the Palace, and many more were employed there in some capacity. Cooks who prepared the food, fullers and laundresses who

---

[56]   Constantinople was dedicated on 11 May, 330.

did the wash, seamstresses and tailors who cut and sewed the garments, footmen and porters and butlers and valets and maids who carried and cleaned and dusted and swept and mopped, groomsmen who looked after the horses, chauffeurs who drove the royal carriages, ladies-in-waiting who attended the Empress, stewards who attended the Emperor, clowns and musicians and acrobats and lion-tamers who entertained the court, a veritable army of eunuchs of various ages and levels of experience who conducted the court ceremonial, an actual army of Varangian Guard who offered protection, and any number of courtiers, courtesans, princes, princesses, other dignitaries of various rank, ministers, the servants of all of these notable personages, and many more besides, were all present on the grounds of the Palace every day. It was a bustling, busy, noisy place.

The diffident Michael detested the sensory overload, but Maria, like Eudokia before her, thrived on the buzz of activity. Her daily schedule was relentless. She rose at the cock's crow, took a small breakfast of toast and fruit, bathed—the attitude toward bathing varied considerably from person to person, with ascetic types like Psellos and Constantine X forsaking the bath in some misguided quest to be more like Jesus, but Maria, who held with her mother's traditional Alani position on personal hygiene, insisted on quotidien ablutions—and was dressed by waiting-ladies in imperial finery, including her bejeweled diadem. Then it was a full day of events followed by a state dinner, and usually some entertainment in the evening. Michael skipped as much of this as he could manage, although he generally accompanied her to the Hippodrome, as he liked to take in the chariot races, and his imperial box was set so far above the fray that he did not have to interact with a soul.

The one drawback to her new station was the decided lack of privacy. As princess, Maria had participated in many of these same events, but she'd always been able to carve out some time to be alone—or to be alone with Ramwold. Now, her days were full, she collapsed in bed each night exhausted, and she found that from time to time the sheer volume of people she was surrounded by all day made her, paradoxically, lonely. As Empress she was *treated* differently. A remove formed that had not been there before. The location of her new apartments, furthermore, made it impossible to meet her lover there. She had to contrive another rendezvous point. After several more preferable options—the stables, the carriage house, the gardens—were ruled ineligible on various grounds, she decided upon a stratagem oft-employed in her homeland: the church.

"Peasants back in Georgia live piled on top of each other in their little hovels," she explained to me, "and they lack any sort of privacy. During the day, meanwhile, the churches are both unlocked and empty. Many of them simply use the pew as a conjugal bed."

"That is sacrilege," I said.

"Fie. Are they not multiplying fruitfully, in service of God's commandment to Adam?"

"I suppose."

She fixed a strange look on me, uglying her beautiful visage. "Perhaps you are too young to understand," she said. As I was not yet nine years old, this was probably true.

Maria, of course, did not have to take to some dingy municipal church—she could avail herself of the grandest cathedral in Christendom, the Hagia Sophia. It worked like this: Ramwold would sneak into the Empress's Loge and conceal himself in the confessional box. Maria would then arrive and dismiss her entourage, explaining that she needed time to pray in absolute solitude, and was not to be disturbed for any reason. Once the others quit the room, she would draw the curtains for maximum privacy, Ramwold would emerge from the confessional, and they would indulge their base desires upon a pile of pillows. This could not be arranged as often as she desired, but its infrequency only heightened the erotic pleasure she derived from the encounters; the sanctity of the setting only heightened a sense of ecstasy that approached the divine.

But darkness stalked her. For all the fullness of her schedule, her meticulous attention to her duties, and her occasional rendezvous with Ramwold, Maria was wracked by guilt. Some days she could manage the feelings, but on other days they overcame her, and she walked around in gloom. Not guilt about her infidelity; guilt about the deposed Empress.

"Remember that I loved Eudokia," Maria recalled later. "She was a constant presence in my life, and then she was just…gone. If she had died, I would have mourned, but I would have been able to process my grief more easily, because of death's finality. But she wasn't dead. She was still alive, still in possession of her faculties, still living in Constantinople—Piperoudion was a short carriage ride from the Palace. And yet she was dead to me, because I had no way of contacting her. I longed to visit the convent, but it would have been indecorous for an Empress to do so. And I needed to see her, or at least to communicate with her. I needed to know that she wasn't cross with me, that she bore me no grudge. Understand: her rooms were now mine, her wardrobe now mine, her jewels now mine. It was *her* crown on my head, *her* servants at my beck and call, *her* Empire that I ran. How did she feel about this? I had no way of knowing, but I could well imagine. And I did not much enjoy such contemplation. She was locked away in that horrible nunnery. Men were not permitted to see her at all, which meant no visits from her sons—even her littlest ones, Leo and Nikephoros Diogenes. She was the Empress, true, but she was also their mother. That made no difference to the Doukids, and no exception was made[57]. How do you go from being on top of the world to *that*? How do you reconcile such a pre-

---

[57] The two Diogenes boys were living with the Komnenoi, under the careful watch of Anna Dalassene. (A.K.)

cipitous fall from grace? Can you ever recover from such a blow? These were the sort of thoughts that plagued my sleep at that time. None of this was my fault, and yet still I felt that by taking her place, I was somehow complicit in her downfall."

This dangerous idea would soon fix itself in her mind. Almost every night she would dream of Eudokia, a ghost Eudokia, lashing out at her, and she would wake in a cold sweat, alone and lonesome in her perfectly made bed.

"But it was not your fault," I protested. "You were guilty of nothing. What choice did you have?"

"I offered no protest," she said. "I allowed events to unfold. I chose to go along with it, and that is still a choice."

XIX
THE EUNUCH

THE NAME NIKEPHORITZES MEANS "LIT-
TLE NIKEPHOROS," and the eunuch, while
plump, was indeed short of stature; his passing resemblance to the handsome slave Ramwold
did not extend to physical size. That said, there was
nothing small about his intellect, and even less about
his ambitions. While his loyalties lay primarily with
the House of Doukas, it is wrong to believe that he
was merely an agent of that great family. Nikephoritzes had larger aims. He knew that as a eunuch he
was barred from taking the purple himself—in this
way eunuchs are like women—but he nevertheless
could, as chief minister, act as *de facto* regent to an
ineffectual Emperor. Such was the opportunity he
saw with the aloof Michael, whom he viewed as a
damp lump of clay, ready to be molded to his liking.

When a river is dammed up, the gushing waters
do not stop, but merely change course; likewise,
when men are deprived of the source of their

manhood, as with Nikephoritzes, the lascivious passions do not die out, as is commonly supposed, but rather reveal themselves elsewhere. Nikephoritzes lusted not for women but for power. The most quantifiable aspect of power is wealth, and the avaricious eunuch sought to enrich himself as much as he could. Perhaps he saw this as due compensation from the Empire to which he'd sacrificed his ballock-stones. I cannot pretend to understand the exact source of his motivation, but greed is the most alluring of the deadly sins; it takes an one like Christ to renounce material wealth and mean it. Nikephoritzes was an able and shrewd finance minister, yes, but also a rapacious requisitioner of his own hoard.

Not long after the initial ministerial meeting earlier described, Nikephoritzes, acting independently, sought out the Emperor in his stables. As usual, Michael was there, grooming the forelocks of Humility. With him was Ramwold. They had, in fact, completed their shameful obscenity not ten minutes prior, and in the afterglow the Emperor appeared relaxed, almost blissful.

"Your Highness," Nikephoritzes said bowing, "may I have a word?"

Michael's entire being deflated like a popped pustule, but he granted the eunuch an audience. Ramwold, nodding, quit the stable—but remained close enough to the window that he could hear the entirety of the conversation, which he dutifully reported to Maria.

"Forgive my impudence," said the eunuch, recognizing at once, without much surprise, that the two men were lovers, "but I have a proposal that I feel will ease your worried mind."

"Continue."

"From what I knew of you before your coronation, and what I have observed upon my arrival at court, I have concluded that Your Highness would prefer not to involve himself with the diurnal affairs of state."

Michael could not help but chuckle at the phraseology. "That's one way of putting it."

"The construction of your current cabinet is such that there is no chief. Your Highness has four individuals—five if we count the Empress—whispering in your ear. Such an organization will require Your Highness to constantly listen to a host of opinions and then make decisions. In such a system, Your Highness will spend most of his time in the Map Room, conferring with his advisors. Humility the horse will be woefully neglected."

"You speak the truth," Michael sighed. "What is your proposal, sir?"

"Allow me to serve as *Prime* Minister," Nikephoritzes said. "Have the others report to me, and give me the final say. In this way, I can insulate you from as much court intrigue as possible."

"Why you, sir, and not Psellos? Or my uncle the *Caesar*?"

"I love them all dearly," the eunuch said. "But are they loyal to you, or to the House of Doukas?"

"But I am a Doukas."

"No, Your Highness is foremost the Emperor."

Michael nodded. "I suppose if the *Caesar* wished to be *Augustus*, he could have done so," he said. "And my cousin Andronikos, he should not be advanced ahead of his own father."

"And Psellos, while undoubtedly wise, is an old man," Nikephoritzes added. "The stress of the position would accelerate his decline in health, I fear."

"I suppose." Finished with the forelock, he rose, dropping the brush in a bucket. "And what of Maria? My wife is brilliant in her way."

"She has already spoken to me about this," Nikephoritzes said. "I have put her in charge of court ceremonial and given her the run of the palace."

"Capital idea." Michael rose and extended his hand, which the eunuch took as he genuflected. "Let it be done, Mr. Prime Minister."

"Thank you, Your Highness."

"Once a week is sufficient for us to meet, I think, unless the urgency of the situation demands my involvement."

"Yes, Your Highness."

"Now, off with you."

Another rôle Nikephoritzes took on later that month, independently and without mentioning it to a soul, was that of imperial procurer. While Michael's preference for handsome young men was an open secret at court, neither was it ever remarked upon, certainly not to the Emperor himself. There are some topics that decorum prevents one from broaching, in mixed company or otherwise, and buggery was one of them. Nikephoritzes himself was not unfamiliar with such forbidden passions; perhaps he too would have followed that heretical path, had circumstances allowed him to remain intact.[58] So the eunuch took no small pleasure in personally recruiting and selecting slaveboys for that nefarious purpose. He'd have them wait in Michael's salon after dinner, in groups of two of three so as not to overwhelm the socially-uneasy Emperor, and he'd rotate them so often that none of them could develop any special intimacy with the *Augustus*; any slave that dared boast of the encounter was immediately sent to Proti where he was put to death by slow torture. (One poor soul was sent there innocently, in fact, just to advertise to his mates the consequences of trading in rumor.) This was a calculated gamble—the new Prime Minister was only guessing at the potential rewards; Michael could easily have banished the comely slaves from his salon and the audacious eunuch from his post—but as it happened, the Emperor was, as Nikephoritzes had hoped, exceedingly grateful to him for his discrete assistance. His imperial lusts were sated, and the arrangement had the added benefit of chaining Michael and Nikephoritzes together with the shackle of shared secrets.

----

[58]   Like many third and fourth sons of ambitious fathers, Nikephoritzes had been castrated by his parents when he was a child in the hopes of placing him in a coveted position at court, where bright eunuchs were always in demand. (A.K.)

"It was a stroke of genius," Maria told me later. "Michael came to depend on Nikephoritzes not only for the administration of the Empire, but for the satiety of his lust. Plenty of worthy candidates could have served in the former capacity, myself included, but only Nikephoritzes could be trusted with the latter. This made him indispensable. From what I understand, Livia did much the same for her husband Caesar Augustus, although in her case it was swarthy Syrian girls and not pretty blonde boys—this is how Nikephoritzes came upon the idea, from reading his history. Genius, this was. I wish I'd thought of it myself!"

Thus, as the first year of the tempestuous reign of Michael VII Doukas came to a close, the various court struggles for power, prestige, and fortune had more or less resolved themselves. Assured of his influence and his wealth—he was already one of the largest landowners in the Empire—the *Caesar* repaired to his Thracian estates, where he idled in semi-retirement. Andronikos was gifted several robust properties of his own, rich sources of revenue that remained in his (and my) family's possession in perpetuity.[59] Psellos stayed on in a diminished capac-

---

[59]   The Dumbarton Oaks Research Library has documents in its collection attesting to a gift to Andronikos Doukas from the Emperor Michael of income properties. I translated

ity, and it was at this time, genuinely encouraged by the Emperor, that he began work in earnest on his *Chronographia*. And Maria managed the palace, a more demanding and tedious job than she had anticipated, as discussed. Michael avoided all of them as much as he could, preferring to ride, play polo, sail on the Propontis, compose iambics and anapæsts, and avail himself of those handsome slaveboys his Prime Minister selected for his amusement.

Beyond the frontier, Robert the Fox was busy consolidating his position in Italy, garrisoning troops at Bari, organizing clever systems of taxation, and otherwise putting roots down in what had been, not that long ago, the heartland of the Empire. But the graver threat lay to the East. By the time Alp Arslan learned that the new administration had vociferously renounced what he rightly felt were generous terms of surrender, it was well into February, but the cold of winter did nothing to chill his boiling blood. Territories could be retaken without much trouble, of that he was certain, but what particularly incensed him was the loss of revenue. For Diogenes had promised not only a hefty down payment, but a yearly tribute of some thirty thousand pieces of gold—gold the Lion desperately needed to underwrite his expensive campaign to Ægypt, the real prize. In his death-throes on Proti, the sightless former *Augustus* had amassed as much

---

it myself, in fact—so imagine my surprise when I came across this reference!

lucre as he could get his dying hands on and sent the coin to the sultan, with a note explaining the unfortunate situation—a burst of gallantry in an otherwise depraved life. This only increased Alp Arslan's anger. He ordered his troops to raid Byzantine *themata*[60] all across Anatolia. Armeniakon, Charsianon, Cappadocia, Paphlagonia, Anatolikon, Kibyrraiotan. No province was to be spared.

"Be ruthless," the sultan commanded, "and unyielding."

By the time the sun was in the Ram, incursions by marauding Turks began in force, led by an able general called Suleiman, and much of Anatolia was lost to plunder and rapine. The Lion was contemplating whether or not to sack Constantinople on his way to conquer the Ægyptian Fatimids—he knew of the impregnability of the city, girded by choppy water on three sides and on the fourth by the Theodosian Walls, the greatest fortification ever constructed; in seven centuries, none had ever managed to take the Queen City—and had indeed begun exploring just how such a siege might work. Then, in November, God smiled on the Empire. The governor of some backwater town in Turkestan, which the Lion was in the perfunctory process of subduing, refused to bow to the mighty sultan, and after a short and unnecessary battle, was captured. As he was led to his new overlord, this brazen governor

---

[60]   Administrative districts.

brandished a dagger and rushed at him. Now Alp Arslan was the best general of his era, but he was also an excellent shot with a crossbow. He called off his guards, stood on the saddle, took aim at his attacker—and slipped just as he shot his bolt, missing his mark...whereupon the lowly governor dug the dagger deep into his bosom! In December of the Year of Our Lord 1072, the Lion roared his last—an early Christmas present for Byzantium. Or so it seemed to Nikephoritzes, who decided that this moment was the opportune time to strike.

"Alp Arslan has a preponderance of sons," the eunuch explained to Michael, who was not remotely interested, "as well as any number of ambitious generals. If the sultanate is anything like Byzantium, there will be a period of strife and civil war. Sons will take arms against each other, and Suleiman, the rogue who leads the band of plunderers, will likely himself covet the throne."

"Do what you will," Michael said, "and be gone."

And so a force led by Isaac Komnenos, my father's older brother and now the Domestic of Schools, marched on the Turkish marauders, with the aim of regaining lost territory—"rescuing" former Byzantine lands from the infidels, as Nikephoritzes phrased it. "They will greet us as liberators," the eunuch predicted.

On its face, this was not an unwise move. There was bound to be some confusion, if not outright chaos, in the months after the Lion's death. The Byzantine army, while still composed of too many mercenaries from hither and yon, was nonetheless a worthy match for the infidels. And the Christian residents of Anatolia, who'd dwelt for so long under the suzerainty of Rome, would sooner bow to the Byzantine Emperor and the Patriarch of Constantinople than some tent-dwelling Moslem upstart who did not drink wine or eat pork.

Or so it seemed.

If logic was on Nikephoritzes's side, luck was not. The succession from Alp Arslan to his eldest son Malik-shah, not in the same class as his father but still a canny military strategist, was seamless. Suleiman's savvy policy of granting Anatolian peasants more rights over their land, and thus bettering their temporal position, made them reluctant to revert back to the old ways, regardless of which indifferent god their overlords prayed to. And while the brothers Manuel and Alexios Komnenos were both superb generals, this talent skipped the middle brother; Isaac was the tone-deaf child in a family of organum singers. My uncle sailed with his army to Caesarea, the venerable capital of Roman Judæa, with the unconventional plan of attacking the Turks from the south—Hannibal crossing the Alps was his inspiration—and was almost immediately routed and captured.

With the bulk of the Byzantine army thus rendered inoperative, a rebellion broke out in Galatia, not two hundred miles from Constantinople. A Frankish soldier of fortune called Oursel, a crafty mercenary general employed by the Byzantine army, broke rank and declared himself *basileus* of his own little kingdom there, in the Optimaton *theme*.[61] Oursel's renegade troops plundered their merry way to the very shores of the Bosporus, where they put seaside houses to the torch, signalling their ominous proximity to the Emperor. While the Norman rebel knew better than to attack Constantinople itself, his presence a stone's throw from the Golden Horn comprised so exigent a threat that John Doukas himself came out of his Thracian semi-retirement to lead a regiment of the Varangian Guard to subdue the insurgency, with his son Andronikos Doukas as second-in-command. As the forces converged near the Zompi Bridge, victory appeared imminent. The Byzantines had vastly superior numbers, and were fighting close to home. But two simultaneous and unforeseeable complications bollixed the operation. First, most of the *Caesar*'s army consisted of Frankish mercenaries, many of whom defected to the enemy rather than take arms against one of their own. Second, the general Nikephoros Botaneiates, the head of the Anatolikon *theme* who was ordered to attack Oursel from the East, suddenly decided, against all logic, to abort the mission—just as Andronikos had done to Diogenes at Manzikert. With half his army switching sides, and his reinforcements in full retreat, John Doukas had no chance against the clever Oursel. The paltry Byzantine force that

------

[61]   A theme was a division of the Empire, much like a state or a province; *basileus* = king.

remained was defeated, and both John and Andronikos Doukas, astonishingly, were taken prisoner; my grand-father lost his left hand in the fighting, and many pints of blood, and suffered a horrible head wound as well.

This then was the dire situation Michael, or rather Nikephoritzes, faced at Constantinople in A.D. 1073: the Fox fortifying position to the West; and to the East: his best commanders and bosom friends captured by Oursel, another general held by the Turks, and the head of his Anatolikon *theme*, no small threat to take the purple himself, gone rogue. It seemed only a matter of time before the barbarians would take the Queen City, storm the palace, and deprive the negligent Emperor of his sight, if not his life.

But not even impending doom could provoke Michael to engage; if anything, the present danger made him even less inclined to take decisive action. Nikephoritzes, usually imperturbable, was in a state of near panic. The only general available to him with any significant battlefield experience was Nikephoros Bryennios, head of the Eastern *theme*, and this Bryennios, no friend of the Doukids, would just as soon assume possession of the throne himself than defend the poltroon currently occupying it. Also, the expense of the constant wars had depleted the Treasury, which meant that to continue underwriting the war effort, Nikephoritzes had either to raise taxes or debase the coinage. (He would eventually do both).

When Maria went to see the embattled Prime Minister after the disaster at Zompi Bridge, he looked so harried she thought he might burst into tears.

"I was sorry for him," she told me later. "For all his faults Nikephoritzes was a man of great intellect, and thus it must have been clear to him even then that his administration was a complete and utter failure. He had no children, no family, and thus no legacy beyond his political success, and he must have known that the end for him was near."

By this time, Maria had grown accustomed to consoling the broken-hearted. Her cousin Irina, the reader may recall, was married to Isaac, whom the rapacious Turks were holding hostage, and she had spent the last few weeks patiently drying her kinswoman's copious tears, often in the company of Anna Dalassene, as well as negotiating directly with Suleiman for the general's release.[62] She listened patiently as the pitiable Prime Minister unburdened his troubles upon her. And then Maria spoke: "There is only one man who can save us, minister: Alexios Komnenos."

In retrospect, many decades hence, this seems an obvious solution, but at the time it was radical. What Maria suggested was that Nikephoritzes entrust the fate of the Empire to the younger brother of a

---

[62]   This negotiation proved successful; Isaac was ransomed not long after, returning to Constantinople in chagrin. (A.K.)

military failure, a seventeen-year-old lisper with a spotty beard and an even spottier résumé.

"But he is too young."

"And therefore not as likely to covet the throne for himself."

"He is still a boy."

Maria smiled. "He is more of a man than you'll ever be."

This was a low blow, and a risky comment; it might not have had the intended effect. But Nikephoritzes took it in stride. The eunuch smiled pleasantly, and regarded Maria with newfound respect, as if she had revealed herself to be Minerva come down from Olympus. Then he retorted: "I could say the same of you, Your Highness."

And at the preposterousness of the situation—a foreign woman and a eunuch arguing over a military decision involving a teenager that may very well determine the fate of the Empire—both of them burst out laughing.

XX

THE LISPER

I'VE ALREADY EXHAUSTED MANY BARRELS OF INK extolling the exploits of my "old man," the great Alexios Komnenos, and I am loath to revisit the subject in these pages. One cannot, however, write a piece of autobiography without discussing one's father, particularly if one's father is the all-powerful Emperor of Rome—and thus the cause of both one's most grandiose ambitions and one's most heartbreaking woe. Of his military victories, his shrewdness in tactics, and his numerous imperial triumphs, I shall not elaborate on what I wrote in the *Alexiad*. Let us confine ourselves here to speaking of Alexios the man; that is enough to keep us busy!

At fourteen, as we've seen, he'd marched with his brother Manuel to the East, getting a taste of the action, and had borne witness to the ultimate exchange between his brother and Andronikos Doukas; the experience baptized him into the harsh ways of the world and whetted his appetite for revenge.

Three years later, as he stood in the Map Room before the eunuch Nikephoritzes and the Empress Maria, he was, despite his tender age, a fully-formed man, just as the *Augusta* had suggested. Gone, or at least in full retreat, was his lisp. Filling in nicely was his beard. Stocky, on the short side, with a chest like a wine barrel and stout, powerful legs, he had the physique of a wrestler, and he strode around the court like Mars come down to Earth. Alexander the Great was sixteen when he led his first campaigns, a year younger than my father that day, and the latter shared the precocity of the former, as my father would emulate the Macedon's rate of success in battle.

And yet in other ways Alexios was still a child. He did not have his own apartments, but lived with his mother at the Komnenoi palace, in the north-west corner of the city, not far from the Blachernai. His sisters lived there too, as did the little boys Leo and Nikephoros, the sons of Diogenes and Eudokia. There was not yet a question of whom he would marry, or when. On the battlefield he had no equal; off it, he needed all the help he could get. He scarcely knew which clothes to wear for which occasion, he had a terrible memory for both faces and names, and his knowledge of court ceremonial remained pitiably small even after ten years in the purple. But military sagacity is a gown that masks even the most gruesome deformities. And Alexios had several other forces working in his favor. First, unlike the vain and egotistical Romanos Diogenes,

who interpreted even constructive criticism as insubordination and believed himself capable of running
the entire Empire himself, my father was well aware
of his flaws; and his self-regard was healthy enough
that he had no problems delegating. Second, he had,
in the person of his mother Anna Dalassene, the
ideal delegate. She knew nothing of military tactics,
but what ample knowledge she did possess neatly
complemented her son's manifold shortcomings.
Together, they were a perfect circle, a chain—like
the one stretched across the Golden Horn in times
of crisis[63]—with no weak link.

Anna was a full thirty years older than Alexios,
and yet they functioned for all purposes and intents
as husband and wife—so much so that there were
whispers among the more spiteful and envious at
court of an incestuous relationship between mother
and son. Indeed, these rumors plagued them for as
long as Anna was alive. Once Alexios took Maria
as his lover—or, rather, once Maria took Alexios;
the lisper was always the subordinate in that part-
nership!—I cannot imagine that my father forsook
the bed of the youthful Empress for that of his
ancient mother. Before that time, however, when
Alexios was still young and vulnerable and green in

---

[63]   This was an ingenious military defense that successfully
protected the inner harbor from foreign invasion for centuries: a heavy chain that stretched across the entrance to
the harbor and destroyed the hull of any ship that dared
breach it.

the ways of love? As much as I'd like vociferously to protest the innocence of my progenitors, I cannot say for certain that this particular cloud of smoke, noxious though it is, did not emanate from genuine fire. I know for a fact that my father's respect for the fidelity of familial boundaries was suspect. The Theban king who seeks pleasure with Antigone is twice as likely to have also consorted with Jacosta.[64] But once again, I am getting ahead of myself. At this point in the story, Alexios is seventeen, and innocent of at least one of those two cardinal sins.

The most attractive attribute my father possessed, one that served him well both as Great Domestic and as Emperor, was his child-like love of fun. For all his impressive triumphs, he was a man who did not take himself too seriously. Especially when he was young, he regarded the world with a laugh and a shake of his head, as if he himself were amazed at his good fortune, at the perfect and magical alignment of stars under which he'd been born. This jocularity was infectious. It was impossible to spend any amount of time with him and not come away with one's spirits buoyed. Diogenes was the life of the party, too, in his way, but his vanity and capacity for cruelty came through even in his jokes. Alexios could be cruel, too—witness the many rivals whose eyes he'd zealously put out—but for most of his life, his sense of humor remained pure. When he

---

[64]   "The Theban king" is Oedipus.

lost his ability to laugh, late in his reign, around the time of the burning of Basil the Physician—when he began to take himself too seriously—that was when I knew the end was near for him.

When seventeen-year-old Alexios entered the Map Room, the spring in his step was undeniable. There was nothing haughty or off-putting about it; he appeared amusedly delighted by the prospect of addressing the Empress and the Prime Minister. Not that he wasn't there on his own merits. While he was indubitably born of aristocratic stock, the House of Komnenos, infused as it was with Armenian blood, was considered socially inferior to that of the Doukas or indeed the Dalassenos—this is why my mother and grand-mother went by Irene *Doukaina* and Anna *Dalassene*, respectively: the names of their noble birth families held greater currency than those they married into—but the noble circumstances of his birth by no means assured him of military success. The battlefields of Byzantium are littered with the corpses of commanders better born, with lesser ability.[65]

Alexios had been warned that Michael would not vouchsafe his presence in the Map Room, and yet he was still mildly disappointed that the Emperor did not join them. Although perhaps it was for the

---

[65]   My great-uncle Damian Dalassenos, for example, whose pedigree was impeccable, did not inherit a talent for military science; his campaigns against the Bulgarians were incontrovertible failures. (A.K.)

best, as my father's infatuation with the Emperor's wife was in full evidence; beneath his spotty beard he blushed as he bowed deeply before her. His feelings towards Maria had not changed. If anything, the sight of her in the purple, bejeweled diadem on her pretty head, only enflamed his desire. Nothing stirs the blood like power! The difference was that now, some years after their last meaningful encounter, Alexios had grown into an one worthy of her affections. The spark between them was undeniable. Even Nikephoritzes the eunuch noticed it, and it troubled him; a love affair between a sitting Empress and a precocious general could spell disaster for the Emperor his client, and thus for him personally.

"Salutations, Your Highness," Alexios said, working hard to not revert to lisping. "Mr. Prime Minister."

"General," Nikephoritzes said.

"Alexios," the Empress smiled. "What a man you've grown into."

My father had to adjust his standing position so his ardor for the conversation did not reveal itself beneath his tunic. "May I first express my heartfelt gratitude for you both, on winning the release of my dear brother Isaac," he said. For his brother had indeed returned to Constantinople, and the bed of Maria's alluring cousin Irina, a few weeks before. "This is a debt I hope you will allow me to repay on the battlefield."

"In good time," the eunuch said. "I assume you've been briefed on our position."

"I have."

But Nikephoritzes explained it anyway: in Italy, the Fox was marshalling his forces, no doubt preparing for another attack. To the East, much of Anatolia was lost to the Lion's worthy son Malik-shah, and efforts to retaliate had thus far been futile. There was the debacle in Caesarea, in which Isaac had been captured, and the embarrassing rebellion by the Norman upstart Oursel, who now held hostage both the *Caesar* and his son.

"Andronikos has been seriously injured," Nikephoritzes added. "He lost a hand."

I wonder if it is the same hand he used to dispatch my brother Manuel, Alexios thought—but he kept this to himself. "Again I would like to apologize for my brother's dismal showing," he said. "With your kind permission, I would like to raise a new army and march on Oursel. He is clever, but he is blinded by ambition. I've seen his likes before."

"In due time," Nikephoritzes said. "We wish you to be prepared, in case you have to act swiftly, but for now, we are negotiating with the sultan."

"With the sultan? But why?"

"Let the Turks take out Oursel. This will give us time to assemble our army." The eunuch flashed a crooked smile and nodded cheekily, as if this were the most clever piece of statecraft ever devised.

"And what, if I may ask, will we give the sultan in exchange for this service?"

"Nothing. Just some territory in the East that he already controls."

"I see." But see Alexios did not. He glanced at Maria, and could intuit that she, too, did not endorse this plan. "I suppose there is no other alternative."

"There is," the Empress said. "The location of Oursel's ersatz kingdom is in Galatia, halfway across Anatolia—land that has changed hands countless times in the last half century. He has, in short, inserted himself right between the two mightiest nations on Earth. The instant he falls, the Turks will again take the territory. So why are we in such a hurry to remove him? Let Oursel stay. Ransom the *Caesar* and his son, or better yet, exchange them for the promise to recognize his little republic. In order for the sultan to attack us, he'd first have to march through Oursel's territory. The Frank is a buffer between us and them. Do you see? The Turks will remove him anyway, in time, without concessions from us. Patience will win the day."

Alexios nodded approvingly. "That is an inspired strategy," he said. "Who is its author?"

"The Empress herself," said Nikephoritzes. "And while the plan has its merits, it does not allow for certain realities. Public perception, for one. How are we to sell the idea to the hoi polloi that we've allowed a mercenary to establish his own miniature empire? Or to the army? Soon every general will follow suit, and we'll have rebel kingdoms all over the place. No," he said, "the plan has already been decided."

"In that case," Alexios said, "I thank you for your trust in me, and when my name is called, I will be ready."

Maria's smile as he left melted his heart. Although he knew Nikephoritzes's plan was pure folly, all he could think of after his time in the Map Room was that singularly beautiful face.

Alexios had given little thought to the prospect of his marriage—if pressed, he would admit that he was holding out for Maria, long shot though that was—but to his mother Anna Dalassene the question was always in the forefront of her mind. That her son might one day take the purple grew likelier with each dazzling military victory, but a bad match, she knew, might hamstring his chances. The ideal wife had to be from a good family, young, pretty, and if possible shy and reserved and a bit stupid— Anna did not want her future daughter-in-law to dilute her own considerable influence over her son. In this respect, Maria was not an ideal candidate, however much Anna adored her. Although she was the Empress, she was a foreigner, and the influence of her extended family was negligible; if she married Alexios she would have to be either divorced or, more likely, widowed, neither of which were ideal outcomes; and Maria was smart and headstrong and would absolutely divert attention from Anna, which my grand-mother did not want. That Alexios would more or less automatically be made Emperor if he married her, as Diogenes had been when he wed Eudokia, weighed just as little in her calculations as the fact that he was head over heels in love with her. To those of us in the highest circles of society, marriage is about the consolidation of power, alas, and not the consummation of love!

So the betrothal of her third, and most eligible, son was very much on her mind when Anna was visited by another foreign princess called Maria—Maria of Bulgaria, daughter of the king of that land and a Byzantine princess from the Phokas line, mother-in-law of the general George Palaiologos[66]…and the unhappy wife of Andronikos Doukas. While Anna had loathed the Doukas family even before Andronikos slew her son Manuel (which by this time she'd been briefed on; Alexios could keep nothing from her for long), she had a soft spot for this Bulgarian Maria, who, despite being a Doukas by marriage, hated the family almost as much as Anna did.

Understand, court life is miserably insular. The social stratum in which Anna moved consisted of at most five hundred individuals, all of whom were compelled by the dictates of society to spend time together whether they wanted to or not. In those situations, Anna and Maria of Bulgaria often sought each other out. The latter, though plain in appearance, was possessed of a wry sense of humor and liked to grouse about the dissipation of her wanton husband, and the former enjoyed hearing her funnily

---

[66] One of my father's closest friends. (A.K.)

complain. As the son of the *Caesar* and nephew of the *Augustus*, Andronikos had not exactly grown up in privation, but the resources he brought to the marriage were dwarfed by the fabulous wealth of the Bulgarian Maria, who owned large tracts of land around Lake Ohrid in Macedon. His wife's revenues underwrote his lavish excesses, as Andronikos, like Diogenes, was fond of the high life's various inducements: wine, women, dice, horses, and so forth. He was forever on the wrong end of exorbitant bets on the Hippodrome chariot races, he drank too much, and he once contracted some sort of venereal disease from a Bithynian whore that, if my grand-mother is to be believed, turned the tip of his foreskin green. It was when a gravely-wounded Andronikos languished in Oursel's custody, sometime early in A.D. 1074, that Maria of Bulgaria came to the Komnenoi residence to pay a visit to my grand-mother, her eight-year-old daughter in tow.

"My dearest Maria, I am so sorry to hear about your husband," Anna said.

"Don't be," the Bulgarian said, rolling her eyes. "It serves him right. If he took to military strategy like he took to drink, he wouldn't have been captured by that rogue."

"I heard he lost an arm."

"Just a hand. Not the whole arm. Likely a ploy to gain sympathy from his creditors. I'll believe it when I see it."

Anna could not help but snicker.

"With one hand, perhaps he'll be half as keen to play dice. My bursar will be delighted."

"Oh, Maria, I do adore you."

"The feeling is mutual, my dear Anna. You are the sole person in Constantinople with whom I can make light of all this."

"As you know, I am not one of your husband's more fervent admirer's," Anna said smiling. She had never told her friend that Andronikos was responsible for the murder of her son Manuel—that would disturb the delicate balance of their bonhomie.

"Already Oursel has demanded a lavish sum for his ransom," said the Bulgarian. "Likely to pay for all his whores."

At this Anna burst out laughing. "My dear Maria, you are too much!"

"But soft," said her world-weary friend. "There is a reason for my visit beyond the pleasure of your company." She gestured to the window, where, below, her daughter could be found scampering playfully around the courtyard. "Irene is young, but Andy"—that is what she called her husband, as if he were a child, and always with a touch of contempt—"is not long for this world, what with the way he comports himself. I'd like to find a match for my daughter before Death comes for him."

"I'm listening."

"I know you hate the Doukoi. So do I. But the Doukas women are, on the whole, a superior lot to the wretched men. And Irene is only *half* Doukas.

She is also a proud descendent of the king of Bulgaria, as well as the Emperor Phokas himself!"

"I have always adored your little girl. You know that."

"Your son Alexios is not yet betrothed."

Anna smiled. None of this surprised her. "No, he is not."

"Irene is eight, almost nine. In two years' time, she can be married."

"At eleven? Is that not rather young?"

"She is wise for her years. And as I said, I have a sneaking suspicion that her father will not be around much longer."

Anna held up her hand. "My dear Maria," she said, "I think the world of my son, as you know, but the Komnenos name is inferior to your own. Irene will be marrying down. Socially, I mean."

"Alexios is special," the Bulgarian said. "Anyone can see that. Is he even eighteen yet? And he's about to be made Domestic of the Schools—my own husband's job, which his disability will prevent him from further performing, and further botching up. Your son may well be the best general in Byzantium, and his uncle was *Augustus*. The likelihood of him taking the purple is great. Unlike my wastrel Andy, I have not the stomach for gambling, but as to the chances of there being an Emperor Alexios, well, that is a wager I'll gladly make."

These words greatly pleased my grand-mother. She too saw the possibility of Alexios ascending to the loftiest perch, but had taken superstitious care not to discuss it out loud. "Maria," she said, "I am humbled and flattered."

"Bosh," said the Bulgarian. "Alexios possesses all the imperial attributes—he is smart, charismatic, shrewd, and of high moral character. He is also a damned good general, which is the most important thing. Having a Doukas wife will only help him realize the ultimate achievement."

For a full minute Anna said nothing. She sat on her divan and stared at an icon of the Virgin Mary on the wall. Her mind was racing. A smile came to her lips. "My dear friend," she said at last, "I am at a loss for words, so delighted and honored am I by this overture. I must discuss it with my son, of course—"

"Of course."

"—but you have my full and eager blessing." Then her forehead wrinkled. "Attend…have you discussed this with your husband?"

"I have not."

"What if he refuses?"

"Then I will chop off his giblets and feed them to the pigs."

At this the two women caused such a ruckus with their laughter that the servants burst in to make sure they were not fallen ill.

Anna Dalassene and Maria of Bulgaria: my grand-mothers.

XXI
THE BABE

WHILE MARIA'S DALLIANCES WITH RAM-WOLD WERE LESS FREQUENT, still they endured. It had been seven years of this—she knew the date precisely, and the two of them celebrated that anniversary each year—and still Maria was not pregnant. Were it not for the miscarriage, she would have thought herself barren, but clearly she was capable of carrying a child. Had that trauma robbed her of her ability to reproduce? As the months turned to years, she became increasingly desperate.

Her longtime nurse and dear friend, Rona, introduced her to a series of home remedies thought by Georgian mystics to effect conception. There were herbal brews, poultices, elixirs, and strange roots and seeds consumed at specific times of the day, the week, the month. None of these produced a child, although one of the elixirs did give her a welcome boost of energy, and another seemed to enhance her sexual pleasure.

The midwife advised her to keep careful track of her menstrual periods, and also of the phases of the moon. "The moon and the mother are linked," the hoary woman told her. "They are in alignment. What you want to do is figure out when in the lunar cycle your menses comes, and try your luck in the opposite phase. So if your period coincides with the new moon, during the full moon is when your womb will be ripe." No doubt this was good advice, as the midwife was wise in the ways of science, but Maria's cycle did not line up with Luna's at all. Sometimes her menses was during the full moon, sometimes the new, sometimes in waxing crescent, sometimes in waning. There was no rhyme or reason to it that Maria, or indeed the midwife, could divine. The old woman told her to keep her spirits up, but Maria could see the concern in the midwife's ancient, tired eyes.

The court astrologer—the same Antiochene fool who would read my own natal chart, but a decade younger and in marginally better possession of his faculties—highlighted some key transits, conjunctions of Venus and Jupiter mostly, which benefic influence might bring better fortune to the process. Needless to say, this superstition did not work. Venus and Jupiter had larger concerns.

And she tried prayer, as her husband had famously and idiotically advised. She prayed to God, she prayed to Jesus, she prayed to the Madonna, she prayed to St. Peter and St. Paul and St. Elmo and also, on the advice of the Patriarch, to St. Marina of Antioch, who was martyred by the Emperor Diocletian and had once been swallowed by a dragon. Her prayers, however ardent, went unanswered.

It was Maria herself who diagnosed the cause of her infertility: God's wrath. The Maker was angry with her for betraying her mother-in-law Eudokia, now wallowing at Piperoudion, which was less convent than prison with crosses. Eudokia had brought her to Constantinople against all conventional wisdom, Eudokia had looked after her as her own daughter, Eudokia had taught her all about the inner workings of the court. Eudokia had created her, and what had she done in return? Stood idly by as the soldiers took her away. She was no better than Peter, denying knowledge of Christ.

The insidious *idée fixé* tormented her. She lost her bright smile; wrinkles formed on her forehead, and dark circles under her luminous eyes. She could not sleep, for when she slept, she dreamed only of Eudokia, a daemonic Eudokia, her eyes red with flame, cackling madly with demented pleasure at her agony of barrenness.

"What could I do?" Maria recalled later. "I could not visit her at the convent, not as the Empress. Decorum prevented that. I could not even risk writing to her. Eudokia was clever, and she might use my words against me. And writing in Greek has always been difficult for me, frankly."

Unable to communicate with her openly, Maria decided to risk initiating contact via a third party. She sent her nurse, who by now was getting on in years, to the convent, under the pretense of making a donation. Once inside the walls at Piperoudion, Rona was able, after some initial difficulty, to wangle a short audience with Eudokia.

The whilom Empress was pale, her face lined with age and stress, and she must not have been eating, because she appeared frail and thin. The plainness of the nun's habit did not become one so accustomed to regal dress. It was like seeing the crown jewels floating in a bucket of pig slop.

"Maria sends her warmest regards," the nurse said.

"Maria," Eudokia said, practically spitting out the same. Then, with derision in her voice: "The Empress, you mean."

"Yes, she."

"Fie."

"She loves you dearly. All night and all day she frets over you."

"Does she," said Eudokia. "Frets over me in *my* bed, in *my* gowns. Yes, I'm sure this has been *quite* an ordeal for her, the poor deprived creature."

"Believe what you will," said the nurse. "I was sent here to give you that message: that she loves you, that she worries over you, that she prays for you, and that she will do what she can to see that you are released from this place and returned to the Palace, where you belong."

Eudokia laughed, but there was no pleasure in it. "She knows as well as I that this is impossible. I will die in this wretched place. If she wants to pray on my behalf, tell her to petition the Lord thus: to have mercy on my soul and take me quickly."

Rona defended her mistress's position. "She means it, Your Highness. She is sincere. I have known her since she was an infant. If there is anyone on Earth she cares for more than you, I've yet to meet him." Then the good nurse risked her own interposition; this woman was no longer royalty, after all. "I beseech you, Empress, have mercy on her. Lift the curse."

"Curse? What curse?"

"Have not you cursed her womb with barrenness?"

Eudokia did not say anything for some time. She just stared at the nurse with an unknowable expression on her well-lined face. Finally she spoke: "It was inevitable that I would wind up in a convent. I hope that the same fate does not befall our fair Maria, but I know that it will. This is how it ends for us women, all of us, every last one. It is the curse of the purple. That is the only curse I know of, nurse, and its power is too great for me, or anyone else, to command. Do not call on me again." With those words, the ghostly Eudokia disappeared up the creaky stairs.

Maria would see her just one more time, years later—and as her chief rival. But news of the visit lifted her spirits. There was no curse! Eudokia was miserable, but *she did not blame Maria*. She was not the cause of her inability to produce a child.

Although there must have been *some* curse in effect, one Eudokia might not even have been aware of, that was lifted that day. For no sooner did the nurse return to the palace with news from Eudokia than Maria became pregnant.

Following her midwife's instructions, she knew that her last menses came during the waning crescent moon. When the crescent moon came and went again with no discharge, she waxed hopeful with the waxing moon. When another lunar phase passed without blood, she went to see the midwife, who confirmed that she was with child. It would be some months before there was any outward sign, before the bump in her belly could not be reliably concealed beneath the billows of her imperial gowns. This afforded Maria time to solve her next riddle: what to tell Michael her husband. She contemplated arranging a quick liaison with him, a single event at which he could release himself upon her, and thus engender some hope that he was the legitimate father of the child. But this seemed too simple a ruse. He would see through it immediately, and anyway, she had no wish to sully herself with his ejaculate.

Instead, she resolved to give credit to Jesus Christ for seeding her womb. After all, Michael had instructed her, without irony, to pray to Him; well, now her prayers were answered. Who was she to deny His divine involvement? Never mind that her pregnancy was not quite as immaculately conceived as her namesake the Virgin Mother's. The Lord works in mysterious ways.

As usual, she found Michael in the stables. This time it was a different horse of virtue he was grooming, a horse called Chastity. She had last seen him nine days ago at a race at the Hippodrome; he was miserable that day, and she found him now as gloomy and despondent as ever.

"My Lord," she said, "I bring glad tidings."

"Speak your peace and be gone."

"Some years ago, when I inquired after producing an heir for you, you advised me to pray. And I have prayed. Night and day have I prayed to deliver a son to you. After years of dutiful prayer, sire, the Good Lord has at long last answered my prayers."

A wide smile broke across Michael's face. "You are with child?"

"I am."

"But this is wonderful news! Oh, Maria, I am so happy!" He dropped his brushes, rushed to her, and gave her a warm embrace—the first time he'd touched her in months. "How are you feeling? Is there anything you require?"

"I am well so far."

"I can see the change. Maria, you are glowing!"

This made her blush. "Thank you, Michael."

"For the good of the Empire, I hope it is a son. But personally, I'd rather have a little girl, one as beautiful as her mother."

The Empress blushed, smiling. "You should think of names, sire."

"If it is a boy," he said, "we should name it after my father."

Thus the interview ended, a far different result than she'd anticipated. Did Michael really believe that Jesus had some divine hand in all of this? That Maria was Mary redux? Or was he so relieved that she was pregnant, and had silenced or at least quelled the rumors about his own questionable manhood, that he didn't give a whit how she got that way? The Empress did not know, and I can only speculate. But I submit this happy reaction to news of his wife's impregnation by someone else as evidence of his evolved and rarified character. Michael was verily a decent man, saintly in his way, but a terrible Emperor, one of the worst in the long annals of Rome.

Nikephoritzes the eunuch, however, proved more pragmatic. When Michael told him the news, he smiled warmly and offered the perfunctory congratulations, but immediately ordered his network of spies to discreetly discover the identity of the unborn child's father. One of the eunuch guards in the palace, from the days when Maria was not yet Empress, implicated Ramwold; a porter in the Hagia Sophia who'd seen the handsome steward coming and going from the Empress's Loge corroborated the account. Nikephoritzes had both of the informants quietly removed the following weekend. The eunuch guard was drowned in the Propontis, the porter bludgeoned with a mace. There would be no gossip, no rumors. Ramwold was spared for the time being, but he was on borrowed time. The father of the bastard heir to the throne of Byzantium could not be allowed to survive, no matter how high his value to the Emperor and Empress; it was, the eunuch decided, a matter of national security.

By this time, as mentioned, Ramwold was no longer a slave. He'd been freed years ago, just before Michael took the throne, and given a salaried position in the Emperor's personal entourage. There was even talk of his marrying, an endeavor in which both Emperor and Empress indulged him. He still performed his carnal duties for Michael, although far less frequently, and with considerably less gusto.

When he learned of Maria's pregnancy, Ramwold was of mixed mind. He was delighted for her, as he knew how important it was for her to produce an heir; that objective, after all, was the original impetus for their libidinous relations. Once that duty had been discharged, however, he felt melancholy, used, not unlike one of the Emperor's horses sent to stud. And he foresaw, as Maria did not, that the birth of the bastard child would necessitate the death of the father; Ramwold was better acquainted with Nikephoritzes's cruel side, and rightly feared for his life. But when the weeks turned into months, and her belly swelled beneath the purple gowns, and the whole of the nation rejoiced at the prospect of a new crown prince—for the hoi polloi like nothing more than to fuss over royal babies, as such divinely-inspired creatures provide some uplift to their dark and dreary lives—he allowed himself to wonder if he'd been mistaken. Why not let him live? He was not some stranger. He was as close to the imperial couple, as intimate, as anyone alive. Neither Michael nor

Maria would wish such a dismal fate on him. And how lovely it will be, he mused, to meet my child! My own blood and flesh!

The early stages of the pregnancy passed without incident. By Advent, however, Maria was suffering with morning sickness so profound that she was confined to bed-rest. The midwife and the nurse tended to her round the clock. Fever gripped her. She began to have visions. In one such hallucination, her father Bagrat—who'd died of a heart attack two years before, in late November of A.D. 1072, after an impressive reign of 45 years—danced around the room, looking youthful and healthy, and behind him eunuch-like angels summoned her. "To Heaven, my child! To Heaven come!" Whereupon his facial hair morphed into a beard of snakes, and she was convinced that he'd been possessed by the Devil, that he was now roasting in the fires of Hell. All day she lay in bed whimpering, as the nurse pressed cold compresses to her burning forehead and assured her that it had all been nothing but a fever-dream. By the Feast of St. Nicholas, she was so miserable she was actively if quietly praying for death. "Take me, father! Take me!" This went on for a fortnight, with no relent. God was punishing her for her carnal trespasses. There was no other explanation. It was Hell on Earth.

"I've never experienced so much pain, concentrated over such a long period of time," she recalled later. "That must be what Hell is like. I can't imagine how it could possibly be worse. Rona, God bless her, stayed by my side throughout, with frequent visits from the midwife." Privately, both midwife and nurse acknowledged the possibility that the Empress might not survive the ordeal.

It was during this month of agony that Nikeph-oritzes decided to take action against the father of the unborn bastard prince. The last few months had not been kind to the eunuch Prime Minister, either. The hoi polloi regarded him with detestation, blaming him for the staggering rate of inflation that reduced the buying power of their daily wage, and also for the loss of prestige suffered by the Empire at the surrender of so much fertile territory. To alleviate his stress, he ate greedily, even when he was not hungry. Eunuchs have a tropism toward obesity, and Nikeph-oritzes at this time piled on the pounds. From the side angle, it appeared that he, too, was with child.

"Your Highness," he said to the *Augustus*—this was after Michael had just availed himself of an egregiously attractive catamite, a gift from the sultan Malik-shah, so the Emperor was in high spirits—"I have been made aware of a rumor."

"Speak, minister."

"I have heard whispers that the Empress your wife was not impregnated by the Holy Ghost, as we all supposed, but rather that her virtue was com-promised by an intruder."

"An intruder? But how—"

"Let me worry over that. I wanted you to be aware, because when the identity of this despicable creature has been ascertained, I would like to mete out punishment upon him without mercy. Does Your Highness agree?"

"Without question." Michael let out a sigh, half of post-coital pleasure, half of vexation. "Why did Maria not inform me directly?"

"Perhaps she was ashamed. Perhaps she sought to protect you from this rude knowledge. Maria is a good woman and wife, and always behaves with your best interests in mind."

"Locate this foul cancer," the Emperor commanded, "and root it out. I leave it in your capable hands."

"Consider it done, Your Highness."

At the dinner hour on Christmas Eve, Maria felt a gush of warm blood spurt out between her legs. *Here it is*, she thought. *The baby's blood. The infant has died. All of this agony has been for naught!* But the fluid was not red and viscous but clear and watery, a sign that the quickening would happen presently. The midwife summoned her assistants, and all repaired to the Porphyra, the birthing room where all imperial babies, myself included, are literally "born in the purple."

The pain of labor was agonizing, but not as agonizing as the last month had been, and Maria pushed like an automaton, devoid of human emotion. She had nothing left to give. A hush fell on the room as the babe emerged from her splayed legs—an incredible sight to behold! As the midwife caught the child, all were silent, anticipating the newborn's cry. It did not come.

"No," the midwife cried. "Oh, no."

The umbilical cord was wrapped around the poor creature's tiny neck, and this had strangled all life out of it. It was a runt-sized infant, a little girl, pretty as Maria, but dead as Bagrat. All at once the women in the room, proud attendants of royal mothers, began to wail, an ululation of agony and defeat—all but Maria, whose eyes remained closed, who knew better than to look.

As this was happening in the Porphyra, Ramwold was finishing up his duties related to the next day's Christmas feast. He was about to retire for the evening when he was summoned to the Emperor's apartments—unusual at that hour, but not unusual enough to arouse suspicion. Michael was not there. In his place was Nikephoritzes the now-corpulent eunuch, accompanied by a short, ugly man with a slit nose.

"My good Ramwold," said the eunuch pleasantly. "Have you not met Romanos Straboromanos?"

"Not formally," the handsome steward said. "Where is the Emperor? Is there something the matter?"

"An issue of palace security," Nikephoritzes replied. "Romanos will explain."

Ramwold found it hard to read the look upon the face of Straboromanos—the nose is more expressive than we realize. But he knew, on some level, that the end was near. This was the *megas heraireiarches*, the head of the Secret Service, and not a man given to impromptu social calls, even on the birthday of the Risen Christ.

"Merry Christmas," the Prime Minister added, smiling brightly, as he quit the room.

Straboromanos moved to speak, but Ramwold stopped him. "I'm not a child," he said. "I know which way the wind blows. Is it to be the dungeons here, or will we away to Proti?"

"It's a bit chilly tonight," the slit-nosed monster said, "but the air is crisp and clear. I thought you might enjoy one last boat ride."

"Thank you," Ramwold said. "I appreciate that."

"You will come peacefully then?"

"There's no point in resisting, is there?"

"None."

"Does the Emperor know?"

"That I cannot say."

"Because you don't know, or you won't tell me?"

"Both." Straboromanos gestured elegantly toward the door. "This way, please."

Back in the Porphyra, the women wept. The midwife swaddled the stillborn girl and prepared to send her to the priest for blessing before burial. There was still the afterbirth to come, but that was nothing, that would pass without incident.

But Maria's pain had not abated. Still she howled—the nurse and the attendants assumed her cries were for the loss of the child, but no—still her belly ached, like her very body was being torn asunder. It was only when a tiny foot appeared that the others realized what was happening.

"A twin!" the midwife exclaimed. "Get ready!"

Breech births are a bad omen, as every occupant in the room well knew, and the old woman went to work, trying all the tricks of her trade to turn the babe to the proper position. This involved prestidigitation the likes of which the midwife had never before attempted, but she was determined that this second child should survive. A drape was brought and run along Maria's chest, so she could not see what was happening, and the midwife's knowledgeable fingers poked and prodded, coaxed and cajoled. The pain was without precedent, and the herbs they gave her to chew on did nothing. Maria shut tight her eyes and muttered prayers to the Almighty and prepared for death.

Ramwold followed Straboromanos, walking silently a few paces behind, like Eurydice and Orpheus, except that our mismatched pair strode *toward* the Underworld. They spoke not a word, and Ramwold made no attempt to escape.

To the harbor they went, not the Golden Horn but the little imperial landing right at the Grand Palace. A small boat was waiting for them.

They boarded the boat and set sail for the island of Proti, six miles and an eternity away from Constantinople.

The break of day could be seen through the cracks in the draped windows of the Porphyra. It was Christmas morning. Maria had been in labor for twelve solid hours. This is how I will die, she thought, giving birth to a child not my husband's. A just punishment for my grievous sin!

Finally, after many attempts, the midwife succeeded in turning the unborn infant. The Empress's pain subsided at once and she was able to push.

At just before seven in the morning, the second of the twins came into the world. This latter child was alive—indeed, the newborn's cries could be heard all through the Palace—and, unlike its stillborn sister, was a boy.

Ramwold was stripped naked, his hands shackled at the wrist behind his back. A hook was fitted into the rusted chain connecting the cuffs, and that hook jerked by a pulley up to the pillars of the barn-like structure in which he was held, hoisting his arms backwards above his head, lifting him two feet off the dirt floor, and popping his shoulders out of their their sockets. He tried not to scream but could not help himself, the pain was so great.

"I've been instructed to mete out the Frankish punishment for sodomy," Straboromanos said. "Ironic, to be sure, given the name of the Emperor on the seal. But I have my orders."

"I understand," Ramwold said, fighting back tears.

"You are a good fellow," the torturer said. "I will work quickly."

"Thank you."

The slit-nosed freak bound both of his charge's ankles to beams on the floor, steadying the prisoner. From a menacing box of instruments of torture he produced a jagged metal wire. This he wrapped tightly around the top of Ramwold's scrotum. The crude metal edges cut into his tender flesh. Straboromanos pulled hard on the wire, wrapping it around and around like a metal tourniquet, choking off the flow of blood. In a few minutes the sac turned a deep shade of purple not unlike the walls of the Porphyra. By then Ramwold had stopped trying to suppress his screams. When one becomes an intimate of the Emperor, one runs the risk of gruesome death. He'd lived a full life. He gave the Empress a child. Maybe the child would be a son. Maybe the child would take the purple one day. His child, his son, *Augustus*. That was more than he ever would have imagined, when he was captured across the Danube that fateful day all those years ago.

There were dogs in the room now, savage mutts, nasty mottled things, barking and growling. When the wire had done its dread work, and his bits fell to the dirt, the mutts fought for the scraps.

From the box, Straboromanos produced a blade. "The Frankish punishment calls for metal spikes to be hammered into the offending region, and then the prisoner to be dragged by those spikes through the town in humiliating fashion," he said. "It is late, and it is Christmas, so we will abbreviate the process, if you don't object."

Ramwold did not object. He turned his head and screamed as the slit-nosed monster sliced off his "offending region" and fed it to the dogs.

"That will do you," Straboromanos said. "Adieu, Ramwold." And he quit the room.

There was nothing left between the Alan's legs, just a gaping hole from which blood, so much blood, an endless supply of blood it seemed, spurted ceaselessly onto the floor, where it was eagerly lapped up by the wretched mutts. Ramwold could no longer feel the pain. He was numb. He was exhausted. He was suddenly elated that the ordeal was over. He said his prayers. He thought of Maria and of Michael, of the pleasures they had given him and vice versa. He thought of his own parents, so long dead. He would reunite with them soon enough. Light streamed through the open windows of the barn. Christmas Day. His last sunrise. His final morning.

He fell asleep. He did not wake.

The babe was an angel. There was no other way to describe him. His parents were two of the most attractive humans in all of Christendom, and he had inherited their good looks. Blonde hair, blue eyes, superlative features, perfection. To behold him was to fall in love. He was named Constantine, after Michael's father, but Maria called him Tino.

The midwife washed the baby, swaddled him, and prepared to hand him to the wet nurse. Maria intervened. "No! It is my son, and I will give him succor."

"But Your Highness, you are weak from the labor."

"I will survive." Maria took the child and offered it her breast. The process came naturally to neither party, and it took several botched attempts before the cherubic boy's pretty little mouth was latched properly to the royal nipple. After that, all was peaceful as little Tino fed contentedly on mother's milk.

The waiting-ladies watched in amazement. For an Empress to nurse her own baby was quite unheard of. Perhaps it was the custom in Alania? But Rona the nurse smiled. It was plain to her how happy the Empress now was.

Maria had fallen in love with her newborn son, and from that moment on, her life would be dedicated to him. Everything she did would be for his benefit. She was Mary, and this Christmas baby was her Jesus. She worshipped and adored him. No mother ever gave more love to a child.

It was December the twenty-fifth, A.D. 1074. Nine years hence, this angelic Constantine—this fair Tino—would be betrothed to me.

XXII

THE RED ROGUE

OURSEL WAS SO CALLED BECAUSE OF HIS RED HAIR—his Christian name, like his countryman Bohemond's, was Mark—which he wore short, in the Norman style, to accommodate his ridiculous helmet. His face too was red, his fair skin baked pink from too much time in the hot sun. He was the most notable of the Frankish mercenaries come from the West at this time, in that he was a superlative general who commanded a personal army of some three hundred knights, but hardly an outlier. Many Normans arrived in this first wave, a harbinger of the great multitudes that were to follow a quarter century hence. Previously, this Oursel had been one of any number of mercenary Frankish generals in Italy, where he'd served under the banner of Roger, the unfortunate brother of Robert the Fox, in Sicily and elsewhere. Our emissary in Bari brought him East when Diogenes was in the purple, and Oursel arrived with his mannish wife, his litter of children—he had no fortified city like Constantinople in which to safeguard his family, so he brought them along wherever he went—and some fifteen score knights and their retinue. He was at the head of a small regiment of eight hundred soldiers during that last fateful campaign of Diogenes, but owing to the Emperor's poor battle plan, and perhaps to Oursel's good luck, he was separated from the Army of Asia and sat out Manzikert. Instead, he established himself in the walled city of Amaseia,[67] where his ability to repel Turkish raids and his refusal to tax the population in the usual Byzantine manner made him extremely popular with the locals.

Oursel was recruited by, and owed his allegiance to, Diogenes, and thus was in no hurry to bow to a new, reportedly inept *Augustus*. Using Amaseia as a base of operations, he expanded his reach to include much of Galatia. When the *Caesar*'s forces failed to remove him—when, to the contrary, and quite by surprise, both John and Andronikos Doukas were captured by him!—the ambitious Frank devised an inspired stratagem: he would have the army declare his prisoner to be *Augustus*. In this way, his own authority would be legitimized, and the civil war that was bound to follow would make the Byzantines powerless to stop him. He would have his own fiefdom for sure. He might even wind up with more.

---

[67] Now Amasya, and still an important city in northern Turkey.

(Regardless of one's feelings towards the red rogue, one must be impressed by his audacious cleverness.)

In the camp, meanwhile, and as previously mentioned, Andronikos was gravely wounded. Not only had he lost his hand, or rather much of his forearm, but he'd sustained a near-fatal blow to the head, with tragic consequences, as we shall see. The primary condition for John agreeing to participate in the usurpation was that Andronikos be removed at once to Constantinople, where he might receive proper medical attention. After a short interview with the wounded general, Oursel consented.

John Doukas was extremely popular in Asia, and many a Roman soldier flocked to his banner. But to be more than a usurper, he needed to be formally crowned; to be formally crowned, he needed access to Hagia Sophia; and there was no way Constantinople would fall to a bunch of Franks, however brave. The city had never, not once in seven centuries, been successfully besieged; its defenses were too great. The longer John took to take the capital, the less legitimacy his imperial declaration held. As the weeks went on without movement, sergeants began to desert the company, first in a trickle, then in a wave. The hasty coronation at Nicomedia fooled no one. Michael controlled Constantinople, which meant he held the Church of the Holy Wisdom—and also the keys to the Imperial Treasury.

Bumbling as always, Michael through Nikephoritzes sued the sultan for help in crushing the insurgency, in exchange for God knows how many hectares of arable land. (Appealing to aid from the Moslems was, in the eyes of many citizens, an unforgiveable affront to Jesus Christ Himself.) Malik-shah did as he promised, promptly attacking the Franks with an unprecedented show of force—Turks as a rule preferred to dance girlishly around their enemy on their fleet ponies rather than engage him directly on the field. Oursel, the ersatz Emperor John, and all of their men were turned over to my father Alexios. The rebellion, such as it was, was no more.

At Manzikert, Diogenes had been routed, yes, but he had at least fought bravely, and managed through the subsequent negotiations to hold on to the Anatolian provinces. Michael snubbed his nose at those negotiations while declining to send his forces anywhere useful, much less take command of the armies himself, relying instead on help from the infidel and Michael's increasingly mutinous generals. He then surrendered vast tracts of his Anatolian territory in exchange for a single ruddy-faced Norman general. Which Emperor, I ask, was the real failure?

Certainly there were rumblings in the field. The aforementioned generals were taking stock of the situation, rightly concluding that Michael had outlived his usefulness, and that the Empire was better served in more capable hands. John Doukas had already made his claim, albeit under coercion. (It was the peculiarity of the situation, and the *Caesar's* argument that if he'd wanted to be *Augustus* he would have simply married Eudokia when she'd asked, that convinced Michael to overrule Nikephoritzes and allow his uncle to retain his sight.) Botaneiates in Asia and Bryennios in Europe both veered inexorably toward open revolt. Even my father, nobler than the others put together, took pause; he'd left Constantinople dedicated to the sitting Emperor, but after his adventures in the East privately determined that he, despite his youth, was better suited to the throne than Michael, his broke benefactor.

The generals were not alone. The hoi polloi actively loathed the Emperor. The combination of higher taxes, lower wages, and debased currency exacerbated the already-high rate of inflation. Wheat prices collapsed; anecdotally, a bushel of grain was worth seventy-five percent of what it had been two years prior. Blame for this was placed at the feet of the Emperor, who was given the pejorative sobriquet *Parapinakes*, meaning "peck-filcher"—one peck being a quarter of a bushel of wheat, the amount Michael's regressive economic policies cost the average citizen. So firmly did this appellation stick that when I was learning my history fifteen years later, I believed that his actual name was Parapinakes. Nikephoritzes too was singled out for derision; there was not a more hated personage in the Empire than the fat eunuch Prime Minister. Given the chance, the Constantinopolitan rabble would happily tear him limb from flabby limb.

At the Grand Palace, Michael himself—still grieving the loss of his love Ramwold—began to revile his station. He dreamed of leaving the purple behind. In this state of mind he paid a visit on Psellos, his tutor and family friend, who had retired from public life to work on his *Chronographia*.

"Teacher," Michael said, "I need your guidance."

"I don't know that I can be of much help," the old monk replied, although he did not believe that, "but I will try my best."

"I want out."

"Out?"

"I hate my life. I hate being Emperor. It has cost me the only real friend I had"—meaning Ramwold—"and turned the hoi polloi against me. The people detest me. My wife no longer respects me. Even my good uncle has turned on me. This is worse than the most abysmal Hell the Adversary can devise!"

"It is a rare privilege to ascend to the throne," Psellos said. "Are you rather sure you can't wait out this period of unease? Once you leave, you cannot return."

"Nor would I desire to. I would not wish this torment on my worst enemy."

"I see." The old monk ran his fingers through his gray beard and thought through the options. "You have an heir now, young Constantine. You could simply abdicate, make him the Emperor, and let Maria your wife serve as his Regent."

"I thought of that," Michael said, "and Maria no doubt is up to the task. But the situation is so bleak, so fraught with danger, that to do so condemns both of them to death. Neither Bryennios nor Botaneiates will recognize Constantine as the *Augustus*. No, one of them will mutiny and slay him, and the Empress too."

"The Empress is on good terms with Alexios Komnenos," Psellos pointed out. "He is young, and a far better commander than the others. He could protect them."

"To what end? Alexios covets the throne. I agree that he is cut of finer cloth than the other two, but he seeks power. What stops him from marrying Maria and taking the purple himself?"

"Nothing," Psellos said. "But that ensures their protection."

"No, Alexios cannot preside over the throne while Constantine lives. He will have to kill him."

"Or blind him. Alexios is merciful."

"Life in the dark is no life at all."

"I quite agree." Psellos stood up and began to pace the room. "There is another option."

"Name it."

"Valentin, the Metropolitan of Ephesus, is too infirm to continue in that position. You could step down gracefully from the purple and take his place there, claiming religious vocation."

A smile of unmistakable joy crossed the young Emperor's face. Since at least the time of St. Paul the Apostle, whose epistle rebuked its citizens for sexual immorality, Ephesus had a reputation for the tacit tolerance of sodomy. There was no place in the Empire to which Michael would rather retire. "Oh, but what happiness that would bring! How do we proceed?"

"There needs to be a successor," Psellos said. "With the way the winds are blowing, I suspect it won't be long. When the moment comes, we will send word that this is what you seek. It will give the new Emperor more legitimacy if you pass the crown to him peaceably."

"Indeed."

"Although that path will also have its hurdles."

"Hurdles?"

"The new Emperor must agree. But I suspect he will. And the hoi polloi will demand a scapegoat. A prominent member of your administration must be sacrificed to atone for your perceived sins."

"Nikephoritzes."

"Exactly."

Michael nodded. "A small price to pay," he said.

"When the time comes," Psellos says, "I will take action on your behalf."

"Thank you, good teacher."

"You're a good man, Michael. You're better than the lot of them."

XXIII
THE MOTHER

THE BIRTH OF CONSTANTINE IMBUED Maria's life with a new sense of purpose. Her son became her Alpha and Omega, her be-all and end-all. Magi from the East did not follow a star to the Porphrya and present the infant boy with gifts, yet Maria looked upon Tino with the reverence normally associated with the second coming of the Messiah. She doted upon him in ways she previously would not have thought herself capable. Rona as well as a young wet-nurse were on hand 'round the clock, yet still Maria kept Tino with her at all times. She slept in bed with him at her side, always touching her body. She fed him from her own breast, quite against the royal conventions, and caused some amount of scandal when she wrapped him in linens around her person and carried him thus to every event at which her presence was mandatory. Her schedule of events was curtailed so she could care for the child—although with all the bedlam in the realm, most public events were scrapped regardless, for reasons of security. Maria could read the writing on the wall. She knew that Michael's reign would be cut short, due to either abdication or assassination, and she rightly saw baby Tino as her best hope of achieving *de facto* imperial powers herself.

Not that it was all so mercenary. Because it had taken so long to conceive, and because of the death of the twin, she was predisposed to loving the boy. And love him she did, with every ounce of her being. There was nothing she would not do to help him. Marry a senile old man, plot an imperial coup, seduce a lisping young general: she did it all for Tino. And young Constantine, God knows, needed the help. He was a sickly child, pale and prone to rash and rheum and fever. She nursed him through his every infirmity and stayed with him at the expense of her own health, which suffered during the infant years. The result was that Tino survived infancy, but he became an exceedingly spoilt child. He knew his mother would give him the world, and he was not afraid to ask for it.

Michael, cuckolded by his own ex-slave and lover, was nonetheless happy to have an heir to the throne, and the birth of the child did somewhat ease the public's contempt for him; the rabble love a royal bundle of joy. But he personally did not show much of an interest in Tino—except as a tool of diplomacy. Within a week of his birth, young Constantine was betrothed to a daughter of Robert the Fox—the most beautiful daughter, as Maria had insisted. This turned out to be one Helena, then fifteen years of age, who arrived in the Queen City one gloomy autumn day with a retinue of waiting-ladies and a special saddle, so she could ride and shoot arrows at the same time. She was tall and mannish, as the Frankish women tend to be, with strong broad shoulders and a devil-may-care smile. Beautiful, not so much, but she would look presentable in the imperial gowns, and anyway the co-Emperor—for that was now Constantine's official title—was still in diapers. Occasionally Helena would visit the Palace and rock the baby to sleep in her powerful arms—hardly the paragon of courtly romance. And she never did master eating with a fork, preferring instead to use her large, masculine hands. Maria refused to let Helena move into the Grand Palace, so she went to live with Anna Dalassene, along with Leo and Nikephoros Diogenes. Anna took to the girl, and from her learned a great deal about Norman custom. But on the whole, the betrothal was the subject of derision at court. The notion of promising the hand of the infant co-Emperor and heir to the throne of the Equal of the Apostles to the hoydenish teenaged daughter of a Norman pirate-turned-duke—even if it increased the prospect of peace—was widely regarded as a travesty, worse in its way than the soaring inflation or the loss of land to the Turks.

Living in the Komneni palace, then, were two sons of a blinded Emperor, the brute daughter of one of the Empire's greatest enemies, and a wide array of Anna's daughters—my aunts—most of whom would one day marry for political reasons. In the Byzantine court, it was unwise to hold a grudge!

Speaking of my father's siblings, it was at this time that Isaac suffered another humiliating defeat—at Antioch, the inveterate Christian stronghold. With tensions smoothed over in Anatolia, the Turks had turned their attention to Syria, launching raid after raid and conquering the ancient cities of Aleppo and Damascus. Isaac took an army to Antioch to defend against these incursions, and was almost immediately routed. His second-in-command, Constantine Diogenes—son of the slain Emperor and husband of my aunt Theodora—perished, and Isaac himself was wounded in the leg and taken prisoner. The Antiochenes raised a ransom of twenty thousand gold *solidi* to buy his freedom.

My uncle's failure to defend Syria would have disastrous consequences, reaching far beyond the House of Komnenos. Three years later, in A.D. 1077, Malik-shah's Turks would take Jerusalem from the moribund Fatimids—their Moslem Ægyptian rivals, who'd held the place for centuries—and slaughter a good number of the Holy City's Christian inhabitants. It was this change in Jerusalem's infidel authority that would prove the impetus for the influx of bellicose Latin pilgrims twenty years later[68]—that and some brilliant diplomatic maneuvering

---

[68]   i.e., the First Crusade.

by my father. And at the risk of coming off like that self-aggrandizing fool Psellos, candor compels me to point out that the scheme to appeal to the Latins on religious grounds and then play them off against the Turks was, in fact, my own invention, as we shall see.

For the first half of the journey from Amaseia, the bound Oursel rode folded over a donkey, the customary way of humiliating a prisoner. Once they reached Bithynia, however, Alexios allowed his captive to wear proper attire and ride with him.

"Thank you," the Frank said, in broken but proficient Greek, "for sparing my life. I owe you one."

"You owe me more than one," Alexios said. "And I will see that you make good."

"As well you should." Oursel rubbed his neck. The ride upon the ass had made it stiff. "I want you to understand my position."

"I understand it perfectly. You are a man of great ambition. You saw your chance to establish your own little kingdom, and you took it by betraying your paymasters."

"That is slander," the Frank muttered indignantly. Alexios laughed good-naturedly, and Oursel continued: "We were brought here, my men and I, by the *Augustus* Romanos Diogenes. It was to him that I pledged fealty, not the crown itself. So you see that your new Emperor, this usurping molly-boy

Michael, is…what was your phrase? A man of great ambition who saw his chance to establish his own little kingdom, and took it by betraying his paymasters."

Again Alexios laughed. After so many months of grave danger, extreme privation, and constant battle, such jovial amusement was a relief. The truth is that he liked Oursel. They were about the same age, and he saw in him a military peer, someone who might understand him. "You somehow managed not to fight at Manzikert."

"And that makes me a coward?" Again Oursel rubbed his sore neck. "I was ordered to scout the northlands, and became separated from the army. I could not rejoin them without marching straight through Alp Arslan's entire force. What was I supposed to do? Allow my men to die? I took refuge in the walled city, killed any Turks that crossed my path, and waited for word from Diogenes. Word that did not come. And it's rather audacious that you would mention a paymaster," he said. "We have not been compensated for quite some time, and we are men for hire. I understand war sometimes complicates the doling out of wages, but after a full year…"

"You managed to secure enough loot to pay your ransom."

"That was through plunder. I'm not proud of that, but you know as well as I that this is what an army far away from home must do to survive."

"You are a mercenary. Too many of your number turn tail and flee at the first sight of danger."

"Without mercenaries, you would have no army."

Alexios smiled brightly, conceding the point.

"At the end of the day," Oursel continued, "we have to do what we feel is right. No man will follow a dastard, no matter how handsomely he is paid. This is a problem with your Emperor Peck-Filcher. Honorable men will not follow the banner of a poltroon. And if wages are withheld? That's another story."

"Perhaps I should have your tongue," my father said, "for insulting the Equal of Apostles." But his smile indicated that this was a joke. For Alexios agreed with Oursel's analysis. Most of the Empire had arrived at the same dismal assessment of Michael VII Doukas.

"Let *you* be my paymaster," the Frank said, "and I will follow you till the ends of the earth."

"Why should I trust you?"

"You already trust me," Oursel replied. "If I did not have your trust, I would not be talking with you right now."

They sat in silence, the two crafty generals, listening to a song being sung by one of the concubines around the campfire outside. Her voice was angelic, and imbued the moment with an almost religious significance. At last Alexios spoke: "I cannot promise to spare your life. The Emperor takes no stock in such decisions; all power lies with his eunuch Prime Minister, Nikephoritzes. With that caveat established, I will lobby for your release. Good generals are in short supply, and I am not without influence at court. You will likely have to languish in gaol for a spell, even if my counsel is heeded. But I warn you, Frank: recidivism will not be tolerated. Make a fool of me, and it's more than your little fiefdom that will be taken from you."

And this is how Oursel, fighting under the banner of Byzantium, came to command an even larger army that the one he'd left behind in Amaseia.

Almost immediately upon returning to Constantinople from Galatia, and receiving the lavish honors awarded him for a job well done, Alexios resolved to exact his revenge on the despicable Andronikos. This was the snake who had killed his brother Manuel, who had abandoned Diogenes at Manzikert, who had endorsed the *Caesar*'s dastardly insurrection—a traitor in every way. His cowardice and greed had cost untold imperial lives. Andronikos was Michael's cousin, and Michael would not dare harm a fellow Doukid, but Alexios had no such prohibitions. The plan was this: He would pay his respects, disembowel the snake with a dagger, watch him painfully bleed out, and dare the spineless Emperor to punish him.

The long faces of the servants at the magnificent Doukid palace, he later realized, hinted at the sad state of affairs therein. Alexios found Andronikos lounging on a divan on the terrace, looking out at the sea. The former Domestic of the Schools was in his middle thirties but looked like a man twice that age. What remained of his hair was white, his face was wrinkled beyond description, and the nub at the end of his left arm was wrapped in white linen that resembled a funeral shroud.

"Fare thee well, friend Andronikos," Alexios said.

Andronikos looked at him blankly.

"It is I, Alexios Komnenos."

There was no flicker of recognition on the older man's face. Nothing flickered at all, in fact. His eyes were vacant.

Alexios showed him the dagger, which again brought no response. "I've come here to slay you, guttersnipe," he said. "Revenge, for the murder of my brother."

Andronikos did not so much as blink.

"What say thee? Speak, cretin."

But Andronikos did not speak. Andronikos could not speak. Andronikos as Alexios knew him was gone. The blow to his head suffered in battle had killed that part of him. What remained was a husk of a man, incapable of speech. A drooling, feeble creature devoid of thought. Devoid of soul.

The breeze from the Propontis blew in, and Alexios caught wind of a foul stench. He realized, to his horror, that the older man had soiled himself. Andronikos lay there in his own filth, unaware, unthinking, blinking blankly every so often. Alexios sheathed his dagger. To kill him would be an act of mercy; better to let him live in agony.

On his way out, he asked one of the servants what had happened.

"We don't know, sir. He has been like this since he came home."

"Has he spoken?"

"Not a word, sir."

My father was angry as he left the palace, his thirst for revenge unslaked. What pleasure can be derived in dispatching an idiot who does not know why he is being killed? In frustration, he kicked over a barrel in the Doukid garden, stubbing his toe. Vengeance would have to be achieved via a different avenue.

XXIV
THE MISTRESS

IN HONOR OF HER FAVORITE SON coming home in one piece, and in triumph withal—quite unlike the "black sheep" of the family, the wounded and twice-ransomed Isaac—Anna Dalassene gave a lavish dinner party at the Komnenoi palace in Alexios's honor. Among the many guests were Isaac and his wife Irina of Alania; Nikephoros and Leo Diogenes, sons of the late Emperor Romanos Diogenes; Helena, the brutish daughter of Robert the Fox and fiancée of the infant Constantine Doukas; the rakishly handsome young general George Palaiologos, one of my father's closest friends, and his wife Anna Doukaina; Anna Doukaina's mother Maria of Bulgaria and little sister Irene.

My father himself cut a dashing figure. After many months on the road, marching hither and yon short of money and food and leisure time, he was finally able to properly bathe and clothe himself and trim and shape his beard and hair. His flowing red cape and gilt epaulets were as impressive as his regal bearing. He looked the epitome of martial power, like Mars himself come to Constantinople.

"Why did you invite so many from the House of Doukas?" Alexios asked his mother teasingly. "I thought you detested them."

"Not all of them. Most, but not all. Maria is not really a Doukas. In fact, she loathes that family more than I do!"

My father knew this was true, he'd witnessed evidence firsthand many times, and he chortled.

"If we are going to take the purple one day, my son, we must have good relations with the Doukoi, whether we like them or not."

"Soft, mother!" Alexios cried. "Let us not have such rude talk."

"And yet I am right." Anna Dalassene gestured with her head toward Irene, a simpering twig of a girl who soaking wet weighed less than certain Constantinopolitan alley-cats. "What do you make of Irene?"

"What do I make of her? What do I *make*? Nothing. She's seven."

"You exaggerate. She's almost nine, I'll have you know."

"Mother, arrest thine impetuous tongue."

Anna smiled and took a sip from the glass goblet of wine she'd been holding all night. "I mention it because Maria of Bulgaria called on me whilst you were away and broached the subject of a match."

"A match?"

"Her youngest daughter with my youngest son."

Alexios laughed. He laughed loudly and joylessly. He laughed expecting, or at least hoping, that his mother would also laugh, and thus reveal this to be a wry joke. But Anna did not. Alexios stopped laughing. "Mother, no!"

"Well, why not? A marriage into that family would be extremely advantageous to us. We like Maria well enough. And the girl is so young, you can mold her to suit your desire."

"You ask why not? I give you three reasons. First, she is, as you say, so young. By the time she is ready to bear children, I may well be dead. I'm in no hurry to breed, but if God ever does place me on the throne I will need heirs, and sooner rather than later. And you know quite well that I prefer older women."

Anna gave his bum a gentle tap. "Yes, I do."

"Mother, behave! Second, her father is not just a Doukas, but the murderer of my dear brother Manuel. Your first-born son. Surely you remember Manuel! How can I in good conscience wed the daughter of such a monster?" Alexios turned his head and stared wistfully across the great room, where the object of his affection was not. "Finally, my heart is set on another."

"Maria of Alania."

Alexios nodded bashfully and examined the ground.

"We all love her, my son. But she is married to the Emperor!"

"Only for the time being, good mother. Chances are she will soon be a widow."

"Perhaps. And marrying the sitting Empress would be the simplest way to achieve the throne."

"Oh, I don't care about the throne. If I could be with Maria, I'd happily live as a sheep shearer in Bithynia."

Anna cackled, her distinctive too-loud laugh. "Now I know you're in love, because that is pure madness! Let us mingle, my son. We'll resume this discussion later, when we are alone, and prudence has returned to you."

Alexios left his mother's side and worked the vast room, shaking hands with this person and that, accepting praise, laughing at the clever quips of his wittier guests—his dear friend George Palaiologos was particularly arch—and making some of his own. He drank more wine than usual. He even sought out Irene Doukaina, his eight-going-on-nine-year-old potential bride, complimenting her on her gown, with some effort coaxing a smile out of her. He found her dull and joyless, a miserable child. And she looked nothing like her mother, the dark and plain Maria of Bulgaria. Fair in complexion, thin as a rail, and rather tall for her age, she was the spitting image of her father Andronikos, once an agent of evil, now a drooling idiot. How could Alexios possibly marry the daughter of the man he hated most on earth, especially when she looked his double? It was folly on his mother's part to even suggest it.

And yet he knew at once that Anna, as usual, was right.

He was sulking in the corner, all by himself, when he was approached by his sister-in-law, the long-suffering Irina of Alania—wife of Isaac and cousin of the Empress. While not quite in Maria's league, Irina was still egregiously beautiful. This paradigm of pulchritude shares the bed of my feckless brother, Alexios thought, and I must make do with the shapeless, plain child! Irina and Irene: their Christian names are almost identical—but that is all they have in common! But he steeled himself, fighting off his inchoate melancholy, and greeted Irina warmly.

"How fares the Empress? I can't tell you how pleased I was to hear of the arrival of the baby Constantine."

His sister-in-law smiled wanly. "In all honesty, brother, she has been better. The child is often infirm, and she worries over him constantly. Her husband the Emperor is another source of her anxiety. She was beyond relieved to hear that you had returned safely from the East."

"As was I."

Irina laughed, and for a fleeting moment Alexios envisaged himself ravishing her. The wine amplified his soul's lustful whispers into screams of desire. It took all the power of his will to banish these untoward thoughts from his mind.

"I have something for you," she said, and from her gown produced a letter, which she handed to him. "Maria sends her regrets." When he moved to break the wax seal, she cautioned, "Read it later, when you are alone."

That night, alone in his room, he did:

My dearest Alexios,

It is with considerable regret that I declined the dinner party in your honor. As you are perhaps aware, I am a new mother, and this state of affairs has left me temporarily unable to make social calls of any kind. Ordinarily this is a blessing, as imperial social calls can be tedious; not in this case. Suffice it to say, I trust in God that you will accept my sincerest apologies for missing the festivities. Furthermore, it is my great hope that you will deign to call on me at some point. I want my son to meet you, so that he may see first-hand how men of honor are supposed to conduct themselves.

Until then I remain,

Yours,
Maria

He slept not a wink that night, spending many hours analyzing the strange language of the letter, trolling for deeper meaning beneath the surface. That she'd written him at all was highly unusual. An Empress did not have to excuse herself from any-thing, it was understood that she would have more pressing matters; and her attendance at a dinner party not held at court would have attracted undue attention. But the tone of the note was also highly informal. There was no litany of titles and so-on, as for example in the Diogenes missive to Eudokia. "Deign to call on me" suggested a power dynamic that was inverse to the actual one. What could she mean by "how men of honor are supposed to conduct themselves?" And the tantalizing ambiguity of that sign-off. *Yours.* Was this simple politesse? Or did more complicated passions lurk in her curious choice of words? His ardor was roused, and with no readier outlet available, Alexios was compelled to take matters into his own hand. He abused himself over and over until his body would no longer cooperate, and even then his desire remained unquenchable. It was almost dawn before sleep finally came for him.[69]

Alexios went the next morning to call on the Empress, bearing gifts he'd acquired on his travels for both her and the new co-Emperor Constantine. Kept waiting in the parlor for almost an hour, like some undecorated commoner, he was convinced that he was mistaken, that the missive was a perfunctory burst of kindness and nothing more. But

---

[69]   I should explain that this detail was provided to me by the Empress, who knew of it from my father. I thought it impolitic to ask him for corroboration. (A.K.)

when Maria personally appeared to call him into the Map Room, he reverted back to his original line of thinking.

The Map Room, he noticed, was no longer a Map Room. Gone was the table, the hard-back chairs, the charts and maps. Now there was a desk, and a divan, and several pillowed chairs. Once a manly redoubt, there was now an unmistakably feminine quality to the chamber.

Beautiful beyond description, yet the Empress appeared tired. Her eyes were bloodshot, and she moved as if in a daze. "Forgive me, general," she said. "Tino did not sleep well last night, and I have only now enticed him to take his nap. He has a bad habit of demanding my full attention at moments when I most want to focus it elsewhere."

"There is no need to apologize, Your Highness," Alexios said. "Should I come back at another time? Perhaps the Empress would herself like to rest."

"Nonsense. I've been eager to see you, to hear firsthand of your exploits."

They were not alone in the Map Room, as decorum prevented them from ever being alone. With them were two of the Varangian Guard, as well as a waiting-lady and two eunuch attendants. Maria spoke to all of them in her native tongue, a language Alexios had heard on his travels, but which still sounded, to his Greek ears, like the Devil's speech. "Would you like something to drink?"

"Some water, perhaps." He was a bit parched from all the wine the night before.

She spoke to one of the eunuchs, who poured him a goblet of water. "None of my attendants here speak more than a few words of Greek," Maria explained. "They won't follow our conversation, so you can speak freely."

"Yes, your highness."

"You're a sight for sore eyes, my friend. This place has been appropriated by poltroons. For some years I managed to mitigate the cowardice of the Prime Minister and his men, but the birth of my son necessitated a lengthy absence from court duties. One likes to imagine that one's presence is essential to the workings of the government, and this is usually vainglory, but in this particular case it is so. I was incapacitated for a few months, and the Empire is now on the verge of collapse. My husband will not see me, he's promised my son to some barbarian bitch, and the people call him Peck-filcher! Forgive me, sir. I'm frustrated and tired, and I'm talking nonsense."

"Your highness," Alexios said, moving closer to her, "it is impossible for you to offend me in any way. Unburden yourself upon me. My ears are anxious to hear what you have to say, and my tongue will repeat none of it."

"You are too kind," she sighed. "The truth is that I'm terrified. Michael seems unlikely to retain his position for much longer. Maybe he lasts another year, maybe two, and then what? My son becomes prey to the vulturine impulses of a usurper. O, it is a horrible thing to be a mother, sir. It exposes one's heart to all manner of siegecraft, and leaves it twice as vulnerable to attack. O, Alexios, it is terrible!"

Alexios took a drink of his water and thought about what he should say. He was flattered that the Empress was confiding in him, and dumbfounded that she had breached all protocol by addressing him by his Christian name. And yet he wasn't all that surprised. We all need confidantes, and when one achieves the highest offices, the pool of potential people to talk with frankly dries up considerably. This is how weak-willed men like Michael wind up being led by scheming nebbishes like Nikephoritzes.

"Maria," he said, chancing a reciprocal onomastic intimacy, "I cannot speak for your husband, who I find a decent man but whose motives have always perplexed me. I'm sorry to say that I agree with your assessment. Best as I can tell, he is unpopular here in Constantinople, and I regret to say that he is held in even greater contempt in the provinces. I have captured Oursel, but there are others in the field who may one day revolt. Botaneiates in particular views the Emperor with derision. But if it eases your mind at all, I will make this vow: I, Alexios Komnenos, will protect you and your son. So long as it is in my power to do so, both of you will have safe harbor, and not a single hair on your heads will be harmed. If you wish, I will repair right now to the Holy Wisdom and take that oath before God and the Patriarch."

Maria beamed. "That won't be necessary. I trust you speak in good faith. And yes, the prospect of your protection does indeed ease my mind. Thank you, sir." Then a strange look came over her face, and she wrung her hands. "I only wish…oh, but it is impossible."

"What do you wish, your highness?"

Her lovely blue eyes met his dark brown ones. She held his gaze as if by magic, and as she did, she bit down ever so slightly on her lower lip and let out a little moan. Alexios had to adjust both his tunic and his sitting position to cover his sudden and obvious tumescence. Then her eyelids fluttered a few times, breaking the spell, and she said, "There are rumors circulating that you will marry Irene Doukaina."

The sudden change in subject made him chortle. "Rumors spread by my mother, no doubt."

"She is a nice girl," Maria said. "Young and shy, but possessed of a kind heart."

"Young, shy, nice, kind-hearted…none of it matters," Alexios said. "My heart belongs to another."

"Is that so," the Empress said. "Anyone I know?"

This time it was Alexios who initiated the eye contact, holding his gaze even longer than she had. He said nothing. He did not need to.

"I need to tell you something," Maria said, when the moment had passed. "A confession, if you will. It may change your opinion of me, but with you I want to be candid at all times."

"Yes, your highness."

"What I'm about to tell you, you must not breathe a word to another living soul."

"You have my word."

She spoke then to the attendants. The eunuchs left the room, and the Guardsman stepped outside. Only her monoglot waiting-lady remained as the chaperone. "My son Constantine…the Emperor is not his father."

This did shock the general, although it did not change his opinion of her. If anything, it made him desire her all the more. "Then who…"

"Someone I loved very much. He is gone now. Nikephoritzes the eunuch had him executed when his identity was found out, even though Michael himself did not object."

"He didn't object?"

"Siring children requires the execution of certain activities the Emperor is either unable or unwilling to perform. Michael and I have never, not once, engaged in the compulsory act. Yet he wanted an heir, so I gave him one."

"I see."

"You think less of me. You think I'm a harlot."

Alexios laughed. "I happen to hold harlots in high regard."

"I should not have told you."

"No," he said, "I assure you, the impulse was good. I don't think any less of you. To the contrary, I admire you for contriving a cunning solution to such a conundrum. Michael is lucky to have you," and here he bit down ever so slightly on his own lowr lip, "and a fool to not."

Tears welled up in the Empress's eyes. She fell onto a divan. "I am the fool, it seems."

Alexios rose and walked slowly toward her. "So your son is to be an only child?"

"Apparently."

"That is a pity." He held out his hand. She took it. He pulled her to her feet. For the third time they stared longingly at one another. "I want you to know that I am your faithful servant, and in the service of your happiness, there is nothing that I would not do."

"Nothing?"

"Not a thing."

And there in the Map Room, in the presence of the blushing waiting-lady, and with the eunuchs and guards just outside, Alexios and Maria made love for the first time, and then the second, and then the third.

"Tino was almost a year old by then," Maria told me later. "Meaning Ramwold had been dead for that length of time. It had been a year and a half at least since the last time I indulged myself. I was ripe for the plucking, and your father, bless his heart, was always eager to pluck."

Given that the still-popular Empress and the Great Domestic—for my father would soon be promoted to that lofty post—were in love, logic dictated that Alexios raise an army and usurp the throne himself. Michael, Maria felt, would abdicate without a fight if given the opportunity to retain his eyes; or perhaps he would die in the insurrection, conveniently widowing her. Maria could then marry Alexios, elevating him to the purple, and Constantine could be co-Emperor and heir. The beautiful Empress and the finest general! What could be better?

But Alexios at nineteen was still too young to seriously contemplate a run at the throne (or so he conservatively reckoned). If he acted too early, before consolidating his power, he might fail—and he would only have one crack at the crown before his eyes were put out. Too, Maria's marital status was a real obstacle. She wanted to be with Alexios and remain *Augusta*, but she also loved Michael and did not want him to be harmed. In short, neither of them wished to take on the risks associated with an outright coup—at least not yet.

So they contented themselves with unfettered lovemaking, and could only wait as events beyond their control conspired against their wildest and happiest dreams.

XXV

THE BRIDE

M Y PARENTS' WEDDING TOOK PLACE on Easter Sunday, A.D. 1077. My father was twenty-one years old, my mother just eleven. If anyone in attendance had qualms about the bride's egregiously young age, they kept it to themselves. The tableau was ridiculous—the strapping general Alexios Komnenos, with his dark hair and heavy beard and military regalia, at the altar with what appeared to be a large doll. Stocky and barrel-chested, with strong, stout legs, Alexios must have weighed eight stone more than his child bride, and while he was not particularly tall, the tip of her head only came up to his breastplate. Irene was made up to look older, her face painted in the latest fashion, her hair beautifully set, but she lacked any sort of feminine curves.

As women and mothers, both Anna Dalassene and Maria of Bulgaria must have been, on some level, ashamed of themselves for countenancing such a risible pairing. There is a fine line between sourcing a good husband for one's daughter and acting as her procuress, between matchmaker and whoremaster, a distinction that is blurred when the daughter in question is too young to have her monthly menses. Such was the sad, weakened position of the House of Doukas, that its rehabilitation required the virgin sacrifice of an eleven-year-old; and such was the ambition of the House of Komnenos, that its ascension mandated marriage to a Doukid flower not yet in bloom.

But neither Maria of Bulgaria nor Anna Dalassene could have predicted what happened after the vows were exchanged. For who could have foreseen the callous cruelty exhibited by Alexios in the bridal suite? I have difficulty myself reconciling the events of that night with what I know of my father and mother, both of whom I loved dearly, and who, by the time I was old enough to observe such things, loved each other. One prefers to believe in the inherent goodness of one's progenitors. It is with heavy heart that I tell of what took place, as full disclosure paints my father in an unflattering light, to put it mildly. But I have sworn not to bear false witness, and I will hew to the truth, however unpleasant it may be.

I should also add—Am I rambling now as a means of procrastination? Almost certainly!—that, while Maria is my primary source for much of what I've chronicled so far, this particular tale was unknown to her. Doubtless she'd have been horrified had she known. My mother Irene confessed it to me, not long before she died peacefully in her sleep during the cold night of 19 February, A.D. 1138, at the ripe old age of seventy-two. At first I'd assumed that senility had ravaged her brain, and refused to believe her. But I know now that she spoke the truth; why would she concoct such an abominable story?

"Someday you may wish to write about your father," she told me. "I have kept this to myself for sixty years, and I tell it to you now not for your sake, but that of posterity. I came to love Alexios, and he came to love me. But he was a complicated man, generally kind and generous but capable at times of great cruelty. You saw a glimpse of this dark side of him during the trial and execution of Basil the Physician."

I saw other glimpses, more than glimpses, long before that; but this my mother did not know.

"All great men but Jesus have darkness within them. No one not born of the Virgin is without sin. Your father is no exception. To present him as perfect would be a disservice to him, and to History."

Back to the wedding night. Having just turned eleven, Irene was, as discussed, completely unprepared to be a bride. She had some vague idea of what her primary function might be—that is, the production of heirs—but no inkling of how that function might be executed. Nor was her mother or any of her other relations, Bulgarian or otherwise, particularly concerned about this perilous ignorance. While the nuptial union officially ceded dominion of the woman from father to husband, the tacit understanding was that the groom of so young and green a bride would wait a bit before throwing her to the wolves, so to speak. This was gentlemanly courtesy, and Alexios was nothing if not a gentleman; how could anyone have known he would not extend said courtesy to his own wife?

No sooner did the newlyweds enter the candle-lit bed-chamber that his mood darkened. A charming and charismatic man, Alexios had been, after that first encounter with her at his party, strangely aloof to Irene: curt, unsmiling, almost rude. He had pantomimed contentment before the Patriarch and the parishioners, but now that they were alone together all signs of happiness vanished.

"Alexios," Irene asked, "is something the matter?"

He didn't answer. Instead he began to claw violently at her gown, a white silken garment made especially for the occasion by the best seamstress in the Queen City. He did not have much luck with it. "Take off that horrible dress," he told her.

Irene was scared now, but she prudently decided that obedience was the best course of action. She worked as quickly as she could, but the dress was fantastically ornate, and she needed his help to unfasten all the laces. At last she stood before him naked, her small pale body shivering in the night's chill. Her arms and legs were no thicker than oar-handles, her breasts were like two mosquito-bites, her chest so frail the ribs could easily be seen. And she was short of stature next to him, as eleven-year-olds tend to be. The best word I can think of to describe her body is this: breakable.

"Lay down," Alexios said. Although not a particularly tall man himself, he towered over her, like the Hagia Sophia over the imperial stables. He was still wearing his smart wedding clothes.

Irene took to the bed, reflexively grasping at the blankets.

"No," he said. "No covers. I want your ugly body exposed."

Her heart pounded in her chest like a rabbit's, and she bravely fought off the urge to cry.

"Here is the situation," Alexios told her. "Your father killed my brother. Murdered him in cold blood, because he would not betray the Emperor at Manzikert. You look surprised. You did not know? The snake did not tell you? No matter. Manuel is dead, Andronikos slew him, and the soul of that contemptible scoundrel fled his hideous husk of a body before I could properly exact my revenge. Ah, but there are other ways to sate one's need for vengeance. And here one has been presented to me. You are his daughter, his own flesh and blood, and I will use you as a vehicle of my wrath. Do not speak, wench. I don't want to hear your pleas for mercy. You will say you are innocent. Very true—but so was my brother. You will say you are too young—but so was my brother. And your mother was the one who arranged this, let us not forget. She is your whore-master, your bawd. Do not appeal to me for mercy, you Cyprian cow. Confine yourself to cursing your mother for offering your tender flesh to me, and to praying for your father's eternal damnation, when that drooling imbecile finally breathes his last, for condemning you to your unusual fate. Turn over." He lifted his tunic. "I said turn over."

Still she did not cry. The shock had frozen the well of her tears. For a moment she was paralyzed, but she did not wish to raise his ire any further. She complied. She closed her eyes tight, but could feel her nakedness exposed to the chilly night air—her teeth began to chatter—and she shouted when he spanked her hard on her exposed buttock.

"In time, you will come to enjoy this, no matter how rough it is at first. Women are weak in that way. But I will do my best to defer your pleasure." He was over her now, covering her like a lousy blanket, his lips inches from her ear. "I want it to hurt."

Irene chanced a glance behind her. His long tunic was hiked up to his waist, tucked into his belt. Something between his legs extended at a right angle from his body. To her innocent eyes it looked like an asp, slithering menacingly toward her, ready to strike. She gasped, then gathered herself, lay still and shut her eyes.

There was a jar of a viscous white substance by the bed. Alexios dug his hand into the jar, scooped out some of the stuff, and rubbed it on his manhood. Then he took a larger dollop and applied it to her backside. This confused her. Irene had been woefully underprepared for this moment—her mother had told her nothing, her nurses had been mum;

certainly they had assumed that consummation of the union might wait a bit, given her youthful eleven years, or that her new husband would initiate her himself—but even so, she had some dim awareness of what might transpire. And even her dim awareness was enough to determine that the copulative act did not involve the area of her body in which he was spackling the...lard, it must be, she suddenly realized. Fore, not aft, surely? And yet he seemed to know exactly what he was doing (all soldiers do). His fingers worked with purpose, probing her. The urge came over her to break wind; under the circumstances she could not help but do so. This only made him laugh.

"This is the only use I have for you," he said. "I don't want to see you, I don't want to be seen with you, I don't want to talk to you, and I certainly don't want to give you pleasure of any kind, other than through your acceptance of pain. If I hear word of this at court, from anyone, I will charge that you were not a virgin when we were wed, and you will spend the rest of your life in some godforsaken convent. Do you understand? Nod if you understand."

Irene nodded.

"Good. Now, weep and moan if you must. I want you to suffer."

And without further preamble, he took her, and while she did not want to give him the satisfaction of seeing her break, she could not help but cry out.

⁓

Irene spoke to no one of her ordeal, but whom could she have told? Her father was incapacitated, her mother would have died of shame, and no one else would have believed her. She had no recourse but to endure her plight: a famous and well-regarded husband who ignored her except to sodomize her in the bed-chamber. For months this went on. Her life was a misery, her only recourse, beyond taking her own life or her abuser's, to change the man's mind.

Lesser mortals would not have survived, but my mother was made of purer stuff than most. She contrived a means of escape.

It was now October, the most clement month of the year in the Queen City, when the humidity is at its ebb and a pleasant breeze gusts all day long off the Propontis. One night Alexios, vexed by the latest show of incompetence by the Emperor and his eunuch minister, took her more savagely than usual. By then Irene was accustomed to the act, although she still disliked it. This time she screamed as he entered her, so much that he arrested his assault.

"When will this end?" she shouted, turning over. "Do you really mean to treat me like an animal for the rest of our lives?" In all their time together she'd been too afraid to speak, and her voice, naturally soft to begin with, was whisper-quiet. This was far and away the loudest she had dared address him.

Alexios was taken aback. He had grown to enjoy this expression of carnality, even if the initial impetus for it had melted away somewhat. But he was resolute. "Yes," he told her. "That is my intention."

"Then kill me now, for I have no wish to carry on."

He was waiting for her to cry, as women will at such moments, believing tears lubricate the flow of mercy. But she did not. She was beyond tears. Her anger was too great. "Take your big strong hands and snap my neck, or so help me God I will throw myself off the Theodosian Wall."

"Suicide is a mortal sin," he informed her, as if she did not know this.

"Under the circumstances, Jesus will forgive me."

"Don't be so sure," he said. But he was wavering. Although capable of cruelty, Alexios was not by nature a cruel man, and lately remorse about the abuse of his young wife had begun to wear on him. Second thoughts plagued him.

"I am not my father," she told him. "Punishing me may have punished him if he were able to understand what was happening, but he cannot. All you have done is harmed an innocent girl."

"He knows, wench. His soul is out there somewhere, I know not where, but his soul knows."

"His soul is trapped within that feeble body," Irene said. "The soul is not given release until death. I asked the Patriarch this many times, and that is what he told me. The monk Psellos said the same thing. So did my cousin the Emperor."

"Fie," Alexios said. But my father's understanding of religious doctrine was always limited. Although he fancied himself a great thinker on all subjects, he was a military man, not a theologian.

"I have a proposal," she said. "I implore you to consider it."

"Go on."

"You see me as an extension of my father, is that so? Then I will prove to you that I am not."

"How?"

"Give to me a flagon of poison. I will entice my father to drink it. Thus will he die by my own hand. I can offer no stronger proof than patricide."

Alexios considered this for a moment. The torment of his wife, however cathartic, was not sustainable. Whether he liked it or not, he was married to this Doukid shrew, until Death parted them. If he wanted children, for example, he would have to change course. Furthermore, he did not really want his wife to despise him. "Let it be done," he said, turning her onto her back. "Let this seal the deal."

And so the next morning Irene called on her father, fed him a glass of poison, and quit the house. He died that night, the fourteenth of October, of what the surgeons thought was an edema. Thus did my mother in one fell swoop deliver Andronikos from his prison of broken flesh and herself from the clutches of her tormenter.

After that fateful night, Alexios did not return to her bed-chamber for years. The relief she felt was exquisite.

XXVI
THE REBELS

O N THE DAY ANDRONIKOS DIED, Oursel was languishing in the dank dungeon beneath the Grand Palace where he'd been held since his ignominious arrival at Constantinople. A fortnight later, on All Saints' Day of the Year of Our Lord 1077, Alexios Komnenos, the newly-minted Domestic of Schools and thus the commander of the whole of the imperial army, paid his prisoner a visit. The Frank was well disposed to think highly of my father, who spared him his life, his sight, and his testes—any of which could have been justifiably taken by the Emperor upon his capture—and had furthermore paid out of his own pocket for Oursel to be properly fed.

"My general," the Frank said, rising, "what a surprise. Have you come to escort me personally to the gallows?"

Alexios evaded the question. "I suspect news does not travel quickly to these parts."

"You'd be surprised. I do have some inkling of recent events. Your promotion, for one."

My father laughed in his good-natured way. "At the moment, quite irrelevant, I'm afraid. The Empire is under attack. Two rebellions simultaneously: one to the East, and one to the West."

"Botaneaites in Asia," Oursel said, "and Bryennios in Europe."

"Correct. The Treasury is completely depleted. What money wasn't spent on war has been embezzled by Nikephoritzes and his crooked crew, and with so much land in rebel hands, we have no mechanism to replenish the funds through taxation," Alexios said. "The financial situation is dire, and the city is on the verge of riot. Meanwhile the two generals march on. Bryennios is only a day's ride from Constantinople."

The Frank nodded and began to pace the confines of his cell. "So you've come on orders of the Emperor to eliminate any potential threats. I understand."

"No," Alexios said. "I've come to enlist you."

"Enlist?"

"You're a fine general, Oursel, and I need your help. Will you ride with me?"

"You would trust me to lead an army? After all that has happened?"

"Michael is a brilliant man, but he knows not of the realities of war. He has never so much as visited a battlefield, much less fought on one. He cannot appreciate the subtle twists of fate that compel us soldiers to do what we do. As I see it, all of your actions were justified by the situation on the ground. Are you too ambitious for your own good? Perhaps. But it will do you no good to betray *me*. Your fortunes will always be better off aligned with mine than in opposition. That is the truth, and I suspect you know this."

"I do."

"Will you swear fealty to the Emperor?"

"Of course." Oursel flashed a mischievous smile. "Permit me one question, general, if you would: why not just take the throne yourself? You already lead the army, you're already within the city walls and thus don't have to take it by siege, and the Constantinopolitans have had enough of Michael and his eunuch puppetmaster. There will be a new Emperor soon. Why not Alexios Komnenos?"

This is a question my father had not heard in almost two hours, when his brother Isaac asked the same thing. All of his confidantes struggled to understand his thinking. He answered straight away: "Because I have sworn to protect the Emperor. However I feel about his capabilities as a leader of men, if I betray him, chaos will ensue. The Empire needs stability in order to function. It needs generals to follow orders. Otherwise, we are no better than barbarians." Then he smiled broadly. "No offense."

"None taken."

"The gaoler will free you. Go to your wife and family, restore your health. We march in one week's time."

"Yes, my general."

On Christmas Day, A.D. 1077, Tino would turn three. He was walking, talking, out of diapers and no longer napping, although he was still sleeping in his mother's bed and still nursing. "He was a picky eater, but he ate," Maria recalled. "The breast soothed him, and frankly it soothed me."

Life in the two months leading up to that birthday was anything but soothing. The child had survived bouts of ague and measles and chicken pox, his young life hanging desperately in the balance as his fevers raged—but would he survive the looming insurrection? In the glory days of Rome, Emperors would think nothing of dispatching a three-year-old if he happened to be a legitimate claimant to the throne. Constantine the Great executed *his own son*, Crispus, when he suspected him, wrongly as it happened, of plotting a coup. We Byzantines are more merciful— the sons of Diogenes grew up in the house of my own grand-mother (although one of them wound up being dangerous to my father; perhaps they should have been thrown to the wolves)—but there was a strong probability that the child would be blinded, if not slain, when the curtain fell on Michael's regime.

By the Nativity Fast,[70] Maria knew the end was near. The signs were everywhere, from the demon-

---

[70] The start date of the Byzantine equivalent of Advent: November 15.

strations in the street to the alignment of the stars. Michael's days in the purple were numbered. Six years was too short a reign, but her husband had already lasted twice as long as his ill-starred predecessor, Diogenes. Was it possible for an Emperor to put down two rebellions, a thousand miles apart, simultaneously, while also staving off disgruntled city-dwellers and alleviating financial blight? Alexios could do it, she reckoned, but Michael was simply not up to the task. That he was now openly discussing the possibility of abdication was further sign of his weakness.

"I was sore afraid," Maria told me later, as she stroked my hair. "You are lucky, my peach; your father is a strong Emperor whom none dare oppose. He has brought stability to Byzantium not seen since the days of Basil the Great. You have no idea what it's like to witness the walls around you fall. It's terrifying beyond description. Remember, I watched as Eudokia was swept out of the palace; I did not want that to happen to me. Nevertheless, I made preparations."

At this time, Maria endowed a small convent called Vaspurakan, on Mount Papikion, west of Constantinople. This area, in which she owned two vast estates, was heavily populated by Georgians. Maria was enormously wealthy—the Empress has significant personal revenue, and she was never a lavish spender—and was able to transform the drab place into something palatial. In the event of a coup, she would exile herself to Vaspurakan, which she hoped was far enough off the beaten path to ensure her safety, and that of her young son.

She also began obsessively to plot out various scenarios in her mind, with the aim of being prepared for any occurrence. As she saw it, there were three possible candidates to take the purple when Michael left: Byrennios, Botaneaites, and Alexios.

Although my father had made it clear that he would not seek the throne for himself, there was always the chance that he would wind up occupying it anyway, when all was done and said. That would be advantageous for Maria, in that her personal safety would be guaranteed; and Tino might still be heir; but because Alexios had hastened to marry that shrewish daughter of the House of Doukas (as Maria thought of Irene), Maria would not be able to remain *Augusta*.

Botaneaites was a widower, which left open the possibility of her marrying him to retain her position. Too, he did not have a son, which meant that should said marriage transpire, Tino could be made heir to the throne. But Botaneaites was an old man, well into his seventies, and physically repulsive; the prospect of sharing her bed with him, however remote, was unappealing to the point of nausea.

The least appealing of the three options, from her point of view, was Nikephoros Bryennios. Here was a strong tactical general, scion of a noble family, mature in years but young enough to reign for a decade or more. He was married to a kindly if ugly woman, whose face was akin to a bat's; and he already had five sons, the oldest of which, Nikephoros Bryennios *fils*—called Junior—was then fifteen. If Bryennios took the purple, there was no hope of Maria keeping, nor of Tino inheriting, the crown. Worse, Bryennios was a day's march from the Queen City, well ahead of the Asian forces commanded by Botaneiates. If he prevailed, Maria would have to flee, and may well lose her life. She was much relieved to learn that Alexios, together with Oursel, was raising an army to meet the Thracian rebels.

As the Nativity Fast began in A.D. 1077, Botaneaites was fifty miles from the Bosporus. The general, then *Strategos* of the Anatolian *theme*, enjoyed a sterling reputation on the battlefield, although his war record was littered with instances of cowardice and defeat. From a distance he appeared a viable candidate for *Augustus*—wealth, pedigree, experience, charisma—but his mental faculties were in rapid decline due to his advanced age. Indeed he was so confused much of the time that he increasingly came to rely on the aid of his two chief ministers, a pair of former Sclavonian slaves called Borilas and Germanos, avaricious monsters who valued their own enrichment more than the health of the Empire. Led by the slaves, Botaneaites had bought off Suleiman, a vassal of Malik-shah's who was now the sultan of "Roum"—the name referred to territories long held by Rome—and surrendered even more Eastern lands to the infidels. He was farther from the capital than Bryennios, but that only meant he was in the perfect position to pounce when his chief rival faltered.

The lands beyond the Theodosian Walls to the west, while not technically part of the Queen City, were nonetheless densely populated, with smart houses, small farms, robust places of business, and the occasional villa dotting the lush landscape. These affluent suburbs, so close to Constantinople proper, did not know of war; the might of the Empire had protected them from foreign incursion for centuries. It was quite a shock, then, when the motley Western army under the nominal command of Bryennios—a hodge-podge of Bulgarians, Macedonians, Sclavonians, Franks, Italians, and Turks; truly a loathsome assemblage of lesser humanity—having marched into these affluent little towns and villages, decided *en masse* to put them to the sack. Like a mob, they descended, looting businesses, setting houses to the torch, ravishing unsuspecting females, and slaughtering anyone who dared oppose them. These were not mere peasants, who are so often fodder for invading armies, but rather plutocrats.

One pack of a dozen soldiers—I say "pack" because during the sack, all pretense at military formation fell away—forced its way through a gate and into a handsome house just steps from the Wall. When the owner of the manse, whose name history did not record, attempted with his two sons to talk sense into the intruders, they beat all three of them to death with clubs. Next they trashed the house, smashing furniture, ripping curtains, stealing silver. One of the soldiers defecated in the kitchen. Upstairs they found the homeowner's wife and daughter huddled under some blankets. They beat the wife unconscious and threw her out the window. What befell the daughter, who was perhaps sixteen, was even crueler: they ripped off her clothes and threw her on the straw pallet, four of them held her down, one on each limb, and all twelve of them had their way with her in turn, whooping and laughing and hollering as they came.

The youngest member of the pack, about the same age as the unfortunate girl, was the last to have a go. He seemed reluctant. He'd watched the others unleash their passions, and he thought they looked like savages, like animals. He knew that this was wrong. That he had never before "walked with a woman," as Scripture euphemistically phrases it, meant also that this was his first time attempting such an operation. When the older men exhorted him to take her, he hesitated; this reluctance was interpreted by the wild savages as a deficiency in his manhood.

"Are you a man or not?" one of them snarled.

"Maybe he is ashamed," another suggested.

"His tackle must be puny," taunted a third. "Like his father's." And everyone laughed.

At last he could take it no more. He yanked up his tunic to reveal his impressive anatomical endowment—the others gasped when they beheld its massiveness—and with a silent prayer of forgiveness, thrust himself into the defenseless girl. Lubricated by blood and the ample seed of eleven men, he could not find much friction, and it took him a long time, longer than he would have liked, to finish. But finish he did.

As he withdrew himself from the slag of the poor creature, the older men cheered and chanted his name. *Nik-e-phor-os! Nik-e-phor-os! Nik-e-phor-os!* For this young man was the son and namesake of the great general Bryennios.

And I regret to say that I can report with expert authority on the size and girth of his endowment, because I was myself in the position of that unfortunate girl *vis à vis* Nikephoros Bryennios the Younger, who after that initial taste became well-disposed to rapine. Twenty years hence, you see, I would marry him.

Each of them took another turn with the girl, and then they smashed her skull with a blacksmith's hammer.

XXVII
THE METROPOLITAN

As HE WATCHED THE EMPIRE CRUMBLE AROUND HIM, Michael underwent a profound spiritual awakening. He prayed for six hours or more every day, as a monk does; he abandoned the sybaritic practice of indulging himself with procured slaveboys; he spent more time with his son Tino; he treated his wife with considerable affection, like in the old days; and he freed himself from the influence of the Prime Minister Nikephoritzes. Instead, he turned for guidance to the new Patriarch, Kosmas, who'd held the office since August of A.D. 1075, at the death of Xiphilinos. This Kosmas was born and raised, and lived much of his life, in Jerusalem, and watched with horror as the Lion's Turks took the Holy City and slaughtered many of his friends and extended family members. He was pious but not to a fault, and open to pragmatism when it suited his purposes. Unlike Nikephoritzes, who sought first and foremost to enrich himself, Kosmas had no ulterior motives. He genuinely wished his friend the Emperor to find happiness, and to succeed. While the eunuch—who by this time was grotesquely obese, his very physiology a testament to his gluttony and greed—had trained Michael to doubt his own judgment and rely solely on him, Kosmas encouraged the Emperor to be more assertive.

The change in his personality was marked. It is ironic that in the last days of his time in the purple, with the end in plain sight, Michael was, at long last, acting like a real *Augustus*, an actual Equal of the Apostles, and not a eunuch's lap-boy. This did not change his desire to abdicate to become Metropolitan of Ephesus; on the contrary, all of his decisiveness at this time was actuated by this ultimate objective. By Christmas Day of A.D. 1077, Michael was more than ready to surrender the throne. But the atrocities committed in the western suburbs were so heinous, and thus reflected so poorly on the general whose army was responsible for the sack, that Michael could not in good conscience cede the throne to Bryennios.

"I might just as soon surrender the crown to Lucifer himself," he remarked to Kosmas, who nodded in agreement. He summoned Alexios and Maria to the Map Room for an interview with himself and the Patriarch—the first such meeting he'd personally convened in years.

Alexios was surprised, entering the chambers, that the eunuch Prime Minister was not in attendance. "Where is Nikephoritzes?" he asked, after making his usual ceremonial gestures.

"I have reassigned him," Michael said.

My father practically fell over backwards in shock.

"The eunuch understands finance better than I do," the Emperor continued. "Try as I might, I can't quite sort out why, in order to raise more revenue, we cannot simply mint more coins. Nikephoritzes says that doing so will make the financial situation even worse. I'm sure he is right—he would gain more by righting the ship than I would—and so I've let him invest all of his energy in that arena. Matters of state, and of war, no longer concern him."

"May I say that I admire you for making that decision, Your Highness," Alexios said—and he genuinely meant it.

"Thank you, general. I appreciate your kindness. Is it working out with Oursel?"

"Yes, sire. He is a fine general, and I do not think he will betray us again."

"Excellent news. Please, have a seat."

When the four of them were seated on the divan and the chairs, each with a goblet of wine, Michael continued: "I don't think there's any question that I have made many mistakes during the last six years. I doubt that History will be kind to my memory. This is my fault. Perhaps I was not ready to lead, perhaps I was afraid—no matter. I have no one to blame but myself for the current state of the Empire. I allowed myself to be led, and that is the one thing an Emperor must never do. There is no coming back from that."

Alexios said nothing. He glanced at Maria, for some hint at what might happen next, but her lovely visage was impassive.

"I have decided to retire," the Emperor said.

Alexios could not believe his ears. "Retire?"

"I will abdicate in favor of a chosen successor, who will grant me the privilege of leaving office with my eyes and my life intact. The great city of Ephesus has no Metropolitan. Kosmas my dear friend has nominated me for the position, and I have accepted his kind offer."

"This is God's will," the Patriarch said, in his stilted Jerusalem accent. "His servant Michael is answering His call."

"When first I decided upon this course of action, I planned on nominating Nikephoros Bryennios as my successor. He is, as you know, a cunning general, born of a noble family, and a worthy leader of men. Or so I was led to believe. After this despicable atrocity right outside the Walls"—he closed his eyes and shook his head violently, sadly—"I cannot in good faith endorse him to take my place."

"No," Alexios said. "I suppose not."

"Meanwhile Botaneaites will arrive soon enough, and thus fate will force my hand. Before he does, I wanted to beseech *you*, friend Alexios, to take the purple."

"Me?"

"You are the Domestic of Schools, the best general in the Empire. You are young. Your wife is my cousin Irene, which means the House of Doukas will accept you. In a city of vipers, you have somehow managed to make very few enemies. Even that rogue Oursel has pledged fealty to you! And as my friend, I know that you will bid me farewell without harm."

Maria smiled widely and clapped her hands. "But this is marvelous! What a wise decision you have made, sire." Based on this reaction, Alexios concluded that she was as in the dark as he was about the purpose of the interview.

"The only stipulation I ask," the Emperor concluded, "is that you name my son Constantine as your heir to the throne. What say you, general?"

Alexios said nothing. Before the meeting, he'd been concerned that Nikephoritzes the eunuch had schemed against him, and was on guard should agents arrive to take him away in chains. Never in his wildest imagination had he expected this.

"You Highness," he said finally. "Words fail me, so flattered and humbled am I by this generous offer. It is with great and sincere regret, then, that I must respectfully decline."

The other three at the table were shocked. Maria in particular looked like she might keel over.

"May we ask why?" the Patriarch said.

"I am not ready to take the purple," Alexios said. "And you, sire, are not ready to surrender it. How could I take the crown from you at the very moment when you are most worthy of wearing it?" Whereupon he thanked the Emperor for his consideration, wished him luck, and quit the room. Maria, shaking her head, ran after him.

Kosmas watched her go, and then looked at Michael. "God has spoken," he said. "It is to be Botaneaites."

Michael nodded. "Alas yes. Send the envoy."

"What are you thinking? Why on earth would you turn down such an offer? You may never get a second chance."

"You might have at least told him you'd consider it! What is to be gained by making a final decision on the spot!"

"It would be marvelous if you were *Augustus*!"

"It would be wonderful if you were the Emperor!"

"Now I have to give up my apartments for whatever shrew Botaneaites marries. Or worse, I'll have to marry him myself."

"Botaneaites is a clod. He might destroy the Empire before you ever get a chance to take the purple."

"You idiot!"

"You fool!"

Such was the invective hurled at Alexios in the hours after the interview, as he was double-teamed by the Empress Maria and his mother Anna Dalassene. The clamor from the rooms at the court was so loud that the servants began to whisper.

But Alexios said nothing. He lounged on a chair, eating a bunch of grapes, and moved only to spit seeds into a gilt spittoon. After an hour of shouting, the two women had spent their frustration. Now it was his time to talk.

"There is more to being Emperor than just taking the crown," he said. "Look at what's happening now. Inflation has ruined the markets, so much so that they now call the Emperor 'Peck-filcher,' a most unappealing sobriquet. I believe the worst is yet to come. Economic chaos brings food riots. That has not yet happened, but it will. And the Treasury is severely depleted. If I take command now, all of those problems will reflect onto me. Also, I have no soldiers with which to work. Botaneaites is old, but he has good lieutenants, and a legitimate army, and many years of battle experience. He would rout any slipshod forces I managed to raise, and then what? He'd be Emperor, and I'd lose my eyes. Do I want to take the purple? Of course. But I want a long and prosperous reign. I don't want to be removed in a few months. And that is precisely what will happen, if I succeed Michael now."

Maria looked at Anna. Anna looked at Maria. Neither of the could muster much of a defense.

"The key is Bryennios," my father continued. "He's the real threat. If he somehow succeeds, he'd reign for many years potentially. He's the one who must be stopped. And I will stop him. Whether I do so as Emperor or as Domestic of Schools is irrelevant. If anything, it's easier for me to operate as Domestic. I have someone to blame for when things go awry. Botaneiates is seventy-seven years old. When last I saw him, he appeared to suffer from memory lapses brought on by senility. He has spent the last year or so in the field, living off the land. That is not a salubrious way to live. No, the old general is not long for this world, I assure you. He has no wife, and he has no heirs. Let him come, let the rehabilitation of the Empire continue under his watch. When the moment is right, either when he meets his Maker or when his rule becomes intolerable, then and only then will I take command." He then spat a final grape seed into the spittoon for emphasis.

Neither his mother not his lover spoke a word.

They didn't need to.

They knew he was right.

XXVIII
THE TRANSITION

LO, EVENTS UNFOLDED EXACTLY AS ALEXIOS HAD FORETOLD. Wheat prices collapsed yet again, and desperate peasants showed signs of revolt; the fat eunuch Nikephoritzes was burned in effigy in a demonstration just beyond the imperial walls, which Michael did nothing to quell. The end days, he knew, had come.

Disgraced by the behavior of his savage soldiers (not to mention his own flesh and blood), Bryennios beat a hasty retreat to Dyrrachium, the ancient city on the Via Egnatia[71] that was his base of operations, under the fictive pretext of a barbarian threat in Thrace. Oursel's regiment gave chase, then marched back and set up camp at Athyra, a small port on the European side of the Sea of Marmara. There the Red Rogue remained on guard, should Bryennios again attempt to attack

---

[71]   An important highway that ran from the Adriatic Coast eastward to Constantinople.

from the West. Meanwhile, Botaneaites continued his slow and inexorable march toward Constantinople. He sacked Nicaea but was nonetheless greeted as a conquering hero; on the last day of Christmastide,[72] A.D. 1078, at the behest of Kosmas the Patriarch, Botaneaites was elected *Augustus in absentia* by the spineless poltroons in the Senate and the Synod; two days later he was at the Bosporus.

But Michael refused to surrender the throne until his modest demands were met, the Varangian Guard refused to let the usurper Botaneiates land, and for the next two months there was an excruciatingly tense period of stalemate. The old general agreed to let Michael and his son Constantine flee to Ephesus unmolested, and the Emperor in exchange consented to crown his successor personally. The impasse concerned the issue of marriage. Botaneiates, a widower, was in need of a wife. And he knew exactly whom he wished to marry: the Emperor's estranged mother, Eudokia, who when Empress a decade hence had spurned him for Diogenes.

Michael steadfastly refused. For one thing, he did not wish to act as his mother's procurer. For another, he had neither seen nor heard from Eudokia in six years, since her banishment to the convent, and he could not be sure she would not seek revenge on him. Filicide is not uncommon in the sad annals of Rome.

Riots broke the stalemate. Unrest in the city devolved into violent anarchy. There was much

---

[72]   January 7.

looting and destruction of property, and angry mobs gathered just outside the imperial walls, demanding that the Prime Minister be turned over to them at once. (Nikephoritzes seized that moment to cravenly flee the city, of which more shortly).

It was determined by both sides that a face-to-face meeting was indicated, but the logistics of such an interview were complicated. Michael rightly feared that if he crossed the Bosporus to see Botaneaites, the general would simply arrest him on sight and end the matter. Botaneaites had similar qualms. Eventually it was agreed that the meeting would be held at sea, aboard a neutral vessel, under cover of night, and mediated by the Patriarch Kosmas; underhandedness would thus be subject to the wrath of God. Not a soul who was not a participant knew of this meeting, and those who attended were tight-lipped about the details. I only learned of the proceedings years later, when I asked Maria about the exact circumstances of the transition, and it was with great—and for her rare—reluctance that she sated my curiosity.

Aside from a handful of monks from the Patriarch's trusted entourage, none of whom were in the galley, there were eight people aboard the ship: Kosmas; Botaneaites and his two closest advisors, the Sclavonian ex-slaves Borilas and Germanos; Michael, Maria, and Alexios. The eighth guest was a surprise, arranged by Kosmas: the erstwhile Empress and current nun Eudokia.

Maria gasped when she saw her. Michael wept. Skin and bones, she had withered away to almost nothing. Her shoulders drooped. Wrinkles lined her face and hands. The hair peeking out from the habit was stark white. The fire in her eyes, once so bright, had smoldered away. She was a husk of her former self, a broken woman. She was not yet fifty, but she looked more ancient than Botaneaites, who at seventy-seven was thirty years her elder.

The presence of Eudokia made Michael forget the grave purpose of the meeting. "Mother," he said, embracing her. "Oh, Mother, forgive me."

"My son," she said simply, "you are forgiven." And she meant it.

Then she turned to the ancient general, who in the dim light of the ship's lanterns looked like Lazarus just come back from the dead. "Nikephoros," she said to him, for Nikephoros was his Christian name. Politesse demanded that she instead employ some or other title, but Eudokia was at the stage in her life—one I know too well—where she was no longer bound by such silly conventions. For years she had been silenced; now she would speak her peace. "Oh, Nikephoros. It is sweet of you to ask for my hand, but as you can see, I am not worthy."

"Nonsense," he said. "You have come from that convent straight away. A few days of proper care, a change of clothes, some paint on your face, and you will again be the Eudokia I know." Then his voice got quiet: "And love."

Maria had assumed, as all of them had, that Botaneaites had insisted on Eudokia's hand because he believed that the marriage would legitimize his claim to the throne. Never in a million years would any of them had thought that his intentions were not mercenary but romantic!

"I say again, it is sweet of you to ask, Nikephoros. But I cannot accept."

The old soldier looked like his heart had been broken in two.

"This is all very heartwarming," said one of his slave ministers, who with their blonde hair and evil grins may as well have been twins, and operated as a sort of two-headed monster.

"Indeed," said the other snidely. "But we have more pressing matters to discuss."

"The time has come," the first slave said to Michael. "Take the crown off your molly-boy head and give it to a real man."

Alexios slammed his fist on the table. "You will show respect," he told the slave, "or so help me God I will throw you overboard."

"Take care, general," the second slave retorted, "or we'll have your eyes."

During this exchange Botaneaites sat as if in a daze. Could he not hear what was being said? Or was he too addled to understand? Studying him in the dim light, Alexios began to have second thoughts about turning down Michael's offer. For a moment he contemplated killing the two slaves and Botaneiates with his bare hands and taking the crown himself—nothing would have been simpler—but prudence prevailed.

"Gentlemen," Kosmas implored.

Then Michael spoke: "I suggest you apologize to the Domestic of Schools," he said, referring to my father. "He is far and away the finest general in Christendom, and if your master is to retain the crown, he will have to rely on him."

Botaneiates suddenly clued in, admonishing them with a glare, and Borilas and Germanos offered perfunctory apologies.

"You have guaranteed safe haven for me and my family," Michael said. "And now my mother has herself decided against the marriage. If you drop that stipulation, we are in accord."

"But the general needs a wife," the first slave said. "The Empire needs an Empress."

"The Empire has an Empress," Maria said, her voice full of fire. "Me. I would have gladly stepped aside for my mother Eudokia, but I will not surrender my tiara to any other woman in the world."

"Oh, but that is a capital idea," Eudokia said, clapping her wrinkled, liver-spotted hands.

"Idea?" Michael asked. "What idea?"

"I believe the Empress is suggesting that she herself marry the general," the second slave said.

"She's certainly possessed of the requisite beauty," added the first.

"But Maria is my wife!" Michael exclaimed.

"Metropolitans do not take wives," Eudokia said. "To take the post at Ephesus, you will have to take a vow of chastity, which would render your marriage null and void. Is that not correct, Father?"

"I suppose so," said the Patriarch. "Although I do not believe in divorce."

"This is a special case," Eudokia said. "For the good of the Empire, you must grant an exception."

Alexios did not much relish the idea of the love of his life marrying the decrepit old general. But the other viable alternative—her exile to some nunnery—was unquestionably less appealing. And in order to have her for himself, he'd have to slaughter every other person on the ship, which he did not have in him. He withheld comment, and instead spent his time glowering at the two impudent slaves.

"It is decided, then," Eudokia said. "Michael will divorce Maria to become Metropolitan of Ephesus. Nikephoros will marry her. And Alexios will set off at once to put down Bryennios in the West."

Botaneiates looked at her longingly. "Are you sure you won't change your mind?"

"I'm afraid not."

He nodded sadly. "As you wish." Then his eyes brightened. "Is there anything else I can do for you?"

"Now that you mention it, yes." Eudokia asked that she be allowed to transfer from the prison-like Piperoudion to a less restrictive convent, where she could take social calls, live less austerely, and have access to the research materials she needed for a book she planned to write, a sort of pagan demonology called *Bed of Violets*.[73]

---

[73] A real tome. There is some question of its authorship, but Anna's account confirms that Eudokia did indeed write it.

The old general immediately agreed to her modest demands. "Anything else?"

"There is one more thing…"

By this time, the former minister Psellos had retired from public life—removed from day-to-day detail after the botched usurpation attempt by the *Caesar* John Doukas—and was hard at work on what would be his magnus opus, the *Chronographia*. He was in his study, a small room in the monastery piled high with manuscripts, working on a section of the history concerning a letter Michael had written to an exile called Phokas: *If you stand in awe of the Judgment of God*, he wrote, *if you expect Him to pass sentence on your deeds, then tremble for the success of this enterprise. Let wisdom guide your steps, let prudence direct your plans. Discretion before disloyalty! He who follows bad counsel plots, from the very beginning, his own destruction!*[74]

He dipped his pen into the inkwell, mulling the next few words, when there came a knocking at his door. Psellos, now well into his sixties and mostly deaf, started at the unexpected commotion. He put down the pen. He opened the door.

---

[74] The *Chronographia*, published in English as *The Fourteen Emperors*, really does end abruptly, with that somewhat ironic line.

The two men at the door looked eerily the same. Both were tall, with whitish blonde hair and pale blue eyes, and both smiled menacingly. "Father," the first one said. His voice betrayed a thick Sclavonian accent. "Come with us."

Psellos looked at the two rogues, puzzled. "Go with you? Where?"

"To Hell," the second one said, brandishing a dagger and driving it beneath the old monk's ribcage.

"That is for the Empress Eudokia," said the first. "She asks that you bid the Devil good day."

And the odious pair stood and watched, amused, as the old minister bled out on the cold stone floor.

The eunuch Nikephoritzes, meanwhile, had fled the city during the riots. His plan was to journey to the East and offer his services to Bryennios, whom he'd known for many years, in the hopes of salvaging his reputation in a new regime. His route to the Thracian hinterlands led him to the walled town of Athyra, where he fatefully stopped to spend the night. He was surprised to find the town occupied by mostly Frankish troops—the regiment of the ex-rebel Oursel.

Nikephoritzes was so fat by now that he had difficulty moving. He could not ride a horse, because he could not mount one, and if he had, the unlucky steed might have broken its back. The red Frank greeted him warmly, but there was no obvious indication that he knew who the fugitive visitor was. Oursel fed him a hearty meal and plied him with wine, so much wine that the fat eunuch fell asleep at table.

The disgraced Prime Minister woke up the next morning in a prison cell, naked as the day he was born. Panicked hands clutched the bars and he shouted to be released. Nothing happened, and he eventually gave up. He remained in the cell for three days, speaking to no one, his only visitor the gaoler who brought him his daily gruel and bucket of water.

On the fourth day, he finally had a visitor: an ugly man without a nose. He screamed, as the evidence was now incontrovertible that Oursel had not incarcerated him in error.

"Hello, eunuch," the torturer said. "By order of the Emperor, you are to come with me."

"Michael would not deliver me to you," Nikephoritzes said.

"You are referring to the Metropolitan of Ephesus," Romanos Straboromanos said. "I speak of the *Emperor*, Nikephoros III Botaneiates."

I cannot verify what exactly became of Nikephoritzes the eunuch. Some say he was drawn and quartered in the public square at Proti; others, that he was gutted, and his skin flayed. I've even heard it said that Romanos bound him to a stake, jammed an apple into his mouth, and roasted him over an open fire. Perhaps this is hyperbole, I cannot say. But it is safe to assume that the unfortunate Nikephoritzes died a particularly agonizing death.

At the crack of dawn on the last day of March, A.D. 1078, Michael repaired to the Studion monastery, taking his son Constantine with him for safe keeping. That afternoon, his wife—or rather ex-wife—was wed to the new Emperor.

It was a joyless ceremony, presided over with thinly-veiled disgust by Kosmas himself. The only guests who seemed to be having any fun were the Sclavonian slaves, the blonde rogues who cackled derisively throughout the proceedings. Royal weddings run the risk of ridiculousness, as the pairings tend to be comically mismatched; witness the nuptial ceremony of Alexios and his child bride. Even so, this was a ludicrous tableau. Because she was Empress, and divorced, and the mother of a young son, Maria refused to wear white, opting instead for the most modest of her imperial purple garments, and she did not once smile. As for Botaneiates, he'd spent much of the last decade in Asia, and this was the first time anyone had taken a good look at him in years. He was seventy-seven years old and looked a decade older, Methuselah come to Byzantium. He was almost completely bald, and his scalp was wrinkled and covered with unsightly liver spots. A preponderance of long white hairs gathered at his ears, his nose, and his eyebrows. And he stooped to walk, which, because he was tall, gave him the aspect of one of those scavenging birds that haunt the coast of the Propontis.

Alexios seethed throughout. He could not believe his unhappy turn of fortune. The crown could have been his! Instead he exercised caution and bided his time—and for what? So the love of his life, a paragon of beauty at twenty-seven, could wed this gruesome man fifty full years her elder? The thought of Maria subjecting herself to his lustful advances, if in fact he was still capable of them at his advanced age, filled him with both rage and disgust. His stomach began to ache—it was hot in the cathedral—and for a brief moment he feared he might throw up. That he was seated next to his own wife, who was all of twelve, did nothing to ease his mind. Botaneaites, he resolved, would need to go, and sooner rather than later. At the first available opportunity, he decided, he would make his move, prudence and patience be damned.

He needn't have worried about the old man forcing himself upon his lover the Empress, as he had upon poor Irene. Maria took care of that matter herself. For Botaneaites did indeed visit her bed-chamber on their wedding night. He had been drinking, and the wine enflamed his lust. Yes, he was decrepit, but he was still a man, and thus incapable of resisting his new wife's charms, however careful she was to conceal them.

"What are you doing here?" she asked, annoyed.

"Why, I've come to consummate the marriage," he said.

"Absolutely not," she told him. "You took my hand to legitimize your claim to the throne. That is quite enough."

"What, what?" he cried—this was a pet expression of his that drove her crazy. "Undress yourself, woman. I aim to make you mine."

"Are you even capable of that?" she retorted. "At your age? From what I understand, you've not been able to perform up to expectations in many years. You look surprised; I assure you, your profound impotence is well known to every soldier under your command. They snicker at you when you are out of earshot. They call you 'Soft One' and 'General Wet Noodle.' But if you ask me, I think your decrepitude is just an excuse. I think you've *always* had difficulty pleasuring a woman. You are half a century older than I, and where are your children? You have none. Pathetic, truly. Don't cast aspersions on your deceased wife, either. I'm sure it was not her fault. That's why you were so ambitious on the battlefield—to compensate for your shortcomings. And I do mean short," and to punctuate this last insult, she held up her smallest finger and wiggled it limply at him.

The new Emperor said nothing. Whatever difficulties he may have had conceiving with his departed helpmate, never did that unfortunate woman—nor any woman!—address him so. He stood there stunned, as if he'd taken a blow to the head.

"Why don't you doff your smelly clothes, and let's see what we're working with," Maria said. "I want to see if it's as paltry as everyone claims."

Botaneaites did not know what to do. For a moment she thought he'd had a stroke. Then he lifted his tunic.

"Jesus, Mary, and Joseph," Maria said, cursing. "That's *it*?" And she burst out laughing—the same cruel, derisive sort of laughter favored by the Sclavonian slaves. "How in Heaven's name do you expect to consummate the marriage with *that*?" More spiteful laughter. "For your sake I hope it expands a *little* bit." Then she giggled and said, "A little *bit* indeed!"

By now the old, new Emperor was staggering, like a boxer who's just sustained the knock-out punch.

"Let's see." Maria spat into her palm—most unladylike—and grabbed at his manhood. She kneaded it for a full two minutes, but it remained as soft as wet clay. The serpent did not rise.

"That's what I thought," she said, releasing him. "If you would like to tell your friends, or anyone else, that the marriage has been consummated, I will not contradict you. But if you ever come into my apartments again for that purpose, I assure you, not a soul in Christendom and beyond will be unaware of your disability. Do you understand?"

At last, the hoary Emperor spoke. "Yes, good wife. A thousand pardons." And he quit the room with the velocity of a much younger man.

Thus did Maria of Alania, twice *Augusta*, hold the dubious distinction of having not one but two unconsummated imperial marriages. The one Emperor who was her lover was not her husband. He was, or would soon be, her son.

Volume Three:
The Komnenoi Revolt

A.D. 1078-81

XXIX

THE BLINDER

IN THE ANNALS OF HISTORY, the succession from one Emperor to the next is presented as a list, Isaac-Constantine-Diogenes-Michael, that suggests a seamless transition, as the notes of a major scale sung by an organum vocalist to warm up. But even the neatest transition has rough edges, and the transition from Michael to Botaneaites was anything but neat. The first two years of the ancient *Augustus's* reign were consumed by the squashing of various rebellions, as no less than half a dozen upstarts all over the Empire[75] brazenly assumed the imperial title; as the decrepit Botaneaites was himself in no condition to put down the insurrections personally, his remaining energies having been sapped by his coup, the "honors" fell to my father. For much of

---

[75] Which was less vast that it had been under Michael, the dutiful reader will recall, as Botaneaites had surrendered so much of Asia to gain the throne for himself. (A.K.)

those two years Alexios marched hither and yon, from Thessalonika to Nicaea, leading his tired army into battle, routing pretenders' regiments, capturing rebel commanders, and perfunctorily depriving them of sight.

The more victories my father won, the more wealth he amassed,[76] but the ulterior reward for all his hazardous work is that most of the viable threats to usurp the throne were removed. When the time came for Alexios to himself move against Botaneaites, there were no remaining third parties to oppose him; this was part of his master plan, which he achieved to perfection—although he was almost defeated before he began.

When Botaneaites took the purple, you see, Bryennios still remained in the field. The Eastern commander controlled a vast army, and he perceived his misstep at the walls of Constantinople as a minor setback. After all, the new Emperor was moribund, his hold on power tenuous, and his popularity already in wane just a few months into his reign, when the economic policies of Botaneaites—which mostly involved legalized looting—caused the already-precarious prices of wheat to collapse completely.

Bryennios was a clever warrior, blessed with an illustrious pedigree, conspicuous by height of stature, and beauty of face, and preeminent among his

---

[76]   A significant portion of my family's wealth derives from my father's defeat of a certain Basilakes, a Byzantine Midas, whose rich lands were seized by Alexios around this time. (A.K.)

fellows by the weightiness of his judgment, and the strength of his arms. He was, indeed, a man fit for kingship, and his persuasive powers, and his skill in conversation, were such as to draw all to him even at first sight; consequently, by unanimous consent both of soldiers and civilians, he was accorded the first place and deemed worthy to rule over both the Eastern and Western dominions. On his approaching any town, it would receive him with suppliant hands, and send him on to the next with acclaim. The odds were good that Bryennios would quickly supplant Botaneaites, Nikephoros III yielding to Nikephoros IV.

And when my father and his lieutenant general Oursel met the Eastern general at Kalabrya, on the banks of the river Almyros, Alexios came the closest he'd yet come to losing a battle—and his life. This was in the late autumn of A.D. 1078. Alexios had spent several months on the march, chasing his opponent across the rolling fields of Thrace, reconnoitering, sizing up his advantages and his disadvantages. The latter outnumbered the former. First, Alexios possessed a force both smaller in number and less experienced, while Bryennios commanded a seasoned and well-trained army. Second, my father was in unfamiliar territory that his enemy knew like the back of his hand. Third, he was fighting on behalf of an unpopular Emperor, while his opponents viewed the battle to come as a fight for freedom, and knew that defeat meant certain death. Fourth, the capture of several dishonourable

Turkish spies meant that Bryennios was informed of my father's sizable disadvantages.

From the beginning, the battle was a disaster. Ranks broke, Franks and Turks traded sides with impunity, confusion reigned in the ranks, and the standards became commingled. In the first hour of combat, Alexios was cut off from his forces and moved about within the rebel army with just a small detachment. Capture seemed imminent, if not death. He cursed, raising his fist at the sky. "O Lord," he cried, "why hast Thou forsaken me?"

But Providence had other plans for Alexios Komnenos. Fate was on his side. No sooner did he shake his fist than he espied one of the royal grooms leading a horse belonging to Bryennios, decked out with a purple cloth and gilt bosses; moreover, the men holding the large swords which customarily accompany the *Augustus* were running close beside it. On seeing this Alexios covered his face with the vizor which depended from the rim of his helmet, and rushing with violence against these men with his six remaining soldiers, he not only knocked down the groom, but also seized the royal horse. Together with it he carried off the swords and then escaped, unnoticed by the rebel army. Arrived in a safe spot, my father started off on the gilt-bedight horse of Bryennios, and the swords which are usually carried on either side of the Emperor. He bid a herald with a stentorious voice to run through the whole army crying out, "Bryennios has fallen! Bryennios has fallen!"

This bit of deception brought back to the battle from all quarters many of the scattered soldiers belonging to the army of the great Domestic of the Schools (to wit, my father), and others it encouraged to carry on. In short, the capture of this horse was a gift from God, and the turning point in the battle.

But Bryennios himself, although beyond weary from fighting, shewed his courage and mettle. He would not go down without a fight. For at one minute, he would turn to right or left to strike a pursuer, and at the next, carefully and cleverly arrange the details of the retreat. He was assisted by his brother on the one side, and his son and namesake on the other, and by their heroic defense on that occasion they seemed to the enemy miraculous.

As Bryennios's horse was now exhausted, and unable either to flee or pursue (in fact, it was pretty well at death's door from continuous coursing), he halted it, and, like some brave athlete, stood ready for combat, and called a challenge to two highborn Turks. One of these struck at him with his spear, but was not quick enough to give him a heavy blow before receiving a heavier one himself from the would-be Emperor's right hand. For Bryennios with his sword succeeded in lopping off the man's hand, which rolled to the ground, spear and all. The second man leapt off his own horse, and like a panther, darted on to that of Bryennios, and planted himself on its flank, and clung tightly to it, and tried to get on its back. Bryennios kept twisting round like a cat chasing its tail in his eager but futile endeavors to stab him with his sword. However, he did not succeed, for the Turk behind his back escaped all the blows by bending aside. Therefore, when his right hand was exhausted from only encountering emptiness, and the athlete's strength gave out, he surrendered there and then to the whole body of the enemy.

The imperial soldiers seized him, leading the captive away to my father, who happened to be standing not far from the spot where Bryennios was captured.

Alexios was busy drawing up his own men, and the Turks, into line, and inciting them to battle. News of Bryennios's capture had already been brought by heralds, and then the man himself was placed before the Domestic, and a terrifying object he certainly was, both in the battlefield and in chains. This was a man my father had known for some years, and as his noble elder had greatly respected.

"You fought bravely and well," the older general said. "That you are so young seems impossible."

"I have learned from the best," Alexios said, gesturing toward Bryennios.

"I don't suppose I could persuade you to join me?"

My father laughed good-naturedly. Then his expression turned sober. "Do you ever wonder if there are different, parallel worlds to the one we're living in now? Sometimes I have that inkling, and right now is one of those occasions. There is an alternative reality in which you and not Botaneaites has taken the purple, and I am your humble servant. But in this iteration, the here and now, that is not to be, happy as it would have made me."

"You are loyal to Botaneaites."

"I am loyal to the Emperor. His identity is not important. My job, after all, is to restore imperial loyalties. Without them, peace is impossible."

"Very well." Bryennios kicked at his legs, which were shackled together. "I then must make an urgent request of you."

"Name it."

"I want you to put out my eyes."

Alexios laughed joylessly, and then understood that Bryennios was not kidding. "You are serious? Sir, I cannot. I would sooner smash the frescoes at Ravenna[77] than take the eyes of an one such as you."

But Bryennios was steadfast. "You must know that old age has addled the mind of poor Botaneaites. He is a dotard. At this point he is a figurehead, a puppet, and his strings are being pulled by the two wretched barbarians, Borilas and Germanos. They are vipers; watch out for them; they will come for you, too, my boy. The vipers want me dead, not blind, and they will effect the latter to achieve the former. I don't want to wind up like Diogenes. You will show mercy in the blinding."

"You insist upon this?"

"I do."

---

[77]   Of Justinian and his advisors, and Theodora and her retinue.

"Very well, it shall be done."

Alexios swallowed hard. He understood the rationale that underpinned the practice of blinding one's rivals—it was more humane than execution, and it made moot their claim to the throne, as blind men cannot serve as *Augustus*—and he'd had plenty of other rebels deprived of sight, but the prospect of achieving the act himself, and upon his respected comrade-in-arms no less, left him queasy. His palms began to sweat. He then said, to press for time, "Any other way I can be of service to you?"

"One last request, general," said Bryennios. "My son Junior. I ask that you look out for him."

"I have heard it spoken of his valor and intelligence. Yes, of course, I will keep an eye on him," and he immediately regretted using the phrase.

Diogenes, the reader may recall, had his eyes gauged out by Romanos Straboromanos with a serrated spoon. But there is a more humane way of achieving the same result. The general and would-be Emperor was bound tightly to a table—this was a kindness, for sudden movement, which would be involuntary in any case, might cause the brand to disfigure his face—and an iron rod heated in a makeshift furnace.

"Are you certain you want me to do this?" Alexios asked. "We might wait. Perhaps the Emperor will be merciful."

"It must be done. You know it must."

"Very well," and he made the sign of the cross and said a little prayer under his breath.

Two men pried open Bryennios' eyelids with iron tongs, and Alexios held the hot brand to the general's face—as close as possible to the eye without touching. For it is not necessary to make contact. As the sun chars the skin even from a great distance, so a hot iron rod in close enough proximity to the eye will put it out. And in this manner did my father, quite against his own wishes, spend the general's light.

When the blinding was done, and the useless eyes bandaged, my father removed the fetters from the ankles of Bryennios and let him walk under his own power back to Constantinople. Alexios summoned the blind man's son, Nikephoros Bryennios the Younger, and installed him in his own tent. Then he prayed, and wept, and set out the next day for Thessalonika, where yet another rebellion was in full swing.

It would be two years before his work was done, and all the rebels defeated. By that time, there would remain just one general in all the Empire with sufficient power, charisma, and wherewithal to usurp Botaneaites: the Great Domestic himself, Alexios Komnenos.

XXX

THE DOTARD

THE FIRST TWO YEARS OF THE REIGN OF NIKEPHOROS III BOTANEAITES—which is to say, A.D. 1078-80—were among the most miserable in Maria's life. Her lover was out of town for much of that time, engaged in perilous work, and she worried for his safety; the libidinous entertainments Alexios provided for her, to which she'd become accustomed, were withheld for the duration. For two years she knew not that joy. Her new husband meanwhile was a dotard. Whatever sense that remained beneath the bald pate had melted away as soon as he'd been coronated, almost as if the crown itself had drawn the waning intelligence out of his senile head. Botaneaites spent much of his time wandering the halls of the palace, muttering to himself, and he referred to her always as "Bebdene," which was, come to find out, the name of the young wife he'd lost to cancer half a century ago. While he did not try again to sate his lust with her, neither did he intervene on her behalf when his feckless advisors, the degenerate slaves Borilas and Germanos—next to whom Nikephoritzes was the paragon of prudence and probity!—stripped her of all of her hard-won duties at court. Too, her son Constantine, again living with her in Constantinople, was often infirm. During those years Tino suffered from, and somehow managed to survive, every childhood malady known to man, and some that baffled the physicians. O, the hours she spent in prayer to the Almighty, appealing to His mercy for her boy's survival!

Then there was her spiritual agony. The guilt that had consumed her when she effectively usurped her friend and mother-in-law Eudokia was nothing compared with the anguish she felt contemplating her decision to divorce one Emperor and marry another. Her reprehensible actions filled her with shame, a shame exacerbated by the fact that the hoi polloi vociferously held with her own malefic assessment. All the goodwill Maria had built up among the common folk, who'd adored her from the moment she arrived in Constantinople, evaporated the instant she was re-crowned with Botaneaites. Coronations are not meant to be repeated in any event, and certainly not with a man old enough to be one's grandfather. If Maria was ashamed, the people were ashamed for her, by her, and of her. She came to be known as Maria the Whore.

The return of Alexios in the late autumn of A.D. 1079, in time to celebrate Tino's sixth birthday, buoyed her spirits, but only briefly. While she remained Empress, she lacked the freedoms granted her by Michael. And what good is a title without power or privacy? By that time, Botaneaites was so senile that he believed her to be his mother—but the ministers Borilas and Germanos, as hateful as they were rapacious, and paranoid besides, put her under surveillance night and day, assigning a small detail of trusted agents just for that purpose. These vultures followed her everywhere she went; even in the Empress's Loge in the Holy Wisdom, where she'd found respite when Michael was *Augustus*, there they were, watching her with beady little eyes.

Only in her private rooms was she left alone. And this presented a major problem, as decorum prevented her from properly entertaining Alexios in those private rooms. When he visited her there, the presence as chaperones of his brother Isaac and her cousin Irina was compulsory. Both of them were well aware of the intimate relationship between the Empress and the Great Domestic, and on at least one occasion they turned a blind eye while Maria and my father fanned the flames of their passion. But that was not a sustainable model. My uncle and aunt were extremely generous people, but generosity has its bounds. How to contrive an avenue for multiple, secret liaisons?

One dismal afternoon, Maria was in her rooms, watching her six-year-old son Tino being entertained by Helena, his fiancée, who by that time was twenty-one years of age. Consider the preposterous tableau: Here was this heavy-fisted brute of a woman, taller than most men, and stronger, seriously contemplating marrying a child young enough to be her own son—in the palace of a royal couple whose gap in age spanned five full decades! This made a mockery of marriage as an institution. An older woman, a younger man; a much older man, a younger woman…all of it made Maria laugh, and then, like a bolt of Jovian lighting, inspiration struck her.

"The Patriarch!" she cried, bolting out of her chair. "We must see the Patriarch!" She turned to her nurse, Rona: "Find the Great Domestic. Have him meet me at the Holy Wisdom. Tell him it is extremely urgent!"

An hour later, the principals gathered before Kosmas, whose stony face betrayed the contempt he now felt for the Empress. "What is it?" the holy man sighed. "What is so urgent?"

"Father, I have decided to adopt the Great Domestic, Alexios Komnenos, as my own son. Please prepare the papers."

Gasps escaped from Isaac and Irina, who were also present, as well as Helena, holding hands with little Tino. But Alexios grinned and, unable to stop himself, laughed. Nothing impressed my father more than cleverness, and this scheme of Maria's was undoubtedly clever.

Kosmas could have protested, on the grounds that Maria was not old enough to be the biological mother of Alexios—eight-year-olds do not produce babies, thank God—but his desire to be rid of the Empress outweighed his usual sense of probity. Women, the Patriarch believed, were prone to such hysterical flights of fancy; best to acquiesce to their more innocuous demands. Kosmas granted the request, and plodded grumpily off.

"And now if you excuse us," Maria said, taking the hand of my father, "my *son* and I would like to be alone."

The aged Emperor gave no objection. To the contrary, when told that his wife had adopted the Great Domestic as her son, Botaneiates did not remember that he had a wife. And so "mother" and "son" were free to spend as much time in her royal apartments as they wished, unsupervised and alone. Every day Alexios visited, even on Sundays and holy days of obligation, and Maria's mood improved.

But two obstacles to her happiness soon emerged. First, the decrepit Emperor, for reasons beyond the reckoning of any sane individual, decided out of the clear blue sky to nullify the succession rights of young Constantine Doukas, electing instead to name as co-emperor and heir his wastrel nephew Synadenos, much to the surprise of everyone at court, not excepting Synadenos himself.[78] This obviated the purpose of Maria's marriage to him, and sealed the Emperor's doom. Too, the twin vipers Borilas

---

[78]   The rumor is that the Emperor, now addled by dementia, confused his nephew with his younger brother of the same name, long since dead. (A.K.)

and Germanos lurked in the background, rightly perceiving this overt alliance between Empress and Great Domestic as a threat to their own lofty positions, and they set their mendacious eyes on the ambitious eyes of Alexios Komnenos.

XXXI
THE FUGITIVES

B Y NOW, THE CAREFUL READER CAN APPRECIATE JUST HOW precarious and mercurial are the forces that make and unmake Emperors (and also, by extension, Empresses!). Consider: If my great-uncle Isaac Komnenos chose not to read a bad weather event as a portent of disaster and a vote of no confidence by the Almighty, perhaps Constantine X does not assume the throne. If Michael VII were a different sort of man—or, to be more precise, if he were *not* a different sort of man—perhaps Eudokia does not see the need to marry Diogenes (or to import Maria to Constantinople from T'bilisi in the vain hope that her beauty would inspire his perverted carnal passions). If Diogenes does not insist upon a great military victory, perhaps Michael does not ever take the purple. If the unruly forces of Bryennios do not rape and pillage just beyond the walls of the Queen City, perhaps he becomes Emperor, and he and not Alexios Komnenos reigns for thirty-seven years. Fate is fickle. When emperors fall, they fall hard, and they fall fast. *Dégringolade* can be set in motion by the slightest push from the smallest personage.

A fourteen-year-old girl, say.

When she took her stand against his sadistic advances, and especially when she followed through on her macabre proposal, Irene had won her husband's grudging respect. From that night on, Alexios stopped visiting her bed-chamber; a few months later, he left for war, and was gone for two years, returning home only for brief visits as he crisscrossed the Empire. My mother was happy in this interval to reclaim her chastity; despite his spiteful pronouncement on their wedding day, she had not warmed to the alternative style of intercourse. While she had technically committed patricide, her conscience was clear. In her view, her father Andronikos was in a state of perpetual suffering, a sort of existential purgatory, from which agony her brave actions relieved him. This was a mercy-killing; mercy-killing requires *sangfroid*, it requires great courage, and like the valiant warrior engaging a stronger opponent, or the pious martyr braving the pyre, she had risen to the occasion. Irene was proud of what she had done. When Alexios left for his campaigns, the change in her personality was marked; in his absence, she comported herself like a mature woman of twice her years, the very model of equipoise. Her days of simpering were over. While she remained quiet and disdainful of undue attention, she was now possessed of a regal serenity. In short, my mother was worthy of the station to which she would soon ascend, and in which ascension she would prove a prime player.

Irene was surprised and not a little scared when she was summoned into the Empress's Loge at the Hagia Sophia to meet with Maria. The relationship between my father's wife and his lover was not strained as much as it was nonexistent. The Empress had not said more than a few words to Irene in the latter's lifetime; a perfunctory congratulations after the wedding, perhaps, and not much else. Maria was kind and gentle to most people regardless of station, but she treated my mother with unveiled annoyance, as she would a mosquito buzzing about the room, or a moth in the granary. Irene was not ignorant of the intimacy between her husband and the foreigner Empress, and regarded it with gratitude; if Alexios slaked his animal urges with Maria, she reasoned, he would leave her unmolested. Yet my mother was also shrewd enough to perceive a threat to her safety. The marriage of Maria and the senile *Augustus* was a sham; everyone knew this; but if Botaneaites were somehow removed from the picture, nothing would prevent Alexios and Maria from assuming the throne together—nothing except Irene's very existence. So my mother was on her guard upon entering the great church, its vast nave empty in the darkling night.

"Up here," a familiar voice called, echoing in the emptiness. "Hurry!" She climbed the stairs two at a time, bursting into the Empress's Loge, where her mother Maria of Bulgaria was waiting for her, along with her mother-in-law Anna Dalassene, her aunt Irina of Alania, the Empress herself and several imperial waiting-ladies. The only non-female in the room was Constantine Doukas, not yet seven, sitting quietly in the lap of an individual Irene at first thought was a man, but then realized was Tino's betrothed, Helena.

"What in the—"

"Soft, princess. We must be quiet."

"But whatever is going on?"

All eyes turned to Anna Dalassene, who flashed a tired smile. "Revolution," she said.

"I don't understand," Irene said.

"Borilas and Germanos, those vile Scyths, have issued a warrant for the arrest of the Great Domestic," Anna explained.

"Alexios? On what possible charge?"

"Sedition."

"But that is madness!"

"Indeed. My son—your husband—has spent the last two years fighting valiantly to defend the throne for Botaneiates, and the Emperor when lucid recognizes this. But lately his mind is not right. Senility has taken hold of him, and the Scyths have used his infirmity to poison him against Alexios. They have forged false documents to implicate the Domestic, and they will not rest until they deprive him of sight. Under the circumstances, Alexios had no choice but to take up arms."

Terror froze her blood, but Irene willed it away. "But where is he? Is he safe?"

"I think so," Anna said.

"He is with Isaac," said Irina, Isaac's wife, "recruiting men for the cause."

Anna crossed her arms, and boastfully added, "If the noble Bryennios did not get him, I assure you, there's no way he falls to the likes of the slave Borilas."

"The generals are coming to Constantinople," Maria of Bulgaria added. "Kyzikos fell to the Turks, so Alexios issued the summons. That was the pretext of his arrest—Borilas argued that the purpose of summoning the army was not to fight the Turks but to topple Botaneiates."

"Kyzikos? But that's so close...." As her voice trailed off, Irene held her tongue for a moment, fighting off inchoate passions as she processed this new intelligence. It was simple, really: Her husband, the Great Domestic, was on the lam, fomenting a revolt; he would either succeed in his attempt to usurp the throne, and make of her an *Augusta*, or he would fail, and make of her a widow. There was no middle ground. It was all or nothing. Was my mother afraid? I'm proud to say she was not. The excitement of the evening—by far the most engaging in her fifteen years upon this terrestrial plane—coursed through her veins, and she was instantly stimulated. "Mother," she said. "We must notify George. My grandfather, too, must be summoned."

"Alexios has been to see George," was the reply from Maria of Bulgaria, referring to her son-in-law, George Palaiologos, the dashing general. "He will lend his aid. But the *Caesar* has not yet been informed. That is a capital idea."

Now Irene turned her newly-steeled gaze to the Empress, who had not yet breathed a word. "Your Grace," she said, "forgive my impudence, but we must know which side you are on. It is your husband, after all, whose throne my husband seeks to usurp."

"You speak falsely," Maria said. "That wrinkled old prune is not my husband, no matter what papers have been filed with the Patriarch." Then her voice took on a tone at once sarcastic, condescending, and melancholy. "This might surprise you, princess, but I did not marry him for love—for my heart belongs to another."

With eyes of fire, Anna glared at the Empress, who pretended not to notice, but nonetheless reverted back to her usual tone of voice. "I agreed to take his hand," Maria explained, "in exchange for the promise that he would name my son co-emperor and heir to the throne. Isn't that right, Tino?"

"Yes, mother," the boy said shyly—he was hiding beneath Helena's skirts. (The idea that the two of them would one day wed never seemed as preposterous as it did at that moment in the Holy Wisdom).

"He lately revoked that vow, choosing instead to nominate his drunken reprobate of a nephew—thus violating our compact, and rendering our marriage null and void, as far as I'm concerned. And if it is proof of my loyalty that you require, well, your husband was only alerted to Borilas's plot because I myself was alerted to it, by one of my Alan kinsmen who overheard the vipers scheming. Were it not for me, his eyes would have already been taken." Then her face softened, and tears welled in her eyes. "I would never harm Alexios. Never."

The young Irene nodded, moved by the sincere display of emotion. "Thank you, Your Grace." Then she turned to the others. "We cannot stay here. The Scythian scoundrels will think nothing of desecrating a church, and anyway, we want to make it more difficult for them to find us. This is the first place they will look."

As if on cue, the doors of the great cathedral burst open, and a dozen of the Varangian Guard burst into the nave.

"Agreed," Anna said, impressed by my mother's decisiveness. "Down the stairs and into the crypt. We take the passage to the Refuge.[79] Quickly."

"Take Tino to the Studion," Maria told Helena, embracing her. "His father's friends will safeguard him." Then, as an afterthought: "And you."

"Are you not coming with us?" Anna asked the Empress.

"I must remain. None will dare lay a finger on me. God speed," Maria said, embracing each

---

[79] The sanctuary of the Bishop Nicholas. It is near the great church and was built long ago for the safety of fugitives charged with arrest for crimes; once they entered its doors, they were insulated from the penalty of law. The Emperors of old, you see, were much concerned for the welfare of their subjects. (A.K.)

of them in turn. Irene she hugged last, and more desperately than the others, kissing her also on the cheek, almost on the lips. "Please be safe, my dear."

The Varangian Guard were at the door of the Loge now. Maria detained them, castigating them for disturbing her while in prayer, while Helena and Tino fled via the secondary passage to the Studion, where both of them would wait out the days that followed.

My mother, my aunt, and my two grandmothers followed closely behind. With the Varangian Guard at their heels, my four kinswomen reached the Refuge. The verger, a hunchback who lived at the place, was not keen to let them in without preamble. "State your name and your purpose," he growled at them.

It was Irene who spoke, perfectly mimicking the Empress's accent: "We are women from the East. We've exhausted our silver and would like to worship quickly before returning home."

The stooped watchman bade them enter, bolting shut the great door an instant before the Varangian Guard appeared. The soldiers milled around a bit, anxious, as if unsure of how to proceed, until their commander appeared. Once apprised of the situation, he rapped urgently upon the door.

"State your name and your purpose," the verger growled, the gruffness of his tone unchanged.

"I bring a summons from the Emperor himself. The fugitives you harbor there are to appear before him at nine o'clock tomorrow morning, on pain of death."

At this point, Anna Dalassene came to the door. She recognized the face peering back at hers.

It was easy to recognize.

It lacked a nose.

"Ah, Straboromanos. I see the ministers have sent an one possessed of common sense. Thank God for that. Tell the Emperor—or, rather, tell those Scythian clowns—this: My sons are faithful servants, having fought bravely hither and yon in defense of Your Majesty. But Jealousy, which cannot countenance Your Majesty's goodwill towards them, has brought the Komnenos brothers into clear and present danger. And when the mendacious ministers did plot to gouge out their eyes, my loyal sons, who had discovered the plot quite by chance, found the threat as intolerable as it was unfounded, and quit the city—not as rebels but as faithful servants with three objectives in mind: to escape imminent peril, to convince Your Majesty of the plot against him, and to implore Your Majesty's protection." She regarded the nose-less man with contempt. "Do you have all that?"

Straboromanos grunted at her.

"Was that a yes or a no?"

"Out of courtesy to you, madam, I will deliver the message, but I'm certain it will fall on deaf ears. The Emperor's mind has been made up."

"By himself, or his horrible ministers?"

The nose-less man ignored the comment. "I will return tomorrow with his reply. Almost certainly it will be to arrest you." He noticed Irene behind her mother-in-law, listening intently to the conversation. He smiled at her—the effect on his deformed visage was less pleasant than he'd intended—and said, in a grave tone, "*Tomorrow* I will return. Tomorrow at high noon. Do you understand?"

Irene nodded, and Anna said, "Yes, I do. Thank you, Straboromanos. You are a good man."

The verger gave them pallets to lie upon, but sleep was elusive. Generally imperturbable, Anna Dalassene began to crack under the stress. She threw herself on her knees before an icon of the Virgin she found in a niche, prostrated herself, and spent most of the night in desperate prayer. Irina did the same on the pews, before eventually collapsing in her sleep. Maria of Bulgaria sang songs to herself, strange and beautiful melodies learned from Bulgarian folksmen; she, too, prayed. My mother paced the room, deep in thought. Some hours before dawn, she sent for the watchman.

"Robes," she told him. "Four of them. Big ones, of the kind worn by brothers of the church. Can you supply them? Your munificence will not go unnoticed by the women in this room."

The verger pondered this. "Yes," he said. "I do have them, although they might be dirty."

"That is of no importance. Thank you, kind verger."

At four in the morning, Irene woke the others, who had all finally fallen into slumber. She distributed the robes given her by the watchman. "We leave here as monks," she said. "We walk in a group, slowly so as not to arouse suspicion, along the Mese, past the Hippodrome and the Forums of Constantine and of Theodosius, to the convent at Myrelaion. With luck, we will make it to our destination unmolested."

"Myrelaion?" her mother asked. "That's the one with the arched windows, yes? And the watchtower?"

Irene nodded. "We leave at first light."

For all the vastness of its beauty, Constantinople is a small city, and the distance between the Refuge and the convent was less than a mile. And yet even at the early hour, the streets were swarming with imperial guard as they made their way across town. The foursome was not terribly conspicuous—monks often troll the streets at dawn—although the hoods drawn over their heads was suspicious enough to attract the attention of three Varangian Guard: tall, blonde monsters with no mercy in their barbarian hearts.

"Ahoy there," the leader shouted. "Ahoy!"

By now the women were in sight of their destination, the venerable convent of Myrelaion. But Irene did not want to lead them right to the destination, so she turned down a side street and picked up the pace. This only aroused further the guards' suspicion. They trotted after the fugitive "monks," but Irene, who led the others during the chase, with careful movements and quick, was able to shake them off by darting into and out of a smaller church, St. Demetrios. Before them, the pink dawn kissed the undulating black sea. The guards, fooled, raced to the strand, believing this is where they were headed; the women meanwhile backtracked, arriving at the convent without being observed.

There are prison-convents, there are school-convents, and there are convents for widows of means who wish to live out their lives in comfort. Myrelaion was one of the last, with a reputation for liberality. Men were permitted in the courtyard, for example, and wine was served at every meal, breakfast, lunch, and dinner. And yet the nun who minded the door, a hoary old crone with more hair on her face than a Judæan priest, was rightly suspicious of the quartet of well-maintained women who arrived at dawn dressed as monks.

"What is your business here?"

"We seek safe haven, sister," Irene said. "The soldiers in the streets are brutes. A pack of them tried to have their way with my mother here," gesturing behind her, and Maria of Bulgaria's face, already full of panic, seemed to corroborate the fib.

"And your solution was to lead armed rapists to the convent? Fie," the nun croaked. "Who are you people? Tell me the truth."

"I do not speak falsely," Irene replied. "Our lives are in danger, although we ourselves have done no wrong."

"Right," croaked the nun, but it was clear from her inflection that she did not believe them or care.

"I implore you," my mother said, "let us in!"

"They're on the street," said Irina, who had been peering out the window. "They will be here anon."

"Let us in, I bid you," my mother said, practically shouting. "Have mercy on us!"

But the nun's mind was made up. (And in the old crone's defense, it must be said that her judgment was sound.) She was not going to admit them—until another nun appeared behind her, taller and more radiant.

"Sister Agatha," the newcomer said. "Let them pass."

"But I..."

"They are here to see me," whereupon the speaker stepped into the dawn sunlight. She was thin and frail, the wrinkles on her face deep. But her smile when she shone it upon Irene lit up the room more than the rising sun.

"My little peach," Eudokia said. "How nice to see you!"

"Good morning, aunt," Irene said, embracing her.[80]

"Please. I bid you enter."

And so Irene, Anna Dalassene, Maria of Bulgaria, and Irina of Alania followed Eudokia into the convent—the more liberal convent she'd been moved to as a result of her negotiations with Botaneiates.

They spent a week in Eudokia's company, holed up at Myrelaion, listening to the erstwhile Empress read fables from her superb work-in-progress, *Bed of Violets*.

---

[80]   Irene's grandfather, John Doukas, was the brother of Eudokia's late husband Constantine X, making Eudokia Irene's great-aunt, by marriage.

"I loved listening to those stories," Irene recalled later. "It was astonishing to me how talented she was as a writer. Therein lies the magic of literature. When Eudokia read to us, our fears melted away, and it was somehow possible to forget all the tumult that was going on all around us."

And tumultuous it was. When they emerged from hiding on the third of April, A.D. 1081, they were fugitives no more; the city of Constantinople was reeling from its sack; and the seventy-fifth emperor of Rome had given way to the seventy-sixth.

XXXII
THE USURPER

As spring arrived in Constantinople, bathing the city in warm rain as it does, Maria knew that her days as *Augusta* were numbered, that this Great Lent would be her last in the purple. While she would miss the prestige and perquisites of the high office, there was much she was eager to leave behind. Borilas and Germanos, the two vile ministers, had already deprived her of her court ceremonial duties, which truth to tell she did not much enjoy regardless; during the short reign of Botaneiates she functioned solely as a figurehead, waving prettily to the increasingly hostile crowds at the Hippodrome. No, it was worth vacating the royal apartments to make way for her adopted son, if that meant her biological son would one day take the purple.

On the other hand, Maria was in a peculiar position, as she was the wife of Botaneiates, but also the mother of his presumptive successor Alexios

Komnenos (both relationships were shams). The odds were good that no harm would come to her. The possibility was high that she would not even have to vacate her apartments; why should she, if her "son" took the throne?

Tino was safe with Helena, *en route* to Ephesus. Her cousin Irina and her good friend Anna Dalassene were safely ensconced in the convent at Myrelaion, under the formidable watch of Eudokia herself. Alexios, meanwhile, had already contrived to assemble his army, and was camped just across the Propontis at Aretas, on the grounds of a country palace built, but not much used, by Diogenes. With him were his brother Isaac, the dashing general George Palaiologos, Oursel the red rogue, and the venerable *Caesar* John Doukas—in short, every military man of consequence left in the Empire. The army had already declared Alexios *Augustus*; all that remained was to storm the city itself and oust the daft Botaneaites. Due to the impenetrable defenses posed by the Theodosisan Walls, the Great Chain, and the swirling currents of the waterways themselves, the former was no small feat; but Maria had every confidence that her "son" would manage. With regard to the removal of her loathsome husband, she would do everything in her power to affect the desired outcome.

Maria called on Botaneaites, although she knew persuading him to do anything was nigh impossible, given the addled state of his senile mind. She was surprised to find him perfectly lucid—the first time he'd been so in weeks—and engaged in a serious discussion with Kosmas the Patriarch. The slithery ministers Borilas and Germanos were also in attendance. Anna Dalassene's impassioned defense of her sons' motives had been delivered to him by Straboromanos, and it was this topic that they were heatedly discussing.

"He is a traitor," Borilas said, in his thick Sclavonian accent, glowering at Maria as she entered. "He raised an army for the express purpose of revolt. There is no viable argument to the contrary, when one considers the troops now massed at Aretas."

"I agree, sire," said Germanos, who more or less did whatever Borilas commanded.

"He has bravely defended the Empire in Your Majesty's name," Kosmas retorted. "For years he has fought, risking life and limb for Your Majesty. At any time he could have joined forces with one of the many rebels to attack Your Majesty and he did not. Your minister Borilas falsely accuses him. What other course is open to the Domestic at this juncture? What else could he do? Wait for Your Majesty to take his eyes? Your Majesty's ministers forced his hand. The choice was blindness or revolt. He chose revolt, as any self-respecting man would."

"I concede that we gave him a pretext," Borilas said. "But that doesn't mean he hasn't been waiting for this opportunity for a long time. Alexios Komnenos is an opportunist and a rogue. He always has been. A leopard does not change its stripes."

"A *rogue* leopard," added Germanos, who was rather stupid.

"A leopard doesn't have stripes," Kosmas pointed out.

Botaneiates listened to all of this patiently, engaged, his dark eyes gleaming with lucid intelligence.

"Forgive my imposition, sire," Maria said, "but it seems to me that the subject up for debate is moot. Whatever motives compelled the Great Domestic to raise the banner of revolt, be they benign or malefic, are irrelevant to the matter at hand. The accusations raised by Borilas, which I know to be false, have indeed forced his hand, and Komnenos has opted for revolt rather than blindness. A similar decision now falls to you, husband. The reality is this: Alexios controls the armies beyond the gates of the city. They have already proclaimed him. All that remains is for my son to take Constantinople—a challenge to be sure, but one within his ample powers. The Varangian Guard are loyal and brave; they will fight till the death. But for what? Even if you somehow prevail, what then? Already in your short reign, four generals have brazenly assumed the imperial title, not counting Komnenos. Surely others will follow. Who will lead an army against them, with the Great Domestic out of the picture? You, Borilas? You, Germanos? And even if you somehow found an able and willing commander, how long could you possibly continue, with the Treasury bankrupt, the food prices sky-high, and the hoi polloi against you? You are not a young man, sire. Will you hold out for another year? For two? If you surrender to Alexios, I will do everything in my power, which I assure you is almost limitless in this case, to ensure that you remain intact. He will not have your eyes, husband. You can retire to a monastery of your choosing, and live out your remaining years in peace. The alternative is a long, bloody siege that may well ruin the city—and you will lose anyway."

Kosmas applauded as she finished. "Listen to your wife, Your Majesty," he implored the Emperor. "She is wise in the ways of the world."

"She is a snake," Borilas said, "and a whore. The seed of the usurper swims in her womb."

"Harlot," added Germanos.

At last the aged Emperor spoke. "Silence!" he commanded. "I've had about enough of your insolence, ministers. Begone, all of you. I need time to think."

And so the four of them filed out of the room, where they continued to debate.

"He won't surrender," Borilas told the Empress. "It's not in his blood."

"Then he will die," said Maria matter-of-factly. "As you will, minister. May God grant that I see the day when you are fed to the lions before a raucous crowd at the Hippodrome." Then she smiled innocently, bade farewell to the Patriarch, and repaired to her apartments.

⁓

Meanwhile, the Great Domestic made a study of the city's defenses from his position at Aretas. Although his forces vastly outnumbered those of the remaining Varangian Guard, there was no hope of taking Constantinople by storm, as discussed; the Theodosian Walls were impenetrable, and the battlements around the rest of the city were sufficient, when paired with the inherent difficulties of sea landings, to dissuade him from such an attempt. To gain access to the city, Alexios had to rely on treachery.

Say this about the Varangian Guard: they are loyal. But there were not enough of them alive to defend the city completely. The Charsian Gate, also called the Gate of Adrianople, was guarded not by Varagians but by German mercenaries, barbarians really, whose leader, Gilpracht, had a reputation for corruptibility. A bag of gold *solidi* and a promise of promotion bought George Palaiologos entrance to the city one rainy evening after second watch. At dawn of the first of April, George opened the Charsian Gate, and my father's troops defiled into the city. Years of fighting had decimated the ranks, and this collection of soldiers—almost all of them mercenaries from lands far away, most of them unfamiliar with the majestical splendor of the city—more resembled a loosely-affiliated mob than a proper Roman regiment. Down the Mese they marched in lockstep, but once the men reached the Forum of Theodosius—a stone's throw, as it happened, from where my mother and other kinswomen were hiding at Myrelaion—the lure of the voluptuous metropolis was too great; all semblance of order fell away, and the soldiers dispensed like wild animals in search of sex and plunder. These beasts were met by the more criminally-inclined members of the native Constantinopolitan rabble, who vied with the mercenaries in license and rapine. Shops and warehouses were pillaged, as were palaces of nobles and houses of wealthy citizens. Neither rich nor poor were given quarter by the lustful mob, who showed as little respect for the inmates of monasteries and convents as for the inhabitants of shops and palaces. It was a sack, simple and plain.

A rabble of lunatics broke down the door of the Myrelaion convent; some of the nuns therein were ravished as they said their morning prayers; by some miracle Irene and the others were spared. My mother was hidden away in her cold, windowless cell, and had no way of knowing that the officer in nominal charge of this heinous crime, who was at that moment having his odious way with the Abbess herself, was Nikephoros Bryennios *fils*—Junior—who had, in his disreputable travels, developed an insatiable appetite for rapine. Had Irene borne witness to his abominable actions that day, perhaps she would have been less eager to marry her eldest daughter off to him—but that sad tale we must defer for now.

Abandoned by the lion's share of his men, Alexios was left in the square with Isaac, Oursel, George, and a handful of his most trusted sergeants. A well-timed assault by the Emperor's Guard would easily have killed off all of them in one fell swoop. Indeed, my father, realizing his weakness, expected this. He looked heavenward and muttered prayers to the Almighty.

"So close," he said to himself. "I came so close…"

But death did not come. What Alexios could not know was that Botaneiates had already abdicated, returning his crown to Kosmas at the Hagia Sophia, and then repairing to the hideous monastery at Peribleptos on the Seventh Hill—not far from the Charsian Gate that the rebels had breached. Thus, when my father reached the Grand Palace, he encountered not a single belligerent soldier in his path; all bowed as he approached, and he met the Patriarch, decked out in white robes, waving his arms in greeting. With Kosmas was the smiling Empress Maria.

It was all over in the blink of an eye.

That day, the first of April, A.D. 1081, as George Palaiologos, Oursel, and Isaac rounded up the misbehaving troops and Romanos Straboromanos hunted down and slew Borilas and Germanos both—they were not fed to the lions, as Maria had threatened, but were rather slowly and methodically disemboweled—Alexios entered the bed-chamber of his "mother," Maria of Alania. All afternoon and into the night they made frenzied love, celebrating the climax of their achievement.

"It was," she told me later—eleven years later, to be precise; for we are now less than three years away from my dilatory arrival at the scene—"the best night of my life."

That Maria was the wife of two Emperors but had only slept with a third—a third who was not her husband but her lawful son!—is an irony that, in the ecstasy of the moment, did not even cross her mind. Euphoria consumed her, rendering her incapable of rational thought. She was never before and would never again be as happy as she was that day, riding atop my triumphant father—the new *Augustus*!—like an Amazon queen astride her trusted steed. The future stretched before her like a lush Thracian orchard, beautiful and ripe and bountiful. Together they'd conquered Byzantium; together they would conquer anything. Nothing seemed impossible. She could have sprouted angel-wings and flown out the window of the Grand Palace, as she did in her fever-dream the night Tino was born, and not been surprised.

The next morning the mood broke, and Maria was in tears, inconsolable.

"My darling," Alexios said, "what is the matter?"

She tried to explain, but it was impossible to articulate the cause of her sudden change in mood. She could scarce understand it herself.

"Nothing," she said. "It's just…"

She'd been Empress for almost ten years. Only now, relieved of that oppressive title, was she on top of the world.

But once on top of the world, there is nowhere to go but down.

Volume Four:
Alexios I Komnenos

A.D. 1081-83

XXXIII

THE PENITENT

MY FATHER WAS TOO BUSY INDULGING HIS LUST with his now-aging-but-no-less-gorgeous lover (Maria was then twenty-nine) to concern himself with the fabric of the great metropolis unravelling around him. As it happened, the marauders—they could no longer be thought of as soldiers by this point—had reached such a dissipated state of wantonness that Alexios was extremely lucky that they did not put the entire city to the torch. My mother Irene would have perished in the flames the night of the coup, and I would not be shivering on this frigid morning, writing this down for some vague and suspect readership we are pleased to call "posterity."

O, but thick was the irony! Consider: When mercenaries under the banner of the rebel Nikephoros Bryennios the Elder plundered the suburbs beyond the Theodosian Wall, their general was held accountable; Bryennios's inability to control his troops cost him (probably) the throne and (certainly) his eyes. When mercenaries under the banner of the rebel Alexios Komnenos plundered *Constantinople itself*—its great palaces and handsome houses, its fine shops and sacred monasteries; not to mention the virtue of countless of its women: wives, daughters, and nuns alike—their general somehow contrived to retain his sight and take the purple withal. One imagines Bryennios in his darkness railing against Fortune's unkind whim, upon hearing the news.

By the grace of God my uncle Isaac, soon to be dubbed *Sebastokrator*—a newly-minted title invented by my father that ranked above *Caesar* and below *Augustus*—kept his wits about him. He took to the Treasury, promising the ruffians a bonus payment of gold in exchange for a suspension of bad behavior (he was astonished by how little gold he found there, about which more presently). By then the collective urge for mayhem had been temporarily sated—one can only ravish so many women, after all; virility has its limits, even when abetted by drink—and the soldiers-cum-criminals took their ill-gained *solidi* and repaired to the barracks to cool off, throwing dice for their newly-plundered loot. The near-sack of the city represented the first crisis of the fledgling reign of Alexios Komnenos, and it was solved with gold rather than iron. This was to prove a policy; my father's rote solution to almost every problem was to throw money at it, with deleterious effects on the already-wanting imperial wallet.

So the dogs were called off, to to speak, but the damage had been done: Homes looted, property vandalized, females despoiled. The atrocity demanded some sort of retribution. But there was the rub: Alexios couldn't very well execute every soldier in his regiment, no matter how degenerate; since even before Manzikert, his army had been decimated by years of neglect and poor battle planning, and he needed every last man willing to fight for him, rogue or otherwise. Some of the most egregious offenders could be dispatched, yes, but would that be sufficient? How to win back the good graces of the indignant Constantinopolitans? It was Maria who made the suggestion: my father should publicly announce his own culpability in the debacle, claim full responsibility, and throw himself at the mercy of the Patriarch, who would determine a suitable penance.

"But *I* didn't do anything wrong," he protested. "Why should I do such a thing?"

"People quickly forgive when their Emperors assume responsibility," she told him. "By admitting that one is not without fault, the idea is projected that *Father* is in charge."

The twenty-one-year-old Alexios, still boyish despite his military adventures, laughed. "I don't have any children."

Maria flashed him a wry grin. "Not from lack of trying."

And so, while preparing for the imperial transition—there were ceremonies to be performed, titles to bestow, coins to be struck, a formal coronation to arrange—my father, as usual, did as his lover instructed.

Unlike his urbane and ambitious predecessor Xiphilinos, Kosmas was a pious man, as Patriarchs go, and not inclined to let personal vanity interfere with the discharge of his official God-given duties. But even he was not without self-interest, and the sight of the Equal of the Apostles prostrating himself before him—in the Hagia Sophia, no less, in full public view—stoked the flames of his own hubris.

"I have sinned, Father," Alexios began, rising, in a prepared speech composed by Maria which he had memorized. He was ostensibly speaking to Kosmas, but he was turned out toward the pews, and his voice was as loud as a stage-actor's. This was, after all, a performance. "Laxly have I overseen my charges, and they have committed grievous acts in this great city that I adore. The fault lies with me, for a commanding officer is ultimately responsible for the behavior of his lowliest foot soldier, and thus I beseech you to grant me penance for their terrible sins. I cannot cleanse the stain of their trespasses; this I know." Now he turned to face the Patriarch. "Tell me what to do, Father, to atone for their, for *my*, sin."

Whereupon Kosmas meted out the penance, as if my father were some lowly commoner petitioning for forgiveness for some petty trespass. A steady diet of bread and water was the first stipulation; no feasting at the coronation! My father was to pray five times a day, here at the cathedral, on bended knee. He was to wear a hairshirt, to scourge himself of the sin. When he slept, it was to be on the hard floor, with a stone for a pillow. All of this he must endure for forty days and forty nights, as Christ in the desert. And of course there was to be—and here Kosmas actually coughed!—financial remuneration to the Church.

When the Patriarch finished, Alexios once again fell prostrate, kissed the hem of the former's cloak, and rose. All who beheld the cynical spectacle—and make no mistake, spectacle was the purpose of this exercise—were moved. The Emperor could not un-break what was broken in the houses and palaces, nor could he wave a magic wand and restore the virtue of the offended women. That was beyond his power. But by this humble display of atonement, he had restored popular faith in himself as *Augustus*. That was what mattered. Forty days would go by swiftly enough.

Alexios ate only bread and water during the day, but had meat secreted to his chambers at night. As for sleeping on the floor, this he actually preferred, as he was accustomed to roughing it from his years in the field, and disdained the softness of pallets. The hairshirt, however, was as unpleasant as it was undignified. My father wore the thing in public— woven of coarse sackcloth, that is, the wiry hair of goats, it clung unpleasantly to his hirsute chest, itching and causing rash—but removed it as soon as he was alone each night. When he tried to doff the hairshirt in Maria's bed-chamber, however, she insisted he leave it on.

"Penance is penance," she told him, smiling. "And I kind of like the idea of you suffering a little while giving me pleasure. Perhaps we should talk to Kosmas and have him insist you wear sackcloth on your loins as well."

This line of dialogue only enflamed his desire. Fortunately for the two lovers, the good Patriarch had neglected to insist upon chastity for the forty-day duration.

All along, my father's intention—although it was more vague notion than well-devised plan—had been to take the purple, annul his marriage to Irene, and wed his lover and "mother" Maria. Emperors, he'd not unreasonably assumed, could bend the rules of domesticity to their liking. Just as Justinian had selected as his queen a foreigner of low birth—a whore, Prokopios alleges, although I suspect this appraisal of Theodora is more calumny than fact[81]—

---

[81]   This "calumny" of Prokopios, writing about the empress Theodora, is worth quoting at some length: "On the field of pleasure she was never defeated. Often she would go picnicking with ten young men or more, in the flower of their strength and virility, and dallied with them all, the whole night through. When they wearied of the sport, she would approach their servants, perhaps thirty in number, and fight a duel with each of these; and even thus found

my father could take advantage of his *droigt d'empereur* to select the wife of his choosing. Or so he believed. The political realities of the day, alas, rendered this impossible. Not only had Maria been married previously, both of her imperial ex-husbands were, most inconveniently, very much alive in the spring of A.D. 1081. A twice-widow may have some hope of landing a third husband; not so a twice-divorcée. Incest was another obstacle. Because Alexios's brother Isaac was married to Maria's cousin Irina, the *Augustus* and

---

no allayment of her craving. Once, visiting the house of an illustrious gentleman, they say she mounted the projecting corner of her dining couch, pulled up the front of her dress, without a blush, and thus carelessly showed her wantonness. And though she flung wide three gates to the ambassadors of Cupid, she lamented that nature had not similarly unlocked the straits of her bosom, that she might there have contrived a further welcome to his emissaries. Frequently, she conceived, but as she employed every artifice immediately, a miscarriage was straightway effected. Often, even in the theater, in the sight of all the people, she removed her costume and stood nude in their midst, except for a girdle about the groin: not that she was abashed at revealing that, too, to the audience, but because there was a law against appearing altogether naked on the stage, without at least this much of a fig-leaf. Covered thus with a ribbon, she would sink down to the stage floor and recline on her back. Slaves to whom the duty was entrusted would then scatter grains of barley from above into the calyx of this passion flower, whence geese, trained for the purpose, would next pick the grains one by one with their bills and eat." (*The Secret History of Prokopios*, chapter IX., translated by Richard Atwater [1927]).

quondam *Augusta* were considered kin in the eyes of the Church and thus prohibited from marrying. That did not even take into account the fact that Maria was now, by the law of the land, the new Emperor's mother (although my father, as I can unhappily attest, was not one to let a wee little social construct like incest hamper his lechery).

Further cloudying the picture was the fact that Alexios was himself married—and not to some contemporary Theodora plucked from the low stage, but to a daughter of the most powerful and wealthiest family in Christendom. The Doukids may have scattered in recent years, but their alliance with Alexios during the revolt only enhanced their prestige. The venerable John Doukas, now in his seventies, was back from retirement and once again *Caesar*. The various brothers and sisters of Irene were all married to important members of the nobility, including George Palaiologos, Alexios's ablest general and bosom friend, without whom the coup itself, nor the salvation of Constantinople from the near-sack that followed, would not have taken place. When the learned Marcus Aurelius, whose wife Faustina was the daughter of the Emperor Antoninus Pius, discovered her rampant infidelities, he declined to divorce her: "If I did, I would have to return my dowry—the Empire!" So it was with Alexios and Irene. Maria's shortcomings as a potential bride were ultimately irrelevant. My father simply could not divorce my mother without jeopardizing, if not surrendering outright, the throne. Although he tried.

The coronation took place on the fourth of April, A.D. 1081—Easter Sunday, a date fraught with terrible significance. As Jesus rose from the dead, so too would Byzantium, under the dutiful watch of Alexios Komnenos…and like Christ's, his kingdom would have no end! Whether my father consciously thought this through, or whether Easter happened to be the Sunday immediately following the coup, I cannot say (although knowing the man as well as I did, I suspect the latter; my father was a believer, but he was no theologian). In the event, there he stood, by the altar at the Hagia Sophia on the holiest day of the year, adulterating the immaculate Divine with his violent terrestrial concerns.

Conspicuously absent from the coronation was my mother Irene. Indeed, she'd not yet moved into the Boukoleon, inhabiting instead a more modest palace on the estate, on lower (and thus less prestigious) ground. Maria, meanwhile, was in no hurry to vacate the premises once occupied by her paragon Eudokia; she had not packed so much as a hairbrush. The Dowager Empress graced the coronation with her imperious and still-beauteous presence, smiling radiantly throughout like the proud "mother" she was.

My mother was almost fifteen at the time, the same age Maria had been when she came to Constantinople to marry Michael, and while Irene had some inkling of the worrisome import of her now-royal husband barring her from his own coronation, of what a terrible omen that was, yet she did not take umbrage. That onerous task was left to her kin: her mother Maria of Bulgaria, her brother-in-law George Palaiologos, and her grandfather John Doukas principally. When the ceremonies were complete, and the newly-crowned Emperor was at rest in his Map Room with his mother and *de facto* Prime Minister Anna Dalassene, those three personages, as well as Kosmas the Patriarch, met with the Komnenoi contingent.

John in particular was livid. "That was an embarrassment," he told the new *Augustus*. "To me, to my grand-daughter, to you, and to the whole of the Empire. You have all but announced yourself to the world as a petty, small-minded creature, ripe for usurpation. I'd sooner wipe my arse with your banner than follow it into war."

"Irene is completely humiliated," Maria of Bulgaria reported. "She spent all day in her bed-chamber, in tears." (This was not, in fact, true—my mother later revealed that she would have been happy to leave the Empressing to Maria of Alania and quit the abusive marriage, were that option available to her. The convent never looked so good. And yet the public humiliation must have had *some* malefic impact on her self-regard.) As my maternal grand-mother spoke, her spleen was vented on Anna Dalassene, whose hatred for the Doukids overshadowed her affection for Maria of Bulgaria. The slight at the coronation would create a rift between the two matriarchs, my forebearers, that would never completely heal.

"Alexios," said George, loyal friend and voice of reason, "we love you and want you to endure. Fix this, sire."

"If your underhanded scheme is to repudiate your marriage to Irene of the House of Doukas," Kosmas was bold enough to say, "and take instead the hand of the erstwhile Empress Maria Botaneaites, that is not something the Church will permit, I'm afraid. It simply cannot be done."

Alexios glowered at his in-laws, hating them all at that moment. O, to be King of Kings and not get one's way! Rage consumed him, rage tinged with chagrin. Had he made solemn vows to Maria of Alania, in the heat of passion? In the sanctuary of the bed-chamber, men promise the world, and then fail time and again to deliver. My father was an exceptional man, true, and the Equal of the Apostles besides, but this particular rock was too heavy for even the mighty Alexios Komnenos to dislodge. Anna Dalassene, longtime loather of the Doukids, had given her tacit consent that Irene should be removed in favor of Maria, but in this case, he had to admit, base emotion had clouded her otherwise-pristine judgment. His wife had to stay. Reparations had to be made. The matter was settled.

Although there were four at the meeting in the Map Room, all of them technically guilty of insubordination, if not high treason, both Alexios and

Anna focused their ire on the only one who was replaceable (and thus disposable): Kosmas. The pious Patriarch, who had lobbied Botaneaites so eloquently on my father's behalf, had outlived his usefulness. At the first available opportunity, they vowed afterwards, the sanctimonious old codger would be relieved of his lofty post. One does not call the Emperor "underhanded."

Maria his lover took the news better than Alexios had anticipated. She didn't seem remotely surprised, or even disappointed. "Of course they want me to leave," she said. "Who can blame them?"

"But…"

"Soft, sire. I hoped your plan would work, verily I did, but I knew in my heart that it would not. A thrice-Empress? The hoi polloi would never accept it."

"Well, but why did not you say so?"

"However lofty our aspirations, we should all strive to achieve them," she said, kissing his forehead. "Besides, one never knows what might transpire. Stranger things have happened." Then she slid down to her knees—he was leaning against the well-used couch—and lifted his tunic. "My love for you remains unchanged, my darling. My place of residence will not alter the intimate nature of our relationship, not one iota." She looked up at him, and he could feel her warm breath on his swaying scepter. "Constantine my son will remain your heir apparent, yes?"

He grunted in assent.

Thus with feminine guile was Maria's primary objective achieved. After opening wide her mouth, but before taking him in it, she added, "You won't object if I take the wardrobe, my lord. Irene will have new dresses made. She won't fit in mine anyway."

"Yes, of course, of course," Alexios muttered, his eyes closed. He would have agreed to almost anything at that moment. Men are ruled by their base desires and thus easily led, if a canny woman has the wherewithal to so lead them.

The egregiously extravagant Mangana Palace was built at great expense by the Emperor Constantine IX Monomachos, so that the family of his own mistress, the uppity Sklerinoi, could live in the lap of luxury. The Mangana was a short stroll from the Boukoleon, also on high ground and thus with breathtaking views of the Bosporus; newer than the Grand Palace, it boasted more amenities if not quite as much cachet. That the Mangana was where Maria moved the second week of April—taking with her the entire imperial wardrobe, most of the jewelry, and indeed much that had not been nailed down—was *apropos*, as the Emperor Monomachos's mistress had also been a foreigner called Maria. The Dowager Empress's cousin Irina and Irina's husband Isaac Komnenos, now the *Sebastokrator*, took up residence at the Mangana with her. I would come to know the place well, as I would spend my formative years there.

"It was strange to leave the Grand Palace, to no longer be Empress," Maria told me later. "But one cannot fall prey to greed. Eudokia was removed in the blink of an eye, from *Augusta* to convent prisoner. I had everything I wanted. My title remained intact—once Empress, always Empress—and I had my fortune, and a grand estate to call home, and the freedom that comes with leaving high office. Now the time I spent running the court ceremonial, which is quite tedious work I'll have you know, could be devoted to founding a proper literary salon. Your father still loved me. So what if our love was not countenanced by the Church? As long as Tino was heir to the throne, I was happy...even happier than I'd been in the purple."

At the end of the fateful first month of my father's reign, Irene, young if not innocent, still painfully shy but resolute, and mortified by the gravity and fuss of the proceedings, was herself crowned at the Hagia Sophia, by a self-righteous Patriarch, before a gathering of family and friends who appeared more relieved than joyous.

"Alexios made a big show, proclaiming his fealty to me, all of that," my mother recalled later. "He was very emotional, and played up his remorse to my family. It was all most affecting. But he could not bring himself to look at me. I could have been stark naked that day and he would not have known. Not once during the ceremony did his eyes meet mine. Not once."

This time Maria stayed away. She may have known rationally that events would unfold in the way that they did, as she'd claimed; but hope is a creature of delusion, and deep down inside, she certainly believed that fickle Fortune would once again smile on her, in some magical way, and prolong her improbable reign as Empress.

Alas, it was not to be. She sat on her terrace at the Mangana Palace, surrounded by gorgeous potted plants and vases of perfumed flowers, weeping, even as clouds rolled in and the rains came, mixing with her own tears, like God Himself was crying.

Constantine, who was now seven—old enough to remember it all, old enough for the day to be written indelibly in his mind—was in her bed-chamber playing his favorite game, which involved torturing a mouse the cats had caught but grown tired of. He was in his own little world, as he often was, delighting in slicing off the poor thing's little gray arm with his dull little blade, when he heard the plaintive wailing of his mother on the terrace. Tino had never seen Maria cry before, and the sight frightened him.

"I wasn't sure what to do," he told me later, in a rare moment of introspection, "if I should try to comfort her, or just leave her to herself. So I stood there like an idiot, watching her weep—granting her neither solace nor privacy. I did not understand the source of her anguish, that came much later, but I intuitively knew that Alexios, that your father, was responsible, that he had hurt her somehow, and not as I had hurt the little mouse, but rather in some way that left no outward sign. He had always treated me with a sort of false jocularity, like he was a fun uncle or somesuch, but the events surrounding the coronation convinced me that he was two-faced, a snake. After that day, while I could enjoy his company now and again, I never could fully trust him."

Maria was unaware that her son was watching her. She had been putting on a brave face for weeks, and now the strain was too much. She wept for what felt like hours. She wept like all of her insides were slowly liquefying and pouring out of her eyes. When the tears at last subsided, she saw things more clearly. Tears purge us of our illusions.

"I knew it was better this way," she told me later. "I knew I would be happier. I did not want to be Empress any longer, not really. I talked myself into it, you see. But our feelings are our feelings. We must honor them. And my heart had been broken."

XXXIV

THE MESSENGER

T HE EFFECTS OF AN IMPERIAL COUP are far-reaching indeed. Consider Helena, the mannish daughter of Robert the Fox. One of seven daughters—and almost certainly not the "most beautiful" as stipulated by Maria; the remarkable comeliness of her older brother Bohemond proved that, however rare, beauty did indeed flow in the Norman bloodlines—she was shipped to Constantinople at age fifteen, knowing just a few stray words of Greek, to marry a prince who was still in diapers. Her footfalls were heavy; she lacked physical grace of any kind; in the nursery she was an elephant. An unlikely nanny, she nevertheless took to the rôle with admirable gusto. Her heart, like the rest of her, was outsized. It was impossible not to like her. Everyone adored her, even my spiteful grand-mother Anna Dalassene, whose capacity for contempt was boundless. After seven years at Constantinople, living first with Anna, then at the Grand Palace with

Maria, and now at the Mangana, Helena was part of the family, no matter who her father was, or how foul. The match between her and young Tino had always been ridiculous; Helena herself recognized the long odds of the marriage ever taking place. And yet there was no doubt where her loyalties lay, even as the aforementioned boulder struck the lake and disturbed the muddy waters.

She appeared in Maria's salon just after luncheon, her face pale, her powerful shoulders quaking, her face streaked with tears. In her outsized hands she clutched a letter.

"Helena? My angel, what's the matter?"

And the Norman princess fell into Maria's tiny embrace, weeping like it was the end of the world—because for her, it was. When she composed herself, she handed Maria the letter. "Here," she said. "See for yourself."

The erstwhile Empress took the parchment, squinted her eyes, and gave it back. "It's in French," she said.

"Pardon?" Helena did not seem to understand. After a few moments, she realized her mistake. "Oh, yes. Of course." Then, in her halting accented Greek, she translated the letter:

Bohemond, Prince of Apulia, son of Duke Robert, to his dearest sister,

It has been too long since we have seen one another! I hope that you are well, and still enjoying life in the ample comforts of the Grand Palace. How strange it all must be! Forgive me for not writing sooner. There is trouble everywhere, and Papa has had me marching this way and that to make war…the last two years we have fought almost constantly, with no respite. You'd think he'd slow down in his Golden Years but no.

But this epistle has greater purpose. I write with news, which I hope you will consider glad tidings. There is a man here in Taranto, a monk it is presumed, who claims to be the deposed Emperor of the Greeks, an one called Michael. This Michael further claims he was ousted by a usurper, and has sought our father's aid in returning him to the throne. Is he a fraud? He almost certainly is—from what I gather, your Michael is alive and well in Constantinople, or perhaps in Ephesus…in the event, Papa has decided that, imposter or no, he will take up this fellow's cause. His appeal to the people is thus: that his daughter Helena, promised to the heir of Byzantium, has been cast out along with Michael, and thus he, Robert the Fox, must take arms against the usurper Botanes? Botash? I'm not sure how to spell his name… the old battle-ax who sits unlawfully upon the throne…and restore his daughter and her betrothed to their rightful position, along with this false Michael. I argued against the scheme, but you know how stubborn Papa can be when he gets an idea in his head.

In the event, the offensive will begin soon, this spring, as soon as the arrangements can be made. I'm sure this will put you in an uncomfortable position, my dear sister, and I'm sorry for that. Papa does not consider these things when composing his devious little plans. He is slave to his ambitions. Please keep this knowledge to yourself—burn this letter, my dear! Into the flames it must go! I will see you soon, and am glad at least for that.

All my love,
Your brother,

Bohemond

The translation complete, Helena burst into a fresh round of tears.

I confess that I cannot well imagine how she must have felt at that moment. True, she was merely a pawn in the chess game, a flesh-and-blood pretext for an invasion that Robert the Fox was determined to attempt regardless of who sat upon the throne. He'd witnessed the success of his fellow Norman, William the Bastard, in the British Isles; he rightly saw Constantinople as a far greater prize, and one within his contemptuous grasp. But how could our Helena live with the dread knowledge? The shame and embarrassment were only exacerbated by the fact that, if we use beauty as a metric, she was, despite her ironical Christian name, no Helen of Troy. And yet like her namesake, a fleet of ships would soon be launched to defend her presumed honor.

"But soft," Maria said. "Your brother says the Fox's aim is to oust Botaneiates. Well, my senescent ex-husband has already been ousted. What claim does your father have now?"

"None," Helena said.

"Exactly. This will come to naught, I assure you. Although I would very much like to meet this brother of yours."

In the years they had known one another, Maria had heard many tales of this Bohemond. The first son of Robert the Fox by his first wife, a Burgundian princess called Alberada, he was christened as Mark, but his father nicknamed him Bohemond, after the legendary giant *Buamundus gigas*, on account of his immense size, even as an infant. While Robert was ruthless in his ambition, as evidenced by the "false Michael" imbroglio, his eldest son was more happy-go-lucky, a ferocious warrior who was possessed of a keen sense of *joie de vivre*. Helena had described him as impressively attractive—"Not at all like me," she said laughing; "I take after my mother, alas; *his* mother is much more beautiful!"—enormously tall and strong, with close-cropped blonde hair and a ruggedly handsome clean-shaved face set with crystalline blue eyes a-gleam with mischief. Sisters, even half-sisters, often boast of the comeliness of their brothers—although in my case, my ugly brother's sobriquet was purely ironic[82]—so one must regard these sororal descriptions with due skepticism, and yet Maria had nevertheless convinced herself that the level-headed Helena, not one prone to hyperbole, spoke accurately of her sibling. She, Maria, had a most favorable impression of this Bohemond, almost as a twittering girl might fawn over a dashing Hippodrome charioteer, and she was most curious to make his acquaintance. This letter only added to his appeal.

"Come, my dearest," Maria said, "we must inform His Majesty."

The two women went immediately to the Boukoleon, where the Emperor saw them at once in the Map Room. Alexios listened intently as they told of Robert the Fox's plan, his face impassive.

"Thank you, Helena," he said when they had finished, "for your disclosure. I know your father's unseemly ambitions have put you in an inelegant position. I recognize the hard choice you have made today, and I thank you for it."

"Bless you, sire."

"Before the coup," Alexios continued, "I met with an envoy, a Frankish knight whose name escapes me. He was here to gauge whether or not to go to war. I managed to convince him that I had no intention of invading Robert's lands, or indeed of engaging him at all. My concern was with Anatolia, with the East.

---

[82]   Anna's brother, the Emperor John II Komnenos, was called "John the Handsome," and not for his looks, but rather his big heart.

Raoul! His name was Raoul. Do you know him? Yes, of course you do. The contents of the letter suggest that news has not yet reached your father of my ascension to the purple. When it does, Helena dear, I'm sure your father will recognize the foolhardiness of an invasion. It's true that my army is not at top strength, but Constantinople itself is impregnable, and our people will fight valiantly in their own defense. Your father's plan is a suicide mission. He is intelligent enough to see this. Raoul will help convince him. Nevertheless, we must make preparations."

"Thank you, sire. Oh, thank you."

"You understand that, should your father's army approach, we must remand you to a convent, for your own safety?"

"I would gladly lay down my life for you, Your Highness, and for Maria and Tino."

"Again, Helena, you have my eternal gratitude."

Thus briefed of the potential invasion, Alexios hurried to mobilize his forces. He signed a hasty treaty with the sultan, and ordered all his men removed from the East to the West (a move that would, in time, have far-reaching consequences, as we shall see). At the urging of his mother and Prime Minister, Anna Dalassene—of her precise function in her son's government, more shortly—he also enlisted the aid of the Doge of Venice

He needed to be extremely careful. Raoul the Frankish envoy might have been swayed by my father's cogent argument and his ample charms. Robert the Fox would not be so easily convinced.

XXXV
THE PIRATE

I N THE SUMMER OF A.D. 1081, as he mustered his forces to invade Byzantium, Robert the Fox was sixty-four years old—just a few years younger than I am now. I barely have the requisite energy to rise each morning and jot down these stray thoughts; the process exhausts me; I nap for an hour or two each afternoon, especially now that the heat has suddenly become unbearable. At sixty-four, one's inclination is to slow from a trot to a walk, not accelerate from canter to gallop! When I try to fathom a coeval with the preternatural stores of vigor compulsory to launch an all-out (and quite unnecessary!) invasion of the greatest empire in Christendom, my wits fail me—but then Robert the Fox was in all ways an outlier.

A Norman by birth, of obscure origin and humble pedigree, Robert was nursed and nourished by manifold Evil. Piracy was his first and favorite calling, a career that suited his lawless nature and informed his rapacious worldview forever after. Wholly incapable of being led, he split with his relations—the House of Hauteville, former mercenaries of the Byzantine Empire; we ourselves created these monsters!—at the tender age of fifteen, leading five knights of sufficient villainy, as well as some two score foot-soldiers, into the mountain peaks and caves and hills of Lombardy, from which base of operations he and his bandits set upon unsuspecting wayfarers, plundering horses, arms, gold, and other valuables, which he piled up into a great hoard. Murder, rape, and pillage occupied much of the next two and a half decades of his life. He become expert at all three.

When criminals, however base, acquire enough money and men they become respectable, if not truly noble, and by A.D. 1050, the Fox was as rich and powerful as any of the lesser aristocrats on the boot-shaped peninsula that was once the heart of the Roman Empire. How the mighty have fallen, as the Scripture says![83] By this time the Fox had carved out a piece of territory all his own, in Calabria, although he lacked an official title. No matter—his wealth and power attracted the attention of a buffoon called Reginald, the Count of Burgundy, whose military situation was so desperate that in A.D. 1052 he married his stunningly beautiful daughter Alberada to this glorified pirate. The couple produced two

---

[83] 2 Samuel 1:27.

children: a daughter, Emma, mother of Tancred (of whom more later); and a son, Mark, whom history knows as Bohemond.

Men do not change, warlike men least of all. A military commander who spends the first four decades of his life fighting, killing, plundering, and raping does not abandon these sinful inclinations at the altar. Once a murderer, always a murderer; once a plunderer, always a plunderer; once a rapist, always a rapist—as one who married a thirty-five-year-old career soldier, I can (alas!) attest to this last axiom personally. In the event, Robert kept not his vows of marriage, but forsook Alberada as soon as it was expedient to do so, consigning her to the convent[84] so he could instead take the hand of eighteen-year-old Sikelgaita, sister of Gisulf of Salerno, in A.D. 1058. This Sikelgaita was no ordinary princess. Tall of stature, powerful of frame, and mannish in mien, she resembled her daughter Helena; but unlike Helena, Sikelgaita was a fearsome warrior, as skilled as any man, who accompanied her new husband into battle. Nothing roused her blood more than unleashing her broad-sword on some unsuspecting knight, or trampling to death a misguided foot-solder with her warhorse. With this advantageous match, the Fox found himself the undisputed ruler of much of southern Italy, the scourge of emperors and popes;

---

[84]   One can only imagine how happy she was upon leaving him! (A.K.)

his name struck terror into the hearts of everyone from York to Damascus.

Robert, it should be noted, shared many similarities with my father Alexios. Both lacked the certitude that comes with being a first-born son (there is no such certitude when one is a first-born daughter, as I can unhappily relate) but rose to the highest power regardless. Both depended on guile and cunning to serve them at war, in both the fighting and in the ally-building. Both had children who figured prominently in their stories. Both detested the families into which they'd married. On elevation to higher office, both took what territories they had and expanded them (although Alexios was merely re-acquiring what was rightly his, not conquering outright lands to which he had no claim). Both had remarkable runs on the battlefield, rarely tasting defeat.

The common ground just described was highlighted in the talks in which the then-Great Domestic Alexios engaged with Raoul, the Norman envoy, to such a degree that Raoul adopted the position himself that Byzantium should be left alone, that Robert should confine his ambitions to Italy.

"The risks outweigh the rewards," the envoy explained, once back in Apulia.[85] "No one has ever sacked Constantinople. It has never been done, in many centuries of trying. Even under weak and ineffectual emperors it has stood fast. A competant

---

[85]   The Italian duchy that was Robert's base of operations.

general like Alexios would never allow those walls to be breached, no matter how pitiful the state of the army and the Treasury."

"Many things were never done before," the Fox coolly replied, "until they were."

"But my lord…"

"Silence, imbecile. My daughter was wronged, do you understand, *salop*? The slight must be avenged."

"It *was* avenged. Botaneaites has been removed, sir, and Alexios has reinstated Constantine Doukas, your daughter's betrothed, as his heir. If the Emperor died tomorrow—and with the seemingly boundless appetite these feckless Greeks have for insurrection, there's a good chance he might—Helena would ascend to Empress. I say again: You have no claim."

"I may not, but Michael does, Michael to whom I have sworn fealty."

Raoul faught back the urge to chuckle, as Robert's vows of fealty were as flimsy as cobwebs. "My lord," he said, "whatever you may protest in public, surely you know that the man you have been parading around Italy is not Michael. Michael is in Constantinople. I saw him there with my own eyes. He lives in a monestary with another monk, a pretty blonde one called Stephen, both in the Queen City and also in Ephesus, where he is the Metropolitan. He writes poetry. He gifted me one of his compositions, in fact."

"Raoul, you cur," the Fox said, "you disappoint me, and I must ask you to leave." Possessed as he was by the Devil, Robert nonetheless checked the urge to slay his subordinate on the spot. Had he done so, no one in the Apulian court would have been remotely surprised. Such was life under the thumb of this petty tyrant. When one blinds the brother of one's beloved wife for no reason other than to extort money and property from him, as this Robert did, there is no limit to the ruthlessness of which one is capable.

In that way, it should also be noted, he was not at all akin to my father. Although a soldier by training, and thus no stranger to bloodshed, Alexios was not by inclination a violent man. His preferred method of war-waging involved cunning, not slaughter, and he abhorred wars of attrition, as indeed most Byzantines did. Another difference: while my father took Maria as his lover even after marrying Irene, Robert's fidelity to his Amazonian wife Sikelgaita bordered on uxoriousness. He would sooner cast off his offending organ, to paraphrase the Gospels, than commit adultery.[86]

The difference most readily apparent to the eye, of course, lay in each man's physical appearance. Alexios was barrel-chested, on the short side, with dark curly hair and beard; his attractiveness, if we may call it that, derived from his charisma; my father had an aura of greatness around him that transformed an otherwise plain man into an handsome one. (As I myself bear a striking resemblance to

---

[86]　See Matthew 18:8-9.

my father—"a beardless Alexios" is how I am often described, to my eternal vexation—I'm well aware of his pulchritudinal shortcomings). As befitting an agent of the Dark Lord, Robert was devilishly, fiendishly handsome. He was a man of immense stature, surpassing even the tallest Byzantines; he would have towered over even Andronikos. He had a ruddy complexion, closed-cut fair hair, broad Atlas-like shoulders, and blue eyes that all but shot out sparks of fire. I never saw the man myself, but I've heard many remark that Robert's son Bohemond was his spitting image; Bohemond was far and away the most attractive man I've ever laid eyes on, and the mind fails to conjure an image of an one more so; but even a less-comely Bohemond, as the Fox must have been, is still a formidable sight to behold.

But enough frivolity. The Fox could have resembled an actual fox, and it would not have changed the state of his diabolical and devious mind. He'd spent the last two years preparing for battle—his own Norman Invasion, like William the Bastard's—but instead of some backwater isle, he would invade, and conquer, Byzantium itself! There was some logic to the scheme, however flimsy. In the south of Italy, Apulia and Calabria and Sicily, most of the inhabitants spoke Greek and took the Greek rite, rightly refusing to recognize the Pope of Rome as the supreme pontiff. If he, Robert, could take the purple, he could install his own puppet as Patriarch, and exert control over his subjects both temporally and spiritually. Liberated from the yoke of the Pope of Rome, he would be the most powerful personage in all of Christendom.

With regards to the authenticity of the itinerant Michael, there is no question that he was a fraud. For one thing, he looked nothing like the former *Augustus*: he had chestnut-brown hair, and a thinning beard, and the skin on his arms and legs was visible beneath his wisps of hair. For another, in his brief "reign" as Emperor in Robert's court, he availed himself of courtesans and strumpets, females all, which our Michael would never have done. Finally, the real Michael died in A.D. 1090, when I was six years old. On several occasions, I had the privilege of meeting him and his constant companion Stephen—a kindlier pair I've never met—and, impudent and curious child that I was, I asked him about this wild tale myself. He laughed good-naturedly, patted me on the head, and assured me that he had never been, and had no wish ever to go to Italy, and that the presumed Emperor-on-the-run was a lesser monk called Raiktor. Straight from the horse's mouth, as Homer says. So: the false Michael was indeed false. Whether the ruse was Raiktor's idea or Robert's I cannot say for certain, but it makes no difference; as soon as the opportunity presented itself, Robert seized it, decking the fraud out in silk and jewels and parading him around the peninsula for all to see.

"This is my kinsman," the Fox proclaimed. "He has been wronged! His crown stolen from him by filthy pretenders! We aim to get it back!"

While this made for good theater, the hoi polloi of southern Italy were largely (and unsurprisingly) unmoved. What did they care about the claim of some pretentious foreigner to the throne of a foreign Empire? Certainly their feelings for Robert the Fox did not veer towards affection. Fear, yes; love, not a jot. When his subjects failed to adequately rally to his cause, he simply forced them to assist. He was at all times a man of tyrannical and very sharp temper, and in this conscription he channeled the madness of Herod. Not being satisfied with the fine soldiers who had followed his fortune from the beginning, and were experienced in war, he recruited and equipped a new army, without any distinction of age, ability, or inclination. He collected every-one, whether thirteen or sixty-three, from all across Lombardy and Apulia, and pressed them into his service. There could be seen children and boys, as well as pitiable old men, who had never, even in their wildest nightmares, encountered a weapon, but were now clad in breastplates, carrying shields and drawing their bows most unskillfully and clumsily, and usually falling flat on their fearful faces when ordered to *hut-to*.

These requisitions were naturally the cause of unending trouble throughout the country of Lombardy; everywhere could be heard the lamentations of men and the weeping of women who shared the misfortunes of their unlucky kinsfolk. One would be mourning for her husband, who was too decrepit for service; another for her untried son; a third for her oafish brother, who was a farmer or engaged in some other peaceable line of work. Death awaited them all, grinning. This decree of Robert's was, as I have said, in the mold of Herod's madness, or even worse, for the latter only vented his spleen on babes, whilst the Fox condemned also young boys and old men. Yet, in spite of his recruits being absolutely unpracticed, Robert drilled them daily, and brought them into passable discipline. This ragtag collection of misfits and rejects comprised the army with which he hoped to topple Constantinople!

The network of spies and informants in the employ of Byzantium was vast and far-reaching, and Alexios knew of these plans long before they transpired. Fox or not, one cannot very well conscript half of Lombardy on the sly. His mother's strategy to enlist the aid of the Doge of Venice was successful. He was more than happy to lend his fearsome fleet in exchange for gold and, more importantly to the venal Venetian, trading concessions in the Queen City. When we marvel now at the wealthy state that wretched rat's nest of canals has become, let us not forget that Anna Dalassene and her son Alexios made Venice's unlikely ascension possible. But once again, I've gotten ahead of the story.

Earlier I have mentioned my father's inappropriately close and co-dependent relationship with his mother. The nature of this relationship did not much change upon his ascension. I know for a fact, for example, that they spent more than a few nights together in the imperial apartments after his coronation, sleeping in the same royal bed, *en deshabillé*. Nothing and no one could come between them—not even the lovely Maria of Alania.

"Your grand-mother was always paramount to Alexios," Maria told me later. "Always. In his eyes Anna could do no wrong. I liked her, too—there was much to admire about her, after all—but his love for her took forms that filial love does not often, and should not ever, take. He loved me too, once, but not like he loved his mother. No, no. In T'bilisi, he's what we would call…" and here she supplied a foreign idiomatic expression whose closest Greek approximation is "mommy's little lover boy."

This grotesque co-dependence revealed itself in the first few years of his reign, unsteady as they were. For as brilliant as he was in the battlefield, as brave and crafty and innovative, Alexios was almost comically inept off it. Charm and charisma he had in spades; what he lacked was patience, as well as the depth and breadth of knowledge necessary to effectively administer an empire. To ameliorate the situation, he assumed the position of commander-in-chief of the military and installed his mother as head of state. Vast and sweeping imperial powers he bestowed upon her. This Alexios achieved by a Golden Bull, signed in purple ink to make it official, just before he left the Queen City to join battle with the Fox. The document read more like *billet-doux* than imperial decree.[87]

---

[87] It read: ""Nothing is equivalent to a sympathetic and devoted mother nor is there any stronger bulwark, be it that danger is foreseen, or any other horror apprehended. For if she decides anything that decision will be a firm one; if she prays, her prayers will be a support and invincible guardians. Such a woman my saintly mother has proved herself actually to me, your sovereign, even from my immature years, and she has been mistress in everything to me, and nurse and upbringer. For though my mother herself was enrolled in the senate, yet her love for her son was her prime course and her confidence in that son was preserved intact. One soul in two bodies we were recognized to be, and by the grace of Christ that bond has been kept unbroken to this day. 'Mine' and 'thine,' those frigid words, were never spoken, and a matter of still greater import is that her prayers, of great frequency throughout her life, have reached the ears of the Lord and have raised me to my present position of sovereign. After I had taken the sceptre of empire, she could not bear to be dissociated from my work and from interesting herself in mine and the public weal, and now I, your sovereign, am preparing, with the help of God, for a sortie against the enemies of Rome, and with great care am collecting and organizing an army, yet I deem the administration of financial and political affairs the matter of supreme importance. And certainly I have found what is an unassailable bulwark for good government, that is, that the whole administration should be entrusted to my saintly and most deeply honoured mother. I, your sovereign, therefore decree explicitly by means of this same Golden Bull that, in virtue of her ripe experience of worldly matters (though she utterly despises them), whatever decrees she gives in writing whether the matter be referred to her by the president of the Civil Courts, or

That Alexios allowed such a mawkish deed into the official record is proof enough of his unholy

by the judges under him, or by any of all those others who prepare registers or demands or verdicts concerning public remissions of fines, these decrees shall have abiding validity just as if they had been dispensed by my own serene Majesty or ordered by my own word of mouth. And whatever solutions or whatever orders, written or unwritten, reasonable or unreasonable, she shall give, provided they bear her seal-the Transfiguration and the Assumption-these shall be accounted as coming from my sovereign hand. And in the mouth of him who, for the time being, presides over the financial department, as also with regard to promotions and successions to the judgeships of the higher and lower tribunals, and with regard to dignities, magistracies and gifts of immovable property, my holy mother shall have sovereign power to do whatsoever shall seem good to her. And further if any be promoted to judgeships or succeed to minor posts, if any receive the highest, lower, or lowest orders of merit, these they shall retain for ever unchangeably. And again with regard to increase of salaries, supplements to gifts, remission of taxes, and retrenchments and curtailments, these my mother shall settle absolutely. And to put it comprehensively, nothing shall be accounted invalid, that she shall order either by letter or by word of mouth. For her words and her commands shall be considered as given by me, your sovereign, and not one of them shall be annulled, but shall remain valid and in force for the coming years. And neither immediately nor in the future shall she ever be called to give an account or to undergo an examination by anyone whatsoever, either of her ministers or by the Chancellor for the time being, whether her decrees appear reasonable or unreasonable. In fine, whatsoever shall be done under confirmation of this same Golden Bull of that no account shall ever be demanded in the future." (A.K.)

devotion to Anna. In effect, he removed his own hands from the reins of Government and let his mother drive the Chariot of State. And this in spite of his having passed the years of boyhood and being of an age when ambitious characters like his are generally obsessed with the lust of power. He did certainly himself undertake the wars against the barbarians, and all the labors and difficulties connected with those, but the whole administration of affairs, the choice of civil officers and the accounts of the income and expenditure of the Empire: all of this and more he entrusted to Anna.

It is hard for me to be objective with regard to Anna Dalassene, but even with that caveat, I will allow that my father's assessment of her talent was not without foundation. I will give an example of what I mean. Contemporary histories often laud Alexios Komnenos for the shrewdness with which he led his allies. His foes were less ardent, grousing that eschewing combat to win wars was "womanly." While intended as disparagement, this fair characterization was nonetheless true in two important ways. First, while a man relying on brawn will defeat a woman in combat every time—or almost every time, as Amazonian warriors like Sikelgaita do (happily) exist—cleverness, canniness, and cunning are qualities that are at best gender neutral, and in my experience, which is to say generally, are displayed more prominently in the "gentle" sex. Put simply: Men may be stronger than women, but women are smarter than men. Second, in the case of my father, while Alexios was given credit for the sly intrigues that marked his reign, said intrigues were more often than not the product of a woman's infinitely more devious imagination. Alexios may have been the builder—and as a builder, an one on par with Herod or Justinian—but Anna Dalassene was the architect.

Alexios was a superb general, as we have seen—luck plays some rôle on the battlefield, admittedly, but no one prevails as often as my father did through luck alone—but haste was his *hamartia*. Too often he let impatience get the better of him. Anna knew this, and sought to mitigate the damage done by her son's tragic flaw through slow, patient intrigue.

Consider her scheme involving the Norman called Abelard, one of countless nephews of Robert the Fox, who was living in Constantinople at the time of the Frank's invasion, having fought many battles previously as a Byzantine mercenary. This Abelard was a rogue, simple and plain, and yet he was wealthy if not rich, sturdy if not handsome, vivacious if not young, and well-regarded among his barbarian cohorts if not beloved. Anna convinced Abelard to return to Apulia with a retinue of knights and a pile of imperial gold (most of what remained in the depleted Treasury, alas) and noisily stake his own claim to the territory. This she engineered through her enormous powers of seduction. She seduced him with money. She seduced him with power. And yes, she seduced him also with sex.

"It was incredible to behold," Maria told me later. "Here was a woman in her fifties, at an age when most of us are either dead or have one foot in the grave, and yet she was still able, through sheer force of will, to make herself attractive to this maladroit Norman. God knows what she did to him in the privacy of their bed-chambers, but when he emerged the morning after their first tryst, he was glowing like Venus on a clear night. He would have marched in full armor straight into the Propontis had she but made the insinuation. I've never seen a man so thoroughly charmed by a woman before."

Abelard took to his mission with ardor, promising not only to foment revolution in Apulia, but also to make Anna his consort if he proved victorious. Lesser mortals might have rested upon the laurels of this signature victory, but my grand-mother did not stop there. One can never have enough allies: this was her credo. She also enlisted the aid of the only other man in Christendom brazen enough to claim the title "emperor": one Henry, the King of the Germans. This Henry had a longstanding quarrel with the Pope of Rome; Robert the Fox, Anna knew, had pledged fealty to the latter, although the pirate did not respond to the Papal summons when the Pope's troops were routed by Henry's at Elster.[88]

News of this battle reached Constantinople anon. Anna Dalassene's shrewd analysis of the situation was this: Henry was more powerful than the Pope; he'd bested the Bishop of Rome on the

---

[88]   14 October, 1080

field of battle, and stood poised to sack Rome itself and thus remove him, Gregory, from the Holy See. Robert, meanwhile, had ignored a direct appeal for help from the Pope he'd sworn to protect; the next time, he would have greater difficulty extricating himself from his agreement. If Abelard succeeded in stirring up trouble in Apulia, and the Pope appealed to Robert for aid with the Germans, the Fox would have no choice but to call off his mission to Byzantium. Aware of this, Anna drafted a letter to the King of the Germans, proposing an alliance.

This would prove her signature achievement as Prime Minister, as we shall see.

On the isle of Corfu, some Byzantine troops were garrisoned—a small number, just enough to prevent the islanders from forsaking their imperial tributes. When they beheld the terrifying sight of Robert's fleet of ships approaching, black sails wisping in the wind, they surrendered at once. The bridgehead thus won, the Fox prepared to attack Dyrrachium,[89] the old Roman garrison town that marked the westernmost extent of the Via Egnatia, the overland highway leading east to Constantinople. If Dyrrachium fell, the Fox could muster his troops there and march toward the rising sun, raping and pillaging and conquering whatever he came across; there would be

---

[89]   Now the city of Durrës in Albania. Also known as Durazzo.

no further need for a sea crossing. Its defense, then, was essential. Robert must be kept off the mainland at all costs. For this reason Alexios dispatched his finest general, George Palaiologos, to Dyrrachium and put him in charge of its defense.

When he heard of the dashing Palaiologos's arrival in Dyrrachium, Robert at once had turrets constructed on the larger vessels, built of wood and covered with hides, and had everything necessary for a siege packed on board the ships. Horses and fully equipped cavalry he embarked on the cruisers, and with wonderful celerity he collected from all sides the full apparatus for war, for he was in a hurry to cross the sea. His plan was to surround Dyrrachium with battering engines both on the land- and sea-side, so as to strike terror into the hearts of the inhabitants and also, by thus hemming them in completely, to take the town by assault.

When his preparations were complete, Robert loosed anchor; the freight-ships, triremes, and monoremes were drawn up in the battle array of nautical tradition, and thus in good order he started on his voyage. Meeting with a favorable wind he struck the opposite shore at Avlona,[90] where he joined forces with his son Bohemond, who had crossed earlier and taken that port city by storm. The Fox now divided the whole army into two parts. With the one under his command he meant to sail to Dyrrachium;

---

[90]   Now the Albanian port city of Vlorë

the other half, under Bohemond, would march to Dyrrachium by land.

The numbers worked to Robert's favor; so too the war plans. Providence, however, had other allegiances. After the pirate had passed Corfu and was directing his course to Dyrrachium, he was suddenly caught in a most terrible storm—a mighty tempest that seemed to rage from nowhere, as if summoned by black magic. A heavy fall of hail and snow and the winds rushing down from the mountains churned up the sea violently. Then the waves rose and roared, and the oars of the rowers were broken off as they dipped them; the gale-force winds tore the sails to shreds; the yard-arms were snapped off and fell on the deck, and sixty-some-odd boats slowly sank into the vasty deep. And yet this was in summer, when the sun had already crossed the Tropic of Cancer and was hastening towards the Lion, just at the season which is called the Rising of the Dog Star (the same season, incidentally, when I am now writing this). A hail-storm in the middle of summer! Poseidon and Zeus joining forces against the Fox! The men—remember, these were raw recruits, not used to soldiering; many had never before been on a ship—were naturally all much disturbed and agitated. There was a frightful tumult, for they wailed and shrieked like women, and called upon the mercy of Jesus Christ to deliver them once again to dry land.

The storm did not waver, as if God were pouring out His wrath upon Robert's insolence and arrogance, and shewing him from the very start that the delusional plan would not succeed. Many of the ships were lost completely, crews and all; others were dashed upon the rocks and smashed to pieces. The hides covering the turrets became stretched by the rain, so that the nails fell out of their holes and the weight of the hides dragged down the wooden turrets, which in their fall swamped the ships. However, the boat which conveyed Robert was saved with much difficulty; and some of the freight-ships with all on board also miraculously survived intact. The sea threw up many of the men and quite a number of pouches and other oddments which the sailors had taken with them, and scattered them like flotsam and jetsam over the shore. The survivors buried the dead with due rites, and consequently became infected with the unspeakably horrible stench, as it was not easy for them to inter so many so quickly. Most of the provisions had been lost and probably the survivors would have died of starvation, had there not been an abundance of crops and fruits in the fields and gardens. (The Lord taketh away and the Lord giveth.)

Now the moral of all this should have been obvious—certainly my superstitious great-uncle Issac would have recognized the hand of the Almighty at work, and stopped the invasion—but none of these fatidic occurrences daunted our steely Robert, for he was quite fearless and only prayed, I believe, that his life might be spared long enough to allow him to make war.

God shook His divine fist at the Fox…and the Fox shook his right back!

In the event, nothing of what had happened deterred Robert from the object he had set for himself. When he had collected his whole army from land and sea—the survivors among his half of the army, stragglers from Brindisi, and troops on the march under Bohemond—he occupied the plain of Illyria, made camp, and waited for just the right moment to strike. The worst of it, he believed, was past.

He liked his chances.

After all, the Almighty tried and failed to strike him down; what chance did a mere *Augustus* have?

XXXVI
THE CONQUEROR

Not one inhabitant of Dyrrachium was unaware of the impending Norman invasion, and yet no one seemed to believe the news. That proud coastal city occupied a strategically vital position, and had been firmly in Roman hands since Caesar did battle with Pompey there a thousand years before. Who would dare attack it? Even when Alexios installed George Palaiologos, his best and most renown general, as commander in charge of its defense—a drastic move akin to dispatching Achilles to break up a skirmish of youths at a gymnasium—the hoi polloi failed to grasp the severity of the threat. "The Emperor is being over-cautious," they groused. "He is new. He will learn."

As it happened, my father had not done enough to prepare for the assault, and would pay dearly for this lapse in judgment.

One ship was spied on the horizon, then three, then a dozen. Twenty minutes later, the entire sea was freckled with ships, black sails snapping in the crisp nautical breeze like the swarm of locusts sent by God to smite Pharaoh. Anyone unlucky enough to be outside the city walls froze, cowering at the fearsome tableau. The threat was real! The warships would arrive anon! Hoes and rakes were cast down, sheep and goats left in the pasture, as Dyrrachenes dashed headlong for the creaking iron gates, for the stony cocoon of the age-old walls. Lookouts atop the parapets of the citadel anxiously awaited the ships' approach. Dogs barked ceaselessly, smelling the danger in the air. Was there enough grain in the silos? Enough water in the cisterns? War was coming, and fast. All could feel it.

And then, suddenly, the Normans made landfall. No sooner did the last wayward peasant cross the threshold, and the gates secured and locked, than a contingent of Robert's officers approached the ancient walls.

"State your business here," the crier, a rotund fellow with a booming voice and a gift for comedy, shouted from the parapet.

"For to restore to his proper place of honor our kinsman Michael, who has been expelled from his Empire," was the reply, in haltingly accented Greek. "For to punish the outrages inflicted upon him. For to avenge him."

George's spokesman knew exactly what to say next: "Very well. Bring forth this Michael. If we recognize him as the Emperor, we will without hesitation make obeisance to him and surrender the city."

At once, as if on cue, "Michael" appeared, decked out in magnificent robes and jewels. He was led out with an imposing escort, including a veritable harem of beautiful courtesans, and loudly acclaimed with all manner of musical instruments, including many clashing cymbals, which further disturbed the dogs.

"I am thine Emperor!" Raiktor cried—and his very voice, which spoke not in the manner of one raised in Constantinople, betrayed him. "I command thee: Open the gate!"

"Thou art emperor of vermin," the crier taunted, "and even the rats betray thee. Begone, mouse king, and take with thee thine whores. The air is thick with the saline reek of their slithery cunts. Or is that perhaps your fetid breath that so offends my nose?"

"The impudence! Open the gate, and I shall have that nose, and your tongue as well."

"No, I shall have *your* tongue, prince of rats, to wipe the shite from my arse!" Whereupon the saucy guards pelted Raiktor with rotten vegetables, and worse. A clump of horse manure the size of a human head landed on the false emperor's back, ruining his fine frock. "Michael" shook his impotent fist. "You shall pay!" he shouted, this monk from God knows where. "I shall hang thee from the thumbs in the square, as God is my witness!"

His duty duly performed, Raiktor returned to the camp, where he availed himself with his harlots, as was his wont. Robert meanwhile readied for the assault. Menacing were the siegecraft constructed by his engineers: creaky towers of knotted wood, eighty feet high, just waiting to be rolled into position. The Fox gave the order, and the siege began.

Dung was set afire and catapulted into the city. Archers volleyed flaming arrows over the walls. All of this was intended primarily as a diversion, so the men could move the siege towers into position, but by some quirk of fate, one of the arrows managed somehow to strike George Palaiologos on the side of the head. The dashing general snapped off the stalk but was unable to dislodge the sharp metal that had lodged itself in his skull. For the rest of the day he fought from the parapets with the arrow in his head—a symbol of his bravery, to be sure, but also a terrible omen.

The Norman siege tower comprised a series of steps and ladders, covered in cow hide as protection, and culminating in a wide wooden door four-score cubits off the ground. Said door opened outward, the better for the intrepid invaders to push through and onto the parapet. But George divined that by simply placing a log in the appropriate position, the door could easily be barred shut. As wave upon wave of Frankish soldiers filed into the tower, the ones at the top were squeezed helplessly against the door. The Byzantines simply doused the contraption with oil and put it to the torch. Thus did many a Norman meet his fiery end at the walls of Dyrrachium.

The Fox was nothing if not stubborn, and it took half a dozen such attempts before he conceded that his siege towers would not work. Thereafter, he stopped the assaults. Instead, he bivouacked his men in a crescent formation, just outside the range of archer-arrows, and bided his time. For cities are taken not by the strength of arms, but the vacancy of stomachs. When the stores of grain run out, when famished citizens begin slaughtering dogs for dinner, when brackish water makes half the population sick—that is how a siege is won. It is a most unpleasant business.

When Alexios arrived at Dyrrachium in the middle of October, two months after the siege began, he immediately took stock of the situation. In his assessment, Robert's forces comprised a poorly-trained lot that included men very old and very young, and any number of mercenaries and lowlifes. They were relatively healthy and well-rested, but also soft and inexperienced. The advantage, the Emperor decided, was his.

The day of his arrival, my father convened a meeting of his best generals to discuss strategy. Among those present was George Palaiologos, who had left his post inside the walls, against his better judgment, at Alexios's urgent insistence. (By this time the arrowhead had been removed from his skull, but he would forever after have a scar beneath his flowing hair.)

"Winter is coming," George said, "and these Franks, while well-led, are not really soldiers. We don't need to crush them, but rather hold our line until the cold weather forces them to retreat. Robert is not going to spend Christmas camped out on this dreary plain."

"But why *not* crush them?" Alexios posed. "As you say, they are not real soldiers. These men are soft. Should we not rout them thoroughly, chase them to the deep dark sea, break their spirit completely, and be rid of them forever?"

"The Fox is an agent of the Adversary," George said. "He is pure evil, and deviously smart. We must not underestimate him. We must not be hasty. You know as well as anyone that a great general can do wonders with even a flimsy force."

But my father was an impatient man, that was his fatal flaw, and he decided to ignore George's sage advice and attack at once. Thus the following morning, 18 October, A.D. 1081, the Norman and Byzantine forces enjoined in battle.

At first, Providence favored Alexios. The right flank of his army, comprised mostly of Varangian mercenaries wielding the massive battle-axes that were their weapon of choice, routed the Fox's left flank, which broke formation and fled to the wind-swept strand. At the Emperor's order, the Varangians zealously gave chase, hacking to bits any unfortunate Normans who stumbled and fell.

Sikelgaita, the mannish wife of Robert the Fox and the mother of our own Helena, met these fugitive forces at the shore. Astride her warhorse she cut a menacing figure; she was another Pallas, if not a second Athena; her steely gaze was enough to give them pause.

"How far will ye flee?" she thundered. "Will ye swim across the channel to Apulia? Art thou men,

or mice? Dost thou wish to die like this, in ignominious retreat, with arrows in your backs? Take up
your arms and fight! Be men!" And she took up her
spear and chased after the fleeing soldiers—there
was no doubt that she would delight in slaughtering
them—whereupon their nerve was recovered, and
they turned to face the charging Varangians.

And now the hurry of Alexios came back to haunt
him. So eagerly did his right flank give chase that,
like Diogenes's regiment at Manzikert, it became
separated from the main force, undermining the
position of the army entire. This was a grievous
error, a blunder of the highest order; it went against
every training manual in existence, and my father,
who'd read all of them a thousand times, and who
had made careful study of his brother Manuel's last
campaign, should have known better. Sword- and
spear-wielding Normans surrounded the Byzantine
flank and began to slowly and methodically slaughter
the Varangians, who were exhausted from swinging
the heavy battle-axes and running in their mail, and
lacked the requisite energy to properly defend themselves. Some of the Emperor's men, realizing their
fatal miscalculation, dropped their weapons and
took refuge in a nearby church, that of the Archangel
Michael, surrendering to the Franks and appealing
for mercy. The Archangel did not hear them, or else
chose to punish them for their sins. The barbarians
burned the church to the ground, consigning their
imperial war-prisoners to the flames.

Like a chessboard deprived of its queenside knight and bishop, the Byzantine right flank was now exposed. Robert the Fox shrewdly exploited this weakness, launching his offensive directly into the soft spot of the formation. He ordered his men to attack with lances couched under the arm, a tactic Alexios had never before encountered, and one that was brutally effective. Just like that, the rout was on. Many a noble Roman lost his life on the outskirts of Dyrrachium, among them Constantius, a son of the Emperor Constantine X Doukas; Nikephoros, the father of George Palaiologos; several cousins from the Houses of Doukas, Komnenos, and Dalassenos; and Oursel, the Red Rogue. It is difficult to determine the exact number of casualties, but I put the count at five mille—many more than were lost at Manzikert.

My father himself came perilously close to joining the ranks of the departed. When the battle lines broke down after the Fox's grand offensive, and chaos reigned, Alexios somehow became separated from his men. Half a dozen of the fiercest Kelts in the barbarian army, spears at the ready, gave chase, determined to hunt him down and send him to his Maker forthwith.

"I remember it like it was yesterday," Alexios recalled. (This was a story I heard many times growing up.) "I was surrounded by these vile Kelts, all of us on horseback, and one of their number lashed at me with his broad-sword. As he did, I leaned back as far as I could on my horse, so I was almost fully reclined upon the saddle. The blade sliced through the strap of my helmet, which fell to the ground, and grazed the side of my neck. The Kelt, seeing the blood and the fallen helmet and the prone position of my body, believed he'd struck a death blow, and arrested his pace. I then sprang back up and galloped off as fast as Dark Bay could gallop—that was the name of my steed, Dark Bay, a name given him by Bryennios, his previous owner. O, how God was with me that day! But they caught up to me eventually, the brutes, in this pass between two giant rocks, where the terrain forced me to to slow Dark Bay to a canter. There was no room for them to ride, so they dismounted and gave chase, half a dozen of them, on foot, poking at me with spears. Straight away I knew what to do. I leapt off the back of the horse and onto the top of one of the rocks—I just cleared it; for a spell my legs were dangling below me, but I was able to grasp a root and pull myself up. To this day, I still don't know how I was able to jump so high—it was as if the Archangel Michael had flown me to safety. Not that I was safe, not by any means. I had no helmet, and blood and sweat were spewing into my eyes. It was a horror. One of the Kelts, their leader, I know not his name, found a suitable place a few yards off, and began to clambor up the rock. Just as he was about to clear the top of the pass, I lopped off his head with my sword. This is not easy to do, you have to strike the neck in just the proper way, the chances of me achieving such a death blow were fantastically small, but as I said, God was on my side that day."

Here I would interrupt my father's retelling, as I always did: "With *one blow* you severed his *entire head*? I've seen professional executioners with axes unable to do that. And you did this with a *sword*?"

"I swear on the lives of my children," and he grinned at me, "I speak the truth. I allow that it was miraculous, but miracles do happen, good daughter. That is why it had the effect it did on the other Kelts, you see. One swing of my sword, and the brute's ugly head dropped to the ground between the rocks, and his body fell after."

"That must have been a sight to behold," I said, still not quite believing him.

"Verily it was! The sudden and decisive fall of their leader had a magical effect on the other barbarians, who stopped dead in their tracks as if they, too, had been beheaded. They simply could not conceive of such a big brute being cut down so easily. Silence descended on the tribe, they gazed upon me with fear and trembling, and I left them in the dust, my heart racing, my lungs straining to fill. By the time I could have my wounds tended to, I was in terrible shape. I almost bled out, the physician told me. 'You're lucky to be alive, sire,' he said, and I could tell by his grave expression that he meant it!"

Whether or not my father really beheaded the Kelt, he certainly managed to escape the Norman clutches—no small feat. But while this engagement represented a dramatic victory for the Emperor, the encounter took place, we must recall, when

Alexios was in full retreat. The Byzantines lost big that fateful day. Some fifty hundred men fell, as I mentioned, and the remains of the army were in tatters, in no condition to put up any sort of defense going forward. The road to Constantinople would be open to the invaders.

Robert the Fox took the imperial tent, helping himself to the provisions stored there. Fortunately my father was a temperate man, quite unlike the vainglorious Diogenes, and did not bring much booty with him to the field. But the tableau of the vile Frank seated at my father's throne, gorging himself on the imperial foodstuffs, was a travesty.

The besieged city held out for a few more months, well into the winter, this despite George Palaiologos being unable to re-enter the place and re-assume command. The Normans did not surrender their position with the cold, as the dashing general had predicted, but remained at the ready, like house cats waiting patiently by a mouse-hole. In February of the following year, freezing, starving, and parched, the Dyrrachenes were at "the end of their rope," as Homer says. A treacherous Venetian—there are no other kind!—opened the gates to the barbarians, and proud Dyrrachium fell.

Neither the sack of a coastal city nor the defeat of the Byzantine army satisfied the gluttonous ambition of Robert the Fox. He had higher aims: Constantinople itself. No sooner did he garrison Dyrrachium than he headed east along the Via Egnatia, ransacking the fertile lands, overrunning smaller towns and villages, and compelling the citizens to pay obeisance to Raiktor, the False Michael. Claudiana fell, then Masio Skampa. Not since Attila and his Huns had the Thessalian lands known such an adversary. Providence may have dashed his ships and allowed Alexios to escape, but the Fox seemed poised to triumph nonetheless. It was only a matter of time before he reached Constantinople. If not my father, the best general in the realm, who could stop him?

At Lake Ohrid, at an estate owned by his mother-in-law Maria of Bulgaria, my father rehabilitated from his injuries—both healing and licking his wounds. Ten of his twenty-five years had been spent on the battlefield, and in that remarkable decade he'd strung victory after victory together like so many triumphant pearls on a string. Dyrrachium represented his first taste of defeat, and that taste was bitter to the extreme.

"This is my Manzikert," he kept insisting to George, who'd traveled there with him. "We are doomed. Doomed!"

Hysterical as he sounded, his assessment was on target. He was wounded. The army was a shambles. And the Treasury was sorely depleted. In short, there was no extant army, no money to raise another, and no commanding general to lead it into battle. Not only that, but Robert was marching east at the head of a menacing invasion force that looked unstoppable.

"The only saving grace is that the Fox will not have my eyes," he said. "He will put me to the sword and have done with it. Bid me adieu now, George. I will meet my Maker anon."

"Enough," George shot back. "You expect me to show you pity? You are the *Augustus*! The Emperor of Rome, heir to Justinian and Constantine and Trajan! Act like it, or so help me God, I'll dispatch you myself!"

The strong rebuke from his friend seemed to wake him up. The next day he went riding, his first attempt since his injury. Then it was time to put his contingency plans into motion. First, the coffers must be replenished. At the behest of Anna Dalassene, his brother Isaac announced to the Synod that gold would be confiscated from the churches to finance the Byzantine defense, a decree that was met with a mixture of indignation and dread in the Queen City. Then a new army was recruited.

"We will defeat the Frank," Alexios declared, "or we will die in the attempt!"

Robert the Fox, meanwhile, was well into the interior of the Empire. At that moment his camp was at the lovely lakeshore town of Kastoria. He was busily engaged in war planning—the breaching of the Theodosian Wall was very much on his mind— when messengers arrived from the west with urgent news: Apulia was in revolt!

"You speak falsely."

"No, sir. It is the truth."

His kinsman, a bumbler called Abelard, had raised an army and declared himself king of the territory that had been the Fox's base of operations for almost half a century.

"Abelard?" Robert thundered. "That little pipsqueak? *Abelard?*"

But there was more. An urgent summons had come from Rome: King Henry and the Germans were at the gates, threatening to forcibly remove the Pope from office. Robert's aid was required immediately.

"Fools!" the Fox shouted, at no one in particular, and therefore at everyone.

The careful reader will recall that neither Abelard's revolt nor Henry's Papal adventure was an accident; both had been precipitated by the careful and prescient machinations of the Prime Minister, Anna Dalassene (who had, in light of Abelard's surprising success in Apulia, allowed herself to imagine marrying him and being queen of that backwater domain). Cleverness had triumphed over brute force, intrigue over war, and gold over iron. Under the suddenly-changed circumstances, Robert had no choice but to turn the invasion force over to his son Bohemond, and make his way home.

Not that salvation was immediately at hand. Replacing Robert with Bohemond was akin to substituting Mars for Jupiter. Although the former proved more formidable than the latter, even at his advanced age, both were gods among men. It would take another year before the Normans would be repulsed from Thessaly, at Larissa.

Even this victory, resounding as it seemed, was achieved only by aid both terrestrial and divine. First, Anna Dalassene dispatched Helena, Bohemond's half-sister and Constantine's betrothed, with an offer of a hundred mille gold *solidi* to withdraw. No sooner did Helena arrive than the son of the Fox fell victim to a pestilence that was sweeping through his camp. While the sturdy Bohemond survived, he was in no condition to properly lead an invasion, and so in the late spring of A.D. 1083, he returned with his half-sister to his father's Italian principality, bearing wealth beyond his wildest imagination— wealth, it should be noted, appropriated from the churches of Constantinople. The threat was no more. Once again, gold had succeeded where iron had failed.

XXXVII
THE GHOST QUEEN

ALEXIOS HAD BEEN BADLY WOUNDED AT DYR-RACHIUM—more so than he realized. For months after, he suffered from the profoundest headaches, as if Minerva were about to burst forth from his skull; at times the pain was so intense that his vision was blurred. Too, fatigue gripped him. Sleep became a practical necessity. He yearned to return to the battlefield, to command his troops, to know again the pleasures of the camp. But his body would not allow it. With no other recourse, he turned the reins over to George Palaiologos and went home to the Boukoleon, where he was nursed to health by his wife, Irene.

"It was hard for me to see him in such a state," Maria told me later. "His allure lay in his manliness, his charisma, his vivacity, and none of those traits were on much display as he convalesced. He looked older, he looked beaten, and the gash on his neck was unsightly. In short, he was in no condition to be amorous. Not that we could have done much even if he were—his wife did not leave his side, especially when I came calling. Like an old blind dog, or a crusty barnacle upon the hull of a creaky ship, she sat there day and night. By Eastertide his health had improved, and we resumed our liaisons. But things were not the same. He enjoyed himself as he always did, but his heart was not fully in it. This I attributed to the wound. I knew he'd come back to me. He just needed more time to restore his strength—that is what I told myself, and what I desperately wanted to believe."

My mother corroborated Maria's account. "I did not much like your father," Irene explained. (This particular interview took place much later, when we were here at the convent together, years after Alexios had passed.) "He'd treated me like a cur, and I was angry with him. But when he came back from the front, wounded…something awakened in me. I was his wife, and as such, duty compelled me to care for him. I put all my energies into this, neglecting my other court responsibilities to stay at his bedside. I was, if I may say so myself, a very good nurse. And something magical happened. When we were first wed, as I've mentioned before, he viewed me with contempt, as if I were my own father in female form. And after Andronikos passed, he simply ignored me. I was his Ghost Queen. But during those months together, after his defeat at Dyrrachium, he came to regard me as my own person, as one worthy of affection. His stance toward me softened. I won't say he fell in love with me, because I do not believe that man ever loved me as he did Maria, or, heaven forfend, his dear mother. But he became fonder of me, he certainly came to appreciate me, and he began to treat me with kindness." Here my mother, who was now very old, broke into the smile of a little girl. "If that barbarian had not struck him with the sword, you would never have been born!"

The summer of A.D. 1083, Maria told me, was the happiest season she'd ever known. By that time, she was fully adjusted to her life as Dowager Empress, and had even come to prefer it to her former rôle. She enjoyed all the perquisites of life in high office—the palatial residence, the vast wealth, the jewels, the prestige, the respect of the court and the hoi polloi—without any of the anxiety that marked her uneasy life in the purple. The Emperor was her lover, which was never the case when she was *Augusta*, and she had more influence over him than she'd had over her two husbands. She spent her days reading, writing, and hosting literary salons, none of which she had time for as Empress. Above all, her boy Constantine was co-Emperor and heir to the throne. That was not likely to change, so long as Alexios did not have a son of his own—that, indeed, was her greatest fear, and inspired her to feign passion even on nights when she did not feel it. So long as Maria consumed all of her adoptive son's libidinal energies, her actual son would take the purple one day. It was simple as that. Or so she thought.

One sunny day in late August, a week before Alexios was to leave for his first military engagement since Dyrrachium, the longtime lovers lay on silken sheets on the strand, watching the ships navigate around the Boukoleon landing. Not a cloud dotted the perfect blueness of the noonday sky. They'd been out there for a few hours, alternating between the sun and the shade of palm fronds borne by servants, when Irene came running toward them. Maria and Alexios shaded their eyes with their hands and looked up at her.

"Forgive my imposition," Irene said, out of breath from the exertion, but beaming. "I've just come from the midwife, and I bring good tidings: I am with child!" And she watched with some satisfaction as the blood drained out of Maria's pretty face.

Alexios must have known that this would upset his lover, but he made no attempt to conceal his joy. He jumped to his feet and embraced his wife, covering her forehead with kisses, shouting to all who could hear that he would soon be a father.

Maria, for her part, managed to stem her panic. The little brat in Irene's womb could spoil everything, as she well knew. Alexios would never permit Constantine to take the throne ahead of his own bouncing baby boy, the fruit of his own prodigious loins and one *born in the purple*, no less! And so she too rose and embraced Irene—this had all the warmth of two gladiators shaking hands before a fight to the death.

"Isn't it delightful?" My mother's eyes never wavered from Maria's, and she took particular relish in remarking, "You're going to be a *grand-mother*."

"Yes. Isn't it wonderful."

As soon as she could leave tactfully, Maria went directly to the Hagia Sophia, and spent the next six hours on her knees before an icon of Jesus Christ, praying that the baby, if it lived, would be a girl.

BOOK TWO

THE LOST QUEEN

Volume One:
My Early Years

A.D. 1083-95

I

THE
PORPHYROGENNETOS

T HE SUMMER SOLSTICE IS TODAY, I believe, or maybe it was yesterday? Basil the Physician would have known for sure, but his "heretical" body has long since been consigned to the flames. (A question for the philosophers to argue over at the next salon: Can one descend to Hell if one denies its existence?) In another week it will be the Feast of Saints Peter and Paul.[91] After that the relentless north winds will abate, and the summer swelter will descend upon Constantinople like the Plague of Justinian. Chilled by the wind or baked by the sun: the binary climes of our intemperate metropolis.

In my youth, I disdained the breezeless broil of July and August, but now the stifling heat will bring

---

[91] I always found it curious that two luminaries of such enormous stature have to share a feast day! (A.K.)

me some respite, for always I am cold. My fingers are icicles clumsily gripping at the quill, my hand trembles, shaky are the lines on the page. Perhaps this is the year that the summer will not warm me. Perhaps my days of warmth are over, and only the dirt will bring relief.

Let me write faster, then: the only recourse left to me. When I have finished this second and ultimate history, to that dirt I shall return.

Late in the night of 30 November, A.D. 1083, Alexios Komnenos returned to Constantinople from the Western front. He'd spent much of the previous three years at the head of the imperial army, fighting all manner of foe foreign and domestic. He was fortunate to have such ample opportunity to lead the troops. In the persons of his irrepressible mother Anna Dalassene, the Prime Minister, and his dutiful brother Isaac, the *Sebastokrator,* who proved infinitely more capable as an administrator than he'd ever been as a general, the Emperor found proxies both formidable and loyal enough to dissuade any and all Constantinopolitan rivals challenging the throne during those lengthy absences—an anomaly in the deceit-riddled annals of Rome, and a principle reason why his thirty-seven-year reign was one of the most durable in those same annals.[92] Indeed,

---

[92] Six years longer than Constantine, and one year short of Justinian. (A.K.)

the three Komnenoi, the mother and her two sons, complemented one another so seamlessly—three sides of a right triangle of which my father was the hypotenuse; one greater than the others, yes, but all three interdependent—that an impartial observer would suspect that Providence had created the troika for the singular purpose of imperial rule. If Anna were a typically submissive woman, if Isaac were not such a battlefield bumbler, if Alexios were remotely interested in diurnal governance—or if their older brother Manuel had survived, to say nothing of their father and Anna's husband—history would read quite differently!

So: my father returned late in the night of that last day of November to find his waifish wife so immensely pregnant that her silhouette resembled a pumpkin walking upon forelegs of twig.

"Looks like I got here just in time. You're about to burst."

"I was waiting for you," Irene whispered, patting her bloated belly. "Your *son* was waiting for you."

"Get some rest," he commanded, as if this imperial chrysobull could dispel her terrible night sweats and perpetual urge to vacate her bladder, and magically find a position for her to find sufficient comfort to rest. Then he retired to his own chambers and fell into a deep and dreamless sleep.

The next morning, he summoned Maria to the Map Room, in which he'd installed an even more sumptuous divan—ostensibly to rest his sore feet, as he clumsily explained to Anna Dalassene, who thought the choice of furniture odd; this was the hallowed historical chamber in which wars were planned!—although its actual purpose, as his mother and everyone else well knew, was to make more comfortable his unsavory dalliances with his other "mother," Maria of Alania. He could not marry his lover, yet he could entertain her in the requisite luxury.

But on that particular morning, Maria was in no mood for *amour*. Although Alexios had written to her during his time away, as he always did—how I wish she'd shared those letters with me ere she furiously fed them to the flames!—words on a page, however poetical or heartfelt, were insufficient to the occasion. Every day of his long absence made her less sure of her position, tenuous even on its best day. She needed reassurance, as women will.

"My peach," Alexios said, playfully stroking her hair. "Whatever's the matter?"

Could he really not know? Perhaps not. The ability to fully empathize with another's position was sorely lacking in my father. Such subtlety of feeling puzzled him. His own feelings were a prism through which all experience was reflected. He thought only of himself, not because he was selfish *per se*, but because he simply could not think otherwise. Some birds cannot fly.

"Well…" While she did not wish to disclose how much anxiety the imperial pregnancy had brought her, the stakes could not be higher. A bouncing baby boy, born in the purple, would likely shatter her dreams of Tino's ascension to the throne.

Contrariwise, Irene and her detestable spawn dying in childbirth would help realize them. Not that Maria prayed for such an outcome; that would be sinful, this she recognized. But news of a dead Empress would not be unwelcome. She found herself staring at Irene's frail little-girlish body, with its belly ballooning uncomfortably out, and wondered at its capabilities, its limitations. Would the whelping wound her mortally? Would God smite her and her unborn brat?

"I have missed you so," Alexios cooed, his lips at her ear, his whiskers tickling her soft and sensitive lobe.

At this point, they had been lovers for years. He knew how to make her body respond as he wanted, just as he'd known how to coax Dark Bay, his warhorse, to a more furious gallop. He nibbled at her ears, her cheek, her neck. He rubbed her shoulders with mighty hands that had slain many enemies. When he felt her tension begin to wane, he slid down to his knees, spread her goose-pimpled legs, and made like a pig hunting for truffles. Years of dutiful practice and patient training made him expert in this obscene operation which flummoxes most men who dare attempt it. With savage fingernails Maria clutched at his curly locks—grayer than they once were, and thinning at the top, but still a formidable head of hair. At one point she yanked so hard that he gasped. She was on the verge of a tentative *jouissance* when the bumbling astrologer, the ancient Antiochene, made his ill-starred ingress.

"What news?" the *Augustus* cried, withdrawing his ruddy face from between her legs, his beard shiny with her nectar. (Maria, for her part, screamed an obscenity in her native Georgian, but made no move to cover her shame; let the old fool behold her wonders!)

"The child is born," the old man said, unabashed by the interruption, as if walking in on the Emperor so engaged was a commonplace. "And Your Excellency, the stars are a thing of wonder!" He went on to analyze the natal chart of the Emperor's first-born and heir to the throne. "The position of Mars in the first house, so close to the horizon…Your Grace, you could not ask for better placement." Mars, the astrologer explained—although the Emperor was himself familiar with Ptolemy, and did not require remedial instruction—was ruler of war, and thus its position on the Ascendant indicated an assertive, self-confident aspect well-suited to command. This child was a natural-born leader, the sort of man others would happily follow into battle, even into certain death. "Not unlike yourself," he added, in a tone of well-practiced obsequity.

The Emperor nodded, and the old sycophant continued: "And Jupiter, also so close to the horizon…Jupiter is the Great Benefic. This is a lucky child, Your Grace. Lucky indeed."

"It is a son, then?"

"Yes, sire."

"This pleases me," the Emperor said. "Thank you, sirrah. That is all."

He moved to follow the old fool out of the Map Room, but Maria bid him stop. "Finish," she commanded, her voice as icy as he'd ever heard it, and on the verge of breaking. "Do not leave me in such a state."

"What's that?" He glanced at the door, where his attention if not his heart had left with the astrologer, but to placate Maria, fell back upon his knees and picked up where he'd left off.

This time she did not dig her nails into his scalp. She did not move at all, in fact, just lay back still, with her eyes sealed shut. She did not make a loud exclamation, as was her wont, at the apex—indeed, he only knew she had finished when she did not detain him further—and Alexios found it strange that when he withdrew, she was shaking like a wind-blown leaf on the Map Room couch, her eyes welled with tears.

"At that moment, I had no wish to live on," Maria told me later. "To continue to exist seemed at once foolish and humiliating. I considered *mortem sibi consciscere*.[93] Why not hurl myself off the terrace? I am grateful to the Lord for granting me the strength to check that horrible impulse. And look at how I was rewarded! With you, my peach!" And she petted my matt of unruly black hair, so similar in look and feel to my father's own.

---

[93]   One of several Latin expressions for suicide.

Needless to say, the astrologer was wrong, as astrologers too often are. Irene's child was a girl. Was me. And no outcome, not even the tragic demise of me and my mother, could have proved more beneficial to Maria's lofty ambitions. A princess posed no viable threat to take the purple herself—in ten centuries, a woman had never once assumed sole possession of the throne.[94] Not only that, but the baby girl could be betrothed to her son Tino, cementing his status as co-Emperor and heir apparent. (The radiant dowager Empress would have preferred a more comely baby, to be sure, one that did not bear freakish resemblance to a gorilla, but she was happy enough with this particular gift horse to keep her disappointment in check.) This is exactly what came to pass: Alexios immediately announced the engagement of his newborn daughter—of me, Anna Komnene—to his "mother's" son, the co-Emperor, the eight-year-old ne'er-do-well Constantine Doukas. Legally, this was incest, but the Patriarch, by now too exhausted by my father's shenanigans to raise a fuss, shrugged and granted the match.

Tino was my first and only fiancé. Both of my actual marriages happened too quickly, alas, to allow for the customary period of engagement.

---

[94] It could be argued that Irene of Athens ruled by herself from 797-802, during the Iconoclast crisis, but her son Constantine VII, whom she had blinded and imprisoned, was nevertheless alive during that span.

II
THE MOOR

I N PRACTICAL TERMS, MY IMMEDIATE BETROTHAL meant that, in keeping with long Byzantine tradition, I would spend my early childhood not with my own mother, but with my mother-in-law-to-be: Maria of Alania. My engagement was announced the day after I was born, and after a few weeks in the dutiful care of the gaggle of wet-nurses at the Boukoleon, I was removed, with that same nursery gaggle, to the Mangana Palace. The arrangement was unusual in that I was still a newborn, but hardly without precedent, and suited the seventeen-year-old Irene just fine. The maternal instinct did not come naturally to her, she did not particularly like babies, and she furthermore had no desire to spend the remainder of her prime years confined to the nursery. When the noisy circus left, when the cacophony ended, Irene breathed a long sigh of relief.

"It wasn't that I didn't love you," she told me later. "But I was very, very young, and my life until that point had not been easy. I took great pride and pleasure in performing my imperial duties, tedious and silly as they were. None of it was important, don't get me wrong—your grand-mother would never cede any actual power to a Doukaina—but I felt it was necessary work just the same, and I could not bear to give it up. And while Tino was only eight years old, or maybe he was nine, it was already clear to me that he lacked the necessary mettle to be an able emperor—or, indeed, emperor at all. Your father was blind to his faults because he was in love with Maria, but I saw them clearly. Even then, I knew he was no good. Not cruel, not evil, but inept, and slave to his petty desires. A wastrel. He reminded me of my own father, your grand-father, ruined by drink and dice and wanton women. To me, Tino's weaknesses were a good thing, because they meant that *you* could take the crown. And I wanted *you* to be the one, Anna. I didn't care that you were a girl. I wanted *you* to succeed Alexios when he passed. At the time, I did not believe I would have any more children, at least not with your father—ours was never an amorous union, as you know—so it had to be you. Moreover, I thought it was your fate to do so. I thought it was Divine Providence. I thought it was written in the stars."

This was not just a quaint expression. For it was at this time that Irene developed a keen interest in astrology, an interest nurtured masterfully and self-servedly by the new court astrologer, one Saddiq.

The careful reader will recall that the hoary Antiochene, who despite his vast intellect and wealth of stellar knowledge could not correctly determine my newborn sex, was removed to Proti the day after I was born, once my father learned of the gravity of his error. Alexios was not inclined to replace him, his faith in horoscopy forever shattered, but Anna Dalassene insisted upon the appointment. "How will we know which days are favorable and which are not," she argued, "without a learned astrologer reading our charts?"

The new star-gazer hailed from Cordoba, in al-Aldalus,[95] where he'd studied under the celebrated Moslem philosopher Ibn Hazm.[96] Saddiq was twenty-nine years old when he took the position—the exact date of his Saturn Return, or so he claimed—a full fifty years younger than his dotardly predecessor. He was a Moor, conspicuously tall and regally handsome, beardless and bald, with skin as black as the night sky he so earnestly scrutinized. He looked like no one else in Constantinople— indeed, like no one whom any of the insular court had ever laid eyes on. He may as well have fallen into the Hippodrome from one of the planets that appeared in his charts. His Greek was flawless, his voice deep and rich, and he was egregiously charming. In Cordoba, it was said, he'd had four wives,

---

[95] Today's Spain.

[96] Abū Muḥammad ʿAlī ibn Aḥmad ibn Saʿīd ibn Ḥazm (993-1064).

but he divorced all of them when he converted to Christianity and came to Constantinople.[97] This was easy to believe, as the women at court fawned over him. The extraterrestrial novelty of his physical appearance drew them to him initially, and his genius for seduction held them in his thrall.

"Saddiq had quite a reputation," Maria recalled, and I could tell from her tone of voice that she did not like him. "He'd take your hand in his and read your palm, and he'd spout off all this mumbo-jumbo and make you feel like the most important and special person who ever walked the Earth, like the Lord would select *you* to give birth to the second Christ. Unsurprisingly, the ladies ate this up, and he took full advantage. His penchant for love affairs was prodigious—in a word, Jovian."

While Maria could appreciate the company of the sweet-talking Moor, she saw his act for what it was, an act, and never herself fell for his ample charms. The same could not be said of my mother. Irene was plain in appearance, remember: tall and slender but unremarkable, and, as she would later remind me, very young. She was married to a man who did not love her, who was not attracted to her, who alternated between forcing himself upon her and ignoring her, who'd been kind to her only during one fleeting period after a near-fatal injury, when

---

[97]   Islam in its primitive ignorance is as lenient toward polygamy as it is toward divorce; its practitioners are basic savages. (A.K.)

his kindness would have extended to anyone who nursed him, however ugly. The high rank itself is an aphrodisiac to some men—who would not consider making love to the *Augusta*?—but most of the lecherous fellows at court wisely calculated that the risk of angering Alexios was not worth the reward of a dalliance with his uncomely wife. Consequently, Irene was completely deprived of male attention, and thus highly susceptible to being charmed by it, in the way that an etiolated plant will stretch desperately for a stray beam of afternoon sunlight. Saddiq recognized this desperation immediately, and unlike the Constantinopolitans, had no fear of raising the imperial ire. He knew that the Emperor would not harm him for such a transgression; he'd read it in my father's chart!

But it was *my* horoscope, not Alexios's, that so captivated Irene's attention—and thus, by extension, Saddiq's. "In the *Appendices*, Ptolemy writes:[98] 'Observe the creation of the first king of any dynasty, for if the Ascendant at the creation should agree with the Ascendant of the nativity of the king's son, he will succeed his father.' Your good husband the Emperor was crowned at high noon on Easter Sunday, when Virgo was ascending. And look here," and here he leaned very close to the Empress, so

---

[98] Almost certainly the astrologer was reading the paraphrase of the original manuscript by the great early Medieval philosopher Proclus the Successor (ca. 412-485), who hailed from Constantinople.

close she could feel the warmth of his skin through her purple silken gown: "Anna your daughter boasts the self-same Ascendant: Virgo."

"Does that mean that she will succeed Alexios?"

"That is what the stars suggest, Your Highness." (How it thrilled her that this tall, gorgeous intellectual addressed her so submissively!)

Any half-wit could readily discern the flaws with the Moor's proclamation. For one thing, the mundane event cited in the foretelling—the "creation of the first king," as stated in the thirtieth *Appendix* of Claudius Ptolemy—is not a single, specific moment. When was Alexios "created?" When the soldiers proclaimed him *Augustus*? When Botaneaites abdicated? At the coronation? Even if, by some wild coincidence, all of those events conspired to take place during the two-hour window each day when Virgo was on the horizon, there is still a one in twelve chance that my Ascendant would match— long odds, to be sure, but hardly impossible ones. And yet the normally level-headed Irene believed what the Moor told her as fervently as she venerated the Virgin Mother. One cannot argue against faith; faith trumps reason, sure as a sickle slices through the grass.

Under Saddiq's patient and dedicated tutelage, Irene learned of the esoteric mysteries of the heavens. There was so much arcane knowledge to absorb: attributes of the various planets, signs, houses, angles, and transits; benefics and malefics; tropical, equinoctial, fixed, and bicorporeal signs; triplicities, exaltations, rulerships, and accidental dignities; conjunctions, oppositions, squares, trines, sextiles, and quincunxes; the polarities of hot and cold, and of wet and dry; and any number of observations and theories gleaned from his decade and a half of dedicated study. He also introduced to her, and to the Byzantines generally, the so-called Arab lots—points determined by the sum and the difference of cardinal points, which were, he claimed, essential to proper sooth-saying.

"You see, Your Highness, astrology has two separate but equally essential components," Saddiq explained. "The first is the careful observation of the night sky, and how the heavenly bodies move about the fixed and motionless earth. This requires patience, and it requires knowledge, but the science at its heart is undeniable. The sun rises every morning and sets every evening. The phases of the moon do not change."

"And what is the second component?"

"Interpreting, and in turn predicting, the effect these celestial motions have on us as individuals. The former is a science; the latter is an art; both are difficult to master."

"How can it be so?" Irene asked. "How can the movements of distant Saturn reckon our native personality?"

"My answer to that question is simple: how can it not? Consider, Your Highness: the Sun contributes to the regulation of all earthly things. He engenders the four seasons, bringing to perfection the embryo of animals, the buds of plants, the spring of waters, and the alternation of bodies; and his daily progress operates other changes in light, heat, moisture, dryness, and cold. The moon, being of all the heavenly bodies the nearest to us, also dispenses much influence. By the changes of her illumination, rivers swell and are reduced. The tides of the sea are ruled by her risings and settings. And plants and animals are expanded or collapsed as she waxes and wanes. I'd wager that the cycle of your own royal body is aligned with the moon's."

At this, Irene blushed, for she had realized years ago, and with some astonishment, that her menses came regularly as the moon waxed full.

"So you see," the Moor continued, his eyes twinkling like Venus on a clear night, "if sun and moon exert so much obvious power over us, how could anyone but a fool argue that Jupiter and Mars do not?"

On this particular day, they were in the Empress's Loge at the Hagia Sophia, chaperoned by a yawning pair of Varangian Guard and two waiting-ladies, both busy with their knitting. None were paying attention to the conversation, nor did any of the group notice that the astrologer was sitting so close to Empress that their shoulders grazed.

"My husband does not believe it," Irene said. "He did not want to bring you here. My mother-in-law insisted."

Saddiq nodded sagely. "I respect his judgment," he said. "Plenty of skeptics do not believe. And it's not difficult to see why. Astrology demands the greatest study and a consistent attention paid to a multitude of different aspects. As all persons who are but imperfectly practiced in it must necessarily commit frequent errors, it has been supposed that even such events as have been verily predicted have taken place by chance only, and not from any cause in nature. But it should be remembered that these errors arise not from any deficiency in the art itself, but from the incompetency of untutored persons who pretend to exercise it. Manzikert, for example: my predecessor, the Antiochene, foretold of the catastrophe. I have his papers that prove it. But the Emperor Diogenes did not heed his warnings."

"You speak falsely!"

"Not at all. It was a foolish and distorted reaction to banish the man for mistaking the sex of the baby, especially in the case of the princess Anna. Gender is not something that can be divined from the stars; his ancient ears betrayed him, not his wisdom."

"*Especially* in the case of the princess? Whatever do you mean?"

By Saddiq ignored her question, adroitly changing the subject. "There is something else he predicted."

And here he showed Irene a date, scrawled in a shaky hand on a piece of parchment. A frisson of excitement coursed down her spine at the prospect of a shared, and possibly forbidden, secret.

"November the first, *Anno Domini* 1096," she read. "All Saints' Day."

"Commit it to memory," the Moor told her. "For on that day, the Emperor Alexios will die."

III
THE INFANT

I WAS A FUSSY BABY, they tell me, a bundle of colic and gas that refused to properly latch—and when finally I did find purchase, the tooth I was born with cut savagely into the teat. This natal tooth was the subject of some controversy among the nurses, all of whom espoused some cockamamie theory of its larger meaning. "Death by violence," Rona told Maria. "The child will grow up to be a killer." Others had similar variations on this bloody theme. Patricide, matricide, suicide. Only the midwife offered a more pacifistic take: "Fear not. It only means that the Empress will be pregnant again soon," she said—presciently, as it happened.

What I'm about to reveal next I have never before told anyone. It is a subject that fills me with shame and embarrassment; given that I am the only living person burdened with this particular knowledge, the temptation is strong to redact it from this history, and let it die with me. But no, I swore to tell all, and because this detail, I think, provides no small insight into my character, I must relate it, however loath I am to do so.

The tooth, alas, was not the only peculiarity about the newborn Anna Komnene. I was a gigantic baby, corpulent and long—unusual for a girl—and matted in dark black hair. In that hirsute lining, I bore resemblance to the erstwhile Emperor Michael, who was, after all, my blood relation.[99] There was hair even upon my face, I'm told, a visage which was already the spitting image of my father's: rugged, severe, not at all soft or pretty. My eyes were black as coal, my lips thin and pale, my skin splotchy. Then there was the anatomical curiosity between my legs: the protrusion situated above the pudenda that looked for all the world like a baby carrot—a comparison later made independently by both Maria and Irene. The male member in macabre miniature? Or the largest womanly bit in Christendom? Other signs indicated that I was a girl, albeit an extremely boyish one—this is what the midwife said—but what was the meaning of this bizarre formulation? (As Saddiq remarked to Irene, the Antiochene astrologer was not as far off as it seemed, you see, in reporting my masculine sex to the Emperor. How history would have been different had he not been banished, and the Moor not come to replace him!)

---

[99]   First cousin once removed.

Immediately there rose a debate about what to do. Some believed that the growth—that is what they took to calling it: The Growth—should be pruned away at once, while I was still an infant, and thus more likely to survive its excision. The new astrologer was of this mindset, and his influence, as we have seen, held great sway over my mother. Moslems mutilate their babies as a matter of course, he explained, as a sign of their covenant with their bumbling god, called Allah; as with the barbarous Jews, the foreskin of every newborn boy is sliced away, and many of their baby girls undergo a similar procedure, as female circumcision is held to promote modesty and virtue. Islam is the retrograde faith of Abraham, we must bear in mind, and mutilation of this kind is far less savage than that to which said Biblical forefather was prepared to subject Isaac his son. Or so went Saddiq's jumbled justification for his culture's institutionalized butchery—but it was enough for Irene, who was inclined to agree with the learned Moor. Alexios had no opinion on the matter; his interest in me waned when my true gender was divined, and would not reignite until I was older and more possessed of womanly charms, such as they were. But Maria, who by that point had already taken possession of me, flat-out refused to subject me to the procedure.

"Anyone raising a knife to my daughter-in-law will be executed on sight," she announced. And while she may not have had the legal right to have this done, no one felt strongly enough about the matter to test her authority, thank God.

To be fair, her motives were not purely altruistic. If I did not survive the operation, Tino's future would be much less assured. So the outrage she displayed when the subject was broached was, perhaps, somewhat feigned. Nevertheless, I remain grateful for her protection, and grateful also for the privilege of my royal birth. Were I not *porphyrogennetos*, were I some tanner's daughter with the same freakish anatomy, I would have been left for dead in the forest, food for the wolves.

All of my earliest childhood memories involve Maria. This is to be expected. Not only did I live with her at the Mangana Palace, but the dowager Empress did not outsource my care to the aforementioned gaggle of wet-nurses, but saw to it personally. With the aid of some elixirs prepared for her by the midwife, and also by what must have been hours of painful if dutiful coaxing, she endeavored to make milk flow again from her own breast, and herself gave me suck. For the first year of my life she barely let me out of her sight. Even when my father came to call—remarking amusedly, as he himself partook of the mother's milk, on the gashes on her bosoms made by my sharp natal tooth—I lay in a bassinette adjacent to the royal bed. To this day, a whiff of sandalwood, which Maria burned daily in her boudoir, summons a nostalgic sense of peace and serenity. Too, I recollect the sounds issued by Maria and my father, his guttural grunts, her gentler groans, as they consummated their love. I even have one memory of myself cradled in Mother Mary's arms, my face nestled cozily by her breast. How tiny I must have been, to have fit there so snugly, like the missing piece to a great puzzle!

My early development was much remarked upon. While I was fully ambulatory a few weeks shy of my first birthday, I spoke not a jot. Most babies manage a few stray words, *mama* and *dada* and *cat* and so forth, but I held my tongue all through my second year, and well into my third. My father began to worry that I was dumb, although all who spent time with me insisted that intelligence flickered in my dark eyes. Then one summer day in A.D. 1086, when I was about two and a half, I woke in the morning, gazed out at the blue sea and bluer sky, and said to Maria, in whose bed I slept, "Mother Mary, it is such a fine day. Let us go to the beach."

Or so I am told. The exact words I uttered that morning have perhaps been exaggerated through the years. But I did begin speaking at that time, in complete sentences, my tiny voice confident and sure. Within a year I was reading, both Greek and some Latin, and was engaging in theological discussions with the new Patriarch, Nicholas the Grammarian, who struggled to explain to me the paradoxical mystery of Christ's dual nature. By then I could already cite Scripture, and some at court found common ground between the young princess Anna Komnene and another precocious child who thrilled at Biblical debate with the elders, Jesus of Nazareth.

Anna Dalassene took an active interest in me at that time, as my inchoate genius reflected well on her. She dispatched a team of eunuch tutors to the Mangana Palace, and I spent an inordinate amount of time at their collective elbow, soaking up disparate knowledge. Literature, history, mathematics, science, medicine, astrology, theology: no discipline was kept from me, although my father was not keen on my reading the naughty Greeks at such a tender age.

I had no coeval playmates. My life was constructed so that I rarely encountered another child. The only non-adult I saw regularly was Tino, whom I adored as a god, but who showed little interest in his youthful fiancée; he was otherwise engaged, as we shall see, and anyway much older. My circle was small: Maria, Rona her nurse (until she passed), my grand-mothers Anna Dalassene and Maria of Bulgaria, the Emperor, the Patriarch, Tino, the teachers, the waiting-ladies, the eunuch servants, and the half-dozen cats who prowled about the Palace.

Often in my early childhood, my father was off fighting some or other enemy—even after the sudden and God-given death of Robert the Fox from plague in the glorious spring of A.D. 1085, there were any number of Pecheneg incursions and frontier revolts to put down. When in Constantinople, Alexios was a frequent visitor to the Mangana Palace. His travels had not dulled his ardor towards Maria, the love of his life, and he took every opportunity to call on her.

What I most remember about my father from this time is how much hair he had: on his head, his face, his arms and legs, his chest. Next to the hairless women and eunuchs who populated most of my life, he seemed to me like a whole other species, however similar his face was to my own. He treated me with muted affection, probably forced for Maria's benefit, and regarded me always with puzzlement.

"Will she always look like that?" I heard him ask Maria, concern in his voice.

"Like what?"

"Like a little man. She looks so old. So *hard*. She reminds me of the *Caesar*."

On more than one occasion I woke in the night to the sounds of their love-making. I shared a bed with Maria until I was seven, and my slumbering presence was not enough to dissuade my father from slaking his lust in that same bed. I would lie perfectly still, trying not to breathe, beseeching God to help me keep shut my curious eyes, in the way Lot's wife could not. In my recollection, these dalliances went on for hours, but Maria later told me, laughing out loud, that my father never once, in all their years together, took longer than five minutes to complete his task. When he did finish, he fell instantly asleep, as if by Circean sorcery, and the three of us would spend the night in the bed, the Emperor flanked by his daughter and his lover. Never in my life did I feel as safe and secure as on those nights.

As for my own mother, I have virtually no memory of her from my early childhood. When she sent me away with Maria, or rather when Alexios did, it was as if she had given me up for adoption, or abandoned me on a pile of rubbish, as was routinely done with unwanted babies in Old Rome. She simply banished me from her mind. To be fair, that mind had much with which to occupy itself. In addition to all that study with the Moorish astrologer, Irene became pregnant in the summer of A.D. 1084. This happened during a month-long period during which Maria's mother, Borena, visited from Alania, when my father's customary means of sexual satiety were unavailable to him.

"Five or six times that month, he polished off a jug of mulled wine, stumbled drunkenly into my bed-chamber, and demanded satisfaction," Irene told me later. "I knew better than to resist. He'd done far worse to me, I assure you."

So it came to pass that Irene bore a child—another girl, much to Maria's relief—on the eighth of June, A.D. 1085. The baby was called Maria, after Irene's own mother Maria of Bulgaria, and was as dainty and beautiful as I was coarse and ugly. But daint and beauty do not beget sturdiness, and my infant sister was frail and weak. She caught a fever when she was a month old, and after a few days of perilous struggle, burned herself out. Irene had formed a strong attachment to this second child, and she took her death hard. Already ensorcelled by Saddiq the astrologer, she fell even more deeply under his spell—with far-reaching effects on the Empire, and indeed on History, as we shall see.

IV

THE BASTARD

B Y THE TIME MY MOTHER WAS NINETEEN YEARS OLD, she'd endured enough hardship to fill a lifetime. She was a parricide, first and foremost, as well as a chronic victim of spousal rape that had begun at the tender age of eleven. She'd endured the humiliation of her husband barring her from his coronation, as well as his frequent dalliances with Maria of Alania and also, she suspected, with his own mother Anna Dalassene, which unseemly infidelities he never bothered to deny. She'd allowed her first child to be taken from her at three weeks old to be raised elsewhere, and now watched helplessly as her second breathed its last. Yes, Irene was no stranger to heartache. But the death of the infant girl affected her as nothing else had.

"Like childbirth itself, it's easy to understand the concept, but impossible to know what it actually *feels* like when one of your own issue dies," she explained, many years later, at Kecharitomene.

"You're fortunate, Anna, not to know." And even as she spoke those words, all those decades hence, an old woman waiting out her last hours on this dull terrestrial sphere, she was visibly distressed by the memory.

Alexios, unsurprisingly, did not countenance her despair. Once he realized the new babe was another girl, of no use to him for at least another decade, he lost interest in it entirely, and was unmoved at its passing. The sudden loss of loved ones is a hazard of the military life, and he'd inured himself to Death's callous and indiscriminate famishment, insofar as this is possible. Far from eliciting sympathy, Irene's prolonged and histrionic grief irritated him.

"Irene," he rebuked her, "it's been months now. Pull yourself together! Little Maria was with us for just a few weeks. It's not like you got to know her in any meaningful way. You are the *Empress*, woman. You must move past this."

She said nothing, crossing her arms in front of her chest.

He clutched at her elbows, pulling her closer. "We can make another baby," he said, seemingly pleased with the sagacity of this suggestion, as if babies could be so easily made, or so easily replaced.

"Not now," Irene said, pushing him away—one of the few times she'd ever managed to refuse his advances. "I'm not ready."

This confounded him. To stoical men like my father, who view the world with cold calculation, women like my mother are as mysterious as sphinxes.

Men want only to fix what is broken, and too often do not realize that they are themselves the ones responsible for the breaking.

In her anguish, Irene turned first to God. Many days were spent on her knees before stolid icons, in desperate, tear-stained prayer. She fasted, she rent her garments, she wailed. Nothing happened. In her hour of need she beseeched the Almighty, but He was silent as stone. None of the Church rituals eased her mind; to the contrary, she saw, for the first time, how risible the entire enterprise was. What was the Hagia Sophia but a well-constructed pile of rocks and glass? What was the icon but oil on wood? What was Jesus but a fictional character writ large, the made-up Homeric deity of the new age?

She posed the question to Nicholas the Grammarian that so many who are suffering put to holy men: If there is a just and merciful God, how can He permit such tragedy? How can He be its author?

"I am a good person," she told him. "Why has this befallen me?" And as the Patriarch opened his mouth to respond, she added: "And don't tell me that it is *not for us to understand*, or that *God moves in mysterious ways*. I'm not a child."

The corpulent Patriarch nodded grimly and ran his short, fat fingers through his graying beard. By heart he recited the Pauline epistle: "'There is no one righteous, not even one; there is no one who understands, no one who seeks God. All have turned away, they have together become worthless; there is no one who does good, not even one. Their throats are open graves; their tongues practice deceit. The poison of vipers is on their lips. Their mouths are full of cursing and bitterness. Their feet are swift to shed blood; ruin and misery mark their ways, and the way of peace they do not know. There is no fear of God before their eyes.'[100] What does Saint Paul mean by this? That we are all flawed vessels. That every one of us, without exception, deserves nothing more than to be flung into Hell. That we are only spared eternal damnation by the Grace of God. And that for us sinners, therefore, to question the nature of the unknowable Grace that is our salvation is *itself* sinful. Do you understand, Your Highness?"

"Come, Father," she said. "That is a rather bleak view, don't you think?"

The portly man chuckled pleasantly, his body undulating like a bowl of congealed pig-fat. "I am not here to think, Empress. I am here to atone."

But Scripture or no, my mother refused to believe this. God was just and merciful, God was good. God was love. He had some grand plan, surely—some pattern written into the seeming randomness of the Universe. And if this pattern could not be found in the Bible, then perhaps it could be gleaned in the stars.

Her relationship with Saddiq the Moor was already friendly enough to rouse suspicion among the more priggish at court. After the death of little

---

[100]   Romans 3:10-18.

Maria, Irene spent even more time with the ambitious astrologer, who was only too eager to help her in her quest for enlightenment.

"It must not be imagined that all things happen to men as though each individual circumstance were ordained by divine decree and some indissoluble supernal cause," Saddiq told her—ably paraphrasing his Claudius Ptolemy, although she did not realize it at the time. "Nor is it to be thought that all events are shown to proceed from one single inevitable fate, without being influenced by the interposition of any other agency. The stars *suggest*, Your Highness; they do not compel. We must also bear in mind that man is subject not only to events applicable to his own private and individual nature, but also to others arising from general causes. He suffers, for example, from pestilence, from fires and floods, from the tide of war, from famine, all generated by certain extensive changes in the stars, and destroying multitudes simultaneously. Since a greater agency must logically supersede one that is smaller and less puissant, it follows that in great changes, where a stronger cause predominates, more general affections are put into operation, but affections which attach to one individual solely are excited when his own natural constitution peculiar to himself may be overcome by some greater impulse of the stars, however small or faint. In the case of our poor lost daughter Maria, the pestilence was stronger than her own life force. It is a horrible, unspeakable tragedy, but this is why such things transpire." And he rested his enormous and dark hand, so silky, so soft, on her bony, goose-pimpled knee.

As he did so, a wave of indescribable energy surged through her entire body, as a tall spire struck by lightning. She moved her own hand to his; for a moment, he thought she was doing so to remove it, and began to withdraw; but she instead pressed down, holding his against her knee. "Saddiq," she said. "I don't know how I'd manage this without you."

"I am your faithful servant, Your Highness," he told her, his piercing black eyes locked with her own. "I will do whatever is necessary to ease your mind. Anything that you desire, I will undertake." He took a long pause, as they gazed deeply into each other's eyes. "Anything."

Irene leaned toward him, closing her eyes, and angled her head to facilitate the kiss, as she moved his hand, or rather allowed him to move his hand, up her thigh. The astrologer, to his credit, did not waver despite the enormous personal risk. (The audacious have no shortage of nerve, as the tragedian wrote).[101] He returned her kiss with apposite imperial authority, and when granted her tacit permission to move his dexterous hand, he knew exactly where to put it.

"Most men would have cowered and run," she told me later. "There's no question that Alexios would have put him to death immediately if our

---

[101] It is unclear which tragedian Anna refers to here.

liaison was discovered. Not because he cared about me—he did not—but out of sheer principle. To this day I am grateful to Saddiq for his strength, his courage, and his compassion."

Their subsequent and torrid love affair, which would last for several years, was to have far-reaching impact on the Empire, more than either of them could ever have dreamed: For on the thirteenth of September, A.D. 1087, Irene gave birth for the third time, under a cloud of suspicion. For one thing, while Alexios was in Constantinople during most of the previous winter, not once during that entire season had he called upon his wife in the night; Maria had slaked his lusts completely. For another, the new baby's skin was impossibly dark— Armenian blood ran in the Komnenoi line, as my own coloring shows, but that swarthy race did not produce infants as coal-black as this newborn brat. My father had to know that the child was not his own—it was literally black and white!—but to take any sort of retributive action in this regard would be tantamount to a public admission of cuckoldry to a Moor; and this humiliation his outsized pride would not allow. Thus we all operated under the illusion that the new baby was the product of his own, fairer loins. Perhaps his reaction, or lack thereof, would have been different had the newborn been a girl, like me or my late sister Maria. But the baby, fatefully, was a boy. He was called John, after Irene's moribund grand-father the *Caesar* (who would die soon after), and the little bastard would be the bane of my existence: a living, breathing obstacle to all my hopes and dreams.

If the rest of the Empire was willing to indulge Alexios's obvious fantasy that his wife's bitumen-black baby was somehow his own issue, Maria would not hold her tongue. The infant John, born as he was in the purple—"born purple, in the purple" was the running joke among the wags at court; his skin, indeed, was the very shade of aubergine—threatened, by his perfectly innocent existence, her own son's ascension to the throne.

My father called upon his "mother" one morning in late summer, not long after his "son" was born. This time, Maria rebuffed his advances.

"I make love to men," she told him, "not spineless little poltroons."

"Excuse me?"

"You heard me. Are you the Equal of the Apostles? Or some common catamite?"

Alexios raised his hand as if to strike her.

"Go ahead, hit me. If that's what it will take to make you feel like a man again. I did not realize that eunuchs were permitted to be Emperor. I guess the protocols have changed."

Whereupon he took her suggestion and slapped her hard across the face, leaving a red imprint of his palm on her dainty cheek. I was playing in the next room, a toddler not yet four, and while I do not recall the details of the conversation, I remember the sound when he struck her—it was loud enough to make my little ears perk up.

She ran her hand along her hot, red cheek and laughed balefully. "Good for you, mighty *Augustus*. Your own wife whelps a Moorish brat, evidence of her despicable infidelity, and all you can do is strike *me*, your lover and friend. You cuckold. You laughingstock. You eunuch."

He hit her again, harder this time, spilling her onto the floor and drawing blood from her nose. His cheeks flushed red with rage, and he may well have beaten her further, had I not toddled into the room at that moment, found her invitingly sprawled on the floor, and jumped on top of her.

"Look, Anna," she said, sniffling but refusing to cry, "Papa is here."

I ran to him, and he hoisted me up, effectively ending the violence.

"It is remarkable," Maria said, still prone on the floor, "how similar the two of you look. Anna, you are your papa's spitting image. And yet your 'son' does not resemble you in the slightest, Lex. Oh, but Mother Nature is a capricious witch."

My father petted my hair and showered me with rough kisses, perhaps as a way of stemming his anger. "What would you have me do, then? Expose the fraud?"

"Why not? Call her out as a whore, divorce her, and let us be together, as we should be. As we *are*, in the eyes of everyone but the pitiless law."

A grim smile appeared on his rugged face as I tugged playfully at the hairs of his beard. "First of all, the Patriarch will not allow us to wed. You are my mother, remember?"

"Fie," she said. "Your mother is alive and well."

"More to the point, if I divorce Irene, the Doukids will turn against me. My hold on the Empire is not entirely secure. Surely you recall what *that* feels like, oh ex-wife of Michael Parapinakes. Every spring, it seems, some provincial ingrate declares himself *Augustus*, demanding my urgent attention. No, I need them in my court, however much I despise them."

"That filthy, disgusting ape of a baby, that Moorish gorilla-boy bastard, cannot be heir to the throne," Maria said. "Promise me. Swear in the name of the Lord Jesus Christ. Let the succession go to my son and your daughter."

"Of course that is how it will be," he said. "When have I indicated anything to the contrary?"

"The situation has changed, Lex. Irene has cause now," Maria said. "You must resist."

"Maria, come," and his eyes shone with the usual submissive loyalty, all anger evaporating in the hot afternoon, leaving nothing behind but molten lust.

"Anna, run along and play," she said.

My father set me down, I scampered off, and Maria, still on the ground, rose to her knees and beckoned him to come closer.

V

THE CONFIDANTE

THE BEAUTIFUL WILL, ON OCCASION, GIVE BIRTH TO THE PLAIN CHILD, just as the strong will breed the weak child, the smart the stupid, or the short the tall. In the case of Tino, however, the acorn—to borrow Homer's phrase—did not scatter far from the oak. His parents were astonishingly attractive, and so was he. Tall and slender, with dirty blonde hair that hung insouciantly over dreamy sea-blue eyes, Constantine Doukas was Nature's masterpiece, a triumph of God's handiwork, and the object of desire of every girl at court. Not that he showed much interest. I don't mean that he did not find pleasure with women, like his legitimate father Michael—for he did; rather that he seemed to care about exactly nothing. Indeed, "Who cares?" was his favorite expression, peppered from time to time with a shrugging, "So what?" He greeted the world with a roll of those gorgeous eyes and a snort of derisive dismissal, as if he always, no matter what, had something better to do, somewhere better to be. He was the co-Emperor, after all, the presumptive heir to the throne. He lazed around court in his purple-lined tunics and enviable violet shoes, and when his subjects showed him respect, he never once returned it. He was not, I should make plain, evil or cruel. He no longer tortured mice. He would never use his influence to, for example, exile an enemy, or have a rival arrested just because he didn't like his looks. He was merely slothful, vain, arrogant, and mean in a general, petty sort of way. Most of that meanness he reserved for Maria, whom he regarded with overt contempt.

"My mother is a whore," he would remark to his friends, or indeed to anyone within earshot. "Jezebel has nothing on her. Take a look—that is what an aging strumpet looks like." (To which they almost certainly thought, "My, how well do strumpets age!")

More than once, when my father called at the Mangana Palace, I heard Tino say, "The Emperor has come, Maria." (he always addressed his mother by her Christian name, a brazen show of filial disrespect, as if daring her to do something about it.) "To the bed-chamber go! Open those bony legs and let out the reek of the fishy sea." Whereupon he would plug his nose and run around the room as if fleeing a specter. At first I found this highly amusing, as he seemed to be playing this up for my benefit, to make me laugh (or so I gathered at the time; remember, I was just four years old). By the time I was six, however, and probably sooner, I'd perceived the underlying viciousness of his mockery, and no longer found it funny. But when I was very young, I believed Tino was doing this just for me, and it made me love him all the more.

He was prudent enough to contain himself when Alexios was around; the Emperor had the power to banish him outright or worse, and would be prone to make use of said power if he observed Tino openly maligning his mother. Even so, my father recognized the boy's scurrilous attitude. "What that kid needs," he remarked on numerous occasions, "is a swift smack in the jaw." I have no doubt that if Alexios ever overheard Tino insulting Maria, he would have beaten him to a pulp.

It was heartbreaking to witness. Maria loved her son with all her heart. She nursed him herself, as already related, until he was five or six years old. She shared a bed with him until I came along and pushed him out, when he was nine. She pampered him, doted on him, gave to him whatever his heart desired. Unwavering was her kindness, limitless her love, and saintly her patience. And her only reward was to be derided, disrespected, and dismissed. For she could not control him. He came and went as he pleased. The older he got, the more he roamed; Tino at fifteen and sixteen would vanish for days and sometimes weeks at a time.

All of which suited me perfectly. The palace was enormous, but empty. The *Sebastokrator*, my uncle Isaac, who nominally lived with us, spent most of his time with his mother Anna Dalassene at the

Boukoleon, where they oversaw the day-to-day operations of the Empire; he had rooms there, of which he often made use. My aunt Irina went where Isaac went, and their children, my cousins, were older and had "left the nest" years ago. Rona, the beloved nurse who'd moved from Georgia with Maria, died when I was two. And even when Tino was around, he kept his distance from us. In practice, then, the vast dwelling was occupied by a small clutch of eunuch servants and waiting-ladies, Maria, and me. The dowager Empress was one of the most desirable women in Christendom, and I had her all to myself!

Despite the many stories in circulation concerning the intellectual prowess of Anna Komnene, appraisals of my acumen are generally exaggerated. Genius abounded in Byzantium. Basil the Physician, Anna Dalassene, the deposed Emperor Michael, the bevy of writers and philosophers who attended the salons sponsored by Maria and later by me—all of these individuals boasted intelligence that far surpassed my own. Saddiq the astrologer was brilliant, as was my mother…as was Maria, in her inimitable way. The reason I have stood out among my impressive coevals, I think, is because my own genius, if we may bequeath my modest gifts such lofty characterization, revealed itself very early. At three, I could read and write and speak as if I were ten; at seven, I demonstrated the intellect of a gifted teenager. In a word, I was precocious. But precocity and genius are not the same thing, alas, and should not be conflated! I mention this now not to boast—I have been confined to this convent for almost half my life; fat lot of good my big brain has gotten me!—but to set the scene for what followed.

My dissolute fiancé, as mentioned, was almost never home, meaning Maria and I were together all the time, often with no one else around except a eunuch or three. From A.D. 1090-93, while I was six, seven, and eight years old—a little girl—my ability to carry on sophisticated conversations, and more importantly to *understand* what was being told me, belied the greenness of my youth. Thus was I able, despite my tender age, to act as confidante to this lonely forty-year-old woman. I took care of Maria, in my humble and priestly way, as Maria took care of me.

That three-year span comprised the happiest days of my life. How could it be otherwise? I would wake at dawn, or soon after, make my toilet, and read quietly by the window as I listened to the soothing sound of her sleep-breaths. (Maria owned several books of Georgian poetry, written in her strange and beautiful native tongue, which mysteries I set myself to unlocking). When she rose, we would break our fast together, dress (she would carefully and patiently brush my rat's-nest head of hair), and go to the Hagia Sophia to pray together. After lunch, if weather permitted, we'd take a stroll around the well-manicured grounds. And we would talk. Or rather, Maria would talk, and I would listen.

No detail was spared, no unpleasantness sugar-coated to allow for my unblemished youth. She was brutally honest in every way. Frequently I would ask questions, if I did not grasp the motive behind an action, or, more often, to ensure that I understood. She liked this, because she could tell that I was not only listening, but comprehending. (When she began these confessions, she probably assumed I'd not be able to take any of it in—just as Eudokia had assumed she could not understand Greek, all those years ago—so Maria'd really be talking for her own sake; once she realized my enormous capacity for retention, her tongue really let loose.) After a few weeks of this, I began to take notes—surreptitiously, in the morning hour before she woke, and in Georgian script, lest my papers were discovered by one of the eunuch servants or waiting-ladies. What a perfect cipher her native language made! (I still have those ancient notes, here on my desk—they are, appropriately, the basis for this secret history—and I cannot handle them without smiling.)[102]

In the late afternoon guests would call. My father was a frequent visitor, of course, as was my grand-mother Anna Dalassene, although she never stayed long. I don't recollect Irene ever once setting foot at the Mangana Palace, and I only saw my half-brother, the bastard John, at large events at the Hagia Sophia or the Hippodrome. My aunt Irina was often at the palace, and a host of Constantinopolitan intellectuals, writers, philosophers, and artists that gathered once a week at Maria's salon. Ioane

---

[102]   These notes, alas, have been lost to history!

Petritsi was a permanent fixture—he was in love with Maria, I believe—and the great Theophylact, who hailed from my maternal grand-mother's hometown of Ohrid. The dowager Empress would preside at the salon, cracking jokes, offering insights, asking questions, and drinking copious amounts of white wine. It was at Maria's salon that I first met Saddiq, the court astrologer and father to my nemesis. This encounter I well remember. His skin was black as night, unlike anyone else I'd ever seen, and he spoke eloquently and at great length, I recall, about the familiarity of the regions of the Earth with the triplicities and the planets, a lecture I found fascinating. But when I remarked upon his prodigious learning afterword to Maria, she scoffed.

"He is a fraud," she told me. "Every word that fell from his deceitful lips is a paraphrase or a direct quotation from Ptolemy. Here," and she handed me the *Tetrabiblos*, "see for yourself." And indeed, in the third chapter, I found a section titled "The Familiarity of the Regions of the Earth with the Triplicities and the Planets," which he seemed to have quoted more or less verbatim in his lecture.

After supper, on rare occasion joined by Tino, when he was not out with his low-life friends, we'd retire to the bed we shared. Sleep would come for her first—by then she would have consumed at least a bottle of Caecuban,[103] which hurried the

---

[103] A sweet white wine.

process—and I would curl up against her, listening to her uneven breaths, fragrant with the sweet reek of white grape. She was so beautiful, I would think, so very beautiful, and I was such an ugly little runt, and yet she somehow loved me anyway!

I knew, even at the time, that this arrangement was not sustainable, that it could not last. Happiness is fleeting, even for princesses and erstwhile empresses. What I could not have foreseen—for such tumult could not be divined by the most expert astrologer—is how suddenly the end would come… and by what sinister method.

VI

THE OPIUM EATER

PONDERING THESE EVENTS IN RETROSPECT from my creaky desk at the convent, I realize that it was a wonder that Maria's long-odds ploy to install her son on the throne made it as far as it did. Even under the most favorable conditions, succession is a crap-shoot. My nephew Isaac, for example, eldest son of my half-brother John, was himself denied the crown in favor of our current *Augustus*, his younger brother Manuel, on the death-bed whim of his dying father. And Isaac had as good a claim as any: he was the first-born son of the Emperor! Supposedly John felt that Isaac's hot temper and propensity for rash action would prove disastrous for the Empire, and that the more circumspect Manuel was better suited to the task. We will never know what a reign of Isaac II Komnenos might have looked like, but the six years of my younger nephew's reign have been, it must be conceded, prosperous ones, despite his personal eccentricities.

Tino Doukas had no such natural-born advantages. His mother was twice Empress; now she was the Emperor's lover, and legally his mother, although my father's actual mother was very much alive; he was thus Alexios's "brother," meaningless in the grand scheme of things. Being the son, biological or otherwise, of Michael VII Doukas was little help, as the Peck-filcher remained the object of universal scorn. Moreover, there were plenty of other imperial sons who had just as strong a claim as did Tino, starting with the Diogenes boys, Nikephoros and Leo, both of whom grew up with Alexios in my grand-mother's house. That the sitting *Augustus* now had a male child of his own all but eliminated the already-slim chance that Tino would ever take the purple; the Roman Emperors of old often adopted their successors, most of whom bore no blood relation, but that custom has died out through the centuries—wisely, in my estimation.

Still, all of these hazards might have been surmounted had Tino shown the beatific temperament of Manuel, or even of his licit father Michael. Justinian himself came from common stock, the reader will recall, and his elevation to the highest rank came about not because he was the nephew of the usurper Justin, but because he took to the position like no man ever had.[104] Constantine Doukas lacked

---

[104] Had the plague not ravaged his Italian troops, Justinian would likely have re-conquered the lost Western Roman territory held by barbarians. (A.K.)

these bona fides. He was a wastrel, in every possible way. Vain, arrogant, not as smart as he thought he was, lazy, derisive, disrespectful of others, spoiled, entitled: he was, in short, singularly unworthy of the office.

He ran with a hapless crew of like-minded individuals, coarse and ornery brutes of good pedigree but bad temperament. One was a cousin of the sons of Diogenes, another the nephew of a former Patriarch. Their ringleader, insofar as any of their number could be led, was one Ali, son of a Saracen mercenary. I remember him distinctly, because his black and immaculately-lashed eyes were too close together—always the sign of the Devil, as Maria explained—and on one occasion, after giving me a long, appraising look, he remarked to Tino, "You really have to marry that thing? I'd sooner abdicate." It was Ali who supplied the crew with *kannabis*, that favorite weed of the Scyths, which fragrant smoke they would draw into their lungs by use of a bowl and a hollow reed. Many nights did they repair to one of the stables at the Mangana Palace, inhale their *kannabis*, and shoot dice till dawn. Much money was lost this way, for Tino was a luckless gambler. He would emerge at sunrise from the stables, his eyes bloodshot, and stagger back to his apartments, where he would sleep away most of the day. Other times, he passed out upon a bale of hay in the stables.

The warm pungent tang of the *kannabis* pleased the nose, I'll allow, mixing as it did with Maria's sandalwood incense, and its overall effect was not unpleasant on his disposition. Tino was softer after he smoked, kinder to his mother, quicker to laugh. Had he confined himself to its exclusive use, perhaps he would have grown out of this immature phase and developed into a viable candidate for kinghood; not all imperial childhoods are spent in serious preparation for the purple, nor does serious preparation guarantee ascension to the throne (as I know too well!). Alas, he did not. The serpent Ali one fateful evening brought with him opium to eat. Like Eve, Tino partook of the forbidden fruit. Like Eve, he did not recover.

Years later, when I ran the hospital that my father founded in Constantinople, I became better acquainted with opium. With analgesic properties that border on the magical, the drug was provided to patients in extreme pain: amputees, burn victims, dying men ravaged by cancer. The proper dosage eased their torment and helped them sleep. But so powerful a substance as this was also dangerous if not used properly. What can relieve pain can also cause it. What can help a man survive can also kill him. At hospital, I took care not to dole out too much of the drug, or for too long, because after repeated use, the effect was muted; higher dosages were subsequently required to achieve the same effect. I remember one poor wretch who'd somehow survived a house fire. Hideous burn scars covered most of his body, and his hair had been singed off. When the opium wore off, he'd scream like Lucifer had come up from Hell to deliver him. One of the nurses gave him a double dose, and then a second nurse inadvertently did the same; he died in the night with a peaceful smile across the charred wreckage of his face.

But I did not know any of this when I was eight years old. And Tino was not in pain, at least not in a medical way. He loved the substance because it brought out in him a euphoria that he could otherwise not achieve. When under the influence of the drug, he was a somnambulist, one moving through a dream. A ghoul.

"You don't understand," he told Maria. "This is what Heaven feels like."

"Heaven is for when you die!" she retorted. "Although in your case, I'm not so sure that's where you're headed."

With my already-encyclopedic knowledge of Roman history and Greek tragedy, I was not the typical naïve eight-year-old. I had some inkling of the manifold horrors of the world. I did not rattle easily. But Tino in his opium-fueled ghoul-state terrified me. He was like an one possessed by a cacodemon. Were Jesus to have visited Constantinople, even He would have put His hands on him to cast out the demon, because drug and demon were one and the same. When my fiancé emerged from the stables like this, I hid myself in the wardrobe.

Maria, for her part, enabled her son's weaknesses. What she should have done, I now know from my days at the hospital, is to, first, banish Ali and the rest of the crew from the city—I myself would have had the contemptable Saracen executed, on general principle—and second, have Tino confined to the imperial dungeon for a period of six months, until all traces of the opium had vanished from his body. There is no other way to break the spell. Prayer does not work, nor exorcism. But Maria did not do any of that. Instead, she covered for him. She bribed servants to keep quiet. She paid a bodyguard to track his movements and intervene when he was too dazed to walk home. When Alexios inquired about his odd behavior, she denied it. She simply could not face the fact that her only begotten son was a drug-addled malingerer.

Late in the Year of Our Lord 1091, after my eighth birthday but before Tino's seventeenth—he was born, the retentive reader will recall, on Christmas Day—Maria was summoned to the monastery at Stoudios by the monk called Stephen. Michael, the ex-Emperor and her ex-husband, was gravely ill; she was to come at once. I've never seen her wail like that, not before or since. She wept for half an hour, inconsolably, and then Tino and I accompanied her to the monastery.

Ringed by a menacing wall that cut off the outside world, the austere building was fashioned of hard brick and cold stone, and looked like an enormous crypt. I clutched Maria's hand tightly as we approached. Tino walked a few paces behind, lost in thought, or perhaps still numbed by the opium. At that point, I did not yet know that he was not Michael's biological son; was he himself aware? I could not say, and I never got the chance to ask him. With his thick matte of hair and his swarthy complexion, the dying Emperor bore a far greater resemblance to me, his cousin, than to Tino.

Women were not permitted inside the monastery proper, so they'd had Michael transferred to a room just off the courtyard, where he could entertain visitors. Stephen, a kindly fellow, short, with graying blonde hair, met us at the door. He and Maria embraced warmly, which surprised me. Then he put his hand on my head and said, "It's nice to see you again, little one. I wish it were under less dire circumstances."

Michael lay on a simple pallet, swaddled in sweat-soaked blankets—the adult version of the baby Jesus in the manger. All color had gone from his face, his hair was white as the froth on a wave, his eyes yellow and rheumy. Just three years older than Maria, he looked ancient, as Noah must have at the last of his nine hundred fifty years on this dread planet. But a gentle smile crossed the wide expanse of his face as Maria came near.

"Michael," she cried. "Oh my God, oh my God!" And she fell to her knees at his bedside, weeping uncontrollably. The tableau was reminiscent of a pietà. This was her first husband, her best friend and constant companion during the years after her emigration to Constantinople, the kind soul who taught her to speak Greek, who protected her, who loved her dearly if sororally. Death only becomes manifestly real when it takes those close to us, those our own age or younger especially.

At this point, Stephen tactfully ushered my fiancé and I into the hall, and enjoined us to make ourselves comfortable on the wooden benches there. "They need time alone," he explained, before offering us something to drink.

When the monk left to fetch a jug of water, a visibly shaken Tino left, too. "I've had about enough of this," he said. "To hell with both of them. May Satan have mercy on their souls." Off he went, leaving me alone on a bench in the dark and eerie monastery, quiet as death but for the wailing woman in the next room.

I did not hear every word that was said, just fragments: *I never should have left you* and *I should have been with you to the end* and *You are the light of my life* and *I am a terrible person for abandoning you* and *Thank you for everything my love* and *Please forgive me*. I could not make out Michael's responses; perhaps he was too ill to speak. But he must have made some gesture to expiate her guilt. He was, above all else, a kind man.

Stephen returned with my glass of water, and I had just taken a sip when Maria came outside. "He is gone," she said. "I'm so sorry for your loss, Stephen." And she fell into his arms, and the two of them wept and wept, and wept some more.

VII
THE KISS

A FEW DAYS BEFORE CHRISTMAS, no more than ten days after Michael passed, a waiting-lady woke Maria in the wee hours of the morning. I was having trouble sleeping that night, and had only just nodded off, so I remember it distinctly.

"Milady," the servant cried, her voice full of anguish, "there has been an accident. Come, come quickly!"

Maria jolted out of bed, suddenly wide awake. She had been having a bad dream, she told me later, and upon rising merely drifted from a sleeping nightmare to a waking one. Without looking at me, she put on her robe and her slippers and followed the waiting-lady down the hall. I waited for them to leave, counted to three, and tiptoed after them.

Sprawled face-down on the floor in the hallway, head cocked at an unnatural angle, lay Tino. His eyes were sealed shut. White froth spumed from the corner of his mouth, the color and smell of sea foam. He did not appear to be breathing.

Maria screamed and fell to her knees. Her fingernails dug into her scalp. She began to mutter unintelligibly in Georgian. "*Es meti*," she said, over and over again. "*Es meti*." The lady-in-waiting stood dumbly behind her, patting her hair.

The scream caught the attention of one of the Varangian guard, who marched noisily into the hall, the metal on his mail clinking as he came. He was a Saxon, this fellow, with pale skin and red hair—tough in battle, I'm sure, but useless in a medical emergency. He glanced at Maria, who had entered a sort of fugue state, and then at the waiting-lady, who did not meet his glance, and finally at the still form of Tino on the cold ground. He had no idea what to do, poor fellow.

"Water," I cried, emerging from the shadows.

An eight-year-old girl barking out orders! He would not have been more surprised if the icon of Jesus Christ came to life at that moment bearing loaves and fishes. And to be honest, it did feel as though the Son of God had appropriated my tongue and given it voice.

"Fetch a pail of water," I told him again, trying to keep my voice level. "Please, sirrah."

With no better course of action available to him, he said, "Yes, princess," and raced off.

I would prefer to say that I "raced" to Tino, but in truth I walked tentatively to where he lay. I was scared, I cannot lie, and my fear intensified with the stench as I cautiously approached. I knelt down beside him and called out his name. He did not respond. I picked up his arm, held it aloft for a moment, and let go; it fell to the stone floor with a thud. I placed my left hand on the small of his back. He was warm to the touch, despite the chill in the air, and I interpreted this as an optimistic sign. Was he breathing? This I could not divine. I shook him, again calling his name; again, silence.

The froth seeping like lava from his mouth, the source of the rancid odor, was not, I saw, just foamy bubbles of sputum. There was density to it. I made the Sign of the Cross and said a little prayer. Then I reached into his mouth with my little hand cupped, and I scooped the foul stuff away. It took some doing. Density there was, and also volume. Much of his dinner, it seemed, had come up chewed and bilious, lodging itself in his mouth and his throat. Several times I had to check my impulse to retch. After the fourth or fifth scoop, he let out a loud gasp and began to violently cough. By then the guard had returned with the bucket of water.

"Set it down," I told him. He did, and I washed my hands.

"Turn him over." That was impossible for me at my size, but to the big, strong guard, Tino was a sack of turnips.

"Pour it on him." The guard looked at me quizzically, but I held my ground. "Pour it on him. On his head. Do what I say."

The douse of cold water had the desired effect. Tino sat bolt upright, coughing and cursing. I became aware of Maria and the waiting-lady behind me, joined now by several eunuch servants, as if I'd come out of a trance.

"You did it," she cried. "You saved him!" She gave me a hug so strong I could not breathe. Then, after releasing me, she turned to her son, who sat soaked and sloppy on the stone floor. She smacked him across the face so hard that the thwack echoed off the stone walls. "Ingrate," she spat, striking him again. "Bounder. Slugabed. Good-for-nothing, deadbeat, otiose, useless pile of pig excrement. How dare you. How dare you!" And she kept striking him until he raised his arms and made her stop.

"I'm sorry, mama," he said, sniffling. "I'm sorry. This will never happen again. Never."

Her rage burned out, she embraced him, and mother and son sat there, intertwined on the cold stone steps and covered in vomit, weeping.

The next evening my father called. He'd heard about what happened—the guard had gone directly to the Boukoleon after the incident to file a report— and after a short investigation, concluded that his co-Emperor was a habitual eater of opium, an addict, unable to control his self-destructive urges. Alexios was a temperate man, generally abstemious with regard to drink and drug, but he'd spent most of his life in the army and was no stranger to the del-eterious effects of chronic opium use.

"He needs to stop," he told Maria. "At once, and for good."

"But I'm sure he will," she protested. She simply could not accept Tino's failure, however aware of it she must have been. "Last night scared him good."

"Anna," my father called. "Give us the room, please."

I folded up the book I was reading—Galen, whose physician's wisdom I hoped might offer more insight into my fiancé's condition—and left Maria's bed-chamber. I had my own room, of course, with my own bed, but I almost never used it. I could count on one hand the number of nights I did not sleep in the Empress's chamber, snuggled up beside her.

Alexios shut the door behind me, and after tak-ing a few steps, I went back to the door and listened intently.

"Do you know where he is right now?"

"He took a walk," she said.

"A walk? It's freezing outside."

She said nothing.

"I had him followed," Alexios said. "He is back at the stables with that mischievous Turk."

"No! It cannot be. The…"

"Maria, open your eyes! He is eating opium again, now, as we speak!"

"You speak falsely."

"Would that I were." There was a long, uncom-fortable silence; for a moment I feared they heard me behind the door. Finally he said, "I'm going to take care of this."

"Take care of what? There's nothing to 'take care of,' I assure you."

"Tonight, Tino is going to sail for Proti."

"Proti! But that is a penal colony!"

"There are no distractions there. He will not have access to the drug. He will go there, and he will stay there until the demon is exorcized from his body."

"No," Maria said. "Christmas is coming. His birthday...."

"The boy is a degenerate!" Alexios snarled. "I will not turn the Empire over to a degenerate. I will not do it."

"How dare you call him that. Constantine is co-Emperor. You must show him respect."

"Fie," he said, and laughed derisively. "Respect must be earned. You were married to Michael the Peck-filcher; you know this."

There was a tacit prohibition on any mention of her former husbands. Michael, who had just passed, and whom she genuinely loved, was considered off limits as a topic of conversation. I heard the sound of a scuffle—Maria had tried to smack him, I think, and he had stopped her blow.

"Get out," she demanded. "I mean it. Out!"

I heard the metal-on-metal squawk of the lock unbolting, and I ran down the hall into my own bed-chamber. A perfectly lovely room, but I hated it in there. I did not like to be alone; I was a fearful child when not in the company of my champion

Maria. After pacing around for a few minutes, hoping she would retrieve me, I tried to resume my reading, but my eyes glossed over the letters. Finally I gave up. I lay on the bed, harder and less forgiving than Maria's, and stared at the cracks in the ceiling. A spider had woven an elaborate web in one of the corners, and any number of insects were trapped therein. I traced the spider's movements until I nodded off, still on top of the covers.

When I woke, the room was pitch black. I could make out the outline of the windows, but that was all. Then the flicker of a candle—someone was approaching. Maria, come to bring me back to her room? No: taller, darker, noisier in his movements. I heard the rustle of the tunic, the click-clack of boot-heel on the stone floor.

"Anna," my father said, setting the candle down on the night-stand.

"Papa!"

When he found out that I was a girl, and thus ineligible to take the purple, Alexios lost interest in me, as I've mentioned. I like to think that he loved me, as fathers do their daughters, but nothing he did gave his assumption significance. I was always with Maria, and he preferred Maria to me, a preference he took no pains to conceal. If he treated me always with kindness, the kindness was perfunctory: if not feigned, then forced. I don't know that I had ever been in the same room with him alone before, just the two of us. Imagine my daughterly delight when he took a seat at the foot of my bed!

"I heard what happened," he said. "You saved Tino's life. Whether his life is worth saving: that is a different argument. But there is no question that if you were not there, if you had not taken action, he would have died." He eased back, so he was lying beside me on the narrow bed, both of us on top of the covers. "You have done God's work, Anna. I'm very proud of you." He took me in his strong embrace and kissed me on the forehead.

Oh, the dizzy excitement! The filial pride! Not only had I met with the approval of my father, but with the Emperor of Rome, the very Equal of the Apostles himself! God Himself communicated through the vessel of this maculate being, and here He was indicating His Divine Providence!

I expected my father to release me, to end the embrace. He did not. Instead, he moved his hands all up and down my body.

"You are growing up so fast," he said, stroking my matted hair. "You are practically a woman already."

In the flickering candlelight, his eyes shone black as onyx. A foul reek on his breath, like rotten eggs, assaulted my nose. He kissed me on the lips, gently at first, but he held the kiss, and then, without warning, his tongue burst into my mouth, slithering to and fro like a Cleopatraic asp. My whole body started; I thought I was going to suffocate. But he held me fast, stilling my movements, and kept at it. Finally I thought to rouse my own tongue in self-defense, wagging it desperately back and forth in a vain attempt to fend off his tonsillar advances. This only seemed to excite him further.

As he kissed me—I know now that this, the Frankish-style kiss, is the preferred manner of osculation for grown-ups, but at the time I did not understand what was happening; on the subject of carnal relations my ample reading had failed me—he pawed at me, his plump fingers kneading at my bony buttocks. When he pressed his own pelvis against mine, or more accurately pressed my pelvis against his, I felt something firm between us, the branch of a tree, a section of broom handle, a dog's bone. My first naïve thought was that this was a dagger, or some other small but deadly weapon he'd neglected to disarm ere he lay down. I tried to make him aware of it, but I could not speak with my tongue otherwise engaged. But he knew it was there, because he took my little hand and, to my shock, led it to the obstruction, enjoining me to touch it as he hoisted up his tunic. This I did, tentatively at first. At the slightest brush of my hand, his entire body jolted, as an epileptic having a seizure. The reaction, so disproportionate to what I'd done, astonished me. I squeezed a bit harder, but this did not achieve the same effect as a simple caress, especially when enhanced by the friction created by the movement of my hand.

The candle flickered and snuffed out. One of the cats mewed and scratched at the bed, while another dashed furiously around the room. A mouse, perhaps.

"That feels good," my father moaned. "Don't stop."

Countless times in the course of my life have I tried to recall the exact chronology of what happened next, but the details remain frustratingly fuzzy. Was it a dream? It was not a dream, no, it was not. The blood on the sheets was as real as the pain, incontrovertible evidence that this unspeakable perversion was not the product of a little girl's twisted imagination—that this ancient evil had corporeal form. He was on top of me, and he was inside of me, and that was what Maria witnessed when she marched into my bed-chamber. She screamed, and hurled invective at him, and took a vase from my dresser—a lovely red one painted with flowers, the clay hard and heavy—and smashed it over his head.

Alexios withdrew from me—the suddenness of his egress caused more pain than what had come before, as when an archer's arrow is yanked from the broken flesh in which it has lodged—and in the same motion, lunged clumsily at Maria. He struck her on the side of the head, not as hard as he'd wanted, but with enough force to knock her over. He stumbled to his feet and kicked her; she took the blow but did not give him the satisfaction of seeing her cry. Then he spewed curses, and shook his imperial fist, and angrily quit the room, holding in one hand the still-tumescent object of my violation, as if brandishing a weapon.

Maria came into the bed, the sheets still warm from my father's body, and held me fast. "My peach," she said, weeping. "My poor, poor peach." And she patted my hair and hugged me so tightly I thought all life would be strangled out of me. After some minutes, both of us fell into a fitful, tortured sleep.

It would be the last night I spent at the Mangana Palace.

The dream I had that night is more vivid in my memory than events that happened last week—a strange and inexplicable paradox of growing old, this: Even as the names of new novices float out of my head, I remember a nightmare sixty years past! I am in Michael's cell at the monastery, although the room is darker and drearier than his actual cell, and he younger and more vivacious. *I will protect you*, he assures me. *I won't let them lay a finger on you.* But I know that he has no way to do so, that this platitude lacks the weight of an imperial chrysobull. My fear intensifies. Protect me from what? Who would lay a finger on me? Then the reek of sulfur assaults my nose, and there is black smoke and blue fire, the tortured sounds of screaming. Suddenly and without warning, a quartet of Varangian Guard materializes in the room with us, dressed as the Four Horsemen of the Apocalypse. They've come for me. Michael reaches for my hand. *We are all alone in this lake*, he tells me, *swimming for dear life. Keep yourself afloat or you will drown. Don't let them pull you down.* And then he's gone, and one of the black-clad guardsmen raises his broadsword, and I open my mouth to scream as his weapon slices through my shoulder-blade, and I feel no pain as I watch my own severed arm fall to the stone floor, my dismembered hand clenching and unclenching its fist, as if by dark magic.

I woke with a start; Maria was still asleep, still cradling me, her breath redolent with sweet grape.

Because Michael was recently dead, I knew that his presence in the dream carried especial significance. I wondered at the meaning of his cryptic message. Was his soul in purgatory? Did he require prayerful intercession on my behalf? I decided I would pray for him when I went to church that afternoon. Then I turned toward Maria and closed my eyes, and so did not see the bed-chamber door swing open, and the four Varangian guard enter, with half a dozen eunuchs, my uncle Isaac and my grand-mother Anna Dalassene.

"This charade has gone on long enough," Anna said.

"Nana?" I said, wiping the sleep from my eyes. "What are you doing here?"

"Come, little one," she told me. "Today you come home." And she took my hand and pulled, practically ripping my arm from its socket. I had no choice but to alight, although I was ashamed that the men saw me in my night-clothes. A pool of dried blood stained the white sheet, and the pain when I got up reminded me of what had happened the night before.

Maria woke then, and at the sight of the soldiers, she scampered back to the headboard and pulled her legs up, wrapping her arms around them protectively. Her radiant blue eyes darkened with fear.

"Sister," Isaac said. "I regret to inform you that the betrothal of your son Constantine Doukas to the princess Anna Komnene is hereby null and void. This morning, the Emperor named his own son John co-Emperor and heir to the throne. As a show of good will, the Emperor will allow Constantine to retain his purple shoes and other garments."

I glanced at Maria, expecting to see tears, but she was expressionless, like all life had been drained from her—she looked, in fact, like Tino when high on opium. She must have known deep down that this day would come, but that knowledge did not make the realization any easier to accept. With the benefit of decades of hindsight, informed by my experiences at the hospital, I now know that she was "in shock."

Isaac looked over at me and wanly smiled. He looked embarrassed. "As the princess is no longer betrothed to your son, she will come back to the Boukoleon to live," my uncle continued. "As for you, sister, you are hereby ordered to leave Constan-tinople, or else to remit yourself to a convent. The Emperor leaves the choice to you." Then he added, in a softer voice, "I'm sorry, Maria."

Re-animated, Maria let out a derisive snort, sounding not unlike her rude son. "I'm not surprised that Alexios sent you to do his dirty work," she said.

"A real man would have had the decency to tell me himself. You were always a better person than he, Isaac. I pity you."

"Maria," Anna Dalassene said. "It's over."

"Yes," she said. "So it appears. I will leave at once for Myrelaion. You can have Alexios all to yourself now, *Jacosta*." Anna did not appear to understand the insult. Maria turned to me. "Goodbye, my peach. Please know that I love you most of all." She hugged me, and showered me with kisses, and then my grand-mother tugged again at my arm, harder this time, separating us.

Only then did the great and life-altering moment of the occasion dawn on me. This was goodbye! I screamed, as loud as I could, and the sheer volume caused my grand-mother's hand to recoil. I raced back to Maria, hugging her tight around the leg, like a barnacle clinging to a pier. My eyes were closed, I was weeping, I refused to let go. When Anna tried to grab me, I turned and bit her hand.

"Bring her," she commanded the guards, shaking her wounded hand—I had drawn blood. All four of them were required to subdue me, I'm proud to say, but subdue me they did, whisking me out of the room and away from the Mangana Palace.

They put me down when we got outside—the temperature was below freezing—but I made a break for it, and one of them, a veritable Goliath, hoisted me up over his shoulder and thus conveyed me, kicking and screaming, to the Boukoleon.

"I hope you are not always this insolent," my grand-mother said, smacking me across the face. "It was a mistake to entrust that whore with your care."

"Don't you dare call her that!" I spat.

She fell away, and Isaac vanished too, and the Goliath carried me through the warren of rooms comprising the women's apartments, past eunuch clerks and waiting-ladies, past flowerpots and dour saintly icons, to parts of the palace in which he was generally not permitted to set foot. In the last of the rooms he set me down, turned round on his heel, and marched off, closing the door behind him.

A tall, slender, sad-looking woman sat on the side of her bed, cradling an infant. On the floor, a dark-skinned toddler played some sort of game, the objective of which was to smash his enormous and malformed head against the stone wall, repeatedly, as hard as he could.

"Welcome home, Anna. Come. Meet your brother Andronikos." Irene gave me the baby to hold, and the little guy immediately burst into tears. "He's a fussy one," she said, handing the swaddled infant to the wet-nurse, who sat quietly in the corner of the room. "What happened there?" she asked, pointing at my navel. The front of my night-gown, I saw, was stained with blood.

"I cut myself," I lied. "I tripped getting out of bed." The toddler, meanwhile, was aggressively banging his head against the wall, affording me the opportunity to change the subject. "What is he doing?" I asked. "Isn't he going to hurt himself?"

"John is not terribly smart," she explained. "It's too soon to tell, but I think he may be daft."

"But he is co-Emperor now, and heir to the throne!"

"Yes," Irene said, shaking her head. "So it appears." She glanced up at the icon of Christ on the wall above her bed. "May Heaven help us all."

VIII
THE DIVINE PLAN

TO THE OUTSIDER, OR EVEN TO THE SERVANT, the transition from life with the former Empress at Mangana to life with the sitting Empress at Boukoleon would seem like hopping between heavenly clouds. *Our privileged princess proceeds from one palace to another*, the porter would have been forgiven for thinking: *What's the difference?* Indeed, my schedule remained more or less the same, and at neither address did I want for anything material. I remained the envy of every little girl in Christendom.

Beneath the surface, however, in the vasty deep of my tortured feelings, the changes were intense and difficult and emotionally draining. Maria had been my touchstone; now, just like that, my touchstone was gone. The loss was profound. As in that horrible nightmare, I felt like I'd lost a limb. Not only was she gone, walled up in that drafty convent, but all contact with her was forbidden me.

"She doesn't want to hear from you now," my mother told me. "She has given herself to God and has no excess energy for further distractions."

I suspected that my mother spoke falsely—Maria would never willingly submit herself to God, as her relationship with religion had always been practical rather than spiritual; nor would she willingly sever contact with me, the object of her profound affection—and yet I hadn't the opportunity to prove otherwise. Eventually I stopped asking after her, although she remained always in my thoughts, as the voice of God hummed constantly in the ear of Moses.

My mother was not as warm as Maria, not as demonstrative in her affections, but she was loving in her tempered way, and I know she enjoyed my company. If Irene had not been eager to raise me when I was a baby, she was now ready to "make up for lost time," to use Homer's phrase. Where Maria was garrulous and warm, Irene was quiet and reserved—as I was. The holes in conversation, the awkward pauses, were mitigated by the presence of my baby brother Andronikos—Andy, as the family called him—who was a delight to us both. When we didn't know what else to discuss, we'd turn to him.

But my mother and brother were but a bandage over a gouging wound; they offered some protection, but lacked the healing power to fully restore me to health. For my father had hurt me: deeply, painfully, horribly, permanently. At the time, I did not fully grasp this. The incident befuddled me. I'd always sought his approval, and my uneasy submission to his base desires had won it; thus I was both pleased with myself for, and horrified at the grotesque method of, my sad little victory.

The notion of incest, meanwhile, was not unfamiliar to me, voracious reader that I was. The Greeks sang incessantly of fathers fornicating with daughters, mothers with sons, brothers with sisters; Oedipus was the best-known example, but hardly unique. And did not the Bible teach that inebriate love between Noah and his daughter produced Lot, the sole spared Sodomite, from whom we are all descended? If this were all true, why then did I not thrill completely to my father's touch? Wherefore my squeamishness? To a separate point, if intercourse was supposed to be a source of great erotic pleasure, as Maria indicated that it was, why did I feel only stabbing pain, each and every time my father attempted it? And he attempted it more frequently after the sudden relocation to the Boukoleon, given my newfound proximity to the imperial bed-chamber as well as the insuperable rift between him and his longtime lover. How many times I was subjected to this I cannot say. My recollections are hazy. I felt like it was every night, but I'm sure weeks or even months went by in peace—enough time for my insides to heal, only to be broken yet again. I lay in bed like the bound Prometheus, unable to resist the eagle's taloned assault—and it did feel as though my liver was being pecked out, the pain was so great. Unlike that fabled Titan, no Heracles appeared to end my torment, although every time a provincial would-be usurper declared himself *Augustus* in some remote corner of the Empire, I'm ashamed to confess, part of me hoped and prayed that the rebellion would this time succeed.

There was much more stimulation at the Grand Palace, with its court and courtiers, its ambassadors from foreign lands, its lavish entertainments and dinners, than I had known at the tranquil Mangana. As the purple-born daughter of the Emperor, I enjoyed near-universal favor. Not only was it advisable to maintain excellent relations with a princess, but with Tino suddenly removed from the picture, I was now free to marry. Many suitors sought my hand. Alexios considered all the proposals, but Irene, the child bride herself, refused to allow me to be betrothed again ere I turned a more appropriate age.

As far as I was concerned, marriage held no appeal whatsoever. I was much more interested in the inner workings of the Empire. To that end, I spent as much time as possible with the Prime Minister, my grand-mother Anna Dalassene,[105] who took great pains to prepare me for what she hoped would be my life's work. She believed in total immersion. Nothing was kept from me. At age nine I was privy to every imperial secret. I read treaties, chrysobulls, decrees, missives from foreign diplomats and

---

[105]   She'd forgiven me for biting her! (A.K.)

domestic *espions*. In my free time, I consumed as much history as I could lay my hands on.

Anna Dalassene was brilliant in her way, but no great scholar; she relied more on instinct and charm than knowledge. Lacking in these God-given qualities, I compensated with preparedness. If there is indeed nothing new under the sun, as Scripture says, then history is a guidebook by which the dutiful map-maker might use to chart his course. Eschewing the trappings of the princess's courtly life, I spent all of my free time in careful study. I read Prokopios and Psellos, Skylitzes and Nikephoros of Constantinople, Plutarch and Tacitus, and every military manual I could get my hands on. I learned about Octavian and Tiberius, Caligula and Claudius, Trajan and Antoninus Pius, Hadrian and the great thinker Marcus Aurelius; Domitian and the ill-starred Tetrarchy, Constantine the Great and his bellicose sons and heirs, the crises of the third century and the fall of the City of Rome after the reign of Theodosius the Great, the attempt at restoration by the inimitable Justinian and his Empress Theodora; the near loss of Constantinople to the Saracens during the reign of Constantine IV in A.D. 678; the fanatical Iconoclasts and their ultimate defeat by the formidable Empress Irene; the great expansion under Basil the Bulgar-slayer, and all the wars fought by the Byzantine emperors against any number of foes up to the present day.

My encyclopedic knowledge of Byzantine history gave me a "leg up," as they say at the Hippodrome, in analyzing current events. In the sack of Jerusalem by the hostile Seljuk Turks, rightly reviled by one and all, I was able to discern an historical parallel: the conquests of Attila and his Huns in the fifth century—who would easily have taken Constantinople had persuasive appeals not been made to re-direct him instead to Europe. The Byzantine Way is to win through deception, not brute force: better to let proxies fight your battles than risk mortal wounds yourself. I saw an obvious opportunity to apply that axiom when a delegation sent by the new Pope of Rome arrived in the Queen City. I say "Pope of Rome," but this fellow—Odo of Châtillon, who took the name Urban when he took the Papal robes—was barred from entering that venerable city by the antipope Clement, an agent of the loathsome Germans, who occupied the Vatican City at the time of Odo's ascension. Urban spent much of his pontificate on the road, roving from parish to parish, drumming up support for his tenuous authority. He was charismatic, by all accounts, and given to flowery oration. But his position was weak. His delegates came to Constantinople and lifted the ban of excommunication on my father imposed by the scurrilous Gregory; this heavenly concession was made in the hopes of enlisting the Emperor's terrestrial support for Urban's papacy.

Not that Alexios had men to spare for such a trifling cause half a continent away. To the contrary, the imperial army had been actively recruiting Franks from Gaul to fill out its rank and file. On the subject of these *arrivistes*, allow me a brief digression. The Frankish race fancies itself Christian and thus civilized, but make no mistake: they are really barbarians. They are all descended from the tribes of ruthless raiders who swept down years ago from the Norse lands—*Vikings*, these are called, the Norman word for "marauder"—and their manners have not much changed in the interim. They trumpet the King of the Franks as an "Emperor" on par with our own, as if the itinerant Bishop of Rome had the authority to award such a preposterous title, but they are all savages, their alleged "Emperor" included. Their garments are no better than rags, even the best-bred among them; their women are rude and rough—the wives of both Oursel and Robert the Fox rode with their husbands in battle!—and all of them, men as well as women, drink to excess, exacerbating an already quarrelsome nature. And forget having them to dinner. Franks eat with their grubby hands, stuffing their greedy maws with as much meat as will fit, leaving no room to manipulate and masticate the food, as if they suffer from some genetic malady that compels them to gorge as quickly as possible, and they wash it all down with copious amounts of wine, a stronger vintage than what we serve here, and they belch and break wind at table with impunity. Worse, owing to some imbecilic interpretation of Scripture that conflates Christian virtue with dirt—that scoundrel Gregory, I'm reliably informed, was a prime proponent of this unsanitary doctrine, a sad and smelly attempt to emulate the life of Jesus, assumed by these fools to fancy the fetid—Franks do not bathe. All day they ride, or make war, or pillage for food, or otherwise toil in the sun, sweating profusely, the same rotten garments beneath their mail, and they do not wash, they do not submerge their filthy bodies in water, they do not even remove their clothes to let some air in. The result is an unspeakable reek. A pack of Franks stinks like a hundred thousand raw onions delicately chopped on a hot day. It is the most horrific vileness, an olfactory assault of the worst kind. Once in our presence, to be fair, some of them do adopt a civilized attitude towards ablution—Oursel was not so offensive on the nose, and Bohemond smelled like a rose—but most are content to live in dirt and muck and grime. Even the Turks, whose risible religion at least compels them to wash regularly, do not raise such a stink.

Because the Frankish system of inheritance is flawed, with too much emphasis placed upon primogeniture—it is one thing to dictate that the first-born be the next king, but to leave everything to him and deprive his brothers and sisters of so much as a crust of bread to live on is as stupid as it is cruel—they are constantly at war with one another, brothers attacking brothers on the battlefield for a few acres of rock-strewn real estate: quite the opposite of Alexios and Isaac Komnenos, my father and uncle, whose mutual respect and trust was the rock on which was built the Byzantine Restoration. It was ironic, then, that Urban appealed to *us* for military support, when he had all the able-bodied young men he needed right in his Châtillon back-yard; he lacked merely the ability to organize them into a proper army. As for us, we wanted nothing more than to expel the Seljuk Turks from our former territory, to raise once again our banner over Anatolia and the Holy Land.

Alexios and his closest advisors—Anna Dalassene, Isaac, and Nikephoros Bryennios the Younger—were discussing all of this in the Map Room, from which the couch had by now been permanently removed. I sat in silence, taking it all in, as was my wont, when suddenly an idea came to me, as if by divine inspiration.

"Wait," I cried. Everyone looked at me, as I had never before spoken in the Map Room, not even to excuse myself. "I have an idea."

Discussion ceased. Everyone looked at me. Annoyance crossed my father's face, but only for a brief moment. Then he smiled pleasantly and said, "Well, out with it, then."

"Forgive my interruption," I began. "But I know now what course of action we should take."

"I'll be the judge of that," Alexios said, but he was grinning.

"The vile Turks have taken Jerusalem, the holiest of cities, where they have subjected her Jewish and Christian inhabitants to rapine and slaughter," I said. "We want to remove them, and take the city for ourselves, but such an undertaking is Herculean, and an obvious waste of precious resources. Meanwhile, in Europe, hordes of Frankish knights ride aimlessly about, making war on one another for wont of anything else to occupy their slack attention. What we need to do, it seems to me, is divert those Franks to Jerusalem, and have *them* take out the Turks on our behalf."

"Well, sure," my uncle agreed. "But how? A magic spell?"

"I'm coming to that," I replied. "Here we have a delegation from this new Pope, a gifted speaker who is not afraid to travel hither and yon to disseminate his ideas. He is not in a position of power, this Urban, but if he could bring resolution to the constant problem of internecine war between Frankish cousins, he could at least bring peace to his pontificate. This would help him in his quest to consolidate power."

"Perhaps," my grand-mother said.

"Right now the Pope is calling for help to install him back in Rome," I went on. "A noble cause, perhaps, but not one that plays upon the heart-strings of these Frankish brutes. He needs to take a more selfless stance. He needs to preach about the horrors going on in Jerusalem, in the very City of God, where Jesus Christ preached and suffered and was buried and rose again on the third day in fulfillment of the Scriptures. The infidels now control that ancient and hallowed place! That is the appeal that this Pope must make: that these wastrel Franks should take up arms and go to the Holy Land and re-claim it for Christendom—which is to say, for Byzantium."

My father's fingers probed his beard, as they did when he was deep in thought. "This is an interesting idea," he said. "But aside from the benefaction of Divine Providence, Jerusalem is not a top priority for me. I'm more interested in Syria."

"It may be that the Franks never make it to the Holy City," I replied. "If they do, so much the better. If they fail, they will still make incursions into Syria. Perhaps they will take back Nicaea. Perhaps they will take back Antioch. Once they arrive in Constantinople—which they must do, to pledge obeisance to the Emperor—it will be up to us to guide them. We must be shepherds to their bleating sheep."

Whereupon my grand-mother Anna Dalassene jumped out of her seat and applauded. "Little one," she said, "this plan is a stroke of genius! I will get to work at once, drafting a strategy the Pope can employ!"

That my rough plan succeeded so wildly, vastly exceeding my most grandiose expectations, proves that God favors Christians over Moslems—and also confirms the rank stupidity of the Frankish race.

IX

THE FALSE DIOGENES

IOGENES, THE TRAGIC EMPEROR, HAD A SON CALLED CONSTANTINE. This Constantine was the issue of his discarded first wife—the half-brother of Eudokia's sons Leo and Nikephoros, who lived with my grand-mother at the Blachernai upon the death of their father and banishment of their mother. Through his marriage to my father's sister Theodora, Constantine Diogenes was my uncle. Not that I ever knew him. He fell in battle during the reign of my cousin Michael, in A.D. 1073, valiantly fighting off a Turkish invasion. My aunt Theodora died the following year giving birth to their only child, a daughter called Anna, who was betrothed to the Grand Prince of Serbia, and thus grew up in that faraway land. With all of his immediate family either dead or gone, few recalled that Constantine ever existed—until he declared himself *Augustus* in the Bulgarian marchlands late in the Year of Our Lord 1094. Who this imposter was I cannot say—perhaps he was the actual Constantine Diogenes, conveyed like Eurydice from the Underworld—but he somehow managed to cobble together an army of disaffected citizens and Cuman infidels, making enough noise about an attack on the Queen City that Alexios saw fit to enjoin the fraud's forces in battle.

The False Diogenes was not the only one plotting my father's overthrow. From her dim cell at Myrelaion, Maria of Alania stewed in her anger. She wanted nothing more than to exact revenge upon the man who broke her heart and ruined her life. In the person of Eudokia, the whilom Empress who was Mentor to her Telemachus, she found the perfect partner in crime. This was by design; indeed, it was Eudokia's habitation of Myrelaion that led Maria there to begin with. The two of them concocted a plan to assassinate Alexios during his Bulgarian campaign. That my father planned to lodge at an estate on Lake Ohrid owned by none other than Maria's son and my former fiancé Constantine Doukas afforded a golden opportunity.

"I will to Lake Ohrid go," Maria said. "I will get back into the Emperor's good graces—which will not be difficult, as I am more cross with him than he is with me. Then, in the afterglow of our affections, I will raise a bodkin and play Judith to his Holofernes."[106]

---

[106] Judith 10:11-13:10.

"Not on the first night," Eudokia warned. "The first night, his guard will be up. So too the second. On the third night—that is when you should strike!"

I was not privy to the plan beforehand, for obvious reasons, but my antennae were raised when I received a letter from Maria—my first communication from her since her banishment! O happy day!—via my aunt Irina, her Alanian cousin and bosom friend.

My peach,

How I have missed you! It is cold here at Myrelaion, and I have had to sleep alone for the first stretch of time in many years. I do not like that. How I wish I were back at the palace, with you, where we could talk and be together!

Mightily have we been wronged—me, Tino, you. And you especially…my heart aches at what your father has done to you. I am taking steps to redress this problem and I hope soon, if God allows, we will be together as we were before. Know that I love you dearly, my peach, and the actions I am about to undertake will be done with your happiness and well-being in mind.

Yours,
Maria

Her literary style never approached the level of her discourse, and her handwriting was atrocious, worse than a child's, but how I wept when I received that epistolary embrace, heartfelt as it was! Little did I realize that the "steps" she was taking to "redress this problem" involved imperial assassination. Nothing was further from my mind, in sooth. Even now, I have a hard time believing that Maria would have been capable of murdering my father—indeed, of murdering anyone. She was too kind, too sensitive for such cardinal sin.

As it happened, she never got the opportunity.

Her plan depended on the involvement of her son, Tino, who would, upon the death of Alexios, be proclaimed *Augustus*. Or so Maria convinced herself. What she failed to appreciate was that, while her son enjoyed the trappings of life in the purple, he did not particularly wish to be Emperor. Like his adoptive father Michael, he was not mad for power, and he had seen firsthand how ascension to such lofty heights could destroy a man's joy of life. Furthermore, he refused to betray Alexios.

"Mother," he said, when she informed him of her treachery, "I will not participate in your despicable scheme. I implore you to call it off at once!"

Tino had good reason to protect my father. When Maria was removed to Myrelaion, Alexios had made good on his threat to rid his erstwhile co-Emperor of the scourge of opium addiction. He banished him to Proti, where Tino'd lived for months under the dutiful watch of the aging Romanos

Straboromanos. On that island, far from the temptations of the city, he managed to purge himself of desire for the stuff. This was, as he himself phrased it to me, "tough love," but he was eternally grateful to Alexios for forcing him to embrace a healthier lifestyle. When his mother refused to reconsider her plan, he revealed her treachery to my father, who put an immediate halt to the scheme. It was an ignominious end to Maria's long career in the public eye, a black mark upon her record—although it was, in my view, ultimately forgivable.

The three year span of A.D. 1093-5 comprised busy years in the annals of Byzantium. Alexios slew the False Diogenes and defeated the Cumans. My mother Irene gave birth to another son, called Isaac—easily my favorite of my siblings. Anna Dalassene put into action my plan to liberate the Holy Land by enlisting "Crusader" Franks, with the Pope happily appropriating it as his own idea. Nikephoros Bryennios the Elder, the now-blind general who'd come so close to taking the purple himself, breathed his last. Likewise, the great Eudokia, one of the greatest and most unheralded of Empresses, passed in her sleep at the venerable age of seventy-five. Last, and most tragically: despondent over the rift between his mother and Alexios, Tino, after months of sobriety, sought opium to eat, the better to ease his sorrows. He took too much of the stuff and his heart seized up. He died at his Lake Orhid estate, just twenty-one years old.

Banished forever from Constantinople, with her only son dead, and with his death any hope of re-claiming her position as Empress gone, Maria returned to her childhood home in T'blisi a broken woman. She was forty-four, and would live another dozen years, but the sources of her happiness were exhausted. I exchanged several letters with her in the first few months after her exile. In one of her few missives to me, she wrote: "One day, my peach, you will write about this. You will tell my story, and your story, and you will compose a great history." But after three or four missives, she stopped writing back, suddenly and without warning. This broke my heart, but I forced myself to accept that Maria had had to move on for her own well-being. (It was not until later, the year my father died, that I learned the treacherous truth.)

All these years later, an old woman at the convent, I recall her with nothing but love—indeed, there is no one, not even my own children, not even God Himself, whom I have ever loved more absolutely than Maria of Alania—and when I think of her, I cannot help but weep.

Look! Even now, a teardrop has stained this page. . .

VOLUME TWO:
MY MARRIAGES

A.D. 1096-97

X
THE HEIR

THE UNFORTUNATE SERIES OF EVENTS both preparatory and subsequent to the death of my father the Emperor has besmirched my once-sterling name, and it is commonly assumed that I bore nothing but contempt for my half-brother. This charge is, on its face, preposterous, for one as simple and pathetic as John Komnenos could not engender so much ill will. To be sure, I envied his undeserved status as heir to the throne, a position for which he was uniquely unqualified. But such matters were, frankly, far from my mind in those early days at the Grand Palace. To the contrary, I viewed my brother as my mother did—indeed, as anyone who knew him well did—as a defective creature desperately in need of our collective help: the Komnenoi's flesh-and-blood cross to bear.

As brilliant as the youthful Anna Komnene might have been, as celebrated at court for the precocity of her learning and education, the polar opposite was true of poor John. Irene was fair if not beautiful; Saddiq, exquisitely handsome; both, attractively slender and regally tall. Not one of these superlative traits was inherited by my runtish half-brother. In physical appearance he was pitiable: the deformed skull, the blank eyes, the porcine nose, the contorted posture, the unsightly hue of his skin the same shade as dark clouds before a storm. Were he stripped of his purple robes and sent to live in the barn, one might reasonably have mistaken him for livestock, some exotic animal shipped in from the distant provinces to amuse the children. He did not look like he'd been created to walk upright; indeed, it took him years to manage not to move about on all fours. He spoke in subverbal grunts for almost a full decade, and his vocabulary even in adulthood comprised a pitiably meager stock of words. He never learned to read, never grasped arithmetic beyond simple addition, never understood the complex history of Byzantium; he'd have been hard-pressed to name more than a handful of Roman emperors. As it was, he could not even correctly pronounce his own surname, which he rendered as "Comb-knows," shorn of its second syllable. *John-comb knows*, he would say, when made to give his full name. My grand-mother, aware of the lad's considerable shortcomings, sought to re-cast his imbecility as blissful saintliness by referring to him as "John the Beautiful," an ironic choice to be sure, given his horrific appearance. Historian after sycophantic historian adopted at face value that nickname—Anna Dalassene surely anticipated this—which I never once heard used at court except as a joke. John was beautiful as the dwarf was tall.[107] Their shoddy scholarship, combined with a collective reluctance to publish anything disparaging about the royal family, however valid, means that there are few if any references in the extant literature to John's laughably feeble mind. To the contrary, the credulous Niketas Akominatos,[108] for one, averred that my half-brother was some sort of military genius. A genius! John!

To be fair, by the time he was ten or eleven, John was less bestial than his early childhood presaged. The head was still a monstrosity, the posture stooped, the tone of voice devoid of intellect, but buried as he was beneath his purple robes, surrounded by dutiful eunuchs watching his every step, he was able to fool the hoi polloi—who are, it must be said, far too easy to dupe. When engaged, he would utter one of the clutch of banalities he had at his disposal, a half-dozen responses seemingly chosen at random, as if by the throw of the dice. When asked his opinion of a race at the Hippodrome, he

---

[107] Even artists presented him in the best possible light; the fresco of him at Hagia Sophia, commissioned by his son Manuel soon after his death, was based on another John Komnenos entirely: my first cousin, the eldest son of my uncle Isaac. (A.K.)

[108] Nicetas Choniates, who wrote a well-regarded history of John's reign.

was known to remark favorably on the clement weather, even in a light drizzle!

When one is big sister to such a creature, one falls into the rôle of caretaker—a part to which I was well suited, as my years in the hospital, and later in treating my father's gout, would reveal. Irene was overmatched with John—she was not the sort of mother who was good with little children; and, incidentally, she viewed the prospect of her illegitimate son inheriting the crown with abject horror—but my brother liked me, and I was able to guide him where others failed. There was never animosity between us. Our relationship was more like the nurse to the invalid, or the groom to a sick horse. Even when the horse kicks, the good groom stands his ground.

Had things remained as they were, I would have run the Empire even if John was its nominal head, rather like my grand-mother did for my father. Some equally doltish girl would have been Empress, but Anna Komnene would have "called the shots," in Homer's phrase. As it happened, my hopes were dashed by a "fly in the ointment," to borrow the line from Ecclesiastes—a fellow the same exact age as my brother, an unclean Turk of all things, an orphan whose parents had perished during the siege of Nicaea (of which, more later), where he was personally discovered and adopted by my father in A.D. 1097. Something about this boy attracted the Emperor's attention; Alexios plucked him from that Nicene dung-heap and whisked him back to

Constantinople, to serve as my brother's companion and only true friend. It was as if he'd been delivered there by God Himself. At his baptism, the Turkish youth confusingly took the Christian name John, after his bosom friend. But his birth-name was Axouch, and he was known to one and all as Ax.

My father adopted Ax in the way a soft-hearted individual takes in a sad-faced stray dog. He scarce could have imagined how this singular act of mercy and charity would alter the course of history. Every ounce as fiendishly formidable as Eudokia or Anna Dalassene, as rakishly charming as Diogenes or Saddiq, as precociously gifted as Alexios or myself, Ax would single-handedly ensure John's ascension and the improbable twenty-six-year success of his reign, and prove my greatest rival—and, it must reluctantly be conceded if I am being perfectly honest, my most generous benefactor.

But once again, I am getting ahead of the story. For Ax would never had been found, would have attained his manhood in Nicaea with his parents intact, would perhaps have risen through the ranks to be captain or somesuch, had not the "servants of God" come from the West to do the Lord's—and the Emperor's—bidding. For that fateful event, I have no one to blame but myself.

XI
THE APPEAL

THREE WEEKS BEFORE MY TWELFTH BIRTHDAY, Odo of Châtillon, in his official capacity as Pope Urban II, delivered an address before an adoring crowd of Frankish knights and bishops at Clermont, in the Langue d'Oc region of Gaul. His exact words are the subject of some debate, as there are conflicting sources, and Odo, a gifted orator as previously stated, was given to extemporaneity. But I have reason to believe that he did not much stray from the remarks prepared for him by Anna Dalassene and myself, carefully crafted to exacerbate the feelings of rage already bubbling beneath the surface of every last member of his Frankish audience, and to provide for those feelings an outlet, countenanced by, or seeming to be countenanced by, Divine Providence.

"Most beloved brethren," he began, "urged by necessity, I, Urban, by the permission of God, chief bishop and prelate over the whole world"—subordinate to the Patriarch here at Constantinople, in actuality, but we of course did not mention that![109]—"have come into these parts as an ambassador with a divine admonition to you, the servants of God. I hoped to find you as faithful and as zealous in the service of God as I had supposed you to be. But if there is in you any deformity or crookedness contrary to God's law, with divine help I will do my best to remove it. For God has put you as stewards over his family to minister to it. Happy indeed will you be if He finds you faithful in your stewardship. You are called shepherds; see that you do not act as hirelings. But be true shepherds, with your crooks always in your hands. Do not go to sleep, but guard on all sides the flock committed to you. For if through your carelessness or negligence a wolf carries away one of your sheep, you will surely lose the reward laid up for you with God." He then mumbled a few prayers and quoted a few passages from Scripture, as the priestly members of his audience expected; shorn of the numerous sheep metaphors, the speech might have confused these wooly men of the cloth.

Then his voice adopted a tone of righteous anger. "O race of Franks, race from across the mountains, race chosen and beloved by God—to you Chosen

---

[109] In *The Alexiad*, and again here, Anna makes the assertion of the superior rank of the Constantinopolitan Patriarch. This is historically untrue, although she seemed fiercely to believe it.

Ones our discourse is addressed and for you our exhortation is intended. We wish you to know what a grievous cause has led us to your bucolic country, what peril threatening you and all the faithful has brought us.[110]

"From the confines of Jerusalem and the city of Constantinople horrible reports have gone forth and very frequently been brought to our ears, namely, that a race from the kingdom of the Persians"—Turks, technically, but the ignorant Franks knew not what a Turk was—"an accursed race, a race utterly alienated from Jesus Christ, a generation forsooth which has not directed its heart and has not entrusted its spirit to God, has invaded the lands of those Christians and has depopulated them by the sword, pillage and fire; it has led away a part of the captives into its own country, and a part it has destroyed by cruel tortures; it has either entirely destroyed the churches of God or appropriated them for the rites of its own religion."

Whereupon a hush fell on those gathered. For they had all heard rumors of these barbarous happenings in the Holy Land, scarce believing them. But now that the Pope himself was corroborating the tales of woe, they knew the rumors had to be true. "They destroy the altars," Odo went on, "after

---

[110] There are several extant reports of Pope Urban's address at Clermont on 18 November, 1095. Anna's account bears the most similarity to that of Robert the Monk's, as noted in his *Historia Hierosolymitana*, written ca. 1107.

having defiled them with their uncleanness. With rusted blades they circumcise the Christians, males and females both, and the blood of the circumcision they either spread upon the altars or pour into the vases of the baptismal font. When they wish to torture people by a base death, they perforate their navels, and dragging forth the extremity of the intestines, bind it to a stake; then with flogging they lead the victim around until every last inch of viscera is outside the body, and the poor victim falls prostrate upon the ground.[111] Others they bind to a post and pierce with arrows. Still others they compel to extend their necks and then, attacking them with dull swords, attempt to cut through the neck with a single blow. What shall I say of the abominable rape of the women? And of the children, both girls and boys? To speak of it is worse than to be silent. Know only that the Persians are as animals, unable to temper their sick urges, which they carry out on all of their victims regardless of age, sex, or infirmity."

The gathered Franks, needless to say, savages as they are, were hardly innocent of rapine, and a healthy percentage of those assembled had himself slaked his disgraceful lust on some unfortunate boy from time to time. Norman monasteries were notorious for this sort of thing, in fact. But *Moslem*

---

[111] This is patently false. My sick-minded grand-mother dreamed it up late one night after drinking God knows how many glasses of wine. (A.K.)

men raping *Christian* boys—that was another matter entirely.

"The Kingdom of the Byzantines is now dismembered by these heathens and deprived of territory so vast in extent that it cannot be traversed in a march of two months." This was wild hyperbole. "On whom therefore is the labor of avenging these wrongs and of recovering this territory incumbent, if not upon you? You, upon whom above other nations God has conferred remarkable glory in arms, great courage, bodily activity, and strength to humble the hairy scalp of those who resist you.

"Let the deeds of your ancestors move you and incite your minds to manly achievements; the glory and greatness of King Charles the Great, and of his son Louis, and of your other kings, who have destroyed the societies of the pagans, and have extended in these lands the territory of the Holy Church. Let the Holy Sepulcher of the Lord our Savior, which is possessed by unclean nations, especially incite you, and the holy places which are now treated with ignominy and irreverently polluted with Saracen filth. O, most valiant soldiers and descendants of invincible ancestors, be not degenerate, but recall the valor of your progenitors!"

Odo's words had the desired effect—and then some. For the Franks are a belligerent people, quick to anger, and prone to acts of vengeance. They are furthermore pious, insofar as they idiotically believe all of their actions are governed by celestial forces beyond their control. And here was the one man,

Christ's vessel in their view, who could give those celestial forces both voice and shape! Not one knight in the assembly, even the most peaceable, would have declined the opportunity to slay a Turk just then, if one happened to appear.

But it is one thing to compel a Frank to kill a Moslem in Clermont; quite another to convince that same Frank to leave his homeland—his family and friends, his wife and children, his worldly possessions, and all of them possibly if not probably for good—and trek halfway around the world to kill the same Moslem. Next, Odo had to anticipate their excuses and pre-emptively refute them.

"But if you are hindered by love of children, parents and wives, remember what the Lord says in the Gospel: 'He that loveth father or mother more than me, is not worthy of me. Every one that hath forsaken houses, or brethren, or sisters, or father, or mother, or wife, or children, or lands for my name's sake shall receive a hundredfold and shall inherit everlasting life.'[112] Let none of your possessions detain you, nor solicitude for your family affairs, since this land which you inhabit, shut in on all sides by the seas and surrounded by the mountain peaks, is too narrow for your vast population; nor does it abound in wealth; and it furnishes scarcely food enough for its cultivators. Hence it is that you murder one another, that you wage war, and that

---

[112]   Matthew 10:37-39.

frequently you perish by internecine conflict. Let therefore hatred depart from among you, let your quarrels end, let wars cease, and let all dissensions and controversies slumber. Enter upon the road to the Holy Sepulcher; wrest that blessed land from the wicked race, and subject it to yourselves. That land which as the Scripture says 'floweth with milk and honey' was given by God into the possession of the children of Israel. Jerusalem is the navel of the world; the land is fruitful above others, like another paradise of delights. This the Redeemer of the human race has made illustrious by His advent, has beautified by residence, has consecrated by suffering, has redeemed by death, has glorified by burial. This royal city, therefore, situated at the center of the world, is now held captive by His enemies, and is in subjection to those who do not know God, to the worship of the heathens. She seeks therefore and desires to be liberated, and does not cease to implore you to come to her aid. From you especially she asks succor, because, as we have already said, God has conferred upon you above all nations great glory in arms."

Odo paused now for dramatic effect, before sealing the deal: "Any man who undertakes this Crusade and dies, shall have all his sins forgiven. Any man who trespasses during the Crusade will benefit from remission of his sins, cardinal and venal alike, with the absolute assurance of the imperishable glory of the kingdom of heaven. Take up the cross, my friends. Go ye and take back Jerusalem!"

Whereupon a cry broke out in the crowd, almost as if choreographed—which, of course, it was: "God wills it! God wills it!" If there were any doubt in the mind of any one man there, the sudden, synchronized chant erased it. For only Jesus Christ Himself could have orchestrated such a response, and its meaning was surely to validate every last word Odo had said.

And so the Frankish fools sold their possessions, and put their estates in hock, and bid farewell to their families, and gathered arms and mail and supplies, and prepared for the long journey to the Holy Land—by way of our court in Constantinople, where first they would bid obeisance to the *Augustus*. Little did they know that their heavenly-ordained "Crusade" was conceived, right down to the "God wills it" chant, by an eleven-year-old girl and her grand-mother in faraway Byzantium, for the primary purpose of securing that obeisance.

As for said eleven-year-old girl, she could scarce imagine that this demonstration of political cunning would deliver her, among other things, a husband.

XII
THE SISTER

THE FIRST WAVE OF PILGRIMS TO REACH CON-STANTINOPLE arrived late in the summer of A.D. 1096. Their leader, a city-dwelling fraud referred to without irony as Peter the Hermit, emerged in the wake of Urban's Clermont clarion call. With his long beard, longer hair, tattered robes and sandals, and reputation for piety built on his supposed years living in a cave on some Gallic mountaintop, he looked the part of Jesus of Nazareth, and like Jesus of Nazareth, he proved a capable shepherd. Somehow he managed to round up tens of thousands of disciples—men, women, and children, old and young, poor folk mostly—to take up the Cross and make the pilgrimage to Jerusalem. Along the way they ransacked houses and farms, put the torch to cities, and murdered every Jew they could find, as Moslems were inconveniently unavailable along the land route. What Peter's end-game was, I cannot even guess. Probably he was insane. Less an army than a rabble, a mob of divinely-inspired cretins, perhaps well-intended, but functionally useless against the Turk, its arrival beyond the Theodosian Walls was a sight to behold. One did not realize there was such a multitude of dirty peasants in all of Christendom! The obvious course of action was for the motley bunch to set up camp across the Bosporus and wait until the actual knights arrived, but Peter and his "army" would not have it. These fools had marched hundreds of miles and were desperate to spill the blood of the infidel. And now they waited on our doorstep, getting hungrier and angrier with each passing day.

"What to do?" my father asked in the Map Room, on a particularly scorching August afternoon. Sweat beaded in his beard, I remember, and the chamber reeked of fetid bodies. "Certainly we cannot let them into the city."

"Good God, no," Anna Dalassene said. "There are more of them than there are of us. More likely as not they'll ruin the place, and even if they don't, it will take a full year and a thousand acres of sage to rid Constantinople of their foul stink."

"But they can't make the pilgrimage now," Alexios said. "They are poorly armed, poorly trained. Jesus Christ Himself could come down from Heaven and lead them, and still they would lose. And do we want to tip our hand by sending them onward to Jerusalem?"

"Other forces *are* coming," Isaac my uncle asked of Anna, "right?"

"Hugh of Vermandois," Anna said. "Walter SansAvoir. Godfrey of Bouillon. All three with armies capable of smashing the Turk, and all three on their way. More will undoubtedly follow—the King of France is said to be intrigued, and also the son of William the Bastard—but those three armies for certain are already on the march."

"Whatever you wrote in the Pope's speech, mother," my father said, "it was certainly effective. Your oratory rivals Cicero."

"It was more Anna than I," my grand-mother said, giving me a smile and a nod.

"So: we cannot send them on to the Holy Land," Alexios said, "but we also cannot keep them here. What, then, to do with the miserable lot?"

"Simple," I put in. "Whisk them across the Arm of St. George, as they call it,[113] give them some light provisions, and have them head due east, into Anatolia."

"Anatolia?" my uncle said. "But that's where the sultan's army is headquartered!"

"Precisely," I said. "I'm sure the Turks will take great delight in ridding us both of this rabble. Some will flee, some will survive, most will perish. The infidels will tire themselves out slaughtering so many, and perhaps let their guard down a bit when the legitimate forces arrive."

"Anna!" my grand-mother exclaimed. "That is positively devious! I am very much impressed."

---

[113]   The Bosporus.

"Furthermore," I went on, noting with pride at how my relations were listening so intently to my every word, "we should send an embassy to the sultan, and alert him of their arrival. Secretly, so word does not get out. Let them be prepared. This will ensure that Peter's rabble meets its demise, and it will also buy us some goodwill with the sultan—this will prove valuable, I believe, in the months to come."

Whereupon my father was so proud that he actually clapped his hands together and jumped in the air. (That night, he would further express his affection for me by visiting my bed-chamber, as he still did from time to time; this, too, gave me pleasure—his attention, that is; never the odious act itself.) "God wills it," he said, sarcastically—a quip on the line we'd suggested Urban's planted followers shout at the end of his speech.

The next day, my plan was put into effect. Nikephoros Bryennios the Younger, the son of my father's rival and now his most trusted general, rode off with six knights to inform the sultan of the threat to his western border. Peter's men crossed the "Arm of St. George" and marched to what would be the predicted slaughter. Eager to please and excited to have pleased, I was unable to feel anything other than proud satisfaction with my contributions, although my solution led directly to the death of many thousands of more or less innocents, Christians all.

A few weeks after that fateful meeting, I received a strange letter, delivered by a befuddled Frank whose command of Greek was limited to a few basic phrases and thus could offer no further explanation as to the origin of the post. So thoroughly did he reek that I dismissed him at once, yet the foul stench of his oniony odor hung about the room for hours afterward. The contents of the epistle, however, proved infinitely sweeter:

My dearest princess,

We have not had the pleasure of meeting, although like you, I lived for years with Maria at the Mangana Palace, a victim of my own father's lofty ambitions. Our paths, I regret to say, never crossed. Like Maria, I came to Constantinople as a stranger and was welcomed with open arms, only to be dismissed as soon as I was no longer of practical value. Such is life at court, as you will one day realize (not through direct experience, I hope). I loved Maria with all my heart, Maria loved you, and I have always thought of us as sisters, in spirit if not in biology.

My brother is coming, Anna. He will take up the Cross and join the campaign against the infidels in the Holy Land—the campaign you yourself engineered, if my sources do not speak falsely. He is a mighty warrior, my brother, and I have no doubt that his participation will tip the scales in our favor. With him on the battle-field, Jerusalem will indeed be liberated!

As your spiritual sister, it is my duty to inform you that my brother has ulterior reasons for taking up the Cross. He is hoping that undertaking such an arduous and impossible task, akin to a labor of Heracles, will bring him back into favor with God, and also with the Emperor. For he wants nothing less than to take your hand in marriage. He has heard of your precocious learning and wisdom, and carries with him a charcoal sketch of you done in secret by one of the court artists. "My future wife," he tells all who will hear, "is the most beautiful girl in the world."

I cannot guess how you will feel upon hearing this news, Anna. I assure you that my brother is a kind, strong, decent man, worthy of your affections. I did not want you to be "blind-sided" when it comes out during his visit to Constantinople, which he tells me will come in the late summer or early fall, as soon as he can make preparations.

I pray for you every day.

All my love,
"Sis"

Much as I admired my "sister's" discretion at remaining pseudonymous, I knew at once that this mystery correspondent had to be Helena, the mannish former nanny and fiancée to the late Tino, currently languishing at the convent of St. Stephen of Mangana, a short stroll from the Grand Palace; and that my mystery suitor was none other than the son of Robert the Fox, the legendary Bohemond.

At twelve and a half, I had never been in love, was uninterested in any of the pathetically submissive men who flitted to and fro about the court, harbored no illicit feelings for stray generals, senators, or monks. My mind was focused solely on my studies and my work. But as I recalled Maria's estimation of Bohemond as one of the handsomest and most desirable males in Christendom—and this assessment from a woman not easily impressed!—I must confess that my spindly knees, as the saying goes, became weak as I read and re-read that letter. Plenty of suitors had by that point made their intentions known to my father, my mother, or my grand-mother, but to a man, all of them saw me as a sacrifice to be made in the rise to power, not as a woman to be desired in her—in *my*—own right. This, then, was unprecedented. Was it a prank? Was he feigning his affections to woo me? How could this unparalleled specimen of rugged masculine beauty possibly favor an one as plain and ugly as Anna Komnene?

Unable to contain my excitement, I showed the letter to my mother. I was afraid she would be cross with me, but to my surprise, she was giddy with delight, even more so than I was. "But this is wonderful!" Irene exclaimed. "If anyone can help us realize our ambitions, this Bohemond is he."

"I'm sore afraid, mother," I said. "He has never laid eyes on me. What if this sketch she speaks of is too flattering? What if he takes one look at me and shudders? He is so handsome, and I, so ugly."

"Fie, Anna," she replied, "that is not so. You are not ugly. You are just a more specific type, made for a man with more refined tastes."

"Coat the truth with honey all you like," I told her. "That doesn't change the way I appear."

"Beauty is in the eye of the beholder," Irene said. "Bohemond's father, the dread Robert the Fox, left his first wife—by all accounts a beauty on par with Helen of Troy—to marry Helena's mother, who rode with him in battle and was more manly than most men," and she ran a comb through my rat's-nest head of hair. "Robert was absolutely in love with her. Is it too much to imagine that Bohemond shares his taste in women? As the saying goes, 'Like father, like son.'"

We sat there in silence, both of us pondering the ramifications of this news. Rarely in all my life have I been as excited as I was that hot summer day.

"What now?" I asked finally.

"We go see our friend Helena," Irene said. "And we arrange for a meeting with Bohemond, when he arrives at Constantinople. A *secret* meeting. A *rendezvous*, as the Franks call it." She took my hands in hers. "Tell no one about this, Anna. If you are ever to claim the throne one day, your father, especially, must remain in the dark."

❦

Hardly the most girlish girl in the realm—one will recall the confusion surrounding my sex that led to the old astrologer's fateful banishment—even I was stunned to meet an one as mannish as Helena. Tall, strong, with severe features and no visible hair except the series of short black wires on her upper lip, she looked more like a soldier dressed as a nun than an actual nun. She hugged me with more force than anyone ever had, and her voice was deeper than my father's.

"I hoped you would come," she said. "I knew you'd know at once that I was your correspondent. I didn't sign it just in case someone else stumbled upon the letter first. One can't be too careful."

"That was clever of you," Irene said. "So Bohemond has taken up the Cross. Good for him."

"Good for all of us," Helena said. "My brother is invincible on the battlefield."

"*Almost* invincible," Irene corrected.

"No one can defeat the Equal of the Apostles," the manly nun said, with apparent sincerity. "He was a fool to try. But in his defense, that was my father's doing, not his."

"Is he really sweet on me?" I blurted out, in spite of myself. "Or is he putting me on? Be honest, sister."

"*Smitten* is the word I would use," Helena replied. "My brother has enormous self-confidence, and does not requite some dull and pretty wife to prop up his feelings of self-worth. He is attracted to powerful, intelligent women. I do believe you qualify, princess. Look at how the forces of Western

Europe march *en masse* to Byzantium, at your command! He is a good man, my brother, loyal, strong, kind and generous. He would make a fine husband."

"And together, you would rule the Empire," my mother declared.

"When will he arrive?" I wanted to know.

"It depends," Helena said. "Most likely in September. I will keep you informed as to his progress. Come visit me once a week, or better yet, send a waiting-lady, to arouse less suspicion."

"He will take the Old Road?" Irene asked. "From Dyrrachium?"

"I believe so."

"When he gets to Thrace, we will meet him at one of the Doukas estates. The one to which my grand-father retired."

"I know the place."

"Tell no one."

"Of course."

"And Helena? Thank you."

My "sister" hugged me so tightly as we left that I thought for a moment my head might pop off.

XIII
THE KERATAS

WHILE I STILL MISSED MARIA HORRIBLY, my life was more or less blissful in those days, and yet I knew next to nothing about romantic love. My heart was full of *agápe* and *philia*; of *eros*, I was innocent.[114] While there was no shortage of suitors, as previously mentioned, I did not thrill to any of them—quite the contrary. The acts I engaged in with my father, meanwhile, or rather that my father engaged in with me, were undoubtedly erotic in nature, but they did not consume me with *eros*; my feelings were closer to what the Greeks called *storge*, the "love" one feels for the tyrant.[115] My intimates were all much older than I; the forty-four-year-old Maria had been my closest friend, and now twenty-nine-year-old Irene had

---

[114]   Three of the four ancient Greek words for the various forms of love, per Aristotle's *Nicomachean Ethics*.
[115]   The fourth form of love (ibid.).

taken her place. Most of the older men at court were too intimidated, or too disgusted, to lay eyes on me, although occasionally I noticed Nikephoros Bryennios, the one called Junior, whose appetite for rapine was well known even to me—my mother warned me about him, as did several waiting-ladies whose virtue he'd drunkenly attempted to compromise—glancing longingly in my direction. Such was the extent of my romantic life at that time. The letter from Helena, then, was an arrow from Eros himself that pierced my virgin heart.

Alexios seemed to sense this new rival for his affections, and became even more possessive of me. Usually he'd come to my bed-chamber once a week at most; no sooner did I receive that letter than he visited me with far greater frequency. Every other day the knock would come at the door. Too, his desire was intensified. No amount of scratching could satiate his imperial itch. It was as if he knew, on some level, that my heart was straying, so sought to keep me under his thumb in the only way he knew how.

On one of those occasions, perhaps owing to a surfeit of drink, he did not take the proper precautions. Generally he was the picture of discretion, not wanting anyone at court to guess at the odious nature of his nocturnal visits to my bed-chamber. Not so on this fateful night: All Hallow's Eve, it was, A.D. 1096. He was unusually clumsy, tripping over things in the hallways. He was loud, his voice resounding off the stone walls of the palace. As he approached my door he burst into song, a bawdy bit of ribaldry he'd picked up on some battlefield in his youth:

There's only one place to stick my sword
To stick my sword
To stick my sword
There's only one place to stick my sword
In that wet, wet sheath of hers,
Good Lord!

The immediate result of his carelessness was that half the palace woke up in the middle of the night, wondering at the source of the racket. One of those disturbed was my insomniac grand-mother, Anna Dalassene. No sooner had the imperial sword been stuck in said sheath (unlike in the ditty, the sheath was as dry as the salt into which Lot's wife trans-mogrified, alas) than she burst into my bed-chamber, which door he'd stupidly and unaccountably left ajar.

The admixture of emotions I felt upon this dis-covery is impossible to convey. Shame, certainly, for whatever the Greeks wrote about their incestuous gods, I knew that what we were doing was indu-bitably sinful. Mortification, for who wishes to be seen "making the beast with two backs," as another bawdy tune puts it, with one's venerable relation? Dread, because I knew my grand-mother had the power to punish me. Oddly enough, not all the feelings were adverse. Was I proud that my hand-some father had chosen me, ugly Anna Komnene, as his lover? Did that enhance my own self-regard?

Would that I could lay claim to the contrary. And, yes, as I buried myself beneath the blankets, I felt also something akin to relief—because this discovery must mean the cessation of his unseemly visits, surely? And much as I adored him, I wanted them to cease. Then as now as always, the raw act of love was never not painful for me.

But Anna Dalassene seemed unaware of my presence. She did not so much as glance in my direction. Ire veritably radiated from her, as light from the halo of Christ, but all of it was directed at her wayward son. "How dare you," she said finally.

"Mother," Alexios said, extricating himself from me, "I am the *Augustus*. The Equal of the Apostles. I do what I please." His voice as he spoke slurred badly.

"And whom," she chided. Then, after two shakes of her head, she added, "I don't recall much in the Scriptures about apostles despoiling their daughters. That's an unusual interpretation of the virtue of chastity, *Emperor*," this last word uttered with such malice that it was as if a knife had been thrown at him.

"You can stop feigning indignation," he shot back, sliding his legs over the side of the bed and sitting upright. "I'm not doing anything I didn't learn from you."

"Fie," she spat. "You were a boy. A man. It is different with girls. Girls are more vulnerable, more fragile."

"You know, I've about *had it* with you dictating every move I make." He was now standing fully erect, but made no move to dress. "I am the Emperor, as you helpfully pointed out. It's my visage on the coins, not yours."

"Coins that are debased," Anna spat back. "Just like you."

"Debasing the coinage," he retorted, "was your idea, mother.[116] As was this insane scheme to summon every armed lunatic in Christendom to decamp outside the city walls."

"The latter," she corrected, "to give credit where credit is due, was your daughter's burst of inspiration." For the first time, she looked at me, her expression tinged with disgust and, perhaps, envy. I sat there as if dead, my own expression blank. She added, "The little whore."

"Watch your tongue, mother, or I'll have it torn out."

"Given the uses to which my tongue has so often been put, I'd think twice about that, if I were you." Then I watched in stunned surprise as she reached out her bony hand and, with excruciating gentleness, caressed his naked manhood. One stroke of her index finger was sufficient to give it rise. There

---

[116] This is true on both counts. The debasement of coinage—that is, using less gold and silver in the coin but declaring it just as valuable as it was before—was done at the beginning of Alexios's reign, to finance the many wars going on across the Empire. Gold coins of Alexios were so notoriously shoddy that imperial debts had to be paid with coins bearing the likeness of Michael VII Doukas.

it was between them, bouncing up and down as the bow of a ship in the high-tide harbor. Her voice grew soft, and her tone suggested one who has been betrayed. "What is the meaning of this, Alexios? Am I too old now for your affections? Has my little Jezebel of a grand-daughter replaced me?"

Still I held my tongue. My heart beat in my chest like a rabid animal trapped beneath the floorboards. I pulled the blanket up over my face and shut my eyes. I wanted to melt into the bed and vanish.

"You have not been replaced, mother. You've obsolesced all on your own. Take a gander at the looking glass! You're an old woman with one foot in the grave!"

"How dare you!" She reached out and swatted at his manhood, which, like that same ship at harbor, began to sink.

He tried not to react, although it was obvious she'd hurt him. "Your services are no longer needed at court," he told her. "You will be gone by the time the sun rises, to some convent or other, or so help me God I will banish you to Proti."

"I will do no such thing. I have imperial powers! You cannot remove them. Nor can your government function without me, you *keratas*."[117]

"You flatter yourself, mother. I can run the government just fine."

---

[117] This is a difficult word to translate. It is akin to *cuckold*, but it also implies a dupe, a fool, a weakling.

"Run a government? Fie. You can't even keep a Moor out of your marital bed!"

Anna Dalassene's audacious reference to this taboo subject functioned as the magic words to a nasty spell. He had been drinking, my father, to great excess; he had been interrupted in the satiety of his lust; he had been shamed when his sinful incest had been discovered; his manly bits had been abused; and God knows, the anxiety he must have felt at the unprecedented arrival of the Franks would have felled a lesser man. This messy stew of passions, which had been simmering for hours, suddenly boiled over, spilling its hot mess over everything.

I watched in horror as one mighty blow smashed in her nose.

I saw my grand-mother's blood spurt onto the floor of my bed-chamber, staining the Persian rug.

I witnessed my father wrap his powerful fingers around her throat and lift her half a cubit off the ground.

With my own eyes, I beheld her legs kicking vainly, until all fight was gone and they stilled.

With my own ears, I heard her gurgle and gasp, until all vigor was gone and there was silence.

I saw her dead body collapse to the floor. Alexios regarded it with horror. He muttered obscenities under his breath. Then he said, "I am a monster." At no point did he look at me. I believe that in his state of shock, he forgot that I was in the room.

I watched as he hoisted the corpse into his arms, kissed it once on the forehead, and carried it away.

The next morning—which felt like the same day to me, as I did not sleep a wink that horrible night, but also like a year later, because the time passed with such agonizing slowness—word came around that my grand-mother had died peacefully, in her sleep. As she was seventy-two years old, quite the old crone Alexios said she was, this was entirely plausible, and any suspicions that might have been roused were negated by his obvious grief. Alexios and I were the only ones who knew the truth, and we never once brought up the subject: another of his dread secrets with which I was unduly burdened.

Thus my father slew his mother, just as my mother had slain her father.[118]

When Irene heard the news, she was shocked—not because her eternal mother-in-law had passed, but because her eternal mother-in-law had passed on 1 November, A.D. 1096: the self-same day Saddiq the astrologer had predicted that Alexios himself would breathe his last!

---

[118] One of the many frustrating aspects of *The Alexiad* is that the death of Anna Dalassene is not mentioned. Sources differ on the exact date and cause of her passing, with the best guess being between 1100 and 1102. Certainly she vanished from the records at some point during the First Crusade. The consensus among Byzantine scholars is that Anna Komnene declines to report on this because her grandmother's tenure at court ended ignominiously, perhaps with a charge of heresy. Certainly Alexios committing matricide would explain the lack of mention in *The Alexiad* and clear up the prevailing mystery.

XIV

THE NEWLYWEDS

T HE YEARS SINCE HIS DEFEAT AT LARISSA[119] had
not been kind to Bohemond. Luck deserted
him. Without his indefatigable father Robert the Fox to give shape and purpose to his energies,
he moved about as if lost, like Odysseus ranging to
and fro across the Mediterranean after the fall of
Troy. After some period of dissipation, he'd managed
to oust his brother Roger Borsa to win control of
Taranto, a fortified town of little consequence on
the heel of the Italian boot—not enough to satisfy
the outsized ambitions of this outsized man. His
ultimate aim was nothing less than to succeed my
father, whether by usurpation or inheritance, and
take the purple. Ever since the news arrived of my
birth, not long after Larissa, Bohemond believed,
with the certainty the rest of us believe in the Risen

---

[119] To Alexios and the Byzantine army, after a series of prior
victories.

Lord, that he would one day marry me, and together we would rule the Empire—an ambition almost certainly foisted upon him by his father, but one he'd come to embrace on his own. As the years went by, that scheme seemed more and more grandiose, and he hated himself for ever having entertained the thought, let alone having believed it so fervently. Such was his sorry state of mind in the waning years of the eleventh century.

In A.D. 1096, Bohemond was engaged in putting down a rebellion on the Amalfi coast—ostensibly as a favor to his uncle, the Duke of Sicily, but really to alleviate his chronic boredom. The battlefield was his métier, the arena in which he shone above all others, and to employ him on this sparse if lovely Tyrrhenian beach was akin to Heracles sweeping the well-swept pantry instead of cleaning all of the Aegean stables. That he knew the mission was beneath him did not ameliorate his mood. Once or twice he almost fell prey to a foe's arrow, distracted as he was by his own internal struggle. Twice or three times he earnestly wished that said arrow had found its mark.

And then, just like that, everything changed. Like Saul of Tarsus on the fabled road to Damascus, he saw a sign, an unmistakable sign: pilgrims, Servants of God, traveling under the banner of Godfrey of Bouillon, *en route* to the Holy Land. Recognizing at once that this was his best, and likely his last, opportunity to make something meaningful of himself, to realize the scope of his enormous ambitions, he immediately took up the Cross, taking with him his rapacious nephew and protégé Tancred. His depression faded. His confidence returned. With renewed vigor, he quickly dispatched the rebellion, raised an army of Franks—the smallest but mightiest of the forces that would make its way through our capital city, without question—and prepared to take the fight to the Turks. But not before his appointment in Constantinople. At long last, Bohemond and Alexios would meet: Paris and Menelaus breaking bread years after the latter's abduction of Helen.

Organizing a private meeting with Bohemond required an enormous share of logistical planning, and an even greater supply of luck. None of the other Crusaders could be aware of the *rendezvous*—I do prefer the Frankish term, sounding as it does more exotic to my dull and old-fashioned Grecian ears—nor could anyone in Byzantium suspect that my mother and I were thus engaged, least of all my father. Irene's initial plan was to meet them in Thrace, at her grand-father the late *Caesar*'s estate, but this was ultimately dashed as too public, as well as too close in proximity to the Queen City. Instead, we moved the location further west, to Lake Ohrid, home to my other grand-mother, Maria of Bulgaria, whom I'd not seen in several years. The sudden death of Anna Dalassene provided a useful pretext for our journey (she would have approved!): my grief—as profound as it was sincere, incidentally—could only be assuaged by seeing my other grand-mother. Or so we told Alexios.

And so, in late November of A.D. 1096, a full year after the Pope's fateful exhortation at Clermont, Irene and I arrived at my grand-mother's estate at Lake Ohrid—far and away the most beautiful residence I've ever seen, including the Grand Palace and the Mangana. Two vast and crystalline lakes lay side by side, big and little sister, ringed by splendid mountains. The view from her verandah was extraordinary. We stayed for six weeks, and I spent much of that time listening to tales told by my grand-mother, a gifted and funny storyteller, in her lilting Bulgarian accent, and taking long walks on the bucolic property. I did not so much as open a book the entire time I was there.

Outside of town was a small church, associated in some loose way with a monastery, and it was there that we contrived to meet Bohemond. He and his nephew Tancred were to come alone, disguised as itinerant priests; we would go to them to pray for the soul of my dearly departed Anna Dalassene. Our own security detail, Varangian Guard who'd eagerly accompanied us from Constantinople for a chance to retreat to the tranquil countryside, stood sleepy sentry over the church. These beefy, pink-skinned Northmen drew more attention than the "priests," who arrived on foot, in long gray robes, bearing walking sticks.

Outside the sun shone bright as can be, but little light penetrated the tiny church, with its slits for windows. I could hear some sort of animal clawing beneath the floorboards, redolent of dank earth, but that disturbing sound was drowned out by the fierce beating of my heart. I glanced at my mother, who flashed what was intended to be a reassuring smile, but I could tell that she too was nervous. Our little *rendezvous* was not without risk. What if this meeting were an elaborate ruse? We had only the small company of Varangian Guard—what if Bohemond unleashed the full force of some unseen army and kidnapped us? I trusted that Helena would not lie to me, but what if her brother had lied to her? That was how the Trojan War started, I remembered, sitting in that darkling church: with the whisking away of the wife of a king. Was I just a pawn in the game, and my mother Irene the real prize?

The door creaked open, a cone of light shining across the dark floor. A pair of mice dashed through it, startling me. Two men entered the room, giants both, one bigger than the other. The second bolted the door behind him and stood in front of it; the first approached us, seated in the first pew by the altar as was our custom. We rose to meet him.

"Ladies," he said, doffing the hood of his robe. "It is my sincerest pleasure to meet you." When he was near enough, he dropped suddenly to one knee, bowing his massive head.

"You may rise, sir," Irene said. He did, and I beheld him.

Now Bohemond was such as, to put it briefly, had never before been seen in the land of the Byzantines—he was a marvel for the eyes to behold. He was so tall in stature that he overtopped the tallest by nearly one cubit, and was narrow in the waist and loins, with broad shoulders and a deep chest and powerful arms. And in the whole build of the body he was neither too slender nor overweighted with flesh, but perfectly proportioned and, one might say, built in conformity with the canon of Polykleitos.[120] His skin all over his body was very white, and in his face the white was tempered with red. His hair was yellowish, but did not hang down to his waist like that of his Frankish kinsmen; for the man was not inordinately vain of his hair, but had it cut short to the ears. Whether his beard was reddish, or any other color I cannot say, for the razor had passed over it very closely and left a surface smoother than chalk. His ice-blue eyes indicated both a high spirit and dignity, and his nose and nostrils breathed in the air freely. He was so made in mind and body that both courage and passion reared their crests within him, and both inclined to war. His voice when he spoke was deep and commanding, but also warm and inviting. He was the very picture of charismatic manliness. Beholding him, I swooned.

"Princess," he said, locking his own eyes on mine, "you are even more comely in the flesh than

---

[120] Famous Greek sculptor from the fifth century BCE, known for his bronzes.

your portrait had led me to believe." No one had ever before accused me of comeliness, especially not an one as comely as Bohemond, and yet I detected nothing insincere in his voice. He was either telling the truth or else the best stage-strutter in Christendom.

"You flatter me, sir."

"Thank you for agreeing to see us," he said to my mother, gallantly bowing.

"Not at all." Her voice was remarkably level under the circumstances, but the flush of red upon her cheeks indicated that she was not immune to his ample charms. "We are eager to hear what you have to say."

"As you know, my nephew and I"—and here he gestured toward the door, where Tancred gave a courtly bow—"have taken up the Cross. While we sympathize with our Christian brethren in Jerusalem who have fallen prey to the wrath of the Turk, our motives for joining this Crusade are not, I must confess, wholly religious in nature. You see, I hail from Taranto, and my dukedom there is beneath you, princess. When I conquer the Holy Land, then will I be worthy of claiming your hand in holy matrimony. This is why I have come."

A lump formed in my throat, as if I had swallowed an apple entire. The notion that I would share a marital bed with this man, this god come down to earth, sent tremors up and down my body. I would happily leave Constantinople for Jerusalem—or wherever he established his capital; perhaps, like the Romans, at the more temperate port of Caesarea instead—to spend the rest of my life with him. But this is not what he had in mind.

"Once wed, Bohemond of Jerusalem and Anna of Constantinople would inherit the crown from your good father Alexios, long may he reign, and together, jointly, rule Byzantium. It takes two to accomplish that, as you well know—an Emperor to handle military matters, and an Empress to run the administration. I can think of no better duo in all of God's earth, princess, than you and I."

Irene was smiling. "So your motives are wholly ulterior."

"Not at all." Here he once again fixed his mighty gaze upon me. "None of this would be worth the trouble if I did not hold my betrothed in such lofty regard. The one aspect of women I find singularly attractive is genius. And you, Anna *ma cherie*, are the living, breathing embodiment of genius. It was your idea, was it not, to call upon the Pope for aid, and to base that call upon this unfortunate business in Jerusalem? That was impossibly clever. I would love you forever just for that. You've no idea the effect that has upon me, princess. I would marry you right here, right now, if you would have me, and happily forsake all other women for the remainder of my life."

I thought I heard a repressed chortle from Tancred just then, but when I glanced over, his face was steely and stolid—it must have been my own self-loathing imagination.

"What say you, Empress?"

"It is clear that my son John, although I love him with all my heart, is unfit to rule," Irene said. "If he inherits the throne, the Turks will sack Constantinople within a fortnight. No, Anna simply must succeed her father. And I can think of no one better equipped to help achieve that result than you, duke."

"Thank you for your confidence," he said, gallantly bowing.

"But it is not my decision to make." Irene turned to me. "Having been forced into a marriage I did not want, at an age too tender for such things, I would never put my own daughter in the same position. No, Anna must choose her own destiny. She is young, but as you said, wise beyond her years. What say you, daughter?"

"Yes," I asserted. "A thousand times yes."

"Are you certain?"

"Yes," I said again. "A thousand times yes."

"Then let it be done now," my mother said.

"Now?"

"Here we are in this house of God, and have both the elements of time and surprise working in our favor. What better opportunity will ever present itself?"

"Your husband might object," Bohemond pointed out, although the smug expression on his face suggested that he would not mind if that were the case.

"He most certainly would. But he is not here. And we will not reveal to him that this has taken place until the moment is right."

"A secret marriage."

"Precisely. Tancred, my good man, if you would please fetch us a priest, we can have the ceremony anon."

"Yes, Empress," he said. "As you command."

And so there, in that dank church on Lake Ohrid, Bohemond and I became One. We said our vows to God and to our kin and to each other. He gifted me a ring to seal the promise, a crude circle of hammered iron that I wear to this day. After the ceremony, when we were man and wife, my mother and Tancred went outside with the priest—an old man, half blind, who was sworn to secrecy on the pain of death and given ample coin for his trouble withal—and gave me and my newly-minted husband time alone.

I assumed Bohemond would ravish me, this hulking Frankish warrior, but no—he was gentle. He swooped me off my feet, cradling me in his massive arms, and showered me with chaste kisses.

"You are too young yet for that," he declared. "And I am no savage. I will not rob you of your maidenhood at this tender age, whatever the law allows."

Perhaps he said this to avoid having to make with me "the beast with two backs," as the ribald ditty phrases it. Perhaps he found me as physically repulsive as other men seemed to. But I swear on the lives of my children, he seemed sincere. As my chastity had already been sullied years ago by my own father—which atrocity my new husband had no knowledge of—I had especial appreciation for Bohemond's tenderness. I felt light-headed suddenly, and the last thing I remember before fainting was the look of love, feigned or otherwise, on his gorgeous pink face.

XV
THE PRIME MINISTER

THE MAN WHO EMERGED to discharge the responsibilities of Prime Minister after the sudden death of my grand-mother Anna Dalassene was both a likely and unlikely figure: Nikephoros Bryennios the Younger. Unlikely, because he was the first and only son of the ill-starred general of the same name, my father's greatest rival to the throne, the blue-blood Alexios personally blinded; likely because, as the first and only son of the eponymous Nikephoros Bryennios, he would himself have been *Augustus* upon the death of his father in A.D. 1094, had Fortune favored his father and not the dotardly Botaneaites, had the imperial chips fallen in a slightly different way.

Junior, as he was known to the inner circle at court, had, to the raised eyebrows of some in the Queen City, thrown those same fallen chips in with my father, who regarded him as his own son, as Hadrian did Antoninus Pius.[121] Alexios trusted him implicitly, his loyalty and honor were beyond reproach, and he was, it must be said, both a brilliant general and a talented administrator. That allegations of rapine followed him everywhere; that he was openly feared by maids and waiting-ladies, more than a few of whom had fallen prey to his unwanted advances, with at least two of their number bearing him bastard children; that he was known to encourage the despoilment of women captured in various battles as just another rightful form of pillage, akin to the plunder of silver candlesticks or golden rings—none of this bothered my father, who'd indulged his base desires with both his complicit mother and his blameless daughter, and thus was in no position to lecture a serial rapist on the virtues of chastity. We all have our faults, God knows. In any case, Junior proved a most capable counselor, in every way worthy of succeeding Anna Dalassene. At this time, at the onset of the Frankish quest for the Holy Land, the Empire badly needed skillful management, and he rose to the occasion. I shall give you one such example of his canniness.

One by one the Crusader commanders arrived in Constantinople, where, before undertaking their appointed task, they made obeisance to Alexios. The strategy was to isolate each man, kill him with

---

[121]   Roman Emperors of the second century, not related by birth. It was a custom at the time for the sitting *Augustus* to adopt his hand-picked successor as his son.

kindness, and make him swear oaths before God that any territory he might win during the expedition that had been previously in Byzantine hands—which is to say, any territory at all!—would be restored to the Empire. My father was a military man at heart, more comfortable on his pallet at camp than upon his soft mattresses at the Boukoleon. He would never, as Diogenes had done, travel to a battlefield bearing a gem-laded throne and a gilded chest of crown jewels. He enjoyed the loftiness of his office, certainly, but he was, insofar as it was possible for an engaged Emperor to be, without pretense.

Thus Alexios assumed that the Servants of God, when they arrived, would have an audience with him in the Map Room, designed as it was for that purpose (the couch, you may recall, had been removed years ago, after he quit Maria). But Junior had other ideas.

"Your Highness," he said, "these men are rubes. They are a generation or two removed from living in trees or in caves. Animals, really. A few rotting buildings crammed around a mill—that is a Frankish city. They do not bathe, as we unfortunately know, and have no appreciation for the finer things, because these pigs are unaware that finer things exist. The Huns had more couth than these Norman savages."

"Yes," my father replied, "none of what you say is news to me."

"Their innocent eyes have never beheld a city like Constantinople, a cathedral like the Hagia Sophia, a palace like the Boukoleon. The sheer majesty of the place will put them ill at ease. This is a feeling we wish to intensify when they meet Your Highness."

Alexios ran his fingers through his beard, a gesture he'd been doing more and more lately, as his facial hair grew patchier and grayer. "Continue."

"The Throne Room," Junior said, "has been, in recent years, neglected. Diogenes was not in office long enough to revive it, and neither you nor any of your other recent predecessors could be accused of hubris, and hubris is what is required to make unironical use of that chamber."

"True enough," my father replied. "Botaneaites, Michael, Constantine, Isaac—all flawed men, to be sure, but all of them admirably humble."

"Given the naïveté of these Franks, and our stated purpose to dazzle them, I move that we renovate the Throne Room and have them pay homage to you there."

At this suggestion, Alexios burst out laughing. The jocularity of his younger days had mostly abandoned him after taking the purple, but when my father laughed, his belly shook, his face lit up, and the sound could be heard from far down the hall. "Junior," he said, "that is a capital idea!"

The Throne Room had been constructed almost two centuries before by Constantine VII, who mistook the luck of being born in the purple for proof of his own divinity, and decorated the chamber accordingly. The throne itself was a massive thing, crusted with gold and jewels and upholstered with purple velvet from Cairo (the gold and the jewels had long since been appropriated to finance various crises, and the velvet was moldy and torn), and it was mounted on a dais that, through an ingenious succession of pulleys and levers, made it rise some twelve feet in the air through a switch on the chair's arm. A supplicant would be on his knees before the Emperor, inches away from the imperial boot, and could only watch in awe as said boot suddenly levitated before his eyes, as if by magic! Adding to the effect, a band of musicians blared on trumpets and beat on drums, colored lights streamed, and lions—two of them flanking the Emperor—roared mightily. The inherent godhood of the Equal of the Apostles could not have been communicated more clearly.

And so, under Junior's watchful eye, a team of engineers, artists, and animal trainers set about transforming the Throne Room from dusty afterthought to center of spectacle. Weights and pulleys were greased. Gems—most of them fake; how would these fools know?—were clustered to the throne, which was reupholstered in bright purple velvet. Colored lights were built, and a quick-witted monk in town from Mount Athos figured out how to make white smoke billow from beneath the dais, adding to the effect of bedazzlement. Musicians rehearsed old compositions designed for maximum bombast. Lions could not be found, so bear cubs were used instead—not as majestic, but just as menacing. (One of them almost mauled my idiot brother John, in fact, who'd wandered too close to their ursine

cages.) The royal seamstress designed a new, flash-
ier wardrobe for my father, which included a new
crown twice as tall as the old one. Alexios looked
ridiculous in those new purple-and-gilt garments,
the massive crown on his head, the *globus cruciger*
atop the imperial scepter in his gloved hand. It was
all we could do to keep from snickering.

The first Frank to make obeisance to the
Emperor in the new Throne Room was Godfrey of
Bouillon, who arrived two days before Christmas in
A.D. 1096—some three weeks after my thirteenth
birthday and two months after the death of Anna
Dalassene. This Godfrey was in his late thirties, tall
of stature but not exceedingly so, fine looking but
not exceedingly so. So thick was his blonde beard
that a nest of mice were rumored to live therein; I
personally observed little gnats swarming around his
face. Many of the Franks who took the Cross—my
secret husband, to name but one—did so for temporal reasons, but Godfrey's piety was unimpeachable.
He spoke almost completely in Scripture passages,
found omens in the flight of every cardinal, and
neither married nor took lovers nor entered the
priesthood, choosing to live as a celibate, like the disciples. In short, he was an easy mark. The look on his
austere face when he beheld Alexios on the throne!
How his jaw dropped when the Emperor rose in the
air, as if risen by Christ! Although my father did not
find comfort in such a pose, he played his part to
perfection. Godfrey swore at once to return Byzantine lands to Byzantium. Walter SansAvoir, Hugh

of Vermandois, Raymond of St. Gilles, Adhemar of Le Puy, Robert of Normandy—all had similar reactions. Would Bohemond, my Bohemond, fall for this ruse as well?

How I wanted to send word, to warn him! But his movements were so speedy, there was no guarantee an epistle sent via Helena would reach him in time. Nevertheless, I wrote to my "sister," who was now, in fact, my sister-in-law. And then I waited for my husband to arrive in Constantinople.

XVI
THE WIDOW

THROUGHOUT THE EARLY MONTHS OF THE CRUSADE, my mother remained loyal to, and in love with, the Moorish astrologer Saddiq. Although she and I spent a good deal of time together in those days, she took pains to remain discrete when calling on her lover, or allowing her lover to call on her, with my complete isolation from the Moor being the result. Her motives for setting this boundary are unclear. Perhaps she wished her daughter to remain ignorant of her flagrant infidelity. Perhaps discretion helped alleviate the shame she felt at her sin. Perhaps she sought to protect me from his predatory advances—Saddiq, like many men of talent and ambition, was not in the habit of confining his affections to a single individual, and a princess, whatever her anatomical curiosities or faults, holds a peculiar, inherent allure to those aroused by power. The Moor would have attempted my seduction if opportunity presented itself, without question.

By now, they had been lovers for more than a decade, and I suspect that Saddiq had grown bored of her. Romancing an Empress was difficult enough; *quitting* an Empress—that was nigh impossible. I'm sure that lecherous charmer took more than a few supplementary lovers in those ten years, but Irene remained his primary companion—until the ill-fated day when he turned his libertine attentions to her almost-namesake, my aunt Irina.

Irina, the astute reader will recall, was the cousin of the Empress Maria, one of the Alan contingent that came to Constantinople during the reign of Bagrat in Georgia. No one in Christendom was as beauteous as Maria, of course; nonetheless, her kinswoman was, even in her late forties, a very attractive woman. Unlike the erstwhile *Augusta*—twice married but in neither instance to the man who won her heart—Irina had the good fortune of being in love with her husband. Isaac, unlike his younger brother, was the picture of fidelity, a model mate, kind and gentle and protective. As far as my uncle was concerned, the sun rose and set on his lovely wife, and she loved him dearly in kind. So when Isaac fell gravely ill in the winter of A.D. 1097, Irina became despondent, not least because the nature of his complaint was so puzzling. The fevers, the night sweats, the loss of appetite, the sudden whitening of his hair—all of this was common enough, if no less tragic, even after the symptoms lingered for many weeks longer than normal. But when the blotches appeared on his body, lesions of deep purple, dark brown, and pitch black on his feet, arms, and nose, the medical community was baffled. The fevers were a chronic complaint, but the lesions never went away. We all watched helplessly as my uncle withered away before our astonished eyes. So strong was his constitution, so powerful his will to live, that he endured for five more years in this sorry state. But he was infirm for most of that time, unable to discharge the duties of *Sebastokrator*. (Too, his absence from court, especially after the death of Anna Dalassene, allowed for Junior to expand his own influence over the administration.)

Throughout Isaac's infirmity, my aunt Irina openly grieved. She forsook colors for simple black, as if her husband were already gone. (My grand-mother Anna dressed this way for most of her life, beginning the very day my grand-father died, long before I was born.) She stopped wearing jewelry on her fingers and wrists and neck, and paint on her face. Her hair, still blonde and lustrous even at her advanced age, she pulled back in a tight bun, accentuating the lines of her sad but no less beautiful face. It was as if she were trying to mirror her husband's decline in her own appearance.

The sudden change in Irina's countenance did not escape the notice of Saddiq the astrologer. He began to call on her regularly, under the guise of "checking in on her." There were important transits he had found in her husband's chart, he claimed, that required her urgent attention. Every horoscopical resource at his disposal he used to ingratiate himself to her. Irina's theological worldview was not particularly sophisticated—like her cousin Maria, she prayed and sang and attended Mass, mostly because that was what she had been taught to do, but was too sunny of disposition to require much in the way of spiritual counterbalance—and she knew nothing of the stars and their inclinations. The slick-tongued astrologer arrived at her parlor with an armful of charts and bound volumes, determined to show her the unequivocal evidence that her beloved Isaac would not die anon, that this eventuality was years in the future. (In this accounting, it must be said, Saddiq was correct; my uncle died in late November of A.D. 1102.) What care he took in constructing those charts! What patience he exhibited in explaining it all to Irina, ignorant as she was of astrology!

"Cancer and Leo are the most northerly of the twelve signs," he'd patiently explain, as if stellar declination were somehow capable of easing her suffering. "They approach nearer than the other signs to the zenith of this part of Earth, and thereby cause warmth and heat." On these last words, he inched closer to her, his own leg glancing hers. "They are consequently appropriated as houses for the two principal luminaries—Leo for the Sun, as being masculine, and Cancer for the Moon, as being feminine." Ostensibly Saddiq was discussing the movements of the spheres, but the subtext was obvious, even to Irina. If my plain and unhappily-married mother thrilled at the undivided attention given her by the gilt-tongued Moor, however, my beautiful and happily-married aunt remained, like the earth in Saddiq's charts, unmoved. And when his hand, larger than any hand she'd ever laid eyes on, placed itself on her thigh, Irina screamed. She screamed loud enough and long enough that a detail of Varangian Guard burst into the room.

Clever as he was, Saddiq could offer no defense beyond vehement denial. "It was a misunderstanding," he pled. "My hand slipped off the table."

The holes in his assertion were immediately obvious. First, causing such a scene, and following it up with such a serious allegation, was not in my aunt's nature. A quiet, gentle person who would not harm a fly, Irina would never contrive to invent such a story; she preferred to be out of the spotlight, and certainly would not want it shone on her for such prurient reasons. Second, Saddiq's predilections for lechery were well known to the Empress, who did not react kindly to the news that her Moorish lover, the father of her bastard son withal, was actively trawling for comelier alternatives. Even in his weakened state, Isaac was furious, and my father, as the reader will recall, harbored no particular love for astrologers, and this one in particular.

The torture and death of Romanos Diogenes paled in comparison to the Moor's subsequent ordeal at Proti. The offending parts were removed from his body as slowly and painfully as possible; he was made to watch as said parts were fed to the pigs (pigs were chosen because Saddiq, while a convert to the true faith, still bore a Moslem's aversion to those "filthy" animals—or so it was assumed), and then his eyes were put out. Every bone in his body was broken, every bit of skin scorched. Finally they buried him up to his neck in the sand until the tide came in and put him out of his misery—appropriate enough, as those same tides were actuated by the influence of the Moon, whose movements he knew so well.

There has not been a royal astrologer in Byzantium since—although I would not be surprised if my nephew Manuel revives the obsolete institution, fool that he is.

XVII

THE SERVANT OF GOD

I N A.D. 1097, GOOD FRIDAY FELL ON THE NINTH OF APRIL. It was on that fateful day, fraught with religious significance and, it must be said, inauspicious symbolism, that my secret husband arrived in Constantinople. Unlike his predecessors, who were accompanied by significant armies and arrogant airs, demanding this and that concession to their risible kingship before agreeing to meet with my father the Emperor, Bohemond entered the gates with just a dozen trusted companions, including his nephew and primary disciple Tancred. He forsook arms, armor, and any costumed pomp, appearing as he did on the day of our wedding, in simple gray robes. If the intention was to project humility, his approach could not have been more effective if he'd ridden an ass through the Gate of Charisius the week before.[122]

---

[122] Here, Anna refers to Palm Sunday, when Jesus entered Jerusalem in triumph, riding a donkey.

Whether by careful plan or lucky quirk, he was positively Christ-like in his arrival—although one suspects that Jesus of Nazareth was not the physical specimen my hulk of a husband was. If Bohemond had come to bring the sword, what a sword he would bring![123]

There was something inherently intimidating in his willingness to move about independently of armed guard. Here was a man without fear. Godfrey of Bouillon, shorter than my mother Irene and slender as a cypress, demanded his pomp and his army because he was a weakling and a poltroon. With Bohemond, there was no such illusion. He moved confidently, Goliath among the Jews.

Alexios could not see him on Good Friday, one of the busiest days in the imperial schedule, but granted him an audience the next morning. Bohemond left ten of his knights behind, arriving at the Boukoleon with only Tancred in tow. He'd made careful ablutions. The whiskers on his face were shaved smooth, his short blonde hair was washed and neatly combed, and he wore a new, clean robe so black it shined. He doffed his sandals before entering the Throne Room—none of the others had done that—and fell immediately to his knees, bowing his head deeply at the Emperor's foot.

"Your Highness," he said. "Equal to the Apostles. My eternal thanks for vouchsafing to hold an audience with an one so unworthy."

---

[123] A play on the rather enigmatic line of Matthew 10:34.

The room was nowhere near full, perhaps there were twenty or thirty ministers and eunuchs and other functionaries in attendance, including Junior, my aunt Irina, Bohemond's sister Helena, Irene, and me. All exchanged glances, impressed at the stony disposition of the newcomer, alone unfazed by the Throne Room spectacle. My mother and I glanced at each other every few seconds, nodding our heads, beaming with pride. What a husband we had chosen! Even when Alexios depressed the lever, launching the throne aloft, Bohemond remained stoical.

"You may rise, duke," my father commanded; the command was followed, as his commands generally were.

At that precise moment, one of the bears flanking the throne roared. Everyone jumped at this unusual outburst. Even my father started, perched out of harm's way on his gilded seat. Only Bohemond did not so much as flinch. My mother looked at me and nodded, smiling approvingly.

"Your exploits on the battlefield are well known to me," the Emperor said. "The loss at Dyrrachium remains my worst defeat in all my years as a general. Even at Larissa you fought bravely, though outnumbered. Had your father Robert not abandoned you in the field, it is not difficult to imagine our rôles reversed today."

"You flatter me, Your Highness," my husband said. "At Dyrrachium, as Your Highness will recall, I was the beneficiary of luck, and also of surprise. As the entire endeavor was the product of the outsized imagination of my terminally ambitious father, may Jesus have mercy on his soul, there was never a question that I myself would not prevail against a foe so mighty as Your Highness. I followed my father's orders, as generals in the field must, although I myself found them foolhardy, and Larissa provided me with a merciful opportunity to cut my losses and get back to Taranto." Again he bowed his head. "A defeat to the Equal of the Apostles is not a defeat at all. I was never worthy to make the fight."

They spent a few minutes discussing these battles, each extolling the virtues of the other. Bohemond smartly omitted the moment when my father fell from his horse, took damage to his head, and almost died. From all outward appearances, it seemed that the two great generals genuinely liked each other—Claudius beholding Caractacus.[124] As I watched, I wondered how, and if, my husband would reveal his kinship to his unbeknownst father-in-law.

"I'm sure you are tired from your long journey," Alexios said. "I have prepared apartments for you, your nephew, and your other knights to use for the week-end. You will find it well stocked with good food and strong drink. Let the court recess for now; you and I shall meet tomorrow morning, after you dine and rest, to discuss in greater detail the Jerusalem mission."

---

[124] King of the Britons until A.D. 50, when he was captured and sent to Rome; the Emperor Claudius, as a show of respect, spared his life.

"Splendid," my husband said, again bowing deeply. "My eternal gratitude upon you, Your Highness."

A vicious slander spread about Bohemond that night. It seems that he went to the apartments offered him by my father to find a feast worthy of a king—but he feared foul play. Rather than consume what he suspected was tainted food, he instead gave it to his servants to eat. (In the telling, he did so without alerting them to the possible peril, but this seems unlikely if not preposterous.) In the event, these intrepid servants, famished from many hard weeks on the road, saw the bounty before them, recognized the low odds of Alexios poisoning his guest at the Boukoleon on the first full day of his arrival, and happily chowed down. Did my husband partake of the feast? Who can say. But the pusillanimous slander fed the common narrative of the inherent treachery of Franks, and Bohemond above all. No one excepting me and my mother questioned its veracity.

For myself, I burned for him. Never in my life had I felt such intense longing. All I wanted was a moment in his company à deux. The risks outweighed the rewards considerably—was it worth Bohemond's execution to indulge my desire to spend five minutes with him?—and Irene strictly, and smartly, forbade it.

"I know what you are feeling," my mother said. "Believe me, I know. But if there is ever a hope of you and your husband living together in the open, now is not the time for revelation. Anna, my dear, my poor darling dear, you must control yourself!"

I did not control myself, I regret to say. Instead, I went to my room, locked the door, disrobed, and lay on the bed. I'm waiting for my husband, I told myself. I'm waiting for him to come through that door, see me here at the ready, and take possession of my body. I'm waiting for him to lay claim to me. My heart pounded in my chest. My skin went cold and numb. I ran my fingers all up and down my body—something I never before did, not in that active manner—eventually finding themselves at the *omphalos* of desire, that deformed part of me which Saddiq the astrologer would so casually have excised. The libidinous sensations built to a crescendo, as plainsong vocalists do at key moments in particularly dramatic pieces of music, and I suddenly found myself gasping, my legs twitching, my head beating back, and a coat of fresh sweat spilling across my hirsute nakedness.

This euphoric feeling was almost immediately replaced by shame. What had I done? What had happened here? How would the Almighty judge me for this venal sin? As soon as my breath subsided to normal levels, I rose, put back on my clothes, and went directly to the Hagia Sophia to pray for absolution.

Jesus forgave me; I never forgave myself.

Bohemond met with Alexios the next day—Easter Sunday, as it happened—in the early hours of the morning. They convened in the Map Room this time, and unusually for an audience with the Emperor, they met alone, just the two of them. There was, off the hall, a little closet abutting the Map Room, where one could listen in on the conversations held therein. My grand-mother spent a great deal of time in that room, eavesdropping on "private" conversations. I snuck into that closet as soon as I woke that morning, before even voiding my full bladder, and from that perch heard every word that was said.

"I'm going to be brutally honest with you," my father began, "as we are alone, and can talk like men. I ask that you do the same."

"You have my word, Your Highness."

"You have given me little reason to trust you. I'm sure your faith in Christ is strong, but strong enough to undertake a quest of this kind? I have spent the last few months meeting with a half dozen Frankish nobles, and they all have in common a certain…how shall we say?…ideological purity with regards their faith. One look in their eyes and it is clear that they are doing this for the love of God, and no other reason. A joyless bunch, the lot of them, to be perfectly candid. But you, duke…your ambition radiates from you like light from the sun. Try as you might, you cannot conceal it. Now, I don't object to ulterior motives, so long as they are in concert with my own. So tell me true: what is it you're after?"

"You are perceptive, Your Highness," Bohemond said, "and wise as the Equal of the Apostles should be. It is true, religion is not what motivates me here—not solely, at least, for I will take great pleasure in repulsing the Turk from the City of God in the name of Our Lord Jesus Christ. To your point, I ask: have you ever been to Taranto, sire, to my part of the world? Lovely country, beautiful, but small, and…inessential. For years now I have fought in minor and petty wars, for money and for family honor. And to what end? You are a military man at heart, Your Highness. You well know the ecstasy associated with a major battlefield triumph, how much richer it feels to defeat a formidable foe than some upstart ingrate in the provinces. This Crusade, Your Highness…this could be a battle for the ages. If we are successful in our mission, future generations will sing of our glory! And what military man doesn't pine for that, secretly or otherwise? Glory. Triumph. Immortality. We all want to be Alexander, no?"

Alexios—named, perhaps in some roundabout way, for that great Macedonian king—held his tongue, but I could practically feel him smile.

"If I get nothing out of this but glory, that would sate me. If I find some territory better suited to my needs than Taranto, I would not mind. But let me be clear: I enter this fight as a vassal of Your Highness. Byzantine territory reclaimed will be reverted back to Byzantium, as you have directed. 'Render to Caesar what is Caesar's,'" Bohemond said, and laughed at his joke.

"And what do you ask in return?"

"Your beneficent aid in the mission. The only way this will work—and here I don't know if my fellow Franks fully realize this, having no experience in this part of the world—is if our forces are well coordinated. If the Turk beats us, so be it, but we cannot allow ourselves to fall prey to internal strife."

"Agreed."

"If I may speak candidly…"

"I insist that you do."

"I believe Your Highness fears that I will find some foothold in Syria, and use this as a launching site for an invasion of his Empire."

"*Fears* is too strong a word, duke, but yes, the thought has crossed my mind."

"Upon my life, I swear that this is not my plan, and that that course of action will never be taken."

"If…"

Bohemond was charming, he spoke flawless Greek, and he was a fine military man besides; despite all their chequered history, it was hard for my father not to like him. "You are a wise and canny man, Your Highness; I salute you. You're correct that there is something I want, something I've come to ask for."

"Name it."

"The hand of your daughter, the princess Anna Komnene, in marriage."

So adept was my father at divining the motives of his fellow men that he was seldom surprised. Not so on this day. I heard him gasp. In the closet, I too gasped and almost wet myself. He had done it! He had been brave!

"Naturally, I don't expect you to consent before the adventure is complete," Bohemond continued. "Promise me her hand upon the successful completion of my mission. If I die, you lose nothing. If I fail, you lose nothing. If I succeed, well…then and only then would I possibly be worthy of her." He bowed gallantly. "Your Majesty will need time to consider my audacious proposal, I'm sure."

"Not at all," Alexios said, for his supple mind had already done the requisite calculus. The chances of Bohemond completing this Herculean labor were remote. The likelihood was far greater that he would perish, either in battle or of disease or starvation (he was heading into a desert, after all), that he would break his vow to cede territory to the Empire, or that he would tire of the quest and quit, as he did after Larissa. "I agree to your proposal. But to win Anna's hand, you must succeed *completely*. That means that Jerusalem as well as the cities of Nicaea and Antioch must be liberated from the Turks, and all that territory reverted to Byzantium."

"Shall we put this in writing?" Bohemond offered.

"That will not be necessary. We are honorable men, men of our word."

And they clasped their hands together, these ancient adversaries, thus sealing the compact. In the little nook next door, I hugged myself, tears of joy streaming down my cheeks. I did not yet know that treachery was not the exclusive province of the Franks.

XVIII
THE IDIOT KINGS

Perched on the fertile banks of Lake Ascanius, the ancient metropolis of Nicaea sits a mere hundred miles from Constantinople, as the crow flies. Its tranquil beauty and proximity to the Queen City, as well as its august venerability—whether or not Dionysus founded the city, as local legend insists, the site was certainly well known to Alexander and his generals—led Constantine the Great to convene his famous Ecumenical Councils within its olden walls. That a city of such Christian moment, so close to home withal, had fallen to the infidels was of particular embarrassment to Alexios, who held himself personally responsible; the sultan[125] had, after all, taken advantage of the period of unrest

---

[125] Kilij Arslan I, of the Sultanate of Roum, the rump state established in former Byzantine lands, and called *Rum* for *Rome*.

in Byzantium actuated by my father's usurpation to seize Nicaea in A.D. 1081.

"I don't care one jot about Jerusalem," he remarked to Manuel Boutoumites, his bosom friend and top general, after a visit from one of the Frankish kings. "A sad assembly of oases and ruins in the desert, of no strategic importance whatsoever. Even Antioch, I could live without. But Nicaea? We must re-take Nicaea. We must. It is imperative."

I'm pleased to report that I played a rôle, albeit a vicarious one, in our attempt to re-claim said city. My scheme of sending Peter the Hermit and his rank rabble into the heartland of Anatolia, the teeth of the Turkish army, and certain death, while admittedly cruel, had one unexpectedly happy consequence: So badly did those pitiable fools fight, and so easily did they succumb to the slaughter, that the sultan foolishly assumed that *all* Frankish forces would prove just as ineffectual, and dismissed the threat of the Crusaders out of hand. Surely these Christian bumblers were no match for the mighty Moslem army! So confident was he in his low estimation of the Franks that he removed most of his troops six hundred miles east, to the faraway battlefields of Melitene, leaving his family and his crown jewels behind in his Nicene palace!

To be fair, the sultan's judgment was not as sorry as it appears in hindsight. For all their men, all their will, all their religious fervor, the Franks were led by a motley assortment of effete kings and lesser nobles. Given to soft pillows and shiny jewels, offended by the slightest perceived *faux pas* at court, the likes of Godfrey of Bouillon and Raymond of Toulouse were, shall we say, unaccustomed to the less-than-ideal conditions of an army camp. In the field, it is sometimes necessary to forage for food, for example, and there was a better chance of Godfrey sprouting wings and flying back to Constantinople for luncheon than of his scaring up his own meal in the hinterland. If my secret husband were not among their number—poorer in gold and *matériel* but richer in experience and cunning—the lot of them would have starved.

In May I received the first of a series of missives from my beloved, part of which read:

> We arrived at Nicaea, a small but stately town situated on a gleaming lake, on the sixth of May, having used up our provisions *en route*. It had been a few days since our last proper meal, morale was low, the men gaunt and grumpy. There are six or seven nobles, led by one Raymond, whom you met—a humorless fellow, and old besides, who fancies himself one of the Apostles and behaves accordingly. His brilliant solution to the problem of thirty thousand men on the brink of starvation was to kneel down on a hill and pray to Jesus Christ—as if the Savior would Himself appear with loaves and fishes and maybe some casks of the finest wine! And what do these other imbeciles do? They *kneel down and join him in prayer*! Say what

you will about the infidels, but no Moslem would participate in such a moronic charade. So Tancred and I spring into action. We collect funds from the richer of the praying idiot kings, and use the money to send for proper supplies. And we set the soldiers to work, foraging, pillaging, collecting whatever foodstuffs could be had. In a day's time, we were supping. In a week, the fresh supplies had come back from Constantinople, and we were ready for the attack. But I wonder what the idiot kings would have done if Tancred and I were not here. Would they have starved to death waiting for the Risen Messiah to bring them sardines and dinner rolls? Oh, Anna, would that you could be here to help them!

Once properly provisioned, Bohemond and the "idiot kings" lay siege to Nicaea. Soldiers and generals both tend to prefer pitched battles to siege, as there is far greater freedom of movement for both maneuver and retreat, and the outcome is more swiftly determined. (When the sultan finally returned to Nicaea, realizing his error, he was repulsed by forces led by Robert of Flanders, presumably the least idiotic of the idiot kings, in a pitched battle that lasted long into the night…but only into one long night.) Siege, as I've earlier explained, is not for the faint of heart. My secret husband, ever the contrarian, excelled at the art of siege, as he was possessed of both brute strength and fox-like cunning. He was adept at siegecraft construction, military strategy, and hand-to-hand combat, but unlike his more pious companions, he delighted in the treacherous diplomacy that so often proved the turning point. So it was at Nicaea. As he wrote:

> Sometimes you get lucky with the siege tower, sometimes the people inside run out of food or water and surrender, but the surest way to win the siege is through bribery. I'd found a willing conspirator, a secret Christian in charge of one of the towers to the north of the city, where my men were camped. None of the idiot kings spoke Greek, so it was natural for me to engage him. For some gold and promises of safety for him and his family and friends, he would grant me access. So I set about plotting the final stages of the siege. I would have succeeded, were it not for the treachery of your snake-tongued father.

Of this treachery I was, by the time I received Bohemond's letter, all too aware.

Alexios had dispatched his most devious general, Manuel Boutoumites, to Nicaea to lead the Byzantine forces there, while he himself decamped at Pelekanon, not far from the action.[126] This Boutoumites was thin and swarthy, with enormous beady

---

[126] It was here that my father found my half-brother's friend Axouch. (A.K.)

eyes and a pointed nose, giving him the appearance of a wharf rat. All that was missing was the long pink tail. Fiendishly clever, loyal to my father and no one else, he was unmarried, and like many military men, took particular pleasure in rapine—although his tastes, like those of Roman emperors of old, ran to young boys. Well, this Boutoumites, under orders from Alexios, met in secret with the Nicene leaders, who agreed to surrender the city to him, and thus to the Emperor, directly, rather than to the bestial Franks. Thus Bohemond retired for the evening, secure in his knowledge that the walls would be breached the very next day—and woke to find the Byzantine standard flying over the towers! The Franks had been hoping themselves to sack the city, to carry off money and food for their expedition, to slake their despicable urges upon the Nicene womenfolk. With the place firmly in Byzantine hands, however, they could not do this without incurring the wrath of the Emperor, on whose good graces their ultimate quest depended.

Bohemond in particular was livid. "The snake!" he exclaimed. "The turncoat!"

He and Tancred decreed that the vows they'd made to the Emperor were therefore null and void, and thus repudiated them: any territory subsequently won need not be transferred to the Empire, they declared, as Alexios's treachery had freed them from the compact.

As for me, I suffered too from my father's treachery. Once I knew of my father's deceitful plan, I wrote my husband, hoping to warn him. This letter, of all the letters I'd written Bohemond, was the one intercepted by my father's loyal eunuch steward, one Myron, who had been following my movements and knew of my visits to the convent. Helena was arrested and exiled to Taranto—a supremely merciful act, as Alexios reminded her. My own punishment was far more terrible.

"Why did you do it?" he asked me, incredulous. "Why did you betray me?"

"Why did you betray Bohemond?" I shot back. We were in the Map Room: my father, my mother, and me.

"Bohemond? The son of Robert the Fox, who not that long ago sought to remove me from the throne? I have no allegiance to that asp. And it boggles the mind why you should side with him over me."

I looked at my mother, who shook her head. But I did not heed her warning. "Because I swore to do so," I said.

"How now?"

"Bohemond is my husband," I told him.

"He is not."

"He is. I married him this fall last, during our trip to Bulgaria."

Alexios glanced at Irene, who hung her head in shame. Then he turned his gaze upon me, white-hot anger illuminating his dark eyes. "I say that he is not your husband."

"We married in a church, before a priest, a servant of God!"

"And I say you did not. No such ceremony took place. And I am the Emperor, and my word is law. No, you are my virgin daughter, the princess, and you marry only whom I say." He stepped toward me, so his face was inches from my own. His breath was hot and reeked of scallion. "You will soon be the wife of my trusted advisor Nikephoros Bryennios, Junior."

At this, both Irene and I gasped. "No!" my mother cried.

"We will have a royal wedding as soon as it can be planned, but you will marry him this very day, as soon as possible, in a private ceremony at the Hagia Sophia. That will end, once and for all, this mad notion of my own flesh and blood cavorting with that Frankish swine."

"Alexios," my mother said. "Wait a day. Please. Sleep on it."

"No," he said. "The wedding will take place today. And tonight, Junior will enjoy the affections of his new bride. Now leave me."

So it was that I was married for the second time, to my third fiancé, in a ceremony almost as small and secret as the first one. Irene wept openly, but I kept my composure, I'm proud to say. Even that night, when my new husband ravaged me, his eyes wide with delight, his girth twice what I'd been used to with my father, his stamina approaching the divine—even then, subjected to such unspeakable torture, I shed no tears.

VOLUME THREE:
MY FALL

A.D. 1098-1153

XIX
THE PHYSICIAN

THE SKY IS BLACK. Cold autumnal winds lash the stone walls of the convent. On the Sea of Marmara, the waves smash against each other, the terrible currents ever mysterious to all but the most seasoned sailors. Where has the summer gone? Has it really taken me so long to write so little? I can feel myself fading. My élan vital evaporates, quite unlike the puddles of chilly rain in the little courtyard outside. There is so much more I want to tell of, so much more to impart—I could produce a book just about my experiences at the hospital!—but I don't know that I will have energy enough, or time. The reader will forgive me, I trust, if certain prosaic details of my life fall by the wayside. My children can if they so choose write their own histories, can produce chronicles of their—let's face it, Anna! let's be true!—their boring, humdrum, inessential lives. All perfectly fine people—although they ignore me now, their aged and infirm mother alone in this drafty, cold place—and all of them seem happy enough in their inessentiality. Perhaps inessentiality is a prerequisite to happiness. Perhaps the truly great individuals, the Eudokias, the Marias of Alania, the Bohemonds, must by virtue of their greatness suffer. Perhaps woe is their lot. Happiness? Fie. The hearts of great men were built to break.

Speaking of great men suffering: soon All Hallow's Eve will be upon us, forty-three years since my father strangled the life out of poor Anna Dalassene. Half a blessed century, almost! Let that show how quickly time passes, and how little of it remains for me.

The flame of my life flickers perilously upon its deformed base of melted wax. How it welcomes the wind that will snuff it out!

Enough prattle, Anna. I must finish, I must get to the end of the story, I must tell what needs be told.

The short man in the cold cell is dressed in tattered clothes. Rags, really. He's completely bald on the crown of his head, but the hair that rings that scabbed pate hangs halfway down his back, and is held fast with a piece of string, frayed like the ends of his hair. His beard is long enough that it also requires string to secure it. Time was, he was plump, almost fat, but he's shed a good deal of weight in his year in gaol, and now the excess skin dangles pathetically from his arms. He is withering away before my eyes, despite my earnest attempts to properly provision him. His name is Basil; he hails from Bulgaria, not far from the Lake Ohrid church where I wed Bohemond; he is a physician by training and a heretic by imperial decree.

It is the vernal equinox, the very day when the sun enters the cardinal sign of Aries, in the Year of Our Lord 1107. I am twenty-three years old, a mother of three with a fourth child on the way, and the overseer of the hospital and orphanage built by my father, partly to assuage his nagging guilt at his contemptuous treatment of me, partly to divert my seemingly boundless intellectual energies. Basil is a better doctor than anyone in Constantinople. He taught me how best to treat my father's gout—the only method that brings relief!—yet he languishes in his cell, a prisoner of his own obdurate and profane theology.

"Anna," he says in his heavily-accented baritone. "What's the matter? You look a fright."

I hand him the sweetmeats. He won't eat them. He is too proud, too angry. I bring them to make myself feel better, I think.

"Did something happen? Is Eirene sick again?"

"No, my daughter is fine. It's my mother."

"Has the Empress taken ill?"

"Not that mother. It's Maria. I've just received word. She is gone." And for the first time since hearing the dread news, I break down crying.

"I'm so sorry, Anna," he says. He knows all about my special relationship with the erstwhile Empress

Maria, because I have regaled him with tale upon tale of her exploits. Since his incarceration, Basil has become something of a confessor to me. "You have my sincerest condolences."

Since three months after her self-imposed exile from Constantinople, I have heard nary a word from my almost-mother-in-law. At first I wrote every week, then every month. She wrote back three times, but after that, my letters were never answered, not once. I could only assume that she either no longer had love in her heart for me, or, more likely, found that engaging in correspondence with me was too emotionally draining for her. She had known such profound loss; perhaps she could only endure the heartache by making a clean break. (I myself, at the moribund age of sixty-nine, understand too well the virtues of disengagement; there is a reason monks take a vow of silence. In the green days of my youth, however, Maria's refusal to respond hurt me like a body blow.)

"I just…I wish I could have seen her one last time. Had I known she was ill, I might have journeyed to Vaspurakan[127] to call on her. Perhaps I might have been able to treat her infirmity. God knows what is the state of physic in that backwards Georgian land. But how could I have known?"

"I'm sure she had reasons for not answering your letters, Anna," Basil says. "If I may be so bold, the

____

[127] The convent Maria founded, where she lived out the last days of her life.

most logical explanation is that she never received them."

"What?" This is a possibility I have not considered. "How could that be?"

"Maria was guilty of sedition. She conspired to have your father killed. And your interests and hers were in perfect alignment. He might have intercepted the letters as a matter of imperial security." He picks up a piece of sweetmeat, sniffs it, grimaces, and puts it back in the basket. "More likely he'd do it to punish his former lover for her betrayal."

"He'd never…" My protestation trails meekly off.

"He's done worse to me, your sanctimonious father, for far less cause."

"But…"

Basil says nothing, but his eyes do not stray from mine. The picture of compassion is my condemned friend, as he witnesses my agony.

I decide to change the subject. "Tell me this, then: What happens when we die, doctor?"

"Nothing."

"Nothing?"

"Do you remember the time before you were born?"

"Of course not."

"Right. It is naught, a vast blackness of which we are *blissfully unaware*. If the time before we are born is naught, why should the time after be different? It is arrogant of us to presume otherwise."

"But Jesus died for our sins, good doctor. He died for our sins and opened the gates of Heaven to us flawed mortals."

"Of course He did," Basil says, smiling. "Of course He did."

"You mock me."

"I understand why those of lesser intellect believe in the Resurrection. My dear friend Alexios, for example, for all his success on the battlefield, is no theologian. He lives by his wits, but his intelligence is lacking. He cannot see beyond his own illogical prejudices. But you, Anna, you are smarter than that. Too smart to swallow the falsehoods."

"You are a heretic. I was wrong to come here."

"*Heretic* is another word for *free thinker*. And you come here because deep down, you know that I am right."

"Right that there is no God?"

"Right that we don't know."

I should leave but I don't. Basil is brilliant, more brilliant by far than anyone at court, and I know he has much to teach me, if only as an object lesson. I come here to learn. The accumulation of knowledge, to me, is everything, and I seek it out wherever it takes me, even the theological gutter.

"Does this not scare you?"

"I find no comfort in fairy tales," he says. "The loaves and the fishes, the water and wine, Lazarus, the Resurrection. Fine stories, to be sure, but all of them pleasant fictions. I'd rather know the awful truth than trade in falsehoods. When we die, we *cease to exist.* And that is a relief, dear Anna, don't you see?"

"You are a heretic," I tell him. "My father was right to put you in chains."

"Then he was also right to seize your letters to Maria." In the dim light of the cell, a frown appears on his gnarled face. "I came to the Emperor with an open mind and an open heart. He asked for instruction, and I undertook to instruct him. But his mind was not open, Anna. He resorted instead to trickery and treachery—the Devil's work, as they say, although I'm quite sure that the Devil is also a fiction. He did this because the truth was not on his side. He could not win, so he chose to cheat."

I look away from my friend and teacher in shame.

The Bogomils, followers of the radical teachings of an eponymous priest in the backwaters of Bulgaria, had operated clandestinely in that retrograde region for over a century. The nature of their beliefs was not definitively known by my father, nor indeed by anyone outside their little cult, which had managed to keep its activities more or less quiet for decades. While not a religious man *per se*, Alexios was still faithful to the Orthodox rite. More than that, the existence of a rival strain of Christianity in Bulgaria, however inconsequential, had the potential to erode Byzantine control over the region. The exclusive ability to appoint and dismiss the Patriarch afforded the Emperor with a *de facto* monopoly over the state religion—a perquisite of office he was in no hurry to surrender, even to a small and secretive sect in the provinces.[128]

Quite by chance, a Bogomil cabal was discovered, arrested, put to the torture. One of their number, just before having his tongue plucked out, named as their leader one "Basilos," a physician, who was promptly detained and whisked to the Queen City for an audience with the *Augustus*. Alexios gave his prisoner every indication that the *tête à tête* was to be an intellectual exercise, a meeting of the minds, a friendly theological debate. He entertained Basil in the Map Room, well provisioned with foodstuffs and fine wine; what put the physician's mind at ease was the fact that the two of them were alone. Surely this meant that Alexios was taking him seriously! So Basil spewed out his litany of heresies, the seductively subversive beliefs that had led him to attract so many disciples in Bulgaria. How the sheep are flattered to be told the shepherd's secrets!

"To begin, we must remove all of our preconceptions," Basil began. This was after several glasses of wine helped loosen his tongue, as wine will. "We must forget everything that we have been taught. We must regard the world coldly and objectively. We must at once turn off and turn on our vast powers of imagination. We must assume nothing."

"Very well," my father said, with seeming kindness.

---

[128] It was to establish this religious monopoly over an otherwise disparate Empire that led the Emperor Constantine to "convert" to Christianity in the early fourth century.

"Before the time of Constantine, the Romans had their gods: Jove, Juno, Mars, Venus, and so forth. So too the Greeks, and the Ægyptians before them. A galaxy of gods and goddesses, pantheon upon pantheon. The Bible mentions a number of them: Astarte, Ba'al, Chemosh, Dagon, Marduk, Tammuz. Even now there are plausible alternatives to your Christian god, once called Jehovah or Yahweh. Allah, the god of the Moslems, for example. We are told to believe that these are false gods, that believing in them will mean our damnation. That there is only one true god, the Christian god, whose only begotten Son is Jesus Christ—which itself is a paradox that has never been adequately explained. Is it not far more likely that Jesus too is false? That all gods are false? That all are human inventions?"

Alexios nodded, the picture of imperial patience. "But without God," he said, "and without the Christian faith, what motive would there be for us to do good?"

"I am not a Christian," Basil countered. "And I have lived a peaceable life, caring for my fellow man in my medical practice, seeking esoteric knowledge, practicing humility, generosity, and kindness. Yet here I am, prisoner of a so-called Christian. What good have you done, Your Highness, with respect to me?"

Noticing that Basil's cup was empty, my father refilled it. "Point taken," he said. "Although I do not agree."

"Consider the story of Jesus," Basil went on. "Born of the Virgin. Betrayed by His own people, the Jews. Executed in the worst possible way. On the third day, rising from the dead, in fulfillment of the Scriptures…but revealing Himself only to His disciples, and then vanishing, to Heaven we're told—and we have not heard from Him since. If we were not taught, from a very young age, that this story was Gospel, and moreover that denying its validity was heresy, punishable by death, would not we regard it as just another quaint fiction, not unlike the birth of Minerva from the skull of Jove?"

"You are saying that the Lord Jesus Christ is not real?"

"No—merely that we should approach the story with skepticism. And that, knowing what we know of history, it is far more likely to be fiction than fact."

The Emperor rose, the expression on his face one of intense anger. "I have heard enough," he said. He then snapped his fingers. There was a rush of footsteps, and three scribes burst into the Map Room. "These men were behind that wall," he said, gesturing to the little closet where I myself had often eavesdropped on imperial conversations. "They have jotted down every word we have said. This will be used against you in your trial."

If Basil was disappointed by this turn of events, or scared, he did not show it. He stood up to face the Emperor. "You are a coward," he said. "A coward and a cheat. For your sake, I hope that Christ is real and has mercy on your soul, for you are not a man of your word." And then he spat on the ground, just missing my father's purple shoes. "I came here with goodness in my heart, and you have betrayed my trust."

"It is you who have betrayed *my* trust—by maligning the good name of Jesus Christ. Take this heretic away!"

He has languished in this cell ever since.

"Look at me, princess."

My eyes wander up to meet his.

"You are better than that," Basil says. "Whether you realize it or not. Be glad for the Empress Maria. I assure you, she is at rest now. Whether or not she received your letters, she loved you true, Anna."

"Farewell, doctor."

I am shaking when I leave the dungeon, because I realize, deep down, that Basil is…if not right, more right than the man keeping him in chains.

XX

THE NEWLYWEDS

To marry Nikephoros Bryennios the Younger, as I was forced to at the tender age of fourteen, and then to suffer through that thirty-five-year-old rapist's obliteration of my presumed virtue—the adjective *ruined*, I regret to say, does not confine itself to the metaphorical description of one's reputation, but sadly extends to the entire physical apparatus—all while being denied the chance to consummate my secret marriage with Bohemond, whom I worshiped: in a long life full of disappointment and heartache, this is the second greatest evil that has ever befallen me. Even the predations of my father were not as heinous, as Alexios at least took care to be gentle with me—nor did his nude form resemble something the Emperor Michael might have beheld in the stables. The equine Junior, to the contrary, was a battering ram pounding the wooden gate of a besieged city. Yes, the city opened itself to the besieger, but the gate was damaged beyond repair. My father, to his shame, knew of Junior's libidinal predilections, his yen for brutal battlefield rapine. Why else was such a highly-decorated general and imperial confidante unmarried at thirty-five, but that the courtly fathers of Byzantium loved their daughters more than they pined for social advancement? Alexios arranged the hasty match, at least in part, as retribution for my betrayal. I'm sure of it.

The punishment veered dangerously close to capital. When Junior at last withdrew from me, the horrific night of my second wedding, blood pooled ominously on the bedsheets. I writhed in pain, as my insides felt like the aforementioned broken city gate. Breathing was a chore, walking impossible. He stood over me idiotically, wiping the black-red blood from himself with the linen sheet. I watched as the slow realization came over him that I was his wife, and the Emperor's daughter withal, not some milk-maid whose misfortune was to ply her trade in a sacked city; that as my husband and my senior he was now legally responsible for my well-being; and that said well-being was in grave danger, and with it, his own already-chequered reputation. What would it say about him as a man, as a human being, if his teenaged wife died within twenty-four hours of enjoining him in the marital bed? If he were a widower after a single night? Junior cared not a whit for my health but for his own neck, I'm certain, as he stood there naked, watching my agony. *If the princess dies*, he thought, *I will follow her to the grave.*

A surgeon was summoned, and also the midwife—but quietly, quietly. The bleeding eventually slowed down and then stopped, although blood would spot for weeks afterwards. The stabbing pain in my insides took months to abate completely.

Banished from my father's inner circle, infirm besides, I spent most of that interval in bed, in despair. I even tried my hand at poetry, each poem some variation on the theme of the philandering Jove forcing himself upon Leda. I wrote them in Greek, in Latin, even in Georgian:

> Jove's arms are iron tethers
> Holding Leda in his trap.
> The raging storm she weathers.
> The wings that flap, then cease to flap.
> The linens lined with bloody feathers.

(It was only later, when reviewing the poems, that I remembered that it was Zeus, not Leda, who took the form of the swan, that I'd conflated their rôles somehow.)

Alexios did not question me directly about the incident, but he must have had some inkling of my ordeal. How else could one sustain such intimate injuries on one's wedding night? Whether he spoke to Junior about it, issuing perhaps a stern imperial warning—one is pleased to imagine a threat of exile to Proti, if not castration—or whether my heinous second husband arrived at the same conclusion independently, I cannot ascertain. Either way, Junior took greater care with me going forward, although there were plenty of occasions, during the length of our marriage, that he forgot himself, and subjected me to what he would some luckless piece of battlefield booty. It was my mother, no stranger to marital abuse, who gave me the counsel that would save me on these subsequent occasions.

"When he enters you, you must tightly clench the muscles of the womb," Irene told me. "Try to embrace him with all of your might. That will make it more difficult for him to find his rhythm, and it will cause him considerable discomfort, if not outright pain." This technique, she did not have to tell me, was one she'd employed on her own husband, in the days when Alexios hated her and treated her roughly. (I asked the midwife about it, and she confirmed the viability of this technique, which she said was known as "Eve's revenge.")

Fortunately, Junior found other more suitable outlets for carnal pleasure. He did not find me the least bit attractive—"It is like rutting some uglier version of the Emperor," he remarked to one of his garrulous chums, who repeated the insult enough times that it found its way back to me, and indeed to everyone at court—and would sooner look elsewhere for satisfaction. A stable of regular slatterns took turns absorbing his abuse, all of them far prettier than I, and with physical endurance more saintly. At first, he feigned fidelity, but once his whore-habit was out in the open, and he saw how readily I encouraged it, he was relieved to drop the pretense.

Needless to say, I took no lovers of my own. I was still young, not yet fifteen, and happy to chastely watch, with bated breath, the adventures of my secret husband, whose heroic exploits will be sung of for ages. I was a damsel in distress, and Lord Bohemond, I believed, would save me.

XXI

THE PRINCE OF ANTIOCH

THE LETTERS CAME REGULARLY IF SPORADI-CALLY. Bohemond was in Antioch, leading the coalition of armies against the Turks— armies led by idiot kings who did not fancy being ordered around by one of lesser rank and inferior wealth. Yet there is no question that without Bohemond, the entire enterprise would have stalled at Nicaea. First and foremost, my husband was the only true military man among the well-intentioned but often hapless Crusaders. He was reared on the fields of battle, by his father Robert the Fox, a warrior without parallel; he stood head and shoulders above the effete royals bickering over plumage and protocol. Not only had he fought, but Bohemond, alone among the Franks, had done battle *within the borders of the Empire*. His intimate familiarity with Alexios, and with the godless Turks, provided an incalculable asset to the cause. Finally, Bohemond, and Bohemond alone, spoke fluent Greek, the *langua franca* of our dominions. What a singular advantage this was! True, his rank, his wealth, even the ardor of his Christian faith paled in comparison to that of his confederates. But when battle was enjoined, the veteran knights knew to ignore the others and listen only to him, and the green hands, if they did not know before the battle started, learned to do so once the weapons of war were loosed. The Turks, too, feared him; they would only attack a Frankish army directly if their intelligence revealed that Bohemond was not at its head.

"Dearest wife," he wrote, "I think of you often here in the field, and not just of my love for you. O, my princess, how appalled you would be, were you to grasp the incompetence of the imbeciles who are my fellow Crusaders! All their gold and the esteemed pedigree of their noble births does not help them once the Turks ride against us. One of my confreres, I will not say which out of respect for his station, actually spoiled his linens when he beheld the size of the Moslem army a few days ago! He was an one who made a big fuss before your father the Emperor, insisting on this and that honor at the Grand Palace. Ah, but the battlefield is the great equalizer! Thus they reluctantly fall into line behind me and my fine nephew Tancred, who sends his happy regards. One of my knights was apprenticed to be a scribe, and has taken some notes of the situation at Antioch, which I have enclosed. I know it will make good reading for you. Pray for me, wife, and for my safe return!"

The "scribe," whose identity I never learned, wrote dutifully about the events on the ground—no Xenophon, no Thucydides, but an abler historian that my own "Caesar," Bryennios the Younger.[129] Here is one of his dispatches:

There were assembled, indeed, many Turks, Arabs, and Saracens from Jerusalem, Damascus, Aleppo, and other regions, who were on their way to reinforce Antioch. So, when they heard that a Christian host was being led into their land, they made themselves ready there for battle against the Christians, and at earliest daybreak they came to the place where our people were gathered together. The barbarians divided themselves and formed two battle lines, one in front and one behind, seeking to surround us from every side. The worthy Count of Flanders, therefore, girt about on all sides with the armor of true faith and the sign of the cross, which he loyally wore daily, went against them, together with Bohemond, and our men rushed upon them all together. They immediately took to flight and hastily turned their backs; very many of them were killed, and our men took their horses and other spoils. But

---

[129] This appears to be an early draft of the *Gesta Francorum*, one of the best extant primary sources of the First Crusade, composed by an anonymous soldier in Bohemond's army. It is history's loss that Anna does not identify him.

others, who had remained alive, fled swiftly and went away to the wrath of perdition. We, however, returning with great rejoicing, praised and magnified God, Three in One, who liveth and reigneth now and forever, Amen.

Finally, the Turks in the city of Antioch, enemies of God and Holy Christianity, hearing that Lord Bohemond was not in the siege, came out from the city and boldly advanced to do battle with us. Knowing that this most valiant knight was away, they lay in ambush for us everywhere, more especially on that side where the siege was lagging. One Wednesday they found that they could resist and hurt us. The most iniquitous barbarians came out cautiously and, rushing violently upon us, killed many of our knights and foot soldiers who were off their guard. Even the Bishop of Puy on that bitter day lost his steward, who was carrying and managing his standard. And had it not been for the stream which was between us and them, they would have attacked us more often and done the greatest hurt to our people.

At that time the famous man, Bohemond, advancing with his army from the land of the Saracens, came to the mountain held by Tancred, wondering whether perchance he could find anything to carry away, for they were ransacking the whole region. Some, in truth, found something, but others went away empty-handed. Then the wise man, Bohemond, upbraided them, saying:

"Oh, unhappy and most wretched people! O, most vile of all Christians! Why do you want to go away so quickly? Only stop; stop until we shall all be gathered together, and do not wander about like sheep without a shepherd. Moreover, if the enemy find you wandering, they will kill you, for they are watching by night and by day to find you alone, or ranging about in groups without a leader; and they are striving daily to kill you and lead you into captivity." When his words were finished, he returned to his camp with his men, more empty-handed than laden.

This scribe, whoever he might have been, held my secret husband in the requisite awe. I came to look forward to his dispatches, sporadic though they were.

The situation at Antioch, a city as impregnable as our own Constantinople given its fortifications natural and man-made, grew more dire as the weeks dragged on. Every morsel of food had been eaten from the environs, and the men were famished. The unimaginative leaders of the Crusade, unaccustomed to rumbling bellies, could think of no better recourse than to pray for deliverance. Bohemond and Tancred beheld the others in disbelief. Did these fools expect Jesus Himself to come down from the heavens and offer them divine aid? "On the day of His birth," my secret husband wrote to me, referring to the Christmas of A.D. 1097, "Jesus has better things to do," adding, "God helps those who help themselves."

One of the obstacles to the siege was the presence of one Tatikios, a Turkish slave of my father's age raised in the Komnenos house who'd grown up to be a trusted general in the Emperor's service. Junior loved him as a brother. As a child, I was terrified of him—most of his nose had been torn off in some battle or other, and the prosthetic gold replacement he wore in the middle of a face unhandsome to begin with lent him the frightening air of a daemon.[130] It was whilst playing polo with Tatikios that my father tumbled from his horse; it was this accident that triggered the onset of gout that would plague him until his dying day.

To this noseless freak of a general, Alexios entrusted the Byzantine interests in Antioch and beyond. At the onset of the siege, Tatikios recommended, sagely, that the lands around the walled city should be taken first, so that the armies did not starve; this advice was ignored, and lo, starve the armies did. Men cooked rats on sticks, for wont of a more tempting meal, and the bounty of young bodies freshly dead on the battlefield proved a temptation to the empty Crusader stomachs. (Did the Pope's assurance that sins committed on the quest would be forgiven extend to cannibalism?) Whatever

---

[130] This seemingly-invented detail has been confirmed by other primary sources. While it was more common to behold men (and women) deprived of noses and ears at this time, especially in Jerusalem incidentally, Tatikios must have been quite a hideous sight!

the case, Bohemond seized the opportunity to turn this grave misfortune to his advantage. Over a series of meetings with Tatikios, he convinced the grotesque general that without proper provisions, the movement would die beyond the walls of Antioch.

"You must to Constantinople return, at once, and bring back food," my secret husband said, "or surely we will all perish."

Tatikios considered this. On the one hand, his imperial duty bound him to the Latin armies. On the other, if he did not go back for provisions, Bohemond's assessment was certainly, and sadly, accurate: they would die, and with them, the noble Christian expedition. To tilt the scales, Bohemond had Tatikios followed by a shadowy Frankish operative. On more than one occasion, this operative hurled a blade at the head of Tatikios, intentionally missing; the gold-nosed freak concluded, reasonably under the circumstances, that his life was in danger.

"It may be so," Bohemond said. "There are those in the army who blame you personally for our want, as you are the imperial authority here. For the Emperor has promised us succor on our quest. He has not sent an army to help with the siege; that is perhaps understandable. But to also deny us basic provisions, when Constantinople is but a short journey by sea to our present location? This, sir, the men cannot fathom. As you know, I have ordered my troops to stand down in your presence. But there are men who are not under my aegis, alas, sir."

And so Tatikios, after two days of mulling, set off for Constantinople by sea. His decision, while not entirely a blunder, would prove disastrous for my father's ambitions in the region. No sooner did the sails vanish over the horizon than Bohemond, through his network of spies and informants, spread word of the perfidy of Alexios and his general. "We have been betrayed," he told them to say. "The Byzantine general has turned tail and gone away, leaving us to die alone!" This was, of course, patently untrue, for Tatikios, true to his word, did indeed provision ships and send them back to Antioch as quickly as they could sail. But the damage had been done, and the message received: The Byzantines were not to be trusted. My father was crooked, a liar, and worst of all, a bad Christian, in league with the Turks!

Meanwhile, the situation on the ground only reinforced Bohemond's version of events. The Moslem army, smelling blood, united for one last push against the famished Franks, but Bohemond, that savvy general, rallied the Crusaders and repulsed them.

Removing the Turkish force from the environs of Antioch was one thing; taking the city proper, however, was quite another. Antioch straddled a river, as perilous to navigate as the waters that gird our Constantinopolitan redoubt. On one side, a steep hill serves as a sort of natural shield; on the other, walls of grizzled stone built by the great Justinian ward off advancing armies. There was no way in without treachery; fortunately, in the ways of treachery my secret husband had no equal.

Antioch was accessed by a series of towers studded in the stone walls previously described. An Armenian named Firouz commanded the garrison at one of these, the Tower of the Two Sisters. Over the course of several weeks, Bohemond managed to woo this Firouz, as a groom charms a reluctant bride, promising him gold and a title in exchange for access to the tower. To his surprise, Firouz agreed; probably he was a Christian and loathed the infidels as much as we do; I don't know for certain. "I guard three towers," the traitor said, "and I freely promise them to you, and at whatever hour you wish I will receive you within them."

As this clandestine arrangement was being arranged, a new Turkish army was on the march from Mosul, the largest one yet assembled, led by the fearsome Atabeg,[131] Kerbogha. In a fortnight, the scouts reported, the armies would clash. Knowing of this dread advance, the Crusaders trembled. Time was running out, and the stakes could not have been higher: either they would breach the walls and take the city in the next two weeks, or the infidel army would pin them to the Antiochene walls and rout them. Only my secret husband maintained his composure at this time.

"Friends," he addressed the other leaders, "most illustrious knights, see how all of us, whether of greater or less degree, are in exceeding poverty and

---

[131]　Atabeg = governor.

misery, and how utterly ignorant we are from what side we will fare better. Therefore, if it seems good and honorable to you, let one of us put himself ahead of the rest, and if he can acquire or contrive the capture of Antioch by any plan or scheme, by himself, or through the help of others, let us with one voice grant him the city as a gift."

Raymond of Toulouse was adamantly opposed to the suggestion, insisting that the city, if taken, be handed over to my father, as had been promised.

"What was promised by the *Augustus* was aid," Bohemond replied. "And where is this aid? At the first sign of trouble, the Emperor's general fled."

"Tatikios went to secure provisions," Raymond countered. "At your insistence!"

"So he claims. Do you really expect him to return?"

The others, some reluctantly, some more eagerly, consented to Bohemond's demand, whereupon my secret husband indicated to Firouz, the Armenian guard, that the time had come for action. The treacherous guard allowed some intrepid knights access to the tower; these knights opened a gate for the rest of the army. A bloodbath ensued. After months of siege, Antioch was back in Christian hands in the blink of an eye, led by its new prince, Bohemond. Kerbogha's forces may well have exterminated the Crusaders on an open field of battle, but they now found themselves attempting their own siege of Antioch, and were easily repulsed. By the summer solstice the battle was won. After some recuperation within the ancient city walls, the main Crusader force departed for Jerusalem. But Bohemond stayed behind, establishing a principality in the city built by the great Seleucus, another exemplary general.[132]

Alexios, for his part, was livid when presented with the news that my secret husband planned to hold the city himself rather than cede it to the Empire—although he was not surprised. "Bohemond is a snake," he remarked, "and while a snake might slough its skin, it remains a snake."

Myself, I was overjoyed. With no clear prospect of succession at Constantinople, I prepared myself for the journey to Antioch, where I would surely be embraced as princess. Indeed, my presence there would help ease tensions between my secret husband and my angry father—and in time, could convince the Emperor to bequeath his dominions to Bohemond rather than my feeble-minded half-brother John, whose facility for critical thinking had not improved in the intervening years.

"I await your call," I wrote him, my ardor naked and stark on the page—quite out of character for me. "Send me word, and I shall on the next ship be to Antioch, to take my place beside you, Lord Bohemond! As you took up the Cross and marched to the Holy Land, so shall I take up my retinue and march to your capital!"

I waited…and I waited…and I waited.

The summons did not come.

---

[132]   In the army of Alexander the Great. The city itself is named for Seleucus's son, Antiochus.

XXII

THE MOTHERS AND THE DAUGHTERS

ONE OF THE FEW HAPPY CONSEQUENCES OF MY MARRIAGE is that, in handing me off to his subordinate, Alexios ceded his imperial right to his nocturnal visits. These had waned after the death of Anna Dalassene, but they did not stop entirely until my wedding day. The Emperor's desire too had waned since that fateful night, as if some key component of his libido had perished with his mother, and it was not often that he sought to slake his urges. When he did, he took to calling on his wife Irene.

Saddiq her lover had been dead for some time, the careful reader will recall, after the astrologer's ill-starred attempt to seduce my aunt Irina. The affair caused my mother considerable chagrin, and her feelings of betrayal were so marked that she shut down that part of herself which had thrilled to the Moor's touch. Thus when Alexios appealed to her to discharge her marital duty, unpleasant as it may have been, she did not object. By this time, my father was in his forties, an old man, considerably plumper than he'd been in his prime, with chronic gout in his feet. His virility too was on the wane. These encounters, Irene reported, were mercifully swift; he was generally in and out of her bed-chamber in under ten minutes. Furthermore, his shame at his lack of execution compelled him to behave with extreme gentleness towards her. It was, she told me later, the happiest period in her marriage.

As for what happened next…how the Weird Sisters, gazing at us through their shared and phlegmy eyeball, must have marveled at what they wrought! For in a bizarre quirk of Fate, my thirty-six-year-old mother and I, exactly half her age, were with child at precisely the same interval! In all likelihood we were impregnated on the self-same night, after a raucous ball given for Sviatopolk, the Prince of Kyiv. The Kyivan Rus' imbibe like no other peoples. Their yen for liquor is infectious: both my father and his Prime Minister drank their fill that enchanted evening—enough for the inebriate urge to seek satisfaction from their own wives to win out over their usual disdain for the operation, or rather for the uninspired choice of partners. The notion of motherhood was foreign to me; indeed, I harbored some doubt, on account of my anatomical deformities, that I could ever have children, which skepticism only increased after my wedding night injuries. Thus I was shocked to discover that I was pregnant, still more so that my mother would make the journey with me.

If I was always on good terms with Irene, it was during the twin pregnancies that we became truly close—more sisterly friends than mother and daugh-ter (although there was never any doubt as to whom was the older sister). We spent virtually every hour of every day in tandem, taking our meals, resting our harried bodies, enjoying the cool breezes off the Propontis. She talked a lot, more than she ever had before, regaling me with stories of her youth, her illustrious family, her father and grand-father. And when we knew we were alone, often in the cool of the wine cellar, we spoke in hushed tones of our plans for the post-Alexios future. A fat old man with gout cannot live forever.

"John is unfit," she insisted. "And the other sons, Andy and his brethren, I cannot see how they would survive. It must be you, Anna. You must succeed your father and rule Byzantium!"

My mother was beautiful when with child. The baby-weight complemented her too-slender frame, her breasts filled out her dresses, and her cheeks, usually colorless and sallow, took on a rosy com-plexion. She looked happy and healthy, and this was much remarked upon at court. There is nothing as exciting to the hoi polloi as a royal baby.

I, on the other hand, looked ridiculous. Other than the obvious tumescence of the womb, my body did not change at all, not in any way that I could observe. I cut a mannish if youthful figure.

One court wag put it best: "The princess looks like the Emperor himself having just enjoyed a particularly bountiful supper!" I could not have this merry jokester banished or put to death for his insolence, alas, because he was my own husband.

My son was born on 29 August, A.D. 1102. He was named Alexios, in Byzantine custom, and I called him Lex—the pet name Maria had for my father. Four days later, on the second of September, my sister Zoë was born. The two royal babies grew up together, always in each other's company. They were known as the Twins, and did indeed bear an uncanny resemblance to each other: tall, slender, hirsute.

If I did not know better, I would have assumed my father had sired both.

Junior's behavior improved markedly after the birth of our son. All things considered, he was not the most horrible husband, I suppose. We'd worked together at court long enough that he regarded me as his intellectual equal, if not his superior (although I was that), and he discharged his duties with aplomb, for which I grudgingly respected him.[133] No, his biggest failing as a marital partner would come years later, when my father died. For that, I will never forgive him. But again, in my haste to finish, I am getting ahead of the story.

---

[133] In *The Alexiad*, I refer to him as "my *Caesar*." This was widely interpreted, per my intention, as a display of humility. I did think of him as my *Caesar*—to my own *Augustus*! (A.K.)

XXIII
THE VASSAL

I N HINDSIGHT, THE ONLY KIND OF VISION that does not diminish with age, I see that the day on which I received news of the conquest of Antioch and posted my subsequent missive to Bohemond was the happiest twenty-four-hour period of my young life. I still recall the date: the last day of June, A.D. 1098; five months shy of my fifteenth birthday. O, how the possibilities seemed endless that sunshiny day! Marriage, in the open Syrian air, to the illustrious Crusader. Revenge upon my dull Byzantine husband Nikephoros Bryennios, for his rough handling of his wife, and also upon my father, for arranging that punitive match to begin with. And the dizzyingly delicious prospect of inheriting, upon the death of Alexios, the throne of Rome!

But it was not to be.

"Not yet, my Queen," was Bohemond's reply, three weeks later. "While I long for your sweet embrace, while I yearn to caress your supple skin, the time is not yet ripe. Antioch is taken, but what is Antioch? You cannot leave Constantinople for this place. It is beneath your station, unworthy of you. And you are more useful to us at court. But take heart, my dearest, for your husband will prevail in his ambitions, and together you and I will rule all of Byzantium!"

I did not concur with his assessment. While I oversaw the hospital—that massive complex built by my father to ward the sick, the dying, the indigent—this responsibility gave me little influence at court, where my father did not trust me, and Junior was loath to share information on the goings-on. Wherefore my remaining in Constantinople? How could I help mature the plan here? And part of me began to wonder—to doubt—if he meant a word that he'd written with regards my person, or if he could only suffer to marry an one such as I if the marriage offer were proffered by the Emperor himself, gladly, and meant, explicitly, his eventual ascension to the throne. Had Bohemond, like every other man I'd known, let me down? His actions after Antioch, if not his flowery words, certainly point to that unfortunate if predictable conclusion, and men should be measured by their actions, not their words.

Even as the rest of the Crusaders took Jerusalem, he remained at Antioch, mustering his forces…but for what? His plans defy rational analysis. Military genius *ne plus ultra* though he might be, Bohemond's ability to see the long view was somehow impaired. He could win battles, he could even win wars, but his judgment in selecting which battles and wars to fight, and where, and for what reason, was sorely lacking. For example: when they took Jerusalem without him, his Crusader comrades were undecided over whose head should wear the crown of the newly-conquered City of God. Robert of Normandy stupidly refused the honor. After much discussion, the throne was given to one Baldwin, a cipher compared to my secret husband. King of Jerusalem surely trumps Prince of Antioch! But Bohemond had not made the trek to the place where Jesus had suffered and died. Instead, he bungled about the fringes of his lesser acquisition in a vain attempt to secure more territory.

In the Year of Our Lord 1100, two full years after securing Antioch, Bohemond rode with a few hundred knights—more of an expeditionary force than an army—to Malatia, ostensibly to help defend that strategically-placed outpost from an invasion by one Danishmend Gazi, the Moslem emir of Anatolian lands lost after Manzikert, but actually to expand his own dominions. In his haste, he failed to properly scout the region, and blundered into an ambush. Gazi captured him, slapped manacles on him, and confined him to a rat-infested dungeon in the emir's woebegone capital of Neocaesarea. There my secret husband languished for three full years, enduring God knows what sort of abject misery.[134]

I could not openly plead with my father to secure his release—my ulterior motives would have been

---

[134]   He was, literally, in a Turkish prison.

nakedly obvious—but I did what I could to convince Junior that Bohemond in prison in Constantinople, under the close and watchful eye of the Emperor, was a more advantageous situation than Bohemond in the middle of nowhere, poised to strike at the earliest opportunity. (Did I envision him tattered and torn, too infirm to stand, and my nursing him back to health in the hospital? *Mea culpa*, I confess to entertaining such fanciful thoughts.) In the event, Alexios found wisdom in my line of logic. He negotiated a handsome ransom for the prisoner. His intention, I'm sure, was to bring him to the Queen City in chains, torment him, and send him to Proti forthwith. Before the deal could be consummated, however, Bohemond arranged for his friend Baldwin of Edessa to underwrite his release, and returned to Antioch in August of that year,[135] without my father's imperial involvement.

"Take heart," he wrote upon his release. "Dearest Anna, wait for me a little longer! I am coming for you!"

While I desperately wanted to believe that true love was his sole motivation, I suspected, even at the naïve age of nineteen, that my being born in the purple was more attractive to him than any other virtue I may have possessed. I knew this deep down yet could not give it voice: Alas! Bohemond lusted for the Emperor's throne, not the Emperor's daughter.

---

[135]   1103.

He conquered more Syrian lands, establishing the beginnings of a viable kingdom, but his ambitions faltered when his forces were annihilated by the savage Seljuks at Harran. So total was his defeat that he escaped capture only by an ingenious if morbid stratagem: He started a rumor that he'd been felled in battle, and his "corpse" was whisked out of the city in a coffin he shared with a three-days-dead cock; the foul stench, which reek was detectible from yards away, dissuaded the potentially curious from opening the lid to confirm its contents. God knows how Bohemond managed! At my hospital, patients go into catatonia when experiencing unbearable pain; did his nose go into a similar state of shock, overpowered in that malodorous coffin? Perhaps, as a Frank, he'd developed an immunity to bad smells.

One would be forgiven for imagining that after three full years of confinement in the vile dungeon, followed by the harrowing escape previously described, Bohemond might desire nothing more than a return to his capital city and a reunion with his dutiful and patient wife, to whom he'd vowed to remain chastely faithful. Not so! After the near-disaster at Harran, my secret husband fled to the West, to seek succor with the Pope of Rome and his Frankish associates. When Bohemond left, so did any lingering illusions that he harbored love for me at all. To the contrary, I now doubted that he'd even authored those flowery letters sent from the field. Perhaps the same sad scribe who chronicled the sack of Antioch had also composed them.

After being denied entrance to the Isle of Britain by King Henry—whose older brother, Robert of Normandy, had taken up the Cross with Bohemond, and knew well the threat the Prince of Antioch posed—my secret husband found himself at the court of Philip, the King of the Franks. This Philip also knew of Bohemond's sterling reputation as both a fearless warrior and as an inveterate enemy of the despised Emperor Alexios, and was happy to offer the hand of his daughter, the princess Constance, in holy matrimony. Now, word of the comeliness of this Constance did not escape my attention, even here in Constantinople—but then princesses are uniformly so described. Probably Anna Komnene was in Rouen known as a great beauty. I doubt this Frankish sow was in a league with Maria of Alania with respect to pulchritude. In my mind's eye Constance was plain as plain could be, arrayed in the most garish moth-eaten linens, and reeking of chopped onion like any other Frank.

"Forgive me, my sweet, but I had no choice," Bohemond explained in his subsequent letter. "Just as you had no choice but to marry another."

Fie! The two situations were not even remotely similar. He was a free man, an intrepid warrior, and a prince no less, and could do whatsoever he pleased. I was a teenager, a girl, and the daughter of the Equal of the Apostles; my father's word was law. Did he really believe me foolish enough to swallow this story? No, I unhappily concluded: Bohemond was in thrall to his own grandiose ambition. He cared not a whit for me.

Although I suspected that he might marry another while in Gaul, foreknowledge did not soften the blow. I was in despair. I did not eat, did not sleep, did not leave my bed-chamber for three days. For months after, I did not so much as crack a smile. My infant son John, named for the old *Caesar*, I neglected horribly, as I did his older brother Lex. Alan nurses raised them both.

The end for Princess Constance's new husband was as sudden as it was humiliating. Bohemond once again raised a mighty army, ostensibly to defend the Holy Land, and prepared what would be his final attack on Byzantium. Alexios allied himself with the Venicians, whose maritime skill was unmatched even by our own navy, and who made laughably quick work of the Antiochene prince's fleet. Thus Bohemond's forces were speedily and completely destroyed, and he had no recourse but to sue for peace.

At the imperial camp at Diabolis, the two great men met for the last time, with Junior serving as principal negotiator (How I wished I could have been present that day, to witness my father and my two husbands match wits! But it was not to be.) The picayune details of the treaty are a matter of public record, and I will not get into them here. What mattered was that Bohemond, once an independent operator, was now an imperial vassal—one of the Emperor's employees. This he vowed by solemn decree: "I swear to thee, our most powerful and holy Emperor, the Lord Alexios Komnenos, and to thy fellow-Emperor, the much-desired Lord John

Porphyrogenitos," O how that phrase in particular must have stung!, "that I will observe all the conditions to which I have agreed and spoken by my mouth and will keep them inviolate for all time; and the things that are for the good of your Empire, I care for now and will forever care for; and I will never harbor even the slightest thought of hatred or treachery towards you; and everything that is for the benefit and honor of the Byzantine rule that I will both think of and execute. Thus may I enjoy the help of God, and of the Cross and of the Holy Gospels."

The great Crusader appeared as if he'd swallowed poison when reciting these words, Junior told me later. "It was wonderful to behold!"

Objectively, the treaty was a win for Bohemond, given the ignominious circumstances of his defeat. He retained his principality of Antioch, received pay from the Emperor, and had to surrender precious little territory; Alexios could just as easily have hung him from the nearest branch. But Bohemond was prideful. So intolerable were the terms, so humiliating the defeat, that he could not bear to show his face in Antioch. Abandoning his wife and his two young sons,[136] he retreated to Taranto, and would die a broken man three years hence, on the third of March, A.D. 1111.

Some say he took his own life, but this I could never confirm.

---

[136] The eldest son, also called Bohemond, was prince of Antioch until 1130.

XXIV
THE UNLOVED EMPEROR

I'VE PREVIOUSLY COMPARED THE TRIO of my father, my uncle, and my grand-mother as a right triangle, with Alexios as the hypotenuse. Remove the two shorter sides, and naught remains but a two-dimensional line. The deaths of Anna Dalassene (by her son's own wicked hand!) and Isaac Komnenos (by God's), both of them gone by A.D. 1102, about halfway through his reign, untethered Alexios from his moorings. John my brother was an idiot, Ax not yet old enough or respected enough to make his voice heard, Junior too subservient, too reluctant to give wise counsel rather than telling the Emperor what he wanted to hear. I was the only one in Constantinople who could have helped guide the ship of state, but after the Bohemond imbroglio my father no longer trusted me, and I was relegated to lesser duties. I could treat the gout afflicting his feet, but not the gout afflicting his kingdom, and still less the gout afflicting his mind or his spirit.

However formidable a general and charismatic a leader Alexios might be, there were two inherent obstacles he faced as an usurping *Augustus*. First, he relied unhealthily on the support of the leading Constantinopolitan families, whose sons he was obliged to cosset with fat sinecures and fancy titles. This placed such a burden on the already-depleted treasury that he was forced to raise taxes, and collect them with ruthless vigor. Not only that, but he had no choice but to repeatedly debase the coinage, putting less and less gold in the *solidi* until the coins took on a dullish yellow tone. Imperial payments were issued with the new, inferior money—the soldiers in the army, for example, received their wages in coins bearing the portrait of Alexios—but only older *solidi* were accepted by the Emperor himself. This was nothing less than fraud, as many grumbling payees pointed out, and in time it eroded whatever confidence his subjects had in his administration. Nothing aggrieves the hoi polloi more than cheating them of their money.

Second, by taking the purple through intrigue and daring rather than birthright, he established a precedent by which any hopeful claimant might seek the throne, regardless of pedigree or ability. At the same time, more and more generals and ministers, lifelong professionals who'd ascended to the height of their profession by merit rather than birth, were forced out to accommodate the effete spawn of the noble families. Idle generals and ministers had the incentive then to revolt. No Emperor invested more time and energy squashing insurrections than did Alexios Komnenos. A wealthy cabal of nobles conspired to take the throne the very year of my birth; they were banished and their estates confiscated. Other insurrectionists included the Armenian soldier of fortune Ariebes; my father's friend Constantine Humbertopoulos; the governor of Trebizond and his son, the latter the Emperor's son-in-law, married to my sister Eudokia; a Turkish pirate called Tzachas; a Cretan revolutionary by the name of Karykas, and his Cypriot confederate Rapsomates; Nikephoros and Leo Diogenes, sons of the blinded former Emperor, who'd been raised by my grand-mother Anna Dalassene; the general Katakalon Kevavmenos, who was subsequently deprived of sight; and, most distressingly, my debonair cousin John Komnenos, Isaac's son and the governor of Dyrrachium. And that was all *prior* to the arrival of the Normans in A.D. 1097.

None dared rise up against the *Augustus* during the Crusade—this more than anything testifies to the considerable skill with which Alexios ruled the still-vast Empire. But by A.D. 1106, as my secret husband Bohemond rallied support for his ill-fated attack on Byzantium, imperial hopefuls again raised their felonious banners. The brothers Anemas were joined by a wealthy Senator called Salomon in a plot to murder Alexios; they were found out, their estates confiscated, and the traitors paraded around the Hippodrome on oxen, every hair on their head and face torn out with pitch plaster, bearing crowns of thorns and entrails—an amusing spectacle, to be sure. The assassination plot of one Aaron, bastard son of the Prince of Bulgaria, was so well devised that it failed only because of the unforeseen presence of my mother, the Empress Irene, who happened to be in the imperial tent the night the scheme was to be effected. The irony is that Irene herself was actively plotting to undermine her husband, in league with myself. About the only loyal supporters left to Alexios were his son John, a moron as discussed; John's friend Ax, a political and military genius; and my unambitious husband, Junior. So great was the public loathing for their Emperor that even when he defeated the Sultan of Roum at Philomelion—the last great battle he fought in, at the end of his life[137]—and reclaimed Anatolian lands lost since Manzikert, the hoi polloi still despised him.

Personally, this took its toll on him. Throughout his life, Alexios possessed a healthy self-regard—aware, but not unduly proud, of his considerable talents. He'd always been well-liked. Now that began to melt away. His soul was a house infested by mice; one can bring in the cats, one can set out the poisons, but there will come a time when the mere sound of scratching in the walls can bring on despair. Gone was the youthful sire who'd bedded the beautiful Maria of Alania in the Map Room, the mischievous twinkle in his deep brown eyes forever extinguished.

---

[137] I covered this in detail in the *Alexiad,* and have no wish to revisit the subject here. (A.K.)

I can't recall him laughing during this period, and he had been a jovial man. As a balm for his sadness he turned to drink and, especially, food. His belly grew fat, his hair gray. Gout, once confined to his great toes, encroached upon the rest of his body. The more his joints ached, the less he moved around, and the more he ate; the more he ate, and the less he moved around, the worse his gout became. By the time Bohemond died, in the late winter of A.D. 1111, Alexios was effectively a cripple. His feet had swelled to the size of melons, and only the careful ministrations of Irene, who rubbed them with salve, brought him relief. (I knew how to massage the feet, of course—it was I who showed my mother the therapeutic technique—but her deft touch was preferable to my ungentle kneading.) Indeed, it was to tend to his gouty feet that Irene had come to his tent that night and unwittingly foiled the Bulgarian's assassination plot!

With his physical health failing, Alexios sought to ameliorate his spiritual one. It was at this time, late in his reign, that he began his persecutions against alleged heretics in the Empire. Unloved, unappreciated, he perhaps found solace in extermi- nating the enemies of Orthodoxy in his midst; Jesus would provide for his salvation if his subjects could not. Or his mind might have been slipping along with everything else. In a land as vast as Byzantium, there will always be apostates and blasphemers and cultists hawking their heretical wares; even a Chris- tian Heracles could not cleanse the sinful stables of the collective imperial soul. If a sect grows to such a degree that it threatens the stability of the Empire, by all means, wipe it out. But the Bogomils numbered a few hundred at most, conducting their business in private, and in secret; tales of newborn babes sacrificed and wells poisoned were obviously just that, tales. Why allocate scarce military resources to their destruction? For what purpose, beyond personal and spiritual glory? The whole idea was rubbish.

Yet it was during these crackdowns that Axouch—Ax, the Nicene Turk hand-picked by Alexios to serve as my idiot brother's boon companion—began to show his mettle. He was in his early twenties by the time Basil was captured, tall and dark and handsome, and an obvious candidate for kingship. Only the serenity of his own nature prevented him from usurping my brother when my father's corpse was still cold. Not only would Ax midwife John's impossibly successful and lengthy reign (a quarter century of that dolt!), but he would also ensure that the crown passed not to John's eldest son, but rather his second, Manuel, in accordance with my brother's dying wishes. The wisdom of this bizarre choice is certainly questionable—witness my nephew parading around in his trousers, treating his Frankish Crusader guests with disgusting obsequity,[138] and my idiot sibling's decision looks even more suspect—but

---

[138] What is now known as the Second Crusade took place in 1147-49, about the time Anna was writing her *Anecdota*.

Ax ensured that his master's wishes were granted, as Ax always did. Had he perished during the sack of Nicaea, or simply not been noticed by my father, he would not have been present at the hour of my father's death, and the annals of Byzantine history would read far different.

It is to that hour, and the events leading up to it, that we now turn.

XXV

THE ATHEIST

O N THE EVE OF THE GREAT FEAST OF PEN-
TECOST, in the Year of Our Lord 1118, a
visitor called at the palace. A holy man:
old as the day is long, pate completely bald, white
beard down to his navel, brown robe covered in
dust, sandals held together by tar and the Grace of
God. One gnarled hand clutched his walking stick,
ornately if crudely carved. In the other, a letter.

"My name is Hughes of Payens," he told the
watchman. "I come to deliver this epistle to the
princess, Anna Komnene, may God's blessings be
upon her."

The watchman informed him of the lateness
of the hour and suggested he come back in the
morning.

The old man refused. "I shall wait." And wait
he did, on his feet, quietly and patiently. After an
hour of this wizened stranger loitering in the lobby,
the watchman informed the eunuch steward, who

told the waiting-lady, who roused me. "Can he not give the letter to the watchman?"

"He says his instructions were to deliver it to you personally, and that he took a vow before God to do the same," my waiting-lady yawned. "He's very serious, apparently."

"Very well." I threw on a simple dark robe and pulled my hair back into a scarf—I was dressed, I realized later, just as he was.

An old man in a tattered robe is not incapable of violence, so the mystical stranger was led into an anteroom, under the hawklike eye of some Varangian guard. He remained standing as I approached, then prostrated himself before me—a gesture I had not been subject to since the first days of my life, when I was still engaged to Constantine Doukas.

"You may rise, sirrah," I told him, and he did, making ample use of the walking stick.

"Before I deliver the letter," he told me, in flawless if heavily-accented Greek, "I must confirm your identity."

"Confirm my identity? Why, I am Anna Komnene, daughter of the Emperor Alexios Komnenos."

"So it seems," he conceded. "But you must answer the question I am about to put before you correctly. That was my instruction."

By now the guards and the waiting-ladies were making ridiculous faces at each other, silently indicating that this poor fellow was mad. Probably the servants were right; servants generally are about such things. But I played along. Curiosity seized me:

what could the meaning of this missive possibly be, if such layers of security were attached to it? "Very well," I indulged him. "Ask your question, sirrah."

Whereupon the old man switched tongues, from Greek to Georgian—a language I had not spoken aloud in many years. "Where," he asked, "was the Empress Maria of Alania at the hour of your birth?"

This stunned me. The Georgian phrasing had all the power of a magical incantation, or a fever dream. More surprising was the allusion to my dear Maria. I still thought of her often, every day without fail, several times a day usually, even though she had been dead for ten years. Why had she severed contact with me? Why had she not replied to my letters? Did she go to the grave despising me, her one-time "peach?" Or had sinister forces prevented us from communicating, as Basil the Physician suggested at the time?

"The Map Room," I replied, in clumsy Georgian. "At the Grand Palace. She was with my father in the Map Room."

Whereupon the old man bowed and handed me the letter.

"Thank you, sirrah." I tore open the letter, which date was ten years prior, and read:

Dearest Anna,

I know not why you have ignored my numerous letters. Perhaps your father has poisoned you against me. Perhaps you have determined that I am full of sin and wickedness and not worthy of your affections. I cannot say for sure. I hope that it is because your father has contrived some means of intercepting my letters and that you never actually read them. Horrible as that would be, it is preferable to knowing that you hate me. You, Anna, whom I love most of all.

I am an old woman now, Anna dear, and soon enough Death will send for me. I shall welcome him with open arms, as I once did your father in my bed-chamber. By the time this letter reaches your hands, if in fact it ever does, for there are no certainties in this world, I may well be gone. So be it. Remember me fondly, and my soul will be glad.

The bearer of this letter is one Hughes. He hails from a village called Payens, near the Frankish city of Troyes. He is a palmer, having made the pilgrimage to the Holy City several times. The voyage to Jerusalem, as you know, is fraught with peril. Hughes has established there an order of knights who guard the Holy Temple and keep Christian travelers safe. Jerusalem is the City of God, a portal to Heaven, and there is nothing as important as safeguarding the pious Christians who undertake the arduous journey to that sacred space. I have endowed his mission with ample coin—I have accumulated much in my life, as you know, and no sons or daughters stand to inherit my fortune. I have decided that Hughes and his "Knights Templar" will make better use of the riches than some misbegotten Georgian nephew.

I ask that you please consider joining me in endowing this man's mission. He is worthy, a true soldier of Christ, and his endeavor is an important one. It is rare in this world to find a heart as pure as his, which burns brightly with the love of Jesus the Christ. Thank you, my peach. I love you, now and always, and I look forward to the day when Death shall reunite us (although for your sake, I hope it happens many years hence!).

All my love,
Maria

The emotions coursing through me as I read the letter, written in her unmistakable hand, are impossible to describe. Relief, that Maria's love for me did not wane. Love for her, reciprocally. Gratitude toward this Hughes de Payens, for delivering me something so precious—it was now beyond question that we would endow his mission. Bitterness at having been deprived, for years, of contact with the one I loved most of all in this world. Anger at he who so deprived me. Agony that Maria died not knowing what I now knew, that our bond was true. Desire to join her in death, immediately.

I fell to my knees, collapsing into tears, the servants watching in amazement, as I am not one to show emotion, ever, at all, for any reason. When the tears dried, I prayed, even as the others watched. The old man stood in stony silence, the expression on his face, beneath the white beard, beatific. Finally I rose, and I embraced him—how *that* caused a stir among my waiting-ladies!—and showered him with praise. I instructed the servants to make him a room, the best one available, and spare no expense with regards to his needs. "Prepare supper for him, right this minute, and water and wine."

Alone in the room, just me and my letter and the ghost of Maria, I considered taking a dagger, bursting into my father's room, and stabbing his gout-ridden body as he slept. Alexios Komnenos, author of all of my life's disappointments! He who robbed me of my succession when John was born— John who was not even his own flesh and blood! He who compromised my virtue, night after night after night. He who removed me from Maria's house, and then banished her from the city and then the Empire. He who plucked Axoush from the rubble of Nicaea, ensuring that John would be protected. He who strangled to death my grand-mother and namesake, Anna Dalassene. He who denied me my marriage to Bohemond, and instead wedded me to a despicable rapist. He who excluded me from the imperial ministry, out of pique. He who held my friend and teacher Basil the Physician in a dungeon for years. And now, he who intercepted my correspondence with my one true love in this world, Maria—a petty punishment for her, an agony for me. Alexios, bringer of misery. Alexios, acolyte of the Devil. Alexios, my father, my tormenter. Alexios, monster!

I got as far as his hallway, dagger in hand, but there were too many Varangian guardsmen outside the door, and all the weeping had stalled my nerve. Instead I went to the dungeon to speak to Basil. I told him everything, as I always did.

"Your father is afraid," he told me. "He has always been afraid. And perhaps, in his defense, wearing the crown engenders fear. But there is no excuse for how he's treated you. He calls himself a Christian, and hews to the teachings of his invented Savior, Jesus Christ…and this is how he conducts himself! Meanwhile, here I am, condemned to die for heresy—and yet I have lived more in line with the teachings of this made-up Nazarene than has the Emperor. Oh, the irony, Anna! If it weren't so tragic, it would be funny."

The arrival of Hughes de Payens, and my emotional response to his letter, did not go unnoticed by my father, even as his gout rendered him immobile. Alexios reclined on the couch which had been rein-stalled in the Map Room, albeit for less lascivious reasons, his swollen feet resting in the lap of my mother, who rubbed them gentled with salve. He'd gained so much weight that the rolls of fat on his neck and chin resembled melted clay, and he stunk of stale sweat and garlic. Despite the early morning hour, the skies were overcast, the dim light in the room giving the tableau the look of a death scene.

"You're giving him money?"

"Of course I am. He has the endorsement of the Empress Maria."

"Who's been dead for, what, nine years? How do you know the letter was not forged?"

"I have my ways."

"Don't be a fool, Anna. This man is a charlatan, simple and plain."

I glanced at my mother, who said nothing. Her eyes remained fixed on those horrible feet.

"Where are my letters, father?"

"Letters? What letters?"

"Maria wrote me letters, and I never received them. I wrote her letters, and she never got them. Where are they?"

Before he could respond, I observed his eyes dart quickly to the direction of his desk. Then he directed those rheumy orbs on me. "I have no idea what you're talking about. If you sent letters to Maria, I'm sure she received them and simply chose not to respond. She was very depressed when she left Constantinople, as I recall. Perhaps she shut herself in a convent and did not engage in worldly pursuits."

"That's not what Maria herself wrote."

"In a letter produced by this so-called holy man, nine years after her death? Anna, can you not see how ridiculous this sounds? Tell her, Irene."

My mother muttered some agreement, but I could tell by the wistful look in her eye that she suspected, as I did, that he spoke falsely.

"Very well, father," I said. "I'm sure you're right."

"I am."

I made to leave the chamber.

"One more thing, Anna: this heretic, this Basil the Bulgarian, has filled your mind with falsehoods long enough. It was foolish of me to allow you access to him. I see now the error of my ways. He has meddled in my affairs once too often. You are not to speak to him again."

"But father, I…"

"And he will be executed this afternoon, at the Hippodrome."

"What? But why…"

"He will be consigned to the flames here on Earth, to prepare him for the fires of Hell."

I ran from my father's bed-chamber to the dungeon, but I was too late—Basil had already been removed, to prepare for his fiery ordeal.

Next I called again upon Hughes de Payens. I wished him luck and bade him to leave the city immediately—we were down one "heretic" in the dungeon, and I'm not sure he would have met my father's exacting standards of Orthodoxy. I gave him as much gold as I could scare up on short notice, and promised to send more to Jerusalem when he arrived there. He thanked me, blessed me, and departed at once.

In the afternoon, I went back to the Map Room. My father, I knew, would be taking his luncheon in his apartments, as he always did. Two Varangian guard watched over the door, but they let me through when I claimed I needed ointment for his gouty feet.

His elaborate escritoire had a dozen drawers, some large and some small. I ransacked all of them but found what I was looking for: my letters to Maria. There were three dozen of them, most more than twenty years old. All of them had been opened, read, and filed here in the Emperor's desk. I did not, alas, find her letters to me. Perhaps they'd been intercepted in T'blisi. Perhaps they'd been burned. I would never know what had been on Maria's mind, in the sorrowful September of her life. O, sweet mother! O, how I ache for you!

The urge to weep came and went quickly. All I could do was stare at the parchment, mouth agape, and silently fume in rage. To deny me love, to deny me intimacy, in such a cold and callous way…it was evil. There was no other word for it. Evil. My father was an evil, evil man. A monster. A daemon.

The Devil himself.

XXVI
THE CONSPIRATORS

A LTHOUGH I GAVE LURID ACCOUNT OF IT IN THE *ALEXIAD*, I did not bear witness to the execution of Basil the Physician. Like most of the incidents in that hagiographical history, I relied on some first-person sources but disregarded others, and took great pains to present my father's rôle in the proceedings in the most flattering light, as per my instructions. A monster in so many ways, yet Alexios had no special fondness for execution, preferring instead to blind wrong-doers, or else banish them to Proti. Capital punishment, in his view, was murder, forbidden by the Scriptures, and anathema to his well-held Christian faith. That he chose to carry out the execution of his condemned "heretic" at all was peculiar; but in such a barbaric, awful manner? In thirty-six years on the throne, he'd consigned not a single, solitary prisoner to the flames. Wherefore Basil? Wherefore burning alive? And why now?

I cannot say for certain, but I have my theories. First, my father was sixty-two years old and terminally ill. The dread malady coursing through his moribund body had found its way into his brain, retarding and perverting his ability to reason. Even six months ago, he would never had stooped to such depths. Second, he knew the hoi polloi would thrill to the spectacle. A famous heathen, burned to death at the Hippodrome! O, what good theater that would make! The people had loathed Alexios for years. He knew that he was not long for this world. The love of his subjects which had eluded him for the better part of two decades could be revived, albeit fleetingly, with a simple execution. Burn Basil must. Finally, and above all, my father did it to punish his wayward daughter. He could not bear, even at his advanced age and stage of decrepitude, to share my affections with anyone else. This is why he'd denied my union with Bohemond, why he'd seized all correspondence from Maria. Now, he would take my friend and teacher and confidante from me. Alexios, monster!

The mood at the Hippodrome was dark. Violence hung in the air like a black cloud. Gathered crowds shouted and sneered as the pyre was set alight. Night fell before the prisoner was brought out, but by then the flames burned so high and hot that the whole of the arena was lit up. Rumors flew that Basil believed himself impervious to fire, that angels would swoop down from Heaven and rescue him before any harm would befall him; the

Bogomils had sacrificed human babes to their dark god, in the manner of Abraham and Isaac, and drunk of the newborn blood, which immaculate ichor was the source of his protection. Foul lies, all of this, perpetuated by agents of my father—but there seems to be no end to the perfidious slander that the hoi polloi will believe, and no limit to the depths of their ignorance.

Basil was an atheist; he did not believe in God at all, let alone wingèd agents of His Providence invested with the power and the will to deliver him to safety. He did not willingly walk to the flames, as some asserted, nor did he beg the Emperor for mercy, nor—and here I am proud of his courage—did he recant. If all those years in the dungeon did not change his mind about the appeal of Jesus the Christ, neither would a glimpse of fire at the Hippodrome convince him. He took a few uneasy steps into the arena proper and froze there, absorbing the wild taunts of the raucous crowd, the tears streaming down his cheeks drying immediately in the kiln-like heat of the pyre.

The Hippodrome gendarmes tore off his robe and fed it to the flames; when it caught fire, the crowd roared.

"Enter the flame, heretic!" the Emperor ordered. "Let your god save you!"

But Basil did not move, for Basil could not move.

Ten years ago, Alexios may have spared him. But the Hippodrome crowd was, like the pyre itself, too fired up to ignore. He did not wish to disappoint his subjects, not to save the life of this recalcitrant individual—even if said individual was the only man in the Empire who'd been able to treat his gout.

The *Augustus* gave the signal. Four gendarmes hoisted Basil up and hurled him pell-mell into the fire. His screams of agony were louder even than the roar of the crowd. The flames consumed him soon enough, a single white plume of smoke rising above the black, suggesting for all the world that the eternal soul of this poor heretic was bound to Heaven after all.

The crowd could be heard from the Hagia Sophia, where I knelt in furious prayer, and I could tell from the crescendo of roars when the end had come.

"Basil," I muttered, "O, Basil, Basil, my dear friend," and my own tears were as copious as water in the Nile.

The execution took place on the last day of the month of July, A.D. 1118. The very next morning, the first of August, my father's already-precarious health took a turn for the worse. The gout that rendered him unable to walk without excrutiating pain: this he'd somehow managed to endure. Now the malady, whatever it was, attacked his lungs. He gasped and struggled for breath, and could keep down neither food nor, more ominously, water. It was, as he muttered to my mother, as if a boulder were crushing his breastplate. Not even for a moment could he draw breath freely or fully. He was obliged to sit upright to breathe at all; and if by chance he lay on his back or on one side, the lack of air forced him back upright. For he was unable to draw in or out even a tiny drift of the outer air by the channels for expiration and inspiration. And whenever sleep pitied him and overpowered him, then also he was liable to suffocation; so that at all times whether sleeping or awake, the danger of strangulation hung over him.

Having just burned at the stake the best physician in his Empire, and not fully trusting the second best—which is to say, his own daughter, who hated him—Alexios sent for other doctors, none of whom knew what to do. One dunce suggested phlebotomy, so rather than do nothing, they allowed this charlatan to make an incision at the elbow; predictably, the patient derived no benefit from it, but breathed with just the same difficulty as before, only now his elbow gave him pain also. The infirmity accompanied the Emperor like a noose, and never left off strangling him.

As no remedy could be found for the disease, Alexios was removed to the part of the palace which looked to the south. For during this oppression he found a little refreshment in being moved, and Irene—who never strayed from his side, to the point where her own health suffered—contrived that he should have it continually. For this purpose, she had legs fitted at the head and foot of the Emperor's couch, and ordered the servants to lift him and carry him; there were relays of burly men brought in for this labor. But while this brought some modicum of comfort, it did not contribute to the Emperor's recovery.

When the Empress saw that the malady was gaining ground, she made still more fervent intercessions to God on his behalf, and had numbers of candles lighted and continuous and endless hymns sung in every sanctuary, and largess distributed to the dwellers in every land and on every sea. And all the monks who dwelt on mountains or in caves or led their solitary lives elsewhere she stirred up to make lengthy supplications. But when the Emperor's abdomen had swollen and become very prominent, and his feet had swollen too, and fever roiled his imperial body, then the doctors—fools, all—had recourse to cautery and thought little of the fever. But all treatment was useless and vain, nor did the cauterization help. His digestive and respiratory organs remained in the same perilous state.

For eleven days, my father suffered his asthmatical agony. His body was swollen and bloated, his hair gone completely white, and while I was accustomed, in my years at the hospital, to olfactory unpleasantness, the reek of his moribund body was as unspeakable as any foul odor I'd ever sniffed. I thought of Herod, King of the Jews, builder of the great Temple, as sublime a ruler as that cult of Christ-killers had known since the days of David and Solomon. For all his virtues, Herod was a monster who'd murdered his wife Mariamne. He died of a plague so horrible, so agonizing, that its symptoms have never again been seen. Herod's Evil, it was called. Alexios's Evil: this is what I beheld in those first weeks of August, A.D. 1118. God was punishing him!

My mother, as I said, went above and beyond her wifely duties in that span. The love and care with which she treated her dying husband, her one-time rapist, was as saintly as it was undeserved. Truly this was a woman blessed by the Holy Spirit she so often prayed to.

On the fifteenth of August, the Thursday of the week during which the death of our Immaculate Lady, the Mother of God, is celebrated, it became clear that the end was near. Propped up in a sitting position, Alexios was unconscious, his breathing loud and tortured. Irene's cat, always skittish, always cowering under some or other piece of furniture, came out of hiding and curled himself at his Emperor's swollen, gouty feet. By now, we'd moved him to the Porphyra. Usually reserved for imperial births, its proximity to the medical facilities made it also an ideal setting for imperial deaths.

"The animals know," I remarked. "Come, let us speak."

I sent away the servants from the room, and told the eunuch to summon my husband. When Junior arrived, he held his nose for the stench.

"Is he gone?"

"Soon enough," Irene said. "The question now is, what happens next?"

"Why, John is crowned *Augustus* at the Hagia Sophia," my husband said, stupidly.

"Nikephoros," Irene said. "John is my son, and I love him dearly. But he is a simpleton, mentally unable to perform the functions of the job. Not only that, but he is not the issue of the Emperor. Oh, you can stop looking so surprised; I know you know the truth. Why should we let the Empire fall to a bastard, when he is so uniquely unqualified for the throne? Why should we let this happen?"

"Because it is what Alexios wants," Junior replied, and my father, in his semi-consciousness, grunted.

"He doesn't know what he wants," Irene went on. "He has long been foolish on this issue. The Empire of Christian Rome should not go to the son of a Moor and his bosom friend, a Turk. This pair of blood infidels should rule Byzantium?"

"I don't see the alternative."

"*We* are the alternative," I said. "You and I, dear husband. I, Anna Komnene, the first-born child of Alexios and Irene. You, the first-born son of Nikephoros Bryennios, who, if the chips had fallen at a slightly different angle, would have been Emperor instead of my father. This is a better solution than a Moor and a Turk."

Junior's face was flushed, and I smelled perfume on him. Probably he had been plucked from the sofa of one of his whores.

"Such lofty aspirations cost my father his eyes," Junior said. "And for what? If he'd gone into league with Alexios, pledged himself as his commanding officer rather than his rival, would that not have been a better outcome? I agree that John is an idiot.

We all know this. But what does he have to actually *do*? Wave at the people in the Hippodrome, and undertake the battery of boring civic duties Emperors are obliged to undertake. No jobs for thoughtful men. Meanwhile, Ax and I—and you Anna; and you!—can run the Empire, without the burden of having our faces on the coinage. Don't you see what an advantage that is?"

We stood in silence for a full minute, listening to the dying gasps of my father's rank breath. Irene looked frail and beaten, Junior red-faced and irritable. At last I spoke: "I am not leaving this room until he's dead. When he's dead, I'm taking his ring and sending for you, and you and I will be crowned. If John enters this room, I will kill him myself. The same goes for Axouch. Do you understand?"

"Anna," he said, "you are making a mistake."

"I was born for this moment," I tell him. "Right here, right now. I will not shirk my duties as the *porphyrogennetos*. I cannot. I will not. You will either rule with me, or you will fall."

Tired though I was, sad though I was—Alexios was the author of all my woe, as I said before, but he was still my father—I found myself glowing with excitement. All of my life's disappointments, and there had been many, would soon be blown away with his last, dying breath. His death would be a parting gift to me. I could take the purple myself, as I was born to do—*if* I remained resolute in the coming hours.

Because Alexios had taken so long to expire, and because his heir (if not his flesh-and-blood son) lacked the intellectual capacity to properly assess the situation, John was not at the ready. As the Emperor lay dying, my half-brother was on the polo grounds, playing with his ponies. Axouch, who was without parallel in his facility for management, knew that the *Augustus* was on his "last legs," as the poet says, but all he could do was wait in the wings; my brother's Turkish chum had no conceivable reason to be inside the Porphyra. Claiming medical emergency, I borrowed a dagger from one of the Varangian Guard and hid it under a pillow. I said my prayers to the Almighty, in Whom I still firmly believed. And I waited for the monstrous Emperor to breath his last.

The Ides of August, A.D. 1118. Five thirty in the afternoon. The sun beginning to set over the Anatolian hillside, not that we can see it from the dark confines of the Porphyra. The players: Alexios Komnenos, the Emperor, hunched over himself on the bed; his wife, the Empress Irene, mad with grief, kneeling at his side; a physician, Nicholas Callicles, who had surrendered to the inevitable and is packing his bag of supplies; Myron, the eunuch steward, a smooth-faced shadow by the door; and myself, Anna Komnene, dagger at the ready.

"There is nothing more that can be done," Callicles said. "I will leave you in peace now, to pay your last respects to the great man."

"Thank you, doctor."

We waited by the Emperor's side, my mother and I, each clutching one of his ice-cold hands. After a time, Irene, who by now was half-mad from lack of sleep, signed to me as she wanted me to tell her the state of his pulse. I touched again his wrist and I recognized that all his strength was giving way, and that the pulse in the arteries had finally stopped. I bowed my head and, exhausted, I looked down to the ground, said nothing, but clasped my hands over my face and wept. My tears surprised me, as tears often will. I did not know I possessed a reservoir of grief for this terrestrial Lord who had giveth all to me, and also taketh all away.

My mother seeing my reaction uttered a soul-plumbing, far-reaching shriek. She doffed her royal veil and began to tear the hair from her head as she alternately wept and screamed. She teetered in her purple slippers, swaying to and fro like the mast of a ship at harbor during a rough storm. Irene was in a terrible physical state. She had not slept for more than an hour or two in a fortnight. She'd lost significant weight during the ordeal. Now it appeared that she'd lost her mind as well. What she needed was to collapse into her bed and slumber for twelve solid hours, before she did any more damage to her own weakened body. The deprivation of sleep is no different than the deprivation of food, I'd observed at the hospital, in its deleterious effect on the human physic.

My own tears had subsided, and I saw that the moment of truth was near. I did not want to leave my father's body, not until my idiot brother had his inevitable move, but if there were any questions as to my mother's ill state of health, they evaporated when she found the dagger I'd concealed under the pillow and began cutting off her pretty hair.

By some miracle I managed to disarm her without her doing any more damage to herself, or to me. But the scuffle sapped a lot of my remaining strength—I, too, had not slept well the last few weeks, nor eaten my fill. I wound up carrying her down the hall to her own bed-chamber, tucking her into the bed, and leaving instructions with the waiting-ladies and eunuchs that she was not to leave the room for any reason until my return.

"She is in mourning," I said, "but she is also gravely ill."

One look at her tear-soaked cheeks, her deathly pallor, and the jagged edges of her ruined hair confirmed my diagnosis, and the servants agreed to follow my orders.

When I got back to the Porphyra, Axouch was in the hall outside, chatting with the eunuch Myron. He did not notice me when I turned the corner, and I was able to retreat without him noticing. I went back to Irene's bed-chamber and found a waiting-lady.

"Go now to the hall," I told her. "Tell Axouch that the Empress is about to die and to come at once!"

"Is she…"

"Do as I say!"

Thus afrightened, the servant played the part to perfection, practically screaming as she approached them. I heard the heavy footfalls of Axouch and Myron the eunuch racing. As soon as they rounded the corner, I burst past them, racing down the hall and into the Porphyra, where my father's dead body lay. Before they could give chase, I'd bolted the door.

Inside, my brother John was in the process of wresting the signet ring from my dead father's finger.

"Unhand that ring, pretender," I said to him.

"Anna," he said. The tone of his voice suggested there were more words to follow, but his brain failed to provision him with any.

"You know as well as I that you cannot be Emperor," I said. "You will be the ruin of Byzantium."

"I am oldest son," he managed to retort.

"I am oldest child, and the most capable. Give me my ring, John."

"No."

"I will ask you one last time: give me the ring."

"No."

"Very well. I did not want it to come to this." I darted towards the pillow and removed the dagger. I raised it high, too high, and came at him, slashing down as I ran. He dodged the blow at the last instant—he'd had the benefit of sleep and nourishment in the last few weeks as I had not—and the blade went instead into the breast of the dead Alexios. I pulled and pulled but could not withdraw it.

But I was not done fighting. I leapt at him, baring my fingernails. If I could not slay him with the dagger, I'd scratch out his eyes and disqualify him that way. He fell to the floor, and I fell with him, and for some time we grappled on the carpets, neither of us able to gain the upper hand.

At last there was an urgent rapping on the door. "Open up!" a voice commanded—a voice with no authority to issue commands. "Open this door, Anna!"

Whereupon John rolled us both over and over and over until my dizziness enabled him to break free. He made for the door, as I made for the dagger. He released the bolt as I yanked the blade from my dead father's breast. I whirled around, ready to strike the death blow, as the door opened.

Axouch entered, sword drawn. Beside him was my husband and Ax's bosom friend, Junior, unarmed, in his bed-shirt, redolent with drink and sex—not exactly poised to strike.

John scampered away, cowering behind them.

"Get him!" I urged my husband. "Bring him here!"

I must have looked a fright. A tired, dazed woman, the splitting image of the late Emperor, her hair wild, her eyes shining with madness, brandishing above her head a bloody dagger!

"Bring the coward to me! I will have his eyes!"

Junior looked at me, then at Ax. He made some sort of condescending gesture, as if apologizing for his wife's hysterical flight of womanly fancy, and said, "I'm so sorry, Ax. Please don't hold this against her. She hasn't slept in weeks. She's out of her mind."

"Clearly," Axouch said.

This conversation managed just barely to drown out the sound of John bleating behind them, scared as a farm animal during a thunderstorm. This piece of livestock who would be king!

The course of action was clear. Without Ax to serve as his Prime Minister and principal advisor—his very brain!—John would not manage a single day in the purple. Without Ax, Junior would be forced to take the crown himself, to share with me. Without Ax, and only without Ax, would I be able to claim by birthright.

Summoning all my remaining strength, I leapt at Ax like a panther, muttering prayers to the Virgin Mary as I came. But Axouch, unlike his dim-witted friend, was prepared. With one strike from his sword he knocked the dagger from my hand. Junior then grabbed me from behind, wrapping his burly arms around my neck and squeezing tight.

I tried to resist but could not.

I tried to speak but could not.

I tried to breathe but could not.

Axouch helped my idiot brother to his feet. He made sure the ring was secure on his finger. Then he said, "My *Augustus*! Long live the Emperor John!" and fell prostrate at the sniveling moron's feet.

O, what a terrible thing is primogeniture!

John's confused smile was the last thing I saw before the room went black.

XXVII
THE PRISONER

IT IS SO COLD THAT I CANNOT FEEL THE TIPS OF MY FINGERS. Look—see how my hand wavers as I write down these final pages. November has been particularly cold this year, A.D. 1153, almost a full century after the arrival in Constantinople of the youthful Georgian princess Mart'a. Time has its way of pressing on, most unpleasantly.

I was not quite thirty-five years old when my father died, aged sixty-two, in the middle of August, A.D. 1118—half a life ago. And yet the events of the second volume of my two-volume life can be summarized in a few short paragraphs:

I never forgave my husband for his actions, or more accurately his inactions, on the day Alexios died. He abandoned me, just as my grand-father Andronikos Doukas turned his back on the Emperor Romanos Diogenes at Manzikert. Ax did forgive him, though; by defending the new *Augustus* by attacking his own wife, Junior demonstrated beyond doubt's shadow where his loyalties lay. For this reason, I was spared confinement in a convent, outright exile, or death.

Upon the death of my father, a new Irene was crowned Empress—Irene of Hungary, who had the misfortune of being my idiot brother's wife. My own mother retired to Kecharitomene, the convent she'd erected a few years previous, when the state of my father's health began its rapid decline. I spent most of my time in her company, although my permanent residence remained at the Grand Palace, as if to spite me.

Junior was in his fifties when Alexios died, and he retired from active duty a few years into John's reign. At the behest of Ax, he began working on a history of Byzantium, beginning where Psellos had left off, with the Emperor Michael. As able as he was an administrator, he did not take to research, and still less to writing, and his history was not finished when he passed, of what I'm almost certain was *frengi*, which served him right.[139]

Immediately after Junior's death, Ax informed me that he'd considered banishing me from the Empire entirely, but decided to be merciful. "You can instead confine yourself to Kecharitomene," he gallantly offered, "*if* you finish the work of your late husband."

"And what work is that?"

---

[139] A complication from venereal disease.

"A history of the glorious exploits of your father, Alexios Komnenos."

"Do you wish me to write a history, or an account of his glorious exploits? The two are not one and the same."

"I want future generations to sing the praises of the great man, your father."

With that disappointing directive, I repaired to Kecharitomene, taking a room across the hall from my mother, and set about my work. I sprinkled in as many classical allusions as I could, to stave off my boredom with the project (although this pretentiousness does, I concede, hinder the style.)

Irene died a year after Junior. I wept for her for weeks, and miss her dearly still. She was the last person with whom I shared intimacy. My sons and daughters rarely called on me, as they had their own lives to think about, and I was anathema at court. Speaking with me might be construed as plotting with me, and plotting with me meant exile to Proti. My children! The careful reader will smile at my choice of names: Alexios, John, Irene, Maria.

Of goings-on at court, I gathered what information I could, but I was effectively shipwrecked on a desert isle. That John reigned as long as he did surprised me, but then, Axouch was, it must be said, a gifted Prime Minister—worthy, perhaps, of his own history. Now there, I must concede, was a truly great individual.

Over the course of many years after the deaths of my husband and my mother, I wrote my "history," the *Alexiad*. Ax was enormously pleased with it. "You managed to convey the greatness of Alexios," he wrote, "without coming across as a biased narrator. Well done, Anna!" Xenophon might not agree with this notice, but so be it; better that Ax was pleased than the opposite. Not that he could have punished me worse than he did, associating my name with such a careless and hagiographical document.

What more can be said? Is the reader interested in the sad details of convent life? The coarse cloth that makes up my garments? The gruel on which I unhappily subsist? The mice who live in the walls of my room? A convent is a prison, and nothing more. But then, life is also a prison.

POSTFACE

The stream of time, irresistible, ineluctable, will wash away the dark stain of our delible memory, sure as the rushing river smoothes the stone on its bank. No man mortal or otherwise is impervious to these relentless waters: even gods—those sublime human inventions!—are forgotten. This time-current is powerful, the most powerful force there is, more powerful than love, lust, anger, greed, envy, pride, even faith; my secret history, any history secret or otherwise, is but a vain attempt to dam up its undammable waters. We will all of us drown in the ocean of time: Alexander the Great, Jesus of Nazareth, Alexios Komnenos, you, me, all of us, every last one, without exception. No one lives forever. We are all washed away.

My work here is nigh complete, my second history finished—all for naught, because in the end, all is for naught. None of us Byzantines will be remembered a thousand years hence: an entire civilization, one that proudly endured for centuries, the envy of Christendom and Islam alike, lost to memory. And, as Basil the Physician patiently essayed to teach me all those unhappy years ago, this is for the best! There is comfort, you see, in surrendering to the dread potency of the river of time. Was there darkness before God created the world? I cannot say, but certainly there was personal darkness before I came into it. What did I perceive, before the first of December in A.D. 1083? Naught: a time without time, a place without shape, a soul without awareness. I welcome my return to this time, this place, this state, for only in complete and total unawareness can one truly rest in peace.

Pondering my seven decades in this *vallis lacrimarum*,[140] I am struck mostly by my rank foolishness. What a fool, what a hapless fool, I was! More foolish than Psellos or Diogenes or Saddiq the astrologer or any of the other imbeciles I've rightly criticized in these pages. How gullible! How patently and egregiously wrong! All my life, even after John my brother took the purple, even after Junior died and I was walled up here at Kecharitomene, I clung to the belief that these failures were temporary, that I would one day be Empress. My faith in that risible and damnable falsehood never wavered.

When I contemplate the youthful Anna Komnene, so serious, so ambitious, so sure of her destiny, I am embarrassed to the point of mortification. O, the hubris! O, the misplaced certitude! How could

---

140   Vale of tears. See Psalm 83:7.

I ever have put so much faith in a lie? How could I have dared to presume that centuries of Roman history would yield to a woman on the throne? I, who knew enough of the downfall of Eudokia, of Maria, of Anna Dalassene, to write a history of their exploits, who knew what befell them, all three more formidable than I? How could I have placed so much hope in a feckless father who ruined me? In a philandering husband of similar bent? In a Frankish rogue whose flattering interest in me was clearly and unambiguously ulterior? How could I have trusted *men*? Men, the supposed stronger sex, but really the weaker. What a fool I was. What a damned, accursed fool.

No more.

This afternoon, I will seal these pages—which together comprise a sworn testimony to my loathsome foolishness—in a leaden pot, and wall them up in the wine cellar. Perhaps some brash adventurer will unearth them at some future date, many years hence. More likely they will be lost forever, as all memories are, as all memories perhaps should be. To the dust ye shall return. So be it. So be it.

Tomorrow is the first day of the last month: my seventieth birthday. Seventy years of dashed hopes, of disappointment, of pain, heartache, and misery. As a gift to myself, I will climb to the top of the parapet, I will gaze out at the roiling waters that gird Constantinople, I will offer one last prayer to the Virgin Mary (although I've no doubt that she's as fictive as she is deaf), and I will leap into the wind-swept night—and in so doing, solve the insoluble mystery of mortal man.

If the godly are right, if I am met by Saint Peter at Heaven's Gate and cast into Hell for my sins, then let the Devil do what he will: no infernal torture could be worse than what I've already endured on earth. The odds of that happening, however, are vanishingly small. When the candle burns out, its light is never seen again. So will it be with the flickering wick that is Anna Komnene, the Empress who never was.

Out, candle. Out, Anna.

Farewell.

—A.K.
30 November A.D. *1153*

AFTERWORD

Mea culpa: what you have just read is, in fact, a work of fiction. The translator friend from Georgetown does not exist. There was no codex discovered in Istanbul. I really do work at a coin company—and we really do offer Byzantine scyphates—but my boss did not sell me a medieval manuscript, because there was no medieval manuscript to sell. I just made all that up, to convince you to read a 154,000-word novel about long-dead Byzantine princesses. Sorry! My bad!

Anna Komnene, however, was very real. She really did write the *Alexiad*, a few paragraphs of which found their way into this book. She really was a genius. She really did get screwed over by her old man.

Maria of Alania, too, was real. She really was considered the most beautiful princess in Christendom. She really did marry two emperors. She really did help Alexios take the throne, really did adopt him as her son—and, while we can't be *totally* sure, really was his lover.

The characters in this book are *all* real. Even the ones I invented—the court astrologer, the steward slave, the nurse, the midwife—certainly existed in some form. Moreover, every character is presented faithfully. Every character did what they did when they did it: married who they married, betrayed who they betrayed, killed who they killed, died when and how they died.

To that end, I was meticulous, painstaking. I gobbled up history books and articles, so much so that I began to spot errors. (John Julius Norwich reported the wrong story of the death of Isaac I Komnenos; Wikipedia had the birth year of the Empress Eudokia off by a bit, as she was presumably not having children in her fifties.) Among the many scholars and historians whose work I consulted were Judith Herrin, Lynda Garland, Norwich, Dion Smythe, Stephen H. Rapp, Jr., Avril Cameron, Edward N. Luttwak, Steven Runciman, George Finlay (whose *History of the Byzantine and Greek Empires from 1057-1453* was indispensable), and Edward Gibbon, as well as the primary sources: Psellos and Anna Komnene herself.

The writer of historical fiction is bound by the rigidity of historical facts just as the writer of sonnets must honor the strictures of the poetical form. A sonnet has fourteen lines; Alexios Komnenos took the purple on 4 April 1081; both are inviolable. In historical fiction as in classical poetry, the creativity lies in how one fills in the blanks. This novel is mostly me filling in the blanks. For example: The unparalleled beauty of Maria of Alania is attested in every primary source in which she appears. True, Anna Komnene described all the women she loved as beautiful, but it's clear even in the *Alexiad* that Maria was something special. In short, the historical consensus is that Maria was easy on the eyes. It's also true that, despite being married to Michael Doukas during her prime child-bearing years, in an era when women were almost constantly pregnant, she only bore him one child. That doesn't quite compute; there must be something more to the story. I thought, "What if Michael were gay?" And that unlocked quite a bit of drama.

My original idea was to write a tale of the First Crusade from the Byzantine point of view, centered around a (fictitious) romance between Anna Komnene and Bohemond of Antioch—a big, ambitious work of historical fiction. The original plan was to do this many years from now, when I was retired and had more time to do the research. Then desperation (a novel I'd just finished was rejected by my agent, on account of it being not good) and inspiration (the idea of having Anna be the narrator, and the novel itself being a "real" text) converged, and in 2015-16, I banged this puppy out in eighteen months, writing only in the early morning, reading Byzantine history books in the evening, working a fulltime job, managing a literary website, and coaching several of my kids' basketball teams. The convent-bound princess-cum-nun had infinitely more peace and quiet than I did, but here we are.

Some days, especially early on, I wrote as if possessed. I have never enjoyed writing fiction more than I enjoyed writing this. I never felt more sure of a project I was working on. But my agents couldn't sell it. ("You're not known as a writer of historical fiction" came a few years before "You're not an expert on Trump/Russia" in my numerous rejections by numerous publishing houses and literary agents; maybe if I were a handmaiden Supreme Court Justice or corrupt Trump White House official, I'd have had better luck.) Plus, no one wanted to read it, because, like, it's *long*. The literary appeal of the subject (no one knows anything about the Byzantines!) was also a commercial red flag (no one knows anything about the Byzantines!). Then Trump happened, my writing career went in an unforeseen new direction, and Anna's story really did get buried—on my hard drive, not in a lead-sealed pot, but buried just the same. Until now.

Anna has waited long enough.

A big Byzantine salute to everyone who helped me along the way: my wife Stephanie St. John; my children; Janice & Greg Olear, Franklin St. John, David Laties, Robin Danziger, Owen King, Mary Giles, Denise Wiedemann, Kim Pardi, Lynne Corbett, Ronlyn Domingue, Aja Raden, Stephanie Koff, and Bonnie Savage, who did a wonderful job copyediting the manuscript. Special thanks to Cilla Conway, for letting me use the Empress card from her sublime Byzantine Tarot deck, and to Amanda

Kelly for designing the cover. And much gratitude to everyone who subscribes to PREVAIL.

To my cat Leo, who woke me dutifully at six in the morning every blessed day by licking my face until I had no choice but to get up—I could not have written this without you.

Finally, to Anna herself, 868 years dead: thank you, whenever you are.

—G.M.O.
3 March A.D. *2022*

APPENDICES

HOUSE OF DOUKAS / FAMILY TREE

(* indicates emperor)

Constantine X Doukas* — Sofia Doukas — John Doukas

(m. Eudokia Makrembolitissa) — (m. Manuel Komnenos) — (m. Irene Pegonitissa)

|

Michael VII Doukas* — Isaac I Komnenos* / John Komnenos — Andronikos Doukas

(m. Maria of Alania) — (m. Anna Dalassene) — (m. Maria of Bulgaria)

|

Constantine Doukas — Manuel Komnenos / Isaac Komnenos / Alexios Komnenos* — m. — Irena Doukas

|

Anna Komnene / John Komnene*

LIST OF BYZANTINE EMPERORS

 976-1025, Basil the Bulgar-Slayer
1025-1028, Constantine VIII
1028-1034, Romanos III Argyros
1034-1057, various husbands & lovers of Constantine
            VIII's daughters Zoë & Theodora
1057-1059, Isaac I Komnenos
1059-1067, Constantine X Doukas
1068-1071, Romanos IV Diogenes
1071-1078, Michael VII Doukas
1078-1081, Nikephoros III Botaneiates
1083-1118, Alexios I Komnenos
1118-1143, John II Komnenos
1143-1180, Manuel I Komnenos

KEY EVENTS

And Ages of Key Characters at the Time

		Anna D	Maria	Alexios	Anna K
1025	Anna Dalassene born	0			
1051	Maria of Alania born	26	0		
1056	Alexios born	31	5	0	
1059	Isaac I Komnenos abdicates	34	8	3	
1066	Irena born	41	15	10	
1067	Constantine X Doukas dies	42	16	11	
1068	Romanos Diogenes crowned emperor	43	17	12	
1071	Manzikert; Michael VII crowned	46	20	15	
1074	Tino born	49	23	18	
1076	Winter famine in Constantinople	51	25	20	
1078	Botaneiates crowned; Alexios commander of field army	53	27	22	
1081	Anna Dalassene engineers coup; Alexios crowned	56	30	25	
1083	Anna born	58	32	27	0
1084	Battle of Larissa	59	33	28	1
1087	John born	62	36	31	4
1092	John named heir; Maria banished; Anna moves back	67	41	36	9
1095	Tino dies; Maria to monastery	70	44	39	12
1095	Alexios' ambassadors appeal to Urban II	70	44	39	12

1095	Claremont; Crusade speech by Urban II	70	44	39	12
1096	Bohemond in Amalfi joins Crusade	71	45	40	13
1097	Anna marries Nikephoros Bryennios	72	46	41	14
1097	Nicaea taken by Crusaders	72	46	41	14
1098	Bohemond takes Antioch	73	47	42	15
1100	Bohemond taken prisoner at Melitene	75	49	44	17
1102	Anna's son Alexios born	77	51	46	19
1102	Anna D dies	77	51	46	19
1103	Anna's son John born		52	47	20
1104	Bohemond defeated at Harran; escapes in coffin		53	48	21
1105	Anna's daughter Eirene born		54	49	22
1107	Maria dies; Anna's daughter Maria born		56	51	24
1108	Alexios final defeat of Bohemond/Treaty of Devol			52	25
1111	Bohemond dies			55	28
1116	Alexios terminally ill			60	33
1117	Alexios beats Turks at Philomelion			61	34
1118	Alexios dies; coup attempt			62	35
1137	Bryennios Jr. dies; Anna to convent				54
1138	Irene dies				55
1148	Alexiad published				65
1153	Anna dies				70

DRAMATIS PERSONAE

Ali, an opium eater and friend of Tino

Alp Arslan (Muhammad bin Dawud Changri), a Turkish sultan

Axouch, a Turkish orphan who was Prime Minister for John II Komnenos

Bagrat, king of Georgia, father to Maria of Alania

Basil the Physician, a heretic and atheist

Bohemond of Antioch, son of Robert the Fox, a Norman Crusader

Borilas, Sclavonian ex-slave, advisor to Botaneiates

Botaneiates, Nikephoros III, a dotardly general and emperor

Bryennios, Nikephoros the Elder, a general

Bryennios, Nikephoros the Younger, minister, historian, husband to Anna Komnene

Dalassene, Anna, mother to Alexios Komnenos

Diogenes, Romanos II, rakish emperor who lost at Manzikert

Doukaina, Irena, empress, wife to Alexios Komnenos, mother to Anna Komnene

Doukas, Andronikos, son of the Caesar, father to Irena

Doukas, Constantine "Tino," son to Maria of Alania and Ramwold

Doukas, Constantine X, emperor, husband to Eudokia, father to Michael

Doukas, Irene, John's wife

Doukas, John, the Caesar, brother to Constantine X

Doukas, Michael VII, son of Constantine X, husband to Maria of Alania, emperor

Germanos, Sclavonian ex-slave, advisor to Botaneiates

Giorgi, a monk

Helena, daughter to Robert the Fox, fiancée of Tino

Komnene, Anna, our narrator

Komnenos, Alexios, father to Anna Komnene, emperor
Komnenos, Isaac, hapless brother of Alexios
Komnenos, Isaac I, emperor, uncle to Alexios
Komnenos, John II, son to Alexios, emperor
Komnenos, Manuel, older brother to Alexios
Kosmas, a patriarch
Makrembolitissa, Eudokia, empress, wife to Constantine
    X, mother to Michael VII
Maria of Alania, Georgian princess
Maria of Bulgaria, mother to Irene Doukaina
Nicholas the Grammarian, a patriarch
Nikephoritzes, a eunuch prime minister
Odo, a Pope
Oursel, a Frankish mercenary
Palaiologos, George, a general and friend to Alexios
Psellos, Michael, a minister, monk, and historian
Ramwold, an Alan slave
Robert Guiscard (the Fox), a Norman conqueror
Rona, a nurse
Saddiq, a Moorish astrologer
Sikelgaita, wife to Robert the Fox
Straboromanos, Romanos, head of the state secret ser-
    vice, executioner
Tarchaneiates, a general
Xiphilinos, John, a patriarch
Xiphilinos, Leo nomophylax of the law school, senator,
    brother to the patriarch